Praise for DIS

'A fine, strong story, mysterious and bittersweet, told in a style so economical it almost makes the reader breathless – you just want to keep turning the pages. It's been a time since I was so entertained'

Campbell Armstrong

Disappeared

Colin Falconer

CORONET BOOKS
Hodder and Stoughton

Copyright © 1997 by Colin Falconer

First published in Great Britain in 1997 by
Hodder and Stoughton
a division of Hodder Headline PLC

Coronet edition 1997

The right of Colin Falconer to be identified as the author of
this work has been asserted by him in accordance with the
Copyright, Designs and Patents Act 1988.

10 9 8 7 6 5 4 3 2 1

A CIP catalogue record for this title
is available from the British Library.

ISBN 0 340 65361 2

Printed and bound in Great Britain by
Clays Ltd, St Ives plc

Hodder and Stoughton
A division of Hodder Headline PLC
338 Euston Road
London NW1 3BH

For Cynthia and Guillermo.
And all those who endured and did not disappear.

Acknowledgments

This is a work of fiction. It is not to be inferred that any of the institutions named in this book are currently involved in any of the illegal enterprises I have suggested. Nor are any of the characters in this story meant to represent real people.

However, the background to this story is a matter of recorded history, a nightmare that may have been forgotten by the rest of the world but is still very much alive in the minds of those who were fortunate to survive it. They will never forget it. I have done my best to remain faithful to those events and a number of people helped me in my research. In Buenos Aires I would like to extend my thanks to Andrew Graham-Youll at the *Buenos Aires Herald*. I would also like to thank my good friend Anthea Morton-Saner in London for her contacts in Argentina who were invaluable to me but who would still prefer not to see their names in print. My thanks also to John Challis for his help in Rome. Thanks, too, to George Lucas, my editor in London; and to my agent Tim Curnow in Sydney who helped me immeasurably on this one, and who I value as a friend, despite him being a poor misguided Swans supporter.

And to my wife, Helen, who helps me and loves me more than I deserve. Thank you.

'A belief in the supernatural source of evil is quite unnecessary;
Men alone are quite capable of every wickedness.'

– Joseph Conrad

Prologue

Buenos Aires, Argentina
March 1976

So much death. And yet it began, as it ended, with life. Two lives.

The doctor looked at them over his glasses, his face grim. 'You should prepare for the worst. She has acute respiratory problems and we have noted a cardiac arrhythmia. You must pray for her.'

Rosa stared at him. Someone had scooped out her insides with their fingernails. She clutched at her belly and uttered a sharp cry.

Reuben put an arm around her. He looked down at the child in her arms. She had the softly pink radiance of a newborn. Huge eyes, brown and liquid. She began to cry, as if she understood the death sentence that had been pronounced on her twin. From the first moments it was as if she knew that the world was trying to keep her apart from her sister.

Reuben tried to soothe his daughter's cries, felt her fist close around his finger. So tiny, so delicate. God was warning him. He had placed those he loved at risk and now He was showing him that what had been given could so easily be taken away.

It was all his fault.

'There is no hope?' Reuben heard himself say.

'There is always hope.' The large, black-framed spectacles flashed in the light. 'But I am saying we have done everything we can. Now it is in the hands of God.'

He would not meet their eyes. He was young, not much older than Reuben himself. He had detached himself, wanted just to get this done, move on to another patient. 'You have one healthy daughter, at least.'

'Can I see her?' Rosa said.

*   *   *

Eva had dewlaps at the back of her neck and her brown skin hung
loose on her. She looked like the blind birthling of a rabbit. Reuben
could count her ribs through her skin and the identity tag around
her ankle was barely thicker than his index finger. An oxygen tube
had been taped to her cheek. She was crying; an odd, gasping cry,
like the barking of a seal.

'Eva,' Rosa murmured.

She looked so small, too small even for the humidicrib, adrift
in the vast and white world of the hospital. Her limbs kicked and
flexed in distress, her face screwed up in a monkey-wizened grimace
of pain.

Rosa handed him the twin, Simone. He watched as his wife
patted Eva's bottom, instinct he supposed. She crooned to her
and when that did not work she scooped her up in her arms and
tried to gentle her but little Eva arched her back and screamed
even louder, her face taut and crimson with rage and pain. Her
chest heaved and gasped. Her lips were blue.

'Put her down,' Reuben said.

Eva kicked more desperately. Her toothless mouth gasped for
air, eyes screwed shut.

'Put her down!'

Rosa started to shake. She looked as frightened and as helpless as
a girl. She obeyed, lowering Eva gently into the crib, then stepped
back, a knuckle thrust in her mouth, eyes wet with grief.

Reuben did not know what made him do it. A flash of intuition
perhaps, for a moment seeing himself as Eva, in the pulsing crimson
and jelly warmth of Rosa's womb, feeling the spongy softness of her
twin, her nudge and embrace. From the moment of conception, he
realised, she had always been not one, but one half of two.

Now, faced with this first and desperate struggle, she was cold
and alone.

He placed Simone face down beside her sister in the crib.
Immediately Simone wriggled closer to her twin and as she did so
her left arm somehow draped itself across Eva's shoulder. Almost
at once the terrible crying stopped.

He felt the hairs on the back of his neck prickle.

Rosa's eyes locked with his. Reuben shrugged his shoulders.
Who knows why we do the things we do when we are desperate
this way?

*   *   *

The doctor found the Altmans still at vigil over their daughters.

'Eva is responding well to treatment. You will be able to take her home in perhaps another two days.'

Reuben could not take his eyes from his daughters. They had their thumbs in each other's mouths. 'Thank you, Doctor.'

He smiled, to accept the credit.

'Three days ago you told me she was going to die. It's a miracle.'

'In my experience, children, even small infants, can be very resilient.'

'She stopped crying as soon as we put little Simone in the crib with her.'

The doctor offered him a patronising smile. 'Yes, of course.'

Reuben bent over the crib. The twins were asleep. Reuben, the atheist, said a silent prayer to the God he no longer believed in and vowed he would never put them in danger again.

A vow he knew even then that he could not keep.

I

Argentina, 1974–76

1

Of the fifty or so guests who attended the christening in the San Isidro cathedral that morning, Julio Castro was the only one who had taken carnal possession of the mother of the twin girls now being baptised into the holy faith at the high altar. It was hard for him to concentrate on the words of the priest as he affirmed for the godparents their duties. He kept staring at Rosa and thinking: But I loved you.

The smile had frozen on his face.

But I loved you.

The twins had been dressed in long white gowns, the trains of which trailed over their parents' arms almost to the floor. The thanksgiving hymn rose inside the great vault of the cathedral, the priest's footsteps echoing on the marble steps as he crossed to the font.

A cascade of dark and luxuriant hair fell around Rosa's shoulders, framing a face of angelic beauty. A poor girl's bounty. Do you blame her, Julio? You always knew she would do better than you. But every time he looked at her, he felt a pain deep in the pit of his stomach that burned like an ulcer.

He stepped up to the font with Reuben's brother to accept the duties as godparent to the children. He looked up at Rosa. She offered him a chill smile. He wondered if she could even begin to guess at the pain she had caused him.

They posed on the steps of the cathedral for the photographer. Rosa was wearing a dress of white silk with ruffled shoulders, and long white gloves that accentuated the dark honey of her arms. Julio tried to imagine her naked, but even that memory was fading, unreal now, a distant scent. Reuben stood beside her in his Italian suit and Gucci loafers and Mar del Plata tan, relaxed, contented.

Everyone was smiling. Even Julio: *Those children should have been mine*.

2

September 1974

The history of Buenos Aires can be found in the telephone book: Calderón, Rosetti, Mason, Muller, Levi. Successive waves of immigration from Spain, Italy, Britain, Eastern Europe and Syria have created a hybrid more cosmopolitan than any other South American city. There is a saying in Argentina: Mexicans are descended from the Aztecs, Peruvians from the Incas and the Argentinians from boats.

The inhabitants of Buenos Aires call themselves *porteños*, people of the port, and a *porteño*, they say, is an Italian who speaks Spanish, lives in a French house and thinks he's British. The historical influence of centuries of British investment is evident. The town clock in front of Retiro station is a replica of Big Ben, a gift from the British government. The red London postboxes could have come straight from Oxford Street; and in fact the moulds had been imported from Britain decades before. And there is that most British of institutions, the club; there are polo clubs, rugby clubs and, yes, British clubs. In the twilight of the seventies the small expatriate community still ate afternoon tea from Madeira tablecloths, and drank pink gin and spoke English with Home Counties accents.

But that was just the patina of the city, for underneath the reality was raw and frightening. Most *porteños* still held dual nationality from Spain or Italy and the code of the *porteño* was based on *machismo*. An attractive woman still prompted shouted sexual proposals in the street. It was regarded as an art form and there was even a name for it: the *piropo*. The gut temperament of Argentina did not come from Westminster but from the saddle of the *conquistador* and the bloody sand of the Colosseum. Beneath the skin of the polo-playing *porteño* there beat a savage heart.

But a city is not just a place; it is also a time. For the Buenos Aires of 1974 a monster approached.

Perón, the great General Juan Domingo Perón, was dead. His body lay in state for so long mourners had to be forbidden from kissing the decomposing corpse. His third wife, a former nightclub singer known as Isabelita, took over as President. The worn and fragile fabric that had held the country in place began to unravel completely.

For two years the country had been racked by strikes, student riots and terrorism. The Montoneros, the most radicalised wing of the Peronist Party, had undertaken a bombing campaign. To finance their activities they began kidnapping rich businessmen and foreign executives for ransoms. By that spring they had raised almost forty-three million dollars.

In response Isabelita's Minister for Social Welfare organised the Alianza Anticomunista Argentina, the Triple A, thugs in dark glasses and open-necked shirts who cruised the suburbs in unmarked green Ford Falcons with machineguns, conducting their own abductions for revenge or reprisal. The country plummeted towards anarchy.

No one, rich or poor, was safe from the terror. In Munro, a working-class suburb, the wife of a factory worker had her baby snatched from her arms as she walked into a grocer's shop. In order to get her baby back she was forced to empty the scant contents of her purse on to the footpath. On the same day the owner of a prestigious stud farm was abducted by army officers. The ransom was not paid in cash but by the transfer of ownership of a certain horse, which gave the kidnappers access to the prestigious Tattersall Ring administered by The Jockey Club.

This was the Buenos Aires of 1974, these were the shadows that waited in the background that dark spring when Julio Castro met the woman who was to cost him his life.

He had seen her for the first time in one of those dark little bars on Reconquista. She was easily the most beautiful girl in the place, breathtaking in a swirling red dress and black leather shoes. She was smoking a cigarette which she held between her middle and ring fingers, her left hand poised beside her cheek. Her fingernails were scarlet, her eyes like steel. In a world of men, she had the world by the balls.

She was with another girl, who perhaps on her own might have been thought attractive, but besides Rosa looked merely plain.

The tango singer was singing in *lunfardo*, the Spanish-Italian hybrid that was the patois of Buenos Aires. As she snarled into the microphone, tossing her head in time with the music, a man with long and greasy black hair sat beside her playing the *bandoneón*, a black cloth spread across his shiny black trousers. Like all tango songs it was a tale of a man born under a tortured star, a song of treachery and suffering and unrequited love.

Julio watched as a number of young hopefuls like himself approached Rosa and tried to talk to her, but she ignored them, not even offering them the solace of a glance. He also noticed how, at each approach, her friend bit her lip and gulped at her drink, swallowing back her own disappointment.

She wasn't so bad, Julio decided. She was wearing a short black miniskirt and her low-cut black top revealed a good pair of *bolsas*.

Julio studied his own reflection in the mirror above the dusty bar. He was tall and lean and his long dark hair fell over his collar. He had been told he looked a little like the tennis player, Ilie Nastase. He ran a hand through his hair and liked what he saw. His shirt was open to the second button. He smiled.

He picked up his drink and sauntered across. An idea had occurred to him.

'Would you like a drink?'

Rosa's friend looked up, surprised, and for a moment he thought she was going to spill the rest of her *tinto* over those promising thighs. 'Me?' The eager look in her eyes saddened him. It seemed to him that a certain amount of disdain was more becoming.

He spared not even a glance for the beauty sitting a few feet away on the other side of the table. 'Of course.' He gave her the benefit of his smile.

He bought her a strong red wine, cut with soda water as was the custom, and sat down at their table.

Her name, he discovered with bitter irony, was Carmen. She was a quiet girl with good manners but very shy. She had a full figure and what Julio would have described as a sensual, hungry mouth. Her fair hair was cut to her shoulders. The crucifix that lay between her breasts made him think of sex and the confessional. There was sweat on her lip.

She told him she worked in a bank in downtown Buenos Aires and shared an apartment in Boca with her friend at the table. Julio heard her name for the first time: *Rosa*. Carmen introduced her friend and Julio gave her a nod and a smile and immediately returned his attentions to the unlikely Carmen. But as they talked he watched the beauty out of the corner of his eye. He felt his heart hammering against his ribs, his mouth was dry. He prayed he had not miscalculated.

Indeed, almost every other man in the room must have thought so, for now they descended, thinking that with Carmen entertained, Rosa would be more welcoming of their advances. But she treated their gambits with the same casual disdain.

Now he could feel her watching him, perhaps curious as to why, of all the men in the room, he was impervious to her charm. Beautiful women are so vain, Julio thought. Even when they don't want you, they want you to want *them*.

After half an hour or so Rosa looked pointedly at her watch and whispered something to Carmen. 'My friend wants to go,' Carmen told him. 'She has to get up early in the morning.'

'When can I see you again?'

Even then Carmen seemed surprised that he should have asked her. 'I'll give you my number.' She took a pen from her handbag and scribbled a phone number on the back of a coaster.

They got up to leave and Julio gave Carmen a perfunctory kiss on the cheek. As the two women left the nightclub – men were staring at Rosa like dogs after raw meat – he guessed every other male in the room thought he was blind. He hated himself for his deception but he told himself that he had harmed no one. Carmen had enjoyed her evening and Rosa had learned a lesson in humility. Perhaps.

And as for himself, well, he was a genius.

3

The Café Tortoni was an institution in Buenos Aires. Around the dark-panelled and mirrored walls were black-and-white photographs of the café's famous patrons, writers and former presidents, like Jorge Luis Borges and Pedro Arumburu. There was the murmur of conversation, the whir of the electric fans on the walls, the click of billiards from the back room.

Reuben was reading *La Nación*. The government had closed down the Montoneros' newspaper, *La Causa Peronista*, and their leader, Mario Firmenich, had announced in a closed press conference with foreign journalists that he was taking the movement underground. That was bad news; it meant more violence. Two policemen had already been killed that week in Rosario and Quilmes.

He saw Julio and raised a hand in greeting. He had the waiter bring two more espressos.

Julio flopped down into a chair. There were dark rings under his eyes.

'Look at you. You look like shit. What's the matter? Are you in love?'

'Worse. I'm broke.'

'Where did you go last night?'

'Down the Reconquista. There was this amazing woman.'

Reuben laughed. With Julio there was always an amazing woman. It was nothing new.

The waiter brought their espressos and the scalding, bitter coffee revived Julio's spirits. This friendship he shared with Reuben always surprised him. Although they were fellow students the circumstances of their lives could not have been more different. Julio was poor, smart and gifted; Reuben's father owned a bank and the best that could be said for him by his university tutors was that he was good at rugby. His fair hair he owed to his Polish mother for he was not obviously Jewish. The blue eyes were remarkable in a country of brown-eyed *criollos* and olive-skinned Latins.

Reuben was twenty-three years old and had the world at his feet. Julio was a year younger and had a run-down apartment with rent almost two months in arrears.

Reuben had settled among his less privileged fellow journeymen at the university with the diffident and easy-going charm that money can sometimes bestow. He attracted women without effort. Old money has a scent that sticks to the clothes, Julio observed. It clings to a person like an aura in the holy pictures at church.

Julio had reserved a large measure of contempt for him. Reuben Altman had never had to struggle like the rest of them, because his father paid him an allowance, and had even bought him his own car, a red Chevrolet. Julio had to work nights as a waiter and took the bus.

But because Reuben was neither arrogant nor boastful he was difficult to dislike. He made jokes about himself; he called himself the Brat from Barrio Norte, or Reuben Getty. He was even generous with his money. Julio told himself – and anyone who would listen – that he was just trying to buy friendship and so he spurned the free drinks at the student hangouts in Boca. He treated Reuben Altman with cynical disdain.

It took a broken nose and two cracked ribs to change his mind.

Julio's one passion, aside from women, was rugby. He played wing for the university first team. That year they had reached the final of the inter-university championships where they would play off with Rosario for the trophy. But the night before the game their regular full back was taken screaming to hospital with acute appendicitis. Reuben Altman was drafted in from the reserves as his replacement.

Julio did not even speak to him in the dressing rooms before the game.

It was soon apparent that Rosario's game plan was to target the new full back. In their first attack their five-eighth put up a bomb, a high kick aimed towards Reuben, standing just five yards in front of the goalposts. Reuben waited underneath it, eyes never leaving the ball. He took it on his chest a moment before three big Rosario forwards hit him. He went down under the ruck.

There goes Pretty Boy, Julio thought with perverse satisfaction.

A scrum was called and the maul peeled back. For a few moments Reuben lay unmoving in the dirt, then slowly he got to his feet and limped back to his position on his own goal line. There was a ripple of applause from the crowd.

Twice more in the first half the Rosario five-eighth put up bombs. Twice more Reuben held his ground, knowing what was coming. He never once looked round at the oncoming forwards, nor did he drop the ball under their charge. On both occasions he disappeared under the weight of the Rosario forwards. The last time he got up very slowly indeed, blood streaming from his nose.

Despite himself, Julio experienced a grudging admiration for the spoiled little rich boy.

Late in the game the ball was passed wide to Julio, who sidestepped two Rosario tackles to score. University won the game 17–12 and Julio and Reuben were chaired off the ground by their team-mates as heroes. A bond of courage and achievement was forged between them.

Afterwards, when Julio learned that Reuben had played most of the game with two cracked ribs and a broken nose, his contempt for the Brat from Barrio Norte disappeared. When Reuben shouted drinks that night, Julio accepted. They got drunk together and afterwards fell laughing down the steps of a bar on Reconquista.

'You didn't go to your lectures today,' Reuben was saying to him.

'I had a hangover.'

'How are you going to get through university if you spend all your time in nightclubs? Do you want a degree in the *cumbia*?'

'I don't know. What course do I have to take to get one?'

They talked about university for a while, and rugby, and then the conversation reverted, as it always did, to women. 'I am seeing this woman again tonight,' Julio said, and he held up his hand and shook it as if it were scalded, to let Reuben know that this was special.

They were *all* special.

'Where are you taking her?'

'I don't know. I'm broke.'

Reuben reached into his wallet, slipped a handful of notes across the table. 'Have a good time.'

Julio hesitated for only a moment before he picked up the money. 'Thanks,' he mumbled. He should have felt bad. Reuben was always bailing him out of his financial crises. But he was a spoiled little rich boy. He could afford it.

For two weeks Julio courted Carmen attentively. He took her to the raucous student dives on Reconquista and the fancy all-night tango clubs of San Telmo, living beyond his means, borrowing from friends, mainly Reuben. Without trying to appear too interested, he learned more about Rosa. It was not difficult because Carmen liked to chatter. She told him that Rosa worked in the office of an insurance company on Florida. He also learned that Carmen and Rosa had gone to school together and, like Carmen herself, Rosa had come to the capital from the poorer suburbs of Córdoba, hoping to find a better life. Rosa's parents were both dead. She had a brother in Avellanada, who was married and worked at a big meat packing plant in Boca. Her only real friend in the city was Carmen.

They were rebels after his own heart, for most young people in Argentina at that time lived at home until they got married, and even then did not move far from their families. *But my family don't care about me*, Carmen had said. *And Rosa's parents are both dead.*

Several times when he arrived at Carmen's apartment to pick her up for a date, he caught a brief glimpse of Rosa and his heart beat faster.

One night, when they were out drinking in one of Julio's hangouts on Reconquista, Carmen came straight out and confronted him. 'You don't seem very interested when I talk about Rosa.'

Julio contrived to shrug his shoulders. 'I'm not.'

Carmen looked sulky. She didn't believe him, of course. 'Most men don't see me if I walk into a room with her.'

Julio ran his fingers through her hair. 'I've gone out with a lot of beautiful girls. They are all so vain. It is what is inside a woman that is important to me now.'

He surprised himself with how sincere he made it sound. It was a lie but it was the lie that Carmen had wanted to hear, and so she made herself believe it.

4

One night, as she left the bank on San Martín, she found him waiting for her on the footpath.

'Julio!' Carmen's face lit into a smile and she threw her arms around his neck. Julio ached. He did not enjoy his deceptions, had never thought of himself as cruel. But men were slaves to their desires. Passion was something that could not be controlled. What was he to do?

'*Carmello*, I cannot take you to dinner tonight.'

The smile fell away. 'But you promised.'

'I have a tutorial this evening. It is your fault. I spend so much time thinking about you I have fallen behind with my studies.'

There it was, immediately, that familiar, sulky look. 'So when will I see you?'

'It's all right. I have a better idea.'

'A better idea?'

'Why don't you come back to my place? We can spend some time together right now.'

Carmen understood the nature of the invitation. She readily agreed.

Julio's apartment was in a run-down six-storey block, built in the first drive of expansion under Perón. The sink in the bathroom was stained brown with rust from the pipes and the kitchen window looked on to the concrete wall of a newer, larger block of apartments. There was a table, a poster of Che Guevara and two chairs, one with a broken leg. The bed was a mattress thrown on the floor.

But Julio did not give Carmen time to examine the circumstances of his student life. As soon as they were through the door he pressed her against the wall and put his lips against her neck. 'Carmen,' he growled, 'I am on fire for you.'

He was afraid that Carmen might after all turn out to be a good Catholic girl with provincial morals. But she did not disappoint him. She began ripping at the buttons of his shirt. 'Fuck me,' she whispered in his ear. 'I wanted you to fuck me as soon as I saw you.'

Even Julio, who had once been an altar boy in the family church, was shocked.

The rumble of buses shook the apartment, the commentary of a televised football match drifted from a window in the flat across the road. Julio rose naked from the bed, showered, shaved and patted aftershave into his cheeks. He came back into the bedroom and chose a new pair of jeans and a crisp white cotton shirt. He might not be able to afford a better apartment but his clothes were pressed and hung neatly in the ancient armoire.

Carmen lay under a sheet on the crumpled mess of the bed. She had been a far more energetic lover than he had imagined. With her talent he could imagine her with the gauchos on the *pampa*, breaking in horses.

'You go to a lot of trouble for your tutor.'

Julio ignored the comment. 'I shall only be gone a couple of hours. There's food in the refrigerator and you can watch the TV.' He knelt beside the bed. 'When I come back I will have time to make love to you properly.'

'I thought you did a good job the first time.' She kissed him and tried to pull him down beside her again but he just laughed and pulled away.

'Do you have a telephone?'

'A telephone? How can a poor student like me afford a telephone?'

'I should phone Rosa and tell her where I am.'

'What is she, your mother?' He blew a kiss from the door. 'Keep it warm for me.'

Rosa opened the apartment door with just a bath towel wrapped around her. Julio stood there as if he had been slapped. He stared at the droplets of water on her skin, immediately aroused by the scent of her, wet hair and *mousse de bain*. 'Julio,' she said. A tone she might have used for an idiot little brother. She put one hand on the door, another to the knot of the towel at her breast.

'Is Carmen here? We have a date.'

'She's not home yet.'

For a moment he was afraid that she might close the door on him but then she seemed to make up her mind. She moved aside. 'You'd better come in and wait.'

5

Now he was here he wondered what he was going to do. He had no plan beyond this, a vague notion that once he had her alone he could overwhelm her with declarations of his passion for her. He had even told himself she would be secretly impressed by the trouble he had taken to seduce her. But now he felt only sullied and vulnerable.

'Do you want some coffee while you're waiting? The kitchen's over there.'

She went into the bathroom, leaving him stranded in the middle of the room. She left the door ajar, and he saw a glimpse of brown skin in the margin between the door and the lintel. And then he heard the shower curtain being pulled across the cubicle as Rosa resumed her shower. Julio felt offended that she had left the door open. As if he were a eunuch.

This was not how he had imagined it at all. He had thought she would offer to make him coffee, that they would talk for a while and he would charm her, win her over. He had not believed she would simply walk out of the room and ignore him, that she would treat him like . . . like Carmen's boyfriend.

He looked around the apartment. A mess; some cups with lipstick stains on the rims left in the sink, a few fashion magazines spilled on the sofa. The view from the window was much the same as his own, taking in the air-conditioning ducts and anonymous windows of another block of flats.

He wandered into the bedrooms. He recognised Carmen's room by a familiar dress thrown across her unmade bed. In contrast, Rosa's might never have been slept in, a set from a stage play. The bed had been made with precision. He listened again for the sound of running water and, satisfied that he was safe from discovery, opened the wardrobe, ran a hand across the array of dresses, found the red silk dress Rosa had worn that first night he had seen her in Reconquista. He held it to his nose for the scent of her.

There were no posters of soap opera stars or rock singers as some young women had, no photographs of boyfriends on her bedside table; just a black-and-white portrait of two people dressed in the fashion of the forties or fifties, her parents perhaps. A romantic paperback on her bedside table. No other clues, no keys to her secret.

He heard the shower stop and he quickly walked back into the living room. The bathroom door was still ajar. She was blow-drying her hair in the fogged basin mirror. The towel was very short.

Suddenly he was angry; angry with her, but most of all angry with himself for his conceit. He had thought he was being clever and now he saw he was only arrogant and foolish. He considered walking out there and then, making his statement by slamming shut the door. Instead he stood there by the window, paralysed with rage and desire and humiliation.

Finally he turned back to the bathroom. He could still see her, she had her back to him, leaning towards the misted mirror, wiping away the condensation, smearing lipstick on the bruised, heart-shaped mouth. He imagined how she would look without the towel.

He walked across the room and kicked the bathroom door wide open.

Rosa spun around. 'What are you doing?' But it was not fear he heard in her voice, it was . . . what? Contempt?

'You're driving me crazy. For two weeks I haven't thought about anything except you. I haven't slept because of you. The only reason I asked your friend to have a drink with me was because of you!'

She stood there, droplets of water like diamond chips on the elegantly sculptured shoulders.

'I love you.'

'Get out.'

He stared at her.

'You're despicable.' The insult echoed in his head. 'Carmen's my friend.' She reached behind her to the vanity unit and threw her hairbrush at him. As she did it, the towel slipped and fell around her ankles on the floor.

He should have walked out right then. He would curse himself for his weakness later, many times, particularly in that hot and petrol-tainted darkness as he was dying. But at that moment he told himself that no other man would have acted differently.

His eyes travelled the length of her body. Her dark nipples were erect, from the cold. 'Get out,' she repeated. If she had screamed, if she had been less proud, he would have fled. Perhaps. Instead she just stood there like that, breathing so hard he could see the outline of her ribs through her skin.

He took a step towards her, kicking the bathroom door shut behind him.

6

The moment he had longed for, dreamed about, over in a moment, just a jumble of cameo images, fumbling, violent and confused.

He grabbed her hair and kissed her, hard. She tried to push him away.

He forced her down on to the cold bathroom tiles, fumbling with his jeans. His penis was swollen, the tip already slippery wet. He forced himself inside her, almost at once. She was still trying to push him off, so he grabbed her wrists and held them above her head.

She screamed so he tried to kiss her to smother the sound. She bit his lip and he yelped and pulled away.

'You're hurting me,' she shouted.

He could not help himself. She was too beautiful and he wanted her so desperately. There was a single, shuddering moment, reached too soon. He gasped aloud with the sudden shocking force of it, wondered afterwards if he had withdrawn in time.

When she knew he had finished she stopped struggling and lay still beneath him on the cold, wet floor. Julio felt cheated. Cheated and somehow ridiculous.

Almost at once he regretted it. In his mind he began conducting his defence. But what defence was there? Carmen knew the truth, he could not pretend that what had happened had not been coldly planned. He had made himself not only a brute, but a fool. He had tried to play the role of seducer and instead had needed force to get what he wanted.

'I'm sorry.' He released her arms and rolled on to his side, feeling the sweat chill on the cold tiles. He waited for his breathing to slow. He could not look at her. 'I'm sorry.' He could not think this through. He was too appalled at what he had just done. He could go to prison for this.

He stood up. Rosa did not move. There was a splash of semen on her belly and between her legs on the tile.

He zipped his jeans. There were long strands of her hair still entwined in his fingers. 'I'm sorry,' he said again. He didn't know what to do. He walked out, closed the apartment door gently behind him. He was suddenly a stranger to himself.

When he got back to his apartment Carmen was lying in bed, thumbing through one of his Eduardo Mallea novels, the table lamp that he used for reading propped beside the mattress. 'Julio!' she called from the bedroom. 'How was your tuition?'

'Fine. I learned a lot.'

He went straight into the bathroom and closed the door. It was a mess. Carmen had showered in his absence, had left the mat sopping on the floor, had used his soap and shampoo and neglected to replace the caps. Now she expected him to make love to her, no doubt. He stood with his back against the door and closed his eyes.

Would Rosa go to the police?

When he opened his eyes the stranger was watching him from the mirror. His lip was swollen and bleeding and there were scratches on the backs of his arms from Rosa's nails. The first thing was that Carmen must not know. He sniffed. He reeked of sex, of juices, hers and his. He couldn't go back to bed like this.

I'm not a rapist, he told himself. How is a man supposed to control his passions when he is alone with a naked and beautiful woman? This was passion, not rape. Leaving the door open like that. She was begging for it. He found himself wanting her again, wondering how he could retrieve the situation to his own benefit.

'What are you doing, Julio?' Carmen called through the bathroom door.

'I need a shower. My tutor smokes a pipe. I reek of tobacco.' He peeled off his clothes, stepped into the ancient bath and turned on the taps. A dribble of hot water from the overhead pipe. Julio soaped himself clean.

He stepped shivering from the shower and searched for a dry towel. Carmen had soaked them all. A typical provincial. They had no more manners than a pig. Because one was poor, one should not give up the basic dignities.

He put on a dressing gown and walked, still dripping, into the bedroom. He had rehearsed his story, how he had fallen on the university steps, cut his lip. But Carmen had already turned off the light. There would be no interrogation tonight. She lay in a pool of shadow on the mattress with her head resting on her elbow. He could smell perfume.

'You've been gone such a long time. Are you coming back to bed?'

'I promised you dinner. There is a restaurant just round the corner from here.'

'I've got a better idea. Let me eat you.'

Another man might have found some excuse. But then she would think she was too much woman for him. Troubled and exhausted as he was, Carmen would have to be satisfied.

And so the stranger lay down beside her on the bed, a man whose eyes betrayed nothing, who took what he wanted without thought of the damage. It was a physical chore, and there was little pleasure in it. If anything it was unpleasant and chafing. And as she shuddered and gave a gasp of her small pleasure he knew he had won again. He forced himself on to his own spent finish, for a man cannot fake orgasm without evidence.

This is the last time. I cannot do this to her or to myself. A man must have some dignity.

Carmen lay on her side, asleep. Julio got up and very softly went into the bathroom and slipped into his jeans and shirt. He found some coins in his jeans pocket and tiptoed out of the apartment, closing the door gently behind him. There was a phone over the street in the restaurant.

He dialled Rosa's number.

He looked at his watch. Almost midnight. From somewhere the sound of gunfire, the second shot overlapping the echo of the first. The sound had become so commonplace he all but ignored it.

The phone answered on the fourth ring. She hadn't been asleep, then. 'Rosa.'

She did not answer.

'Rosa, please, I'm sorry for what happened. I have to see you. I have to talk to you.' He had to shout over the chatter of noise in the restaurant. The place was still crowded. Most *porteños* did not eat until at least ten o'clock.

Another silence. He thought she was going to hang up on him. Perhaps the police were there already, listening.

'Tomorrow,' she whispered down the line. 'In the Café Dorego. Ten thirty. Don't tell Carmen.'

And she put down the phone.

It was an unseasonally warm morning and the tall wooden-framed windows had been left open on to the street. Wooden ceiling fans stirred the air, a few students sat around at the tables reading or writing, gazing at the street, the Quilmes ashtrays overflowing with cigarette ash and empty sugar packets. Over the years patrons had scrawled their initials into the wooden tables, even into the bar itself. Dusty bottles lined the glass shelves around the walls, beneath the posters of Gardel and Marilyn Monroe and Chaplin.

Rosa was already there. Her hair was tied in a scarf, she was wearing dark glasses and a blue suit with a hem below the knee. It took Julio a moment to recognise her. This was her day incarnation, he realised, a different Rosa to the one he saw at night.

She had a coffee in front of her and was slowly stirring in a spoonful of sugar.

He sat down and ordered a *café con leche*. They sat there for a long time, like complete strangers, not speaking.

'I wanted to say I was sorry.'

'You're sorry you raped me?'

He looked away. 'Of course.'

'I see. You're frightened I'm going to call the police.'

Was she taunting him? 'If you were going to call the police you would have done it by now.' She didn't answer. The spoon moved relentlessly in her cup. He leaned across the table. 'I never meant to do it. I lost control. I meant what I said. I'm in love with you.'

'I despise you.' She turned her head and looked out of the window. In the plaza the pigeons were flocking around an old woman, fluttering and pecking for the scraps of bread she had brought for them. Finally she said: 'Carmen loves you. If I tell her, it will break her heart.'

'No, Carmen mustn't know.'

'I thought about calling the police, after you'd gone. I had a friend who was raped. A poor girl from the provinces, like me. The policeman who took the report came back the next night and propositioned her.'

'I love you.' It was just a line, a declaration he had used countless times before on many women. This time he believed it was true.

She removed her sunglasses. There was a small bruise over her right eye. He didn't remember doing that. She leaned across the table towards him, lowered her voice, soft as a lover. 'One day I shall get even with you. You are never to come near me again. I have a brother who would kill you if he ever found out what you did. Do you understand?'

She tipped the scalding cup of espresso into his lap and walked out.

'Seen the newspaper?' Julio said.

He pushed his copy of *La Prensa* across the table. Reuben picked it up. A photograph of a charred body beside the burned-out wreck of a car. It had been found in a rubbish dump near the woods out at Ezeiza. The body was riddled with bullets. There were also signs of torture, the newspaper reported.

'Rega's bastards,' Reuben said, meaning the Triple A.

The violence was getting worse, student life was becoming unbearable. The rector of the university had lost his four-month-old son to a bomb blast, he and his wife had been badly injured. A week ago police with riot trucks had moved on to the campus.

The Montos had stepped up their own campaign. A few days before a policeman had been blinded and had lost both arms and legs trying to defuse a bomb. His daughter was four years old.

People were starting to feel they weren't safe anywhere. *La Prensa* carried another report of a seventeen-year-old high school student who had been shot dead as he lay asleep in his bedroom in Barracas in the southern suburbs. His father was a businessman so no one was sure whether the Montos or the Triple A were responsible.

'The country can't go on like this,' Julio murmured.

'I agree. But what can we do?'

'We get rid of Isabelita for a start.'

'I worry who we will replace her with.'

'It's time, you know, that the people had a say.'

'We've been saying that since Evita.'

'She married one of them. This time we need someone completely different. But why am I telling you all this? Tomorrow I'll get arrested.'

Reuben knew there was real concern behind the joke. That was the worst part of the current violence; no one really trusted anyone any more. 'I'm not a Peronist, Julio.'

'You're the enemy, whether you like it or not.' Julio picked up a handful of salted nuts, threw them into his mouth, washed them down with the rest of his beer. He reached for his cigarettes, lit one. His hands were shaking. Not just politics, not just what he has been reading in the papers making him edgy, Reuben thought.

'You okay?'

A shrug. 'Girl trouble.'

'Anything you can't handle?'

'Well, I don't need *your* help.' A nervous grin which vanished as fast as it had come. 'Jesus, women.'

'Who is it this time?'

'You don't know her.'

'Women are like buses, Julio. There'll be another one along in a minute.'

'Thanks, Reuben, but I don't need your platitudes right now.'

Reuben bridled at this rebuke but let it pass. 'Come on, drink up. I'll buy you another beer.'

And there it might have ended. Except for the twist of fate that brought Reuben and Rosa together one evening in Boca.

The restaurant was thick with cigarette smoke, a bedlam of scraping chairs, shouting customers and clattering plates echoing under the dark vaulted ceiling. On a small stage in the corner a singer and a *bandoneón* player battled the noise while waiters scurried to and from the kitchens with plates of pasta and glasses of flaming sambuca.

You are never to come near me again.

It was Carmen's birthday and she had insisted that Rosa join them for her birthday celebration in this teeming Italian restaurant in La Boca. Did she know? Julio wondered. She had accepted his story about the bruised lip, had never asked about the scratches on his arms. Everything was as it had been before. He had got away with it.

And still he burned for her.

Julio sipped his wine, uncomfortable with the stares of the men around him in the restaurant. Rosa attracted such stares wherever she went, tossing the mane of her hair like a wild mare, her red dress riding up her thigh. It was all he could do not to stare himself. The memories of what had happened that night were too raw, too fresh.

And here he was sitting between Rosa and Carmen, their escort and protection. Such irony.

'You're quiet,' Carmen said to him.

'Am I?'

'You've hardly said a word to me all night. Do I bore you?'

'Of course not.' He flicked ash from his cigarette. 'What do you want? That I should act like a schoolboy all the time?'

He looked around. Rosa was watching him, her eyes as hard as flint. And so everything is the same as before, he thought. And still I stay with Carmen because I cling to the hope that you will change your mind about me. Even though I know what a fool I am.

A shadow fell across the table. Julio looked up.

If there was one person Julio had not expected to see slumming it in La Boca it was Reuben Altman; Reuben, elegant in his tan suit and powder-blue silk shirt, a gold Rolex on his wrist. 'For most men one beautiful woman is enough.'

Julio held out his hand, surprised and dismayed. 'Reuben.'

'You are going to introduce me?'

'Reuben, this is a good friend of mine, Carmen Lazzeri.'

Reuben smiled and took her hand. 'So you are Julio's best-kept secret. I have heard so much about you.'

Carmen almost purred with pleasure. The bitch.

'And this young lady is Rosa Gonsalvez. A friend of Carmen's.'

Rosa's eyes glittered with interest. Julio felt suddenly sick to his stomach.

'This is Reuben Altman. He's a grade C student and a hopeless bum, but I support him when I can.'

Reuben laughed easily, leaned across the table and kissed Rosa on the cheek. 'Julio always liked to surround himself with beautiful women. This time he has surpassed himself.'

Julio forced a smile. There was a moment's hesitation and then he asked Reuben if he would join them for coffee and sambuca, hoping that he would refuse.

'There's nothing I would like better but I'm meeting my father here for dinner. He doesn't like to be kept waiting. He's bringing some bankers from São Paulo.'

Julio was both relieved and surprised. 'Here?'

'They want to see some local colour. Besides, this is the best Italian food in Buenos Aires.' He offered the women another powder-white smile. 'It was wonderful to meet you at last, Carmen. And you too, Rosa. I hope we meet again.' He slapped Julio on the shoulder. 'I'll see you tomorrow at university.'

Rosa's eyes followed him as he disappeared into the tobacco and candle haze of the restaurant. 'He dresses well for a student.'

'His father owns a bank,' Julio said, and immediately wanted to bite off his tongue.

'Which one?'

'Well, not the Banco de la Nación. A financial group, I think he calls it. The Altman Group.'

She raised an eyebrow. 'The Altman Group? I've heard of it. The company I work for does a lot of business with them.' Julio knew he had lost her then, although of course he had never possessed her, had never even had a chance. For a poor but sensible girl from Córdoba, Julio's limited charms were small currency to exchange for beauty such as hers.

'Now we have women ringing the office,' Jacopo Altman shouted down the telephone.

'Father?'

'Some woman left a message for you with my secretary. She claimed to be from an insurance company. She wants you to ring her about a disability claim.'

'A what?'

'A disability claim!'

Reuben blinked at the wall, his finger drumming against the telephone cradle. 'What was this girl's name?'

'Gonsalvez. Rosa Gonsalvez. From a company called British-Argentina Assurance. If you've got a pen, I'll give you the number.'

'Rosa Gonsalvez, please.'

'Speaking.'

Reuben hesitated. He remembered her, of course. But what should he say? 'This is Reuben Altman.'

'You're calling about your disability claim.'

'Well, actually, there's nothing much wrong with me.'

Rosa laughed into the phone. 'I believe you are suffering from blindness.'

'Blindness?'

'We met last night in La Boca. And you made no attempt to get my phone number. You *must* be blind.'

Reuben grinned. 'You can tear up the claim, Señorita Gonsalvez. I believe I have just been miraculously cured. Are you free for lunch?'

The Calle Lavalle and the Florida were the city's shopping and pedestrian malls, crowded with pizza parlours, *kioscos* and restaurants. Lovers strolled hand in hand to and from the movies, children ate ice cream on the benches and old men read their newspapers or played *truco* and canasta at the sidewalk cafés, nursing their filtered coffees. It was the haunt of buskers and folk musicians and pantomimists, street artists who performed for a few coins.

'This Rosa Gonsalvez,' Reuben was saying. 'Carmen's friend. I have been seeing her.'

Julio nodded, tried to appear interested, if unconcerned. Suddenly he ached all over. He stubbed out his cigarette. 'You like her?'

A smile played at the corners of Reuben's mouth. *Mierda*. It told him everything he needed to know. 'She's the most beautiful woman I've ever seen.'

'Yeah. I thought she was a bitch.'

He hadn't meant to say that. He saw Reuben raise his eyebrows in surprise at the sudden venom in his friend's voice. 'I think she's quite shy deep down. I guess you don't expect it in a girl like that. I think, you know, coming from the provinces, she's a little self-conscious.' He tapped a finger against his coffee cup. 'I think she likes me.'

'Have you slept with her?' It didn't sound as casual as he had wanted it to. His hands were shaking.

Reuben shrugged. Their eyes locked. He had, of course. No woman was able to resist Reuben, his charm, his money. His father's money.

A street artist stopped by their table, a young man in overalls, his face painted with black and white greasepaint. He was juggling tennis balls. 'Get away from me,' Julio snarled, 'or I'll jam those up your arse.'

The man moved away with a muttered insult.

Julio looked back at Reuben, saw the expression on his face. 'I have a hangover.'

'He's just trying to make a living.'

'I'm a fucking student. What does he come to me for?'

Reuben leaned forward. 'Hey, what are you going to do when you leave university?'

Julio tried to concentrate on this sudden shift in the conversation. All he could think of was Rosa, naked, her long limbs wrapped around his friend. 'I don't know. Get a job on one of the city newspapers, maybe. If I'm lucky. If not, I'll have to go out to the provinces, Córdoba perhaps, or Rosario.'

'Perhaps I can help.'

'With a job?'

'At *La Prensa*. There is someone I know there, one of the senior editors. He's a friend of my father's. His name's Albrecht, Jorge Albrecht. I've talked to him about you. He said he'd like you to give him a call. Perhaps you can work something out.'

A flood of gratitude, diluted with the bitterness of Reuben's conquest. He thought about Rosa, the red skirt swirling around her hips, her long hair around her shoulders, elegant, breathtaking. Walking out of his life. He thought of Reuben, and he felt the impotent bubbling of his anger. Everything was so easy for the bastard: education, money, women.

'Thanks, Reuben. I owe you a lot.'

'Hey, what good is anything if you can't help out a friend?'

He was right. Settle down, Julio. It's just your ego that's bruised. Now you have a job at *La Prensa*, when you could have been on a rape charge. It's not Reuben's fault. You owe him.

Forget it. Two weeks and you won't even remember what she looks like.

March 1976

So here he was, a year and a half later, standing next to Reuben on the cathedral steps, smiling for the camera. He had his job at *La Prensa* and Reuben was installed in his father's banking house, with his comfortable life and beautiful wife and twin daughters. It had all been so easy for him.

But now it was easy for him too, he supposed. Thanks to Reuben. He just had to forget this obsession with Rosa.

But even as they posed on the cathedral steps the shadows were racing towards all of them, like a cloud across the sun. The day of the colonels was coming.

10

They celebrated the christening at Giorgio's, an Italian restaurant in Recoleta. The sound of a guitar and *bandoneón* and the torchy voice of the tango singer drifted through the open French doors on the hot, breathless air. The soft clink of glasses, the clatter of waiters removing plates, the shouts and laughter of men and women dancing.

Outside, on the flagstone patio, the sound was muted by glass, the thick fug of cigarette smoke replaced by the scent of flowers. A white wall was almost obscured by wreaths of bougainvillaea and honeysuckle.

Reuben was on his way back from the washrooms and saw Carmen sitting alone on one of the wrought-iron tables, her heel balanced on a rattan chair, a cigarette in one hand, a glass of wine in the other. She was wearing a black cutaway cocktail dress, her shoulders bare. Pretty, plump, a little blowsy with drink.

Reuben stopped, smiled. 'Where's Julio?'

Carmen nodded towards the windows. He saw his friend, framed by glass in the French doors. He was dancing with a redhead in a green dress. His hand was on her waist and he was laughing.

'I broke a heel,' Carmen said.

'You're wasting your time with him.'

'These shoes are practically new.'

'He's my friend, so I know what I'm talking about. He doesn't like women. Not individually, anyway.'

Carmen looked up at him. He thought she might be about to cry. Instead, she said: 'I never had a chance with him. It was Rosa he wanted.'

'Rosa?'

'You didn't know?'

Reuben did not answer her straight away. 'Yes, I knew,' he said at last.

A wistful smile. 'I don't blame him.'

'It's just the way he is.'

She drew on her cigarette, her eyes never leaving his face. 'Funny, isn't it? I always wanted you. But we don't always get what we want. Well, I don't. Rosa does.'

She was drunk. *I always wanted you.* Reuben knew he should walk away now. 'Julio doesn't know what a lucky guy he is.'

'You're sweet.'

'I mean it.'

She leaned forward, her elbows on her knees, her head wreathed in a chimera of pale blue smoke. 'Well, Reuben, if you ever want to come upstairs you only have to ring the bell.'

His mouth was suddenly dry. He looked over his shoulder. Someone might see them. He could imagine how this would look. 'Forget Julio,' he said, and went back inside.

A storm had swept in from the Atlantic Ocean, lashing the capital with freezing rain, turning the streets black and slick as the belly of a snake. Raindrops wept down the windows of the labour ward as Francesca Angeli threw back her head and screamed.

When the contraction was over she lay gasping and sweating on the hospital gurney. She opened her eyes and saw a doctor staring at the foetal monitor. He shook his head.

'My baby,' she croaked.

He leaned towards her. His face seemed to swim in and out of her vision. 'Señora Angeli. We think your baby is in danger. We have to operate immediately.'

Hadn't she known that, hadn't she tried to tell them? She had felt something was wrong for the past week, deeply, the way a mother knew. And the doctors had smiled and tried to reassure her that everything was normal. Now she stared at the fluorescent striplights and white ceilings and rain-smeared windows, at the tense, sweating faces of the nurses and the doctors, and she groaned with pain and rage and frustration.

My baby.

She clutched the crucifix at her throat and prayed.

She felt someone stick a needle in her arm and there was a buzzing in her ears. It was as if she were falling into a warm bath. Everything faded to rose, then black.

*   *   *

When she woke her husband was sitting beside the bed, whispering her name. The storm was still raging outside. She heard another flurry of rain spatter against the windows. The pains had gone. But there was no relief in that, for in their place was a coldness, a deep visceral ache, which even the morphine they dripped into her vein could not suppress.

'My baby,' Francesca whispered.

Angeli leaned over her. 'It's all right. It's over. You must rest.'

'My baby.' She remembered now, the terrible birthing pains, the tense faces of the doctors, the cold fear. 'Where is my baby?'

She heard a voice, out of her vision. 'Señora Angeli, I am sorry. We did all we could. Unfortunately the infant died *in utero*. There was nothing anyone could have done.'

She could not make sense of the doctor's words at first. She frowned, puzzling over them, trying to think through the buzz of red gelatin that surrounded her. What was he trying to tell her?

'You must rest now,' Angeli whispered.

'Where's my baby?'

'I am very sorry,' the other voice repeated, and then she remembered the contours of her fear, recalled the deep and prescient knowledge she had brought with her to the labour ward. She felt for the pain, searched for it as desperately as she might search through her purse for lost money; but it was not there, the drugs had robbed her even of that fundamental ability to feel. Instead there was just an empty place, a broken nursery where the child of her imagination had played. It was deserted now, inhabited by ghosts.

'I want to say goodbye,' Francesca sobbed. 'Let me hold my baby.'

But then she felt again the familiar prick of another needle and the world of grief and pain slipped away from her for a few more hours.

Francesca never did hold her dead child. Even Angeli did not see her. A priest was summoned to whisper rites over the limp and blue wreckage and then it was burned in the hospital incinerator with other redundant organs. All she was told was that if her baby had lived it would have been a daughter.

It was not until two days later that they told her the full truth of it; that the reason for the premature labour and the child's subsequent death was a genetic defect in Francesca's womb. In order to save the mother's life the surgeons had performed an emergency hysterectomy. She and her husband should reconcile themselves to the fact that they would not now be able to have children of their own.

Francesca bore this news stoically and without tears. Angeli took this to be a good sign.

He was wrong.

11

Rosa sat at the dressing-table mirror, the silk of her nightdress shimmering in the soft glow of the bedside lamp. Reuben leaned his elbow on the pillow and watched her. Her breasts were still swollen with milk. He admired the swell of her flesh as she reached behind her head to brush out her hair.

He drew back the bedcovers.

As she got into bed she flicked off the lamp.

'Don't turn off the light,' he said. 'I want to look at you.'

'I don't want you to. I'm fat.'

'That's ridiculous.'

'I feel fat.'

He nuzzled her neck, his hand on her thigh. '*Cara*,' he whispered.

He was too eager perhaps. It had been so long. But when she did not respond he got angry. He had been patient with her. What was wrong? She was stiff in his arms, perfect, cold, unyielding. She might as well be a storefront mannequin.

He rolled away from her.

'Reuben? Reuben, what's the matter?'

'If you don't want to, why don't you just say so?'

'It's not that. Don't be angry.'

'I'm not angry.' He switched on the bedside lamp and lay on his back, staring at the ceiling.

'I'm sorry. I'm just tired, that's all.'

'You're always tired.'

'It's not easy looking after twins, Reuben.'

'We're not poor. Get a maid.'

'I don't want someone else raising my children. We didn't do it that way where I come from.'

'Where you come from,' he said, slowly.

'What does that mean?' One of the twins started crying in the next room. 'Simone,' Rosa said.

'Let her cry. You can't get up to her for every little sound she makes.'

But Rosa slid out of bed and padded into the nursery. When she came back Reuben was asleep.

Once a month Domingo came.

He had none of Rosa's charm or looks. He was a small, mean-eyed man, with a dark complexion. The look of a *mestizo*. He always dressed in his best suit for these visits, which only served, it seemed to Reuben, to make him appear even more shabby. Often his tie was knotted across his collar or a frayed shirt cuff protruded from his jacket sleeve. He sat perched on the edge of his chair, a man uncomfortable with his surroundings, ready to bolt. He had large, clumsy hands, which hung limp between his knees, as if they were soiled shoes he had taken off at the door and now he did not know where to put them.

He said little, spent most of the hour answering Rosa's questions about distant family members. He never brought his wife or children, although he had been invited to do so many times. Reuben was acutely aware of the gulf that separated them, and it was also an uncomfortable reminder of the divide between himself and his new wife.

Reuben remembered the first time he had come, soon after he and Rosa were married. They had drunk their tea by the balcony, Domingo's eyes restlessly taking in the apartment, the polished timber floor, the Persian rugs, the black leather sofas. As if it were a museum and he had paid admission to see it all.

Reuben felt uncomfortable at these meetings, his liberal views in collision with the reality of his own wealth and privilege.

Rosa had stood up, announcing she would brew more maté. 'Reuben,' she whispered, indicating that she wished him to come with her.

He followed her into the kitchen.

'He needs money,' she said when they were out of earshot.

'What for?'

'Does it matter?'

Reuben felt cornered. 'How much?'

She did not answer. Her expression made him feel mean. He nodded and went into his study, found his chequebook. He wrote out a cheque for fifty thousand pesos, went back into the kitchen

and handed it to her. She took it without a word, folded it neatly
and put it in the pocket of her blouse.

He saw her give it to him later, as he was taking his leave. Their
hands touched for just a moment and the slip of paper disappeared
from view.

He and Domingo shook hands. His were hard, callused by heavy
manual work.

'Goodbye, Domingo.'

He could see his new brother-in-law did not know what to call
him. Señor Altman was too formal, Reuben somehow suggested
friendship and equality. So he just smiled and gave a slight bow
of his head.

After he had gone Rosa started to clear away the cups. Nothing
more was ever said about the fifty thousand pesos, but each
month the ritual was the same. Reuben had accepted an unspoken
agreement to support not one family, but two.

Domingo was not the only visitor from Rosa's other life. One
day, just before the twins were christened, he came home to find
a Catholic priest drinking coffee in his kitchen.

Rosa jumped to her feet. 'Reuben, this is Father Salvatore. He
was our priest in La Boca.'

Reuben put out his hand and the priest took it. A grip as hard
and as firm as Domingo's.

He was a small, slight man with too much hair for so small a
body. It sprouted from the back of his hands and from his neck
where he had stopped short with the razor. He had bright, dark
eyes that burned in his face like coals.

Reuben looked at his wife and a look passed between them:
What is he doing here?

'He got my address from Domingo. He came across town to see
me. To see us.'

'That was very kind.'

They had the guilty look of lovers. If it wasn't for the man's
black clerical suit, he might have been jealous. Reuben knew the
priest did not want his wife's body. He was here to compete for
loyalties of a much more fundamental nature.

'You are not of the faith,' Salvatore said, with a wry smile.

'With a name like Altman?'

'One should never suppose too much.'

'And what are you doing in the Barrio Norte? Aren't you poaching on someone else's turf?' It was meant to be a joke, but it came out with a much harder edge than he had intended.

'I am sure God does not draw boundaries.'

Reuben wondered why he felt this antagonistic. Something to do with being Jewish, he supposed. He had no time for formal Judaism but when he was in a room with a priest something flared in him, some ancient reflex.

'Rosa and I have been discussing your daughters. Have you given any thought to what faith they will be raised in?'

They had discussed it. Rosa attended Mass at the San Isidro cathedral and he had always been content to let her do what she wanted as far as religion was concerned. But something made him say: 'We haven't decided.'

The priest gave him an enigmatic smile that he didn't much care for. 'Well. It is a matter for you and Rosa. I should be going.'

After he had gone Rosa turned on him. 'You didn't have to be so rude.'

'What was he doing here?'

'He's a wonderful man. Sometimes in La Boca, he was the only friend I had.'

Reuben did not answer her.

'I wanted to talk to him about having the twins baptised.'

'I don't care what you do. You know I don't care about any of that.'

But he did care and he wondered why. He always let Rosa do as she wished with her Sunday mornings, as if it were just a hobby. Why should it matter now? Perhaps because it reminded him that he was different to other people. Despite all the pretence, he was still a Jew in a Catholic country. An outsider.

But no one cared about that any more, did they? Not here. Not in Argentina.

They had left all that behind.

12

That autumn fear stalked the streets of Buenos Aires; the city was palpable with it. Like corpse gas it seeped into the houses and the apartments and offices, became as much a part of life as sleeping and eating.

Isabelita's government stumbled from one crisis to another. There had been a wave of strikes and the cost of living had risen three and a half times in a year. There was blood on the streets. Every day the newspapers reported some new atrocity, wives and children of soldiers torn apart by a bomb inside a military base, mutilated bodies found on dump sites or in the woods near the international airport. The killings were variously blamed on the left-wing Montoneros or the right-wing death squads.

And then, late in March, the tanks rolled through the Plaza once more and a military junta under Lieutenant-General Jorge Videla seized power. At first most people were relieved. When the army dissolved the legislature and imposed martial law the *porteños* hoped the coup would bring a return to stability and common sense, as had happened a decade before.

But the junta's 'Process of National Reorganisation' – *El Proceso* – would not prove to be the panacea that everyone had hoped for. The killings went on. Bullet-ridden bodies continued to appear in ditches and rubbish dumps all over the city. While the government blamed communist subversives the violence took a new and sinister twist, for instead of dying in full public view, some victims simply vanished.

Anyone even vaguely identified with the left was targeted. General Iberico Saint Jean, the new governor of Buenos Aires, made the position of the military quite clear: 'First we will kill all the subversives, then we will kill their collaborators . . . then their sympathisers . . . then, those that remain indifferent. Finally we will kill the timid.'

Buenos Aires, the city that never slept, the place where people rarely ate dinner before nine or ten o'clock, became eerily quiet. Buses stopped running after dark because there was no one left on the streets to justify the service. People scurried home after work and locked the doors behind them, dreading the night.

Soon almost every *porteño* had a story of a friend or family member who had been mysteriously kidnapped during the night, never to be seen again. They had even coined a name for them: *los desaparecidos*, 'the disappeared'.

After he married Rosa, Reuben had bought an apartment in Recoleta, one of the most expensive residential areas of the city. Nowhere was Buenos Aires's faded glory more evident than here, among the *fin de siècle* mansions of Italian gingerbread and Victorian Gothic, where the rich colonists and adventurers had built their homes, well away from the silted river with its rats and fever swamps. A stranger to the city might have believed they were in Paris or Madrid.

The apartment was on the fourth floor of a six-storey edifice that might have been excised complete from the Latin Quarter of Paris. A plant-filled wrought-iron balcony overlooked a quiet and leafy street shaded with sycamore and tipuana trees.

Rosa and Carmen sat by the shuttered window, drinking coffee. The twins were down for their morning nap. The city sweated under a lowering sky.

'How are things between you and Julio?' Rosa asked.

'We broke up.'

'Again?'

Carmen shrugged and sipped her coffee, staring down at the quiet avenue of trees. Rosa thought again about that night, what he had done. She had always been afraid to tell Carmen about it, afraid she would not believe her, that she would think she had led him on. It was what he would say. It was what the police would have believed. 'What happened this time?' Rosa asked.

'The usual. I found out he was sleeping with some other woman. I told him it's over. I never want to see him again.'

Carmen had finished with Julio countless times. She always took him back.

'It's for the best.'

Rosa saw the hurt in her eyes. Carmen's trouble was she loved him. Love always got in the way of good sense. 'I guess you're right. There're a lot of men out there. I just have to find myself the right one. Someone like Reuben.'

Rosa forced a smile and looked away.

'Oh,' Carmen said. She knew, had picked up on that look on her face. 'Trouble in paradise?'

There was so much Rosa wanted to say but she hesitated, afraid of where it might lead her. She took a deep breath. 'It will be okay.'

Carmen said nothing. Rosa loved her for not pushing her. After a while, she said: 'We haven't had sex for months.'

'You think . . . he's having an affair?'

Rosa was shocked by the suggestion. 'No. No, it's not that.'

She could see Carmen did not believe her.

'I suppose when I was pregnant everything changed. He said . . . he was frightened of hurting me . . . but I think when I got big he just didn't . . . want to. But then, after the twins were born, I was tired and . . . well, you know, having babies, it does something to you and you just don't feel the same straight away.'

'It will be all right.'

Rosa nodded.

'He loves you, Rosa.'

And now do I tell her? Rosa felt the fears and uncertainties bubbling inside her. She had to tell someone, she felt as if she were going insane, day after day alone here in the apartment with the twins, Reuben coming home late every night, pale, exhausted, hardly talking to her, having dinner and falling straight to sleep. All their friends were his friends. She had never been as lonely in her whole life. Or as terrified.

'It's not just the babies.' She took a deep breath. 'I don't like him touching me.'

Carmen waited, her eyes huge.

'Something happened. Before we were married. Before I even met him. I don't think I ever got over it.' She put her face in her hands.

Carmen put her arms around her. 'Rosa?'

'I was raped.'

A long, aching silence. Carmen rocked her like a child. When she spoke again she measured her words carefully. 'Have you told Reuben about this?'

'I couldn't.'

'Why?'

When she did not answer, Carmen said: 'Julio.'

There were no more words. They held each other in silence and the future was changed, irrevocably.

13

The black limousine cruised through the quiet, leafy streets of Palermo, one of Buenos Aires's premier residential districts, an area of private schools and embassies where many of the military kept expensive homes and apartments. The Mercedes 450 turned through high wrought-iron gates and into the driveway of a large Spanish colonial house with manicured gardens. The driver, a uniformed police captain, got out and walked around the car to open the door for the car's only passenger. Colonel César Angeli stepped out and strode up the front steps to the portico where a white-jacketed servant already held the front door open for him.

Angeli had the face of an aesthete and the hands of a piano player. He looked much younger than his forty years. His appearance and demeanour suggested a man who took care with his hygiene and personal grooming. His fingernails were well manicured and his thick, dark hair was parted on one side with great precision. But his most striking feature was his eyelashes: they were long and thick and black, highlighting eyes of wintry blue.

A woman in a maid's uniform waited for him in the foyer. She wore a black cotton blouse and skirt and a short white starched apron with starched collar and cuffs. This was Antonia, his senior maidservant.

He handed her his gloves and braided cap, looked around the room. 'Where is the señora?'

From Antonia's expression he knew that it had been another bad day. He felt the tightening of the muscles in his jaw. This was not the way it was meant to be. He had not come this far to have the edifices he had built for himself so artlessly destroyed.

'She is upstairs, señor.'

He nodded and took the stairs, two at a time.

*　　*　　*

He found his wife sitting in a chair by the bedroom window, still in her nightdress, her head lolling on her chest. The blinds were still drawn and the room was in darkness. Angeli experienced a flood of rage. It was something hundreds of women in the *villas miserias* did every day, have babies. Why should it be so hard for the daughter of a banker?

'Francesca.'

She woke suddenly, and her fingers went to the collar of her nightgown. For a moment she blinked, startled, then gave him an uncertain smile.

'*Caro*. You're home.'

Her hair was loose around her shoulders and uncombed. It seemed she had started to apply make-up some time during the day and had abandoned the effort halfway through, with bizarre effect. Her face looked grey in the half-light, making her seem much older than her thirty-two years.

His nose wrinkled in disgust at the stale smell of the room. 'It is almost evening.'

The accusation hung in the silence. Francesca nodded, almost as if she understood, then turned her head to stare at the digital clock beside the bed. The numbers glowed like coals in the shadows of the room.

He went to the blinds and threw up the sash. The late evening sunlight flooded golden into the room, on to the unmade bed, the cups of cold coffee on the bedside table.

Francesca squinted against the light. 'I must feed the baby,' she said. She got slowly to her feet and went into the nursery. Angeli followed her.

A few months before, Francesca had employed, at great expense, a private decorator for the nursery. The ceiling had been painted a pastel blue by a professional artist who had added white clouds to the frieze so that their child would always look up at a perfect sky. Soft toys of immense size had been purchased on Florida, and had been placed inside a crib hand-carved from mahogany. The crib itself was on rockers so that the child could be gently lulled to sleep by the servants each afternoon and evening. The pink chenille bedspread and the soft pink coverlets had been added after Francesca had returned from the hospital, without his knowledge.

Francesca sat down on a low stool beside the crib. A toy moon had been attached to its rail. A cord hung from the base of this moon; Francesca pulled gently at the string and the strains of a nursery rhyme filled the room. Francesca sang in time as she rocked the cradle.

Angeli felt the hairs prickle on the back of his neck.

'She's dead, Francesca.'

She looked up at him, her eyes unfocused, almost as if she hadn't heard.

'*Shhhh.* You'll wake her.'

'Who?' he shouted. 'Who is there to wake?'

He had thought she would get better. All right, he had expected her to be depressed for a short time. But she had been home from hospital almost a month now and every day she slipped further away from him.

Weakness. It was the last thing he had expected from his wife, his ice queen. Ever since they were married he had thought her impossibly remote, even cold. A tall and beautiful *criolla*, she had been an impossible prize for a junior military officer of immigrant stock. The daughter of a banker and ten years his junior, she was sophisticated, well educated, seemingly out of his reach. Yet she perhaps divined in him an ambition to match her own. When she had become his wife his life had become a sumptuous and well-ordered room. Now fate had ransacked it.

Francesca looked up at him, her face wreathed in a beatific smile. 'She's asleep now.' She took his hand and led him softly from the nursery.

14

Mar del Plata, Buenos Aires Province

Argentina encompasses some of the greatest natural features in the world, such as the Iguazú falls and the Patagonian Andes, but most *porteños* regard such attractions as quaint and vaguely alien. Every year they take their summer holidays in the same place, on one of the resorts on the Atlantic coast, usually Mar del Plata. It is a sight not unfamiliar to Californians: a strip of endless beach backed by acres of car parks with the hot sun beating down on shimmering windscreens and scalding chrome.

To the south are the more exclusive resorts, the private beaches where the wealthy built their bungalows and villas in the early twentieth century. The red-tiled roofs are shaded by palms and jacarandas, their owners sipping cocktails on the widow walks, gazing at the steel blue of the Atlantic.

Jacopo Altman had purchased his piece of paradise just a decade before, had watched its value soar by as much as a million pesos a week during the years of Isabelita. It was less than thirty years since his grandfather had arrived in Argentina from the Ukraine. His timing had been good. When the Nazis had invaded their village in 1941 they had razed the synagogue and murdered every Jew they found there. Every single one of his relatives had died in that holocaust.

He did not look like a Jew. With his long silver hair and moustache he could have been an ageing Italian gigolo rather than the scion of a small bank.

Now he crossed his long legs and leaned back in the wicker chair beside his son, and sipped his Bodega Lopez 1971. He could see the breakers rolling in from the Atlantic between the pines. Life was sweet. Which made the danger they had placed themselves in even more poignant.

The sun dropped down the sky below the trees, the day reaching that silent silver moment when the afternoon lulls and evening comes. The air turned cool. They listened to the crickets in the trees.

'A friend of mine was smoked yesterday.' Reuben's voice was soft, barely audible. 'Smoked' was a recent slang expression. 'Gone up in smoke' – disappeared. 'I went to university with him. They beat him up, outside his home in San Isidro, in front of his whole family. Then they threw him in a car and drove away with him. His wife has heard nothing of him since. Later the same men came back and looted the house. They took everything. Even the washing machine.'

Jacopo grunted. What was there to say?

'He was a lawyer. He had tried to help this woman take out a writ of habeas corpus after her brother was disappeared. That was his crime.'

'The world has gone mad.'

'Not the world. Just us. Just Argentina.'

The smell of basil and tomatoes rose from the kitchen, warm on the breeze, mingling with the salt smell of the sea. The cook was preparing pasta with fresh mussels. He heard one of the twins crying downstairs, then Rosa's voice gentling her. There were just the five of them at the villa this weekend. Reuben's younger brother, Arturo, had stayed behind in Buenos Aires with his pregnant wife. Their mother had died five years ago.

If she were here now she would never let them risk so much.

'We have to stop,' Reuben said.

Jacopo turned, instinctively, to make sure they were not overheard. Rosa might be Reuben's wife but she was not one of the family. His son loved her and so he had accepted her but in his heart he knew she was just a gold-digger and not to be trusted.

'It's too dangerous,' Reuben insisted.

'It is too dangerous to stop. If we abandon them now, they will betray us.'

Why had they let him talk them into this three years ago? What had impelled Jacopo to strike this deal? Reuben suspected it was guilt. He had run away from the fascists in 1937 and had survived while the rest had died. Now he had marked his ground.

'They're just terrorists.'

'They called Menachem Begin a terrorist. The British had a

price on his head. He founded the state of Israel. Things have to change here.'

'I agree, but we don't . . .' He heard someone enter the room behind him and they both stopped talking. Rosa came out on to the balcony holding the twins. Jacopo smiled and reached out for them. Reuben poured his wife a glass of wine and the conversation turned immediately to the children.

How much do you know? Jacopo wondered, glancing at Rosa as he held Simone and Eva in his arms. You may be the mother of my granddaughters but I don't trust you. I don't trust you at all.

The light filtered away and they went inside, laughing and talking late into the evening. The clink of glasses, the smell of seafood, the rhythmic crash of the ocean beyond the windows. Out there in the darkness, a juggernaut rushing towards them, about to crush their comfortable world of wealth and privilege.

15

One Sunday they drove out to Avellaneda, to visit her brother. Reuben drove through dreary streets, past tired prostitutes who patrolled the pavements, picking up the motorists and truck drivers who cruised past. Near the apartment complex where Domingo lived they passed a shantytown, one of the many *villas miserias* that dotted the city.

'Stop the car,' Rosa said.

Reuben pulled the car over to the side of the road. 'What are we doing?'

Rosa stared at the sprawl of tin and cardboard, brown and half-naked children playing football with an old rag in the dust. They could smell the stench even from here. 'My parents were born in the *villas*,' she said, her voice flat.

'I know that,' he said, impatient with her.

'Yes, but you still don't understand.'

'What does that mean?'

'Your father despises me.'

He looked away. 'Nonsense.' She was right, of course.

'Oh, he has great compassion for the poor in general. He just doesn't like them individually.'

'Don't tell me about my father! You don't know him. You know nothing about him!'

'I know more than you think,' she said, and he looked at her and he wondered. For all his father's warnings about secrecy there was only so much you could keep from your own wife. How much had she guessed, how much had she overheard? But he hoped he was wrong. Unlike his father he kept the truth from her not because he did not trust her but because he knew how dangerous knowledge could be.

There were three of them, and they all carried automatic pistols. They rushed into the editorial offices of *La Prensa* just before

three o'clock in the afternoon, shouting and holding their guns
two-handed in front of their faces, military style. Everyone in the
office froze, paralysed by the sight of the weapons. Julio felt his
own bowels turn to water. He couldn't move.

They wanted Jorge Albrecht.

Jorge was a balding, shambling bear of a man who seemed
perpetually wreathed in a cloud of tobacco smoke, his dark jacket
and trousers flecked with grey from where ash had tumbled from
the cigarettes that dangled from his lip as he battered away on
an ancient Remington. He had been with *La Prensa* for twenty
years and he had a reputation for being fearless. But this day
Jorge Albrecht's terror was only too evident.

He rose from his desk, his eyes wide as a horse running from a
fire. He tried to run for the door but two of the men cut off his
retreat. One of them slammed the butt of his pistol into the back
of his head, the other grabbed him as he fell and started to drag
him towards the door.

'Jorge Albrecht is under arrest for crimes against the state!' the
third man shouted, and backed away towards the elevators, still
holding the gun in front of his face.

There were perhaps two dozen people in the office when it
happened. No one moved. No one did anything to help.

What could we have done? Julio asked himself later. It was his
first real experience of fear. He could not believe how quickly it
could paralyse the muscles and the mind. When it was over he
rushed into the men's washrooms and vomited.

16

The glass door was reinforced with ornate wrought iron. Beside the door was a brass grille with a bank of buttons, a number engraved under each one. Julio pressed one of the buttons, heard Rosa's voice crackle over the intercom.

'Rosa, it's me, Julio. I've come to see Reuben.'

There was a buzz as the gate unlocked. He pushed back the heavy door and went inside. Stairs spiralled to the upper floors around an ornate lift cage. Julio did not trust his legs on the stairs. He hauled back the elevator's shuttered metal doors. Reuben and Rosa lived on the fourth floor.

Rosa opened the door.

Motherhood had changed her. She was fuller now, not plump, but not the sylph of a girl he had first seen in Reconquista. She was not wearing make-up and the hem of her skirt was longer. There were curd stains on the left shoulder of her blouse. She had a safety pin in her mouth and a baby over her shoulder.

'Julio.'

'Rosa.' Even then Julio experienced a rush of pain, as he always did when he met her. And he had once told himself he would forget her in a fortnight!

'Reuben's not home yet.'

'I have to see him. It's urgent.'

'Come in. He should be back soon.'

He had been to the apartment many times, and always experienced this same nagging jealousy. A long and thickly carpeted hallway led past a master bedroom, a nursery and a study and then opened on to a huge living room. The shutters had been thrown back and a pale afternoon sun lent the room a golden luminescence. There were two heavy mahogany-and-leather sofas with a matching mahogany-and-iron coffee table. Julio studied the two latest additions to the furniture, a carved Spanish sideboard

displaying crystal decanters of port and whisky and an expensive
Swedish sound system. Much more than I could ever have given
her. Much more.

He looked down at his feet. There were infants' toys scattered
around the floor, among the pot plants. Julio suddenly felt like
an intruder, a thief.

Rosa had laid the baby alongside her twin in a playpen in the
nursery. As she came back into the room, they studied each other
for a moment. Her face was hard. 'Can I get you a drink?'

'Just coffee.' He followed her into the kitchen. Put his hands
in his pockets, took them out again. Hard to breathe, hard to
relax. That look on Jorge's face when the men came. 'You look
wonderful.'

'Thank you.'

'I mean it.'

'Am I supposed to be flattered?'

He watched her grind the coffee. She seemed nervous, as nervous
as he was. In another room one of the babies had started to cry.
She brushed past him without a word and disappeared into the
hallway.

Julio wandered out of the kitchen, leaned on the balcony rail.
A fine view over Recoleta, Reuben. You have it all. Money, a
beautiful home, beautiful children. Pity they are not sons, of
course, but you'll have other chances. And you have Rosa. Most
of all, you have Rosa.

He turned away, looked around the room. Shelves of books;
Shakespeare, Güiraldes, Dickens, Mailer, Cortázar, Mallea,
Capote, Frost, Lugones. His attention was drawn by some framed
photographs on the walls. One of Reuben with Rosa and the twins
at the christening, another of the University rugby fifteen that had
won the university cup three years before. Julio saw a younger
version of himself grinning from the front row.

Rosa walked back into the room, holding one of the twins. Julio
thought about that time in Carmen's apartment, tried to remember
what she looked like when the towel fell away. He wondered if she
still thought about that. He thought about it all the time. It was
clear to him now that Rosa had wanted it to happen, otherwise
she would never have invited him into the apartment, would not
have left the bathroom door open.

'Why are you looking at me like that?'

'Like what?'

'You're Reuben's friend. So I'll be polite to you. But don't ever think you can lay a hand on me again.'

A moment later he heard the sound of a key in the door and Reuben walked in.

Reuben looked tired. A hard day counting money, Julio thought. His long fair hair hung over the collar of his tan raincoat and his shoulders were hunched. He carried a black leather briefcase in one hand, a copy of *La Prensa* in the other. He saw Julio first, then he looked at Rosa.

'Julio. What are you doing here?'

'I need to talk to you.'

'Sure.'

Julio nodded towards the study. 'Can we?'

Reuben hesitated, turned to Rosa, who looked away and busied herself with the baby. He shrugged, took a decanter and two glasses from the sideboard and led the way into his study.

Julio gulped at the whisky in his glass. 'The newspaper was raided today. These three guys smashed their way in. They had automatic pistols, for God's sake. They took Jorge Albrecht.'

Reuben ran a tired hand across his face but said nothing.

'Eight days ago the Montos put a bomb on the railway line between here and Mar del Plata. The line was closed for three days while it was repaired. The official story was that there was an electrical failure. Jorge found out the real reason and wrote the story. The editor wouldn't run it, and Jorge threatened to resign. So finally it was run, under Jorge's byline.' Julio took another swallow of his whisky. 'And see what good it did him.'

'Do you know where he is being held?'

Julio shook his head. 'After it happened, the editor sent us out to visit every police station in Buenos Aires. Every journalist in the damned newspaper. Everywhere we went they claimed not to have heard of him. We even went to the Ministry of the Interior. They said they had no notification of his arrest on any charges.'

'So what do you plan to do?'

'The newspaper is going to file a writ of habeas corpus with the central law courts. But it won't do any good. Already this month there have been two hundred writs filed. They were all refused

because the police or the military both said they had no record
of an arrest. It's a neat trick.'

The sun had dipped below the city skyline. Reuben turned on
the lamps and sat down on the edge of the desk. 'I never thought
it would come to this.'

'These people are like Nazis. On Thursday all the journalists from
the major newspapers were summoned to the Casa Rosada. We were
given a piece of paper. You know what it said? "It is forbidden
from this date to make any reference in newspaper articles to the
appearance of bodies, or the victims of kidnappings or missing
persons." That's it. No signature, no department letterhead. They
say it's not censorship, it's a security measure.' Julio took another
gulp of his whisky. 'That's why they took Jorge, of course. To
show they were serious.'

'What do you want me to do?'

'He's your friend, Reuben. It's how I got the job. I thought you
would know.'

Reuben just stared out of the window.

This wasn't the reaction he had anticipated. Julio felt an
upwelling of panic. Jorge Albrecht wasn't the only reason he
had come. 'You have connections, Reuben. At least, your father
does. Your uncle was Larusse's finance minister, for God's
sake. You must be able to do something.' General Alejandro
Larusse had been president in the early seventies. Julio knew
that such men might fade from sight but they did not fade
from power.

Reuben ran his fingers through his hair. 'I'll do what I can.'

'For God's sake, this is almost civil war. You can't sit on the
fence for ever.'

'I'm not fence-sitting.'

'No? You've had it easy all your life! Now when people are
dying and suffering, are you still going to sit up here in your
fancy apartment and count your cash?' Julio regretted the words
as soon as they were out of his mouth. Fear, drinking on an empty
stomach, seeing Rosa again, they had all contributed to his idiot
outburst. 'Shit. I'm sorry.'

Reuben shrugged his shoulders. 'It doesn't matter. You're
probably right.' He picked up the decanter and splashed more
whisky into Julio's glass. 'But for a fence-sitter I know more about
what's going on than you give me credit for. I already knew about

Jorge. My father has been on the phone all afternoon. The fact is, if we knew where he had been taken we might be able to do something. But there are goon squads running loose all over the city. Who was it? The army? The navy? The city police? Even if I spoke to Videla himself I could not get him released if he was taken by Massera's men in the navy.' Admiral Emilio Massera was the other key figure in the military junta.

'You *knew* about this?'

'Not too bad for someone who spends his nights in his fancy apartment counting his cash?' He ruffled Julio's hair. 'Come on, don't look at me like that. I've got a thick skin and it's not the worst thing anyone's ever said about me.' He went back to the window. Lights were blinking on across the city. 'Believe me, we'll do all we can, Julio. But saving Jorge Albrecht may not be within our power. There are wars within wars.'

Julio took another swallow of whisky and noted the first lurching anaesthesia of intoxication. He felt alone and uncertain for the first time in his life. 'I'm frightened.'

'We're all frightened.'

'I'll be next.'

Reuben still had his back to him, did not seem to notice the strain in his friend's voice. 'Any of us might be next. These people are crazy. Nobody's safe.'

'You're all right. No one could accuse you of being a subversive.'

Reuben turned round and the yellow arc of the desk lamp threw strange shadows over his face. 'Yes, I'm all right.' His Adam's apple bobbed in his throat. 'And so will you be, if you don't do anything stupid.'

'It's too late for that.'

'What do you mean?'

'You remember at university? I never had any money. Well, I did some freelance work. I thought it would pay the bills and help me get a job with a big newspaper when I graduated.'

'You were going to save the world. Like all of us.'

'I had some reviews published in *L'Opinión*, a few articles in the left-wing press.'

'They won't arrest you just for that.'

'Who knows what they'll do? You only have to say Karl Marx and you've got a death squad beating down the door.' Julio took a deep breath. He felt almost overwhelmed by this desperate need to unburden himself. Almost like the confessional, except this was something he could never tell his priest. Father Montserrat was a bigger fascist than Videla. 'You remember *Nuevo Hombre*? It was one of the independent papers. The government accused it of being subversive and closed it down.'

'They published some of your stuff?'

Julio nodded. 'Sure.'

'What sort of articles?'

'Political pieces. About corruption in the military. I mentioned Massera, even Videla.' Julio put his head in his hands. He had thought he was so clever. He had kept his pay cheques for weeks before cashing them, modest as they were, so he could show his girlfriends and boast to his radical drinking friends. He doubted that more than half a dozen people in all Buenos Aires had read his pieces. But now, three years later, those forgotten articles had assumed a deadly significance.

'*Mierda*,' Reuben murmured under his breath.

Julio wanted to weep. How could he have been so stupid? 'What am I going to do?'

'You idiot.'

Julio could not look at him. Yes, yes, an idiot. If only he could go back, have his time over again. 'They're going to kill me.' He felt the tears welling up in his eyes. He didn't give a shit about Videla or Massera or any of them any more. He just wanted to be left in peace. 'You think they'll come after me?'

'I don't know.'

'They only have to check, don't they?'

'You didn't use a pseudonym?'

'I liked seeing my name there in print.'

Reuben put a hand on his shoulder. 'So much for fame. No one was interested in *Nuevo Hombre* except the fucking police.'

'What am I going to do?'

Reuben considered for a moment. 'If you're really worried, you could get out of the country.'

'How?'

'Ask for asylum. Mexico.'

Julio stared at him. Mexico. The word seemed meaningless. 'Mexico?'

'They have an embassy in Belgrano. You have to go there late at night. Once you're inside, the government can't touch you.'

'How do you know about that?'

Reuben gave him a smile that could have meant anything.

'Mexico,' Julio repeated. He sat for a long time staring into his whisky. 'Perhaps they won't find the articles.'

'Perhaps.' Reuben didn't sound convinced.

'I'm such an idiot,' Julio said. He started to cry. Reuben put an arm round his shoulders as Julio wept, and they stayed like that for a long time, a portrait of misery, as the shadows raced across the room and the night fell on Buenos Aires.

'What did he want?' Rosa asked later, after he had gone.

'Advice.'

'I don't like him coming here.'

He looked up at her, surprised. 'Why?'

'That *chanta*.' *Chanta*. A line-shooter. A guy who thought he was more important than he really was.

'Julio's okay.'

'Sure. Just let him be okay somewhere else.'

Reuben shrugged, bewildered by Rosa's vehemence. Why did he have to endure her family, her priest, but it was not okay for his friends to come here? But he said 'Okay,' and left it there. He was too tired to argue about it right then.

Too tired and too scared.

When Julio left the apartment, he walked aimlessly for a long time, finally found himself back in the city, walking along Florida. The most famous pedestrian shopping mall in South America, it was said. He skirted the mud-covered duckboards that had been thrown over a hole in the pavement outside a glittering shopfront of Italian leather. The contradictions of my country. He stared at the elegant windows with their displays of Calvin Klein and Christian Dior, an illusory world in an illusory country where everything was within reach, but where most people could never do more than stare with their noses pressed against the glass. Inflation was running at over three hundred per cent and the people crowded into the *villas miserias* did not have enough food to eat. But here in the heart of Buenos Aires the rich had their privileges protected by a savage army who railed against the evils of communism while silencing every dissenting voice with murder.

But Julio could no longer summon his student rage at the iniquities of such a system. Now the most precious thing on the Florida was his own life. He supposed that he and Reuben were not so different after all. At that moment he would have given anything to have entrenched himself once more in the former security of his middle-class life.

He wandered for hours, lurching from one *whiskería* to another, haunted by the sweaty dread of torture and death; a green Valiant waiting in the street, men dragging him towards a table with leather straps, the final bullet in the head. Not even Reuben could save him. The world was a black and terrible place and he did not know where to go to save himself.

Doctor Eduardo Artime came out of the bedroom and closed the door gently behind him. He crossed to the study where Angeli stood by the window, looking over the pool and the manicured lawn.

'A drink, Doctor?'

'Thank you.'

Artime sat on the burgundy leather chesterfield and stretched his long legs in front of him, his high forehead creasing into a frown. He had been Francesca's doctor since she was a child, physician to her entire family: he could be trusted. He took out a bottle of Chivas Regal and poured two fingers, neat, into a tumbler. He handed it to him.

'Thank you.'

Angeli sat down behind his desk. He was aware of an uncustomary disadvantage. He did not like talking to any man, especially on a matter of such delicacy, when he had not seen his file. He would make a point of calling a friend of his in the Ministry and having Artime's dossier sent over to him.

'Well, Doctor?'

Artime considered, in his ponderous way. 'There is nothing physically wrong with her.'

'I realise that.'

Artime sighed. 'She has suffered great loss. She is grieving not only for a child, but also for the loss of her womanhood. This is beyond my scope of expertise, I am afraid. I can perhaps refer you to someone who specialises in such things. It can be handled with the utmost discretion.'

'A psychiatrist, you mean?'

Artime sipped his whisky, nodded.

'I don't think so.' Angeli swallowed back his rage. Psychiatrists! Subversives, all of them, spreading the filth of that dirty Jew, Freud!

'Your wife needs help. This tragedy has deeply disturbed the balance of her mind.'

'Is there nothing you can give her to snap her out of this?'

Artime blinked slowly. 'There is no medical solution, no drug to make her the way she was before this happened, if that is what you are asking. I can sedate her if she is having trouble sleeping, but that is only a temporary solution.'

'Sedate her? All she does now is sleep.'

'It would appear she poses no risk to anyone. If, however . . .'

'Go on.'

'If she becomes too depressed . . . well, you should perhaps ask the servants to watch her closely.'

'Suicide, you mean?'

Artime reached into the pocket of his jacket, took out a fountain pen and scribbled a name and phone number into his notebook. He tore out the page and placed it on the coffee table between them. 'I have known this woman a long time. If you change your mind about some . . . therapy . . . she does excellent work. I shall tell her to expect your call. You can be sure of her utter discretion.'

Angeli picked up the piece of paper. *Dr Mercedes Barrington.* An address on Paraguay and a telephone number.

Artime finished his drink, stood up and went to the door.

'Antonia will show you the way out,' Angeli said.

Artime nodded and a moment later the door closed quietly behind him. Angeli stood up and went back to the window, his fists opening and closing at his sides in impotent rage. He picked up Artime's empty glass, weighed it in his hand like a ball and then suddenly, and with great force, he hurled it at the wall.

Julio spent the morning staring at a blank page in his typewriter. By lunchtime the article he was writing on forthcoming preparations for the 1978 World Cup was no closer to being finished than it had been that morning. Although only a casual smoker, he bought a packet of cigarettes at a *kiosco* during his lunch break and smoked them steadily through the afternoon. He looked out of the window, his head wreathed in smoke, his mind blank. He tried not to think.

When he got home to his apartment that evening he turned on the television and stared at it until the end of transmissions. Then he drank steadily until one o'clock in the morning and went to bed.

But sleep would not come. His sheets were damp with sweat, his head ached. It was difficult to breathe, there was a great weight pressing on his chest. This was when they came, the death squads, in the middle of the night, dragging you out of bed and throwing you naked and shivering into one of their green Falcons. He heard a car backfire in the next street and he sat bolt upright in bed.

His heart was hammering in his chest, he could feel it through his ribs, beating so fast it was almost painful.

Perhaps he had already left it too late. Perhaps he was already a dead man.

A crude cardboard sign hanging on the elevator said: OUT OF ORDER. Reuben sagged against the wrought-iron gates. He did not have the strength for three flights of stairs. Not today. He ripped away the piece of cardboard and threw it across the foyer. Everything was to shit in this damned country.

When he reached the apartment he could hear Eva screaming on the other side of the door. *I don't have the patience for this.* Before the twins, he would have got himself a stiff drink, gone into the study, closed the door, wound down slowly. Rosa knew him well enough by the time they were married to let him alone at the end of the day. But now he had no peace at home either.

When he walked in, Rosa was kneeling in the middle of the living-room carpet with safety pins in her mouth, changing nappies. *Everything to shit.*

He threw his briefcase on the floor.

Rosa looked over her shoulder. '*Buenas tardes*,' she said, with heavy irony.

'I said hello. You didn't hear me.'

'Bad day?'

He didn't answer her. He wished she would make the children shut up. He went to the sideboard, picked up the whisky decanter. He poured three fingers in a tumbler and drank half of it in one swallow, neat.

If there had ever been any doubts about the junta's aims, they had been dispelled by what he had seen tonight at the *kiosco* where he stopped each evening to buy his copies of *L'Opinión* and the English-language *Buenos Aires Herald*. Neo-Nazi magazines like *Odal* and *Militia* were being sold openly now. This in a city which boasted the world's seventh-largest Jewish community. He had not set foot inside a synagogue since his bar mitzvah, but he understood that that was beside the point. His name was Altman and that made him a target of this new, government-sanctioned welling of hate. As if they didn't have enough to worry about.

Rosa watched him, warily. She put the girls in a cot by the window. 'Can you watch the girls for me? I'll get dinner.'

'I don't want any dinner.'

He walked past her, threw himself on the sofa. His eyes fell on the newspaper lying on the coffee table, a slim four-sheet with mimeographed pages, *La Voz de La Razón* printed across the top in Gothic typeface. He stared at it, as if it were some grim practical joke.

'What's this?'

Rosa's voice was sulky. 'It's just a newspaper.'

'What's it doing here?'

Eva picked up on the anger in her father's voice and started to cry. Rosa scooped her up and soothed her. 'You don't have to shout.'

Reuben stood up, held the paper in front of her face. 'Are you crazy? Where did you get this?'

'I saw it lying on a chair in a *confitería* on Florida. I wanted to read it.'

Reuben could not believe his ears. Didn't she know what had been going on? Did she think they were somehow insulated from the terror that had insinuated itself into every part of this city? 'How could you be so stupid? Do you know what happens to people who are caught with copies of this?' He took the newspaper into the kitchen, lit the gas burner, and held it over the flames.

Rosa watched him. Eva was still screaming in her arms.

'Can't you shut her up?' he shouted.

'What's wrong with you?'

'What's wrong with *you*? You think it's okay bringing this sort of shit into our home?' He carried the burning newspaper to the sink. 'You want the police knocking on our door in the middle of the night?' He had never imagined she took any interest in politics. As long as they had a nice apartment, as long as she had nice clothes to wear and babies to look after, he thought she was happy. She was just a girl from the *villas*, right?

The flames licked around his fingers. He dropped the remains into the sink and flushed the ashes down the waste pipe. Then he leaned on the edge of the drainer, exhausted by his own rage. He hung his head.

Eva quietened and Rosa took a step closer. She put her head on his shoulder. 'What's wrong?'

Reuben ran a hand across his face. 'Nothing. I'm just tired.' And he turned away from her and went into the study, closing the door behind him.

His nerves were shot to pieces. He didn't know how much longer he could keep going with this.

19

Two mornings a week, Rosa left the children with her new maid and spent a few precious hours shopping, or having coffee and pastries with friends at a *confitería*, or, as she had this morning, at a private health club gymnasium on Esmeralda and Alvear. Her black Citroën was parked in the street outside.

It was a cold autumn morning. Julio turned up the collar of his jacket against the bite of the Atlantic wind. He leaned on the roof and waited for her.

After half an hour she finally appeared. She was wearing a black silk track jacket and pants over a pink leotard, and she was carrying a sports bag in her left hand. There were damp sweat patches on the leotard and her hair was wet.

She was fumbling in her jacket pocket for her car keys when she saw him. She stared at him in surprise.

'Julio?'

'Hello, Rosa.'

'What is it? What's wrong?' Suddenly she looked alarmed. 'Is it Reuben?'

'Reuben's fine.' He nodded towards a bar further up the street. 'Can we go someplace and talk?'

Her face set like stone. 'I don't think so.'

'It's important. Please.'

The steamy warmth and chatter of the *whiskeria* was welcome after the chill of the street. The closeness of her stirred him. Her jacket was open and he could see the tan valley between her breasts.

She felt the direction of his stare and zippered the jacket all the way to her neck. 'What is this about?'

'I had to talk to you.'

The waiter brought two coffees, espressos, with two glasses of water. Rosa pulled her cigarettes from her sports bag and lit one. He smiled.

'What's so funny?'

'You spend all morning in a health club and then you light up a cigarette.'

She let out the tobacco smoke in a long stream and then leaned her elbow on the table, the cigarette poised. A casual toss of the dark hair. He stared at the scarlet fingernails, still long and carefully manicured despite the babies. Her eyes were black. 'Don't play with me, Julio. You said you had something to tell me.'

He leaned closer. The smell of her sweat affected him like French perfume. 'Are you happy with him?'

A quick intake of breath. 'I'm going.' She picked up her cigarettes from the table and tossed them in her bag. Her hands were shaking. 'If you dare show your face at our apartment again I shall tell Reuben everything. Do you understand?'

'Don't worry. You won't see me again after tomorrow.'

That stopped her. 'You're leaving?'

'I'm in trouble with the authorities. Some articles I wrote back in my student days. I'm going to apply for political asylum in Mexico.' He was grandstanding. Even now he wanted to impress her. 'So, you see, you did make the right choice. Reuben won't ever rock the boat. He knows where his bread is buttered. He can sit up there in his nice apartment and admire the view while the rest of us run from the death squads.'

'You are so wrong about him.'

'Would he ever stand up to the government?' *As I did* hung on the silence, suggested but not spoken.

She leaned towards him, their faces now just inches apart. She seemed about to say something, changed her mind.

'Anyway,' he said. 'I just wanted to say goodbye.'

'You think it's going to break my heart to see you go?'

'I'm sorry, Rosa. For what happened.' He drained his cup in one swallow and took a mouthful of water, rinsing away the grounds. 'I hope you'll think about me sometimes.'

'Only in my nightmares.' She stood up. 'I have to go. Goodbye, Julio. I won't wish you good luck because you don't deserve it.' She started to walk off, stopped and turned around. 'He's your friend.'

'I know. And it's killing me.'

'*Cretino*,' she said.

After she had gone Julio sat back and ordered a whisky, even though it was not yet lunchtime. To hell with her, to hell with all of them, to hell with Carmen, to hell with Reuben. To hell with friends, and to hell with women. He would have a few more whiskies and celebrate his last day in Buenos Aires. Tonight he would be begging for asylum at the Mexican embassy.

20

Reuben stood at the window, holding a cup of *café crema*. He looked down into the street. A senior executive from the Ford motor plant lived across the way. Two bodyguards had been hired to protect him and they sat together on the bonnet of a car, smoking cigarettes, their pump-action shotguns resting in the crooks of their arms.

'I may be home late tonight,' Reuben said. 'I have a meeting with some bankers from Indamex this evening. I'll probably take them to dinner.' He kept his face turned away for the lie. A watery yellow sun filtered into the apartment.

'We hardly see you these days.'

'I have a bank to run.'

Rosa sat on the sofa feeding Eva. 'Will you call me?'

'Sure. I'll try not to be too late.'

He went into the bedroom to finish dressing, slipped on a tan camel-hair coat. He picked up his briefcase and went back to the living room.

Rosa gave him a wintry smile. Did she know? Did she suspect? 'Have a good day.'

He kissed her on the cheek. 'Goodbye, *cara*.'

He went downstairs, got into his car, let out a long breath. It was not in his nature to lie easily.

The smell of sex, bodies lathered in sweat, coiling shadows on the wall, colours exploding inside the head. She let him do anything he wanted. Her body's soft openings and fragrances a forbidden haven from the dark world outside. He gripped the wrought-iron lattice of the bed with his fists and rode the waves of his own pleasure, for that moment no longer afraid. Never as beautiful as my Rosa, Reuben thought. She was earthy, plump, without his wife's feline grace. But she's what I need right now.

And when it was over he wanted her again, took her with a slow desperation that measured his guilt and his fear. She climaxed with him, their bodies thrusting violently together. Afterwards he pitched almost immediately into a black and seamless sleep.

21

The twins woke Rosa just before three o'clock for their feed. She rose from the bed, still in a half-sleep. She would often wake in the middle of the night and feed both twins in the dark and not even remember the next morning. But tonight something made her switch on the bedside lamp.

Reuben's side of the bed was empty.

The twins were crying, more urgently now. Rosa forced herself to stay calm. She got up and warmed their bottles in the kitchen. Eva took hers and quickly fell back to sleep in her cot. She had had a fever, and the doctor had prescribed some medicine to bring down her temperature and help her sleep. It was Simone, as usual, the fussy one, who would not settle.

Rosa sat with her on the sofa, gentling her back to sleep.

Try not to think about Reuben. Try not to think about what he's done.

She heard the scream of brakes in the street below. She started with fear and Simone woke and started to cry again.

'Sh, baby, shhh,' Rosa crooned to her.

Moments later she heard the crack of the plastic explosive that tore out the lock on the building's security door. It made her gasp aloud and Simone thrashed her arms and legs in fright.

Rosa rushed to the window. There were two cars slewed across the street, their headlights on. Ford Falcons, standard issue for the police. An armed man was lounging on the bonnet of one of the cars.

She felt a cold stab of fear. No, they had come for someone else.

She heard boots on the stairs.

She looked at the clock. Ten past three.

Someone was hammering on the door. Simone screamed even louder. Rosa snatched up the telephone, her hands shaking.

*   *   *

Reuben was woken from a black sleep by the urgent clamour of the telephone. Carmen groaned and rolled out of bed. He heard her stumble into the other room and fumble for the receiver in the dark.

Reuben heard her say, 'Shit,' very softly, as if to herself. 'It's Rosa.'

'What?' He turned on the bedside lamp. It took a moment for him to remember where he was.

Por Dios. Look at the time!

'It's Rosa!' Carmen repeated, her voice shrill.

Rosa? She didn't know he was here.

He threw himself out of bed, snatched the receiver out of her hand. He could make out Rosa's voice, heard one of the twins crying in the background. 'Rosa?' he said. His voice didn't sound like his own.

'Reuben! The police are here!'

He rubbed a hand across his face. Perhaps he was dreaming this. 'What?'

There were shouts and a loud crash in the background. Someone had kicked in a door.

The line went dead.

22

There were three men in the *patota*, the arresting squad. They were armed with automatic pistols and wore green army-issue bullet-proof vests underneath their civilian clothes. Once inside the apartment they made little noise. One of them came towards her, his pistol held in front of his face. He had a moustache and was wearing a black zippered jacket. 'We are looking for Reuben Altman.'

Rosa could not find her voice.

'Where is he?'

She felt as if someone was choking her. 'He's not here,' she managed.

The man nodded to his colleagues. One of them checked the bedroom, the study, the nursery. She heard him throwing open doors. The other ran into the kitchen and then kicked open the French doors that led on to the balcony.

Simone was screaming in her arms, pink-faced. But Rosa's thoughts were for Eva. Her instinct was to snatch her out of her cot, hold her, try to protect her. But a voice in her head persuaded her that unless Eva made a noise these men might not notice her. There was just one cot, after all, and they could see she had a baby in her arms. If she was arrested, where would Eva be safer? Here, alone, or in some police cell?

She hesitated.

One of the gunmen emerged from the bathroom. 'He's not here.'

The other man turned away from the balcony, also shaking his head.

The man with the moustache nodded. A hood was thrown over her face, Simone was snatched out of her arms. Rosa screamed. But then her wrists were cuffed behind her back and they were pushing her towards the door.

'Simone!' Rosa screamed over and over.

One of the soldiers drove a fist into her stomach and after that it was a struggle just to breathe. They dragged her down the stairs and bundled her into a car.

Stephen Barrington was woken by an explosion. He jumped out of bed, felt his wife's hand on his arm. 'What is it, Stephen?'

'It's just a car backfiring,' he said, without conviction. He slipped on a dressing gown and went to the bedroom window.

'Stephen?'

'There're two cars in the street. There's a man standing beside one of them. I think he's got a gun.'

They heard heavy boots on the stairs and Stephen experienced the first thrill of fear. Like everyone, he knew about the death squads, the disappearances. But that was in another Argentina, a long way from Recoleta. Or so he had thought.

Someone was kicking in a door on the other side of the landing. Mercedes gasped and reached out for him. Stephen came back to the bed, put an arm around her shoulders. They listened to the sounds of the struggle.

'It's the Altmans.' I should go out there, he thought. I should go and help them. He heard Rosa scream and instinctively he got to his feet.

Mercedes clutched at his arm, pulled him back on to the bed. 'Don't go out there.'

'We have to do something.' But now he found he could not move.

'There's nothing you can do. They have guns. They'll take you too!'

Luke was crying in the next room. Stephen went to fetch him and put him in the bed beside his wife. Again he hesitated, caught between fear and duty. 'She has young children.'

'So do we.'

But then it was over, as suddenly as it had begun. He heard shouts below in the street, went back to the window, saw one of the cars drive away. Another man tossed two green plastic bags into the back of the other Falcon. Then it, too, sped away.

A deathly silence.

Mercedes closed her eyes and murmured a silent prayer to the Virgin. Luke was still crying, softly.

'I'm going to see what's happened.'

'Stephen!'

'I'll be right back.'

The door to the Altman apartment hung open, on one hinge. All the lights were on. The telephone had been torn out of the wall but otherwise there were no signs of a struggle in the hallway or the living room. Stephen looked for bloodstains, was grateful to find none.

Then he went into the master bedroom. It had been ransacked. The bedding lay on the floor, the wardrobe doors hung open, the closet drawers upturned. Perhaps they had been looking for something; or perhaps it was an act of frustration at not finding what they wanted.

They had done an even better job in the study. The desk drawers lay on the carpet along with every single file in the walnut three-drawer cabinet. But not one scrap of paper remained. Stephen guessed the contents were in the two plastic bags he had seen thrown into one of the Falcons.

He went into the nursery. A pink rabbit gazed wonderingly back at him through the wooden bars of the cot, a mobile of zoo animals trembled a few inches from his face. Transfers of Mickey Mouse and Donald Duck grinned from the pale blue walls. Fear was replaced by rage as he stared at these icons of innocence. A more savage reality had impinged here, the Devil had left his footsteps in the pink clouds.

The cot appeared to be empty and he was about to leave the room. But then he saw the blankets move.

Dear God.

He took a deep breath. He reached into the cot and pulled back the covers.

The infant had somehow wriggled under the covers, so that the top blanket covered her head. She was wearing a pink flannel jumpsuit. Her cheeks were pink with fever, her thumb in her mouth, her hair damp and tousled. Her toothless mouth was slack in sleep, the rise and fall of her breathing barely discernible. Stephen stared, trying to comprehend the circumstances behind this discovery.

He gently picked up the sleeping child. He heard a noise behind him. He turned around, saw his wife standing, grey-faced, in the nursery door.

'Oh my God,' she murmured. 'Oh my God.'

23

The Mexican embassy was on Arcos Street, a colonial building in the Spanish style with a modest garden in front. Police had been posted on the street corners near the residence. Reuben saw them and hung back in the shadows, waiting a long and desperate hour for his chance. It was almost dawn when he sprinted across the street and rang the bell by the wrought-iron gate, dodging quickly back into the shadows thrown by the wall to avoid being seen. Moments later a guard swung open the gate. Reuben ran inside to safety and asylum.

The room was lit by a naked bulb hanging from a flex. Angeli stood beside the torture table, smoking a cigarette. 'Rosa Altman.'

Rosa turned her head towards the sound. She had been blindfolded. 'Where's ... Simone?' Her lip was cracked, and watery blood oozed down her chin. 'Where is ... my baby?'

Best for now, he considered, to let her wonder. Perhaps later, if she proved stubborn, they might use the infant as a bargaining chip. 'Where is your husband?'

'I don't ... know ... where he is.'

Angeli exhaled, slowly. 'Señora Altman, I am not a brutal man, not a monster. This gives me no pleasure. Just tell me where your husband is.'

She tried to spit at him but she did not have the strength and her tongue was too swollen. The spit dribbled from her lips and ran down her neck.

He took a fistful of her hair and lifted her head from the table. 'Now, I want you to listen to me, Rosa Altman. We don't want to hurt you. We want your husband, not you. Tell us where he is and all this can be over. He has committed serious crimes against the state. We know he is part of a Zionist conspiracy against Argentina. *Your* country. In such circumstances you no longer owe him the loyalties that a wife normally bestows upon a husband. Do you understand? Now then, let me ask you again. Where is your husband?'

Rosa whimpered some reply.

'I didn't hear that, Señora Altman.'

'. . . Simone?'

He let her head fall back on to the table. Somewhere in the next room a man was screaming.

Angeli looked up at Turturro. 'Continue,' he said, and he walked out of the cell, slamming the heavy metal door behind him.

24

'We cannot keep her here.'

A cold grey dawn. Mercedes stood by the picture window, holding the child. Behind her the skyline of Buenos Aires was silhouetted against a fire-and-charcoal sky. Stephen was still in his dressing gown, pacing the room. Luke was finally asleep, tucked into their bed.

'What else can we do? We will have to look after her until one of the family comes for her.'

'They may not even know she's here.' Stephen went to the cocktail cabinet and poured himself another brandy. His hands were shaking. Buenos Aires was the most British city in all South America; the railways had been built by British engineers, its utilities developed with British expertise, its hinterlands opened up with the help of British business and British banks. For a time there had been a thriving Welsh community in Patagonia, there was even a Harrods in Florida Street. Now this. It was like having the Nazis in London. He had read about it every day in *La Nación* and the *Buenos Aires Herald*, knew people who had had cousins or uncles abducted by unidentified men. But it had not touched him personally, until now.

'There is nothing else we can do,' Mercedes was saying.

Stephen knew she was right. But he was afraid. What if those thugs came back, looking for the child?

'What do you think has happened to the Altmans?' she asked him.

'I don't know. Perhaps they are just going to disappear – like all those people they write about in the *Herald*.'

'This poor child.'

'There must be relatives.'

Mercedes sat down on the sofa. A pool of light from the table lamp fell over his wife's face and that of the sleeping child. It seemed impossible that this was happening here, in a security apartment in an exclusive barrio of Buenos Aires.

Stephen decided to go back into the Altman apartment to fetch baby clothes, nappies, toys. He had only been back a short while when they heard men moving about on the landing. They had come back.

This time the Altmans' home was systematically ransacked. Everything of any possible value was looted. Stephen watched them from the window loading the television and sound system into the boot of a green Ford Falcon. They took everything, even the contents of the medicine cabinet.

The Barringtons waited for one of the Altmans' family to appear. By mid-morning, when no one had come, Stephen went down to the lobby. The front door with its heavy wrought-iron security grille still hung open on its hinges. The lock had been blown off with plastic explosives. He saw two men watching the apartment from a parked car across the road.

Some time in the afternoon the caretaker, a tall, hatchet-faced man in his late fifties, came to screw the hinges back on the door to apartment 401. A new security door appeared in the lobby. No one in the building ever mentioned the Altmans again. It was as if it had never happened.

The notion came to him near the end of the day, as he was preparing to go home. He wondered why it had not occurred to him before. He supposed he had been too preoccupied with this Altman affair, the way a man can become too engrossed in a crossword puzzle on a train and forget his stop. His men had raided the Altman Group's offices in the banking district earlier that day, were still trying to piece together the maze of wire transfer records, corporate charter and loan documents and internal memos linking the Montoneros with the Altman financial group.

It was already clear that the information they had been given was correct and that these Jews had betrayed their adopted country. The Altman Group was an established and profitable institution with interests in insurance, shipping and two refrigeration plants. They also had a forty per cent share in two *estançiones* outside Córdoba and had even organised loans and credit facilities for a number of venture companies closely linked to the current military government.

They had also handled almost twenty-one million dollars that had been raised through bank robberies or ransom demands by the Cuban-backed Montoneros. Jacopo Altman had invested this money on their behalf in property in Miami and Tampa. Last month the Altman Group had transferred $142,000 in interest through a numbered account in the Banco de Guadalajara in the Cayman Islands to Havana where the Montoneros headquarters used the funds to buy weapons.

They had learned as much from Jacopo and Arturo and other members of the Altman family, who had all been interrogated downstairs at various times during the day.

Angeli looked at his watch. It was late and he was tired. He had spent the last sixteen hours working on this. He picked up his heavy leather briefcase and went down the concrete steps to the basement.

The guardroom consisted of no more than a desk, a row of metal filing cabinets and a stained bench with a kettle and a few chipped cups. The men ate their lunch from it, but at busy times it served as an additional torture table.

Turturro was sitting at the desk, typing up a report. There was blood on his shirt. Another man, a guard, was making coffee.

They snapped to attention when Angeli came into the room.

'Rosa Altman,' Angeli barked.

'Yes, Colonel,' Turturro answered.

'When you searched the apartment, you found an infant?'

'Yes, Colonel, she was . . .'

'Where is she?'

The sergeant fumbled on the desk for his keys and hurried out of the door. Angeli followed him. Turturro unlocked the door to one of the cells. There were clothes – men's and women's – strewn around the floor and dried bloodstains on a wooden table in the middle of the room and on the cement floor. This was the room where suspects were brought for their initial interview.

The child had been left on a blanket in a corner of the room. She was screaming and kicking frantically in rage and torment. She wore only a simple cloth nappy – soaking wet – and a white vest. She was blue with cold.

'Idiot,' Angeli snarled.

'Colonel?'

Angeli grabbed Turturro by the collar and hurled him against the wall. He slapped him hard across the face. 'The child is innocent.'

'But we . . .'

'In the sight of God she is an innocent! No matter what her parents have done, she is blameless. And you treat her this way?'

The sergeant shook his head. A trickle of blood spilled from his lip down his chin.

'Have you no pity?' Angeli turned away. He went to the corner, bent down and scooped the child up in his arms. 'Get me a blanket.'

Turturro rushed out of the door.

Angeli felt awkward holding the child. He had no idea what he should do to make her stop crying. He knew she needed to be fed and cleaned at least. She smelled vile. 'So this is Simone.' He looked into the infant's face. Brown and wrinkled, like a monkey, a tuft of black hair. Perhaps one day she would grow to be as beautiful as her mother.

Turturro returned with a rough brown blanket. There were bloodstains on it. 'Colonel.'

Angeli snatched it from him. It would do, for now. 'Get out of here.'

Turturro fled.

Angeli looked at the small creature in his arms. 'Simone,' he murmured.

25

'Is Señora Angeli still in her room?'

Antonia nodded. 'Yes, señor, she has not . . .'

'This child needs to be washed and fed.'

Antonia stared in bewilderment at the screaming and filthy bundle the señor thrust in her arms. 'But, señor, we do not have . . .'

'I don't care how you do it. Just do it.' He nodded towards the old servant in the white jacket who was standing in simple astonishment by the door. 'Send Jorge to buy whatever you need. When the child is properly dressed and wrapped in a clean blanket, bring her back to me. And make sure she is no longer crying.'

Antonia blinked and nodded.

'I shall be in my study. And Antonia . . .'

'Señor?'

'Not a word of this outside this house. You understand what will happen to you and Jorge if I discover that you have failed me?'

Antonia turned pale. '*Sí*, Señor Angeli.' She hurried away.

He waited in his study, working on the files in his briefcase. He looked at his watch several times. By the time Antonia returned it was evening and he had turned on the lamps in the room.

There was a knock on the study door.

'Enter.'

The grey-haired Antonia stood in the doorway, as proud as a new mother. 'She is ready, Señor Angeli.'

He stood up and came around the desk. In the soft glow of the wall sconces, the child's appearance was changed utterly. Now that she was warm and fed a healthy pink colour had suffused her skin, and her face had resolved itself into the cherubic serenity of a child. Angeli smelled the warmth of the pink woollen blanket, the faint aroma of curds.

'Jorge bought nappies, some clothes, some blankets,' Antonia gushed. 'And some milk formula. We had to . . .'

'Thank you, Antonia.' He took the child from her arms.

She seemed reluctant to part with her.

'That will be all.'

Antonia nodded and left the room.

Angeli took a deep breath. Holding the child in the crook of one arm, he left the study and went up the stairs to his wife's bedroom.

But Francesca was not in the bedroom. The bed had not been made and there were clothes strewn about the floor. Then he heard his wife's voice, the soft pitch of her singing, in the next room. He looked down at Simone and rearranged the sleeping child's blanket as if primping her before she was to go on stage. Then he went through to the nursery.

Francesca sat beside the empty crib in her nightgown, murmuring a lullaby. With one hand she rocked the cradle, with the other she clutched the neck of her nightgown, as if she were cold.

Angeli's shadow fell across her face. She looked up.

'Little Simone is awake, my love. She was crying for you.' He bent down and laid the infant gently in his wife's arms.

He held his breath and waited to see what would happen.

Francesca gasped with surprise and then her face creased into a beatific smile. 'Why, thank you, César.'

She continued to hum softly as if nothing had happened.

Angeli watched her for a moment, then went out, shutting the nursery door softly behind him. Well, time would tell.

Rosa had been suspended from a hook on the ceiling by her ankles. Her arms were tied behind her back. There were dark, plum-coloured bruises on her back and her ribs and a froth of blood at her nose and mouth. Angeli could hear her breathing from the other side of the room.

He barely recognised her.

Turturro was standing to one side with the doctor. He shook his head. 'She is obstinate.'

'It doesn't matter now. I have just heard from the Ministry of the Interior that her husband has applied for asylum at the Mexican embassy. He is beyond our reach now.' Angeli took the

9mm pistol from the holster at his belt and held the barrel against her temple.

Rosa mumbled something. He leaned closer. Perhaps some last-minute bargain? 'Señora Altman? You wished to say something?'

It was hard to pick out her words. At the third attempt he understood. The word she had spoken was 'Simone'.

'Simone is to go on to a better life. And so must you, my dear.'

He pulled the trigger once. In the confines of the cellar the discharge of the pistol sounded like a cannon shot. Rosa's body jerked on the end of the chain and then was still.

26

A week later the apartment was rented to a new couple.

It was considered too dangerous to ask questions about people who had been disappeared. Stephen reported the incident by telephone to the British embassy but the minor functionary he spoke to was brusque and uninterested. The Altmans, Stephen was informed, were not British citizens and were therefore not the concern of Her Majesty's Government.

The scandal involving the Altman Group was not reported in the Argentine press, but a few days later he learned about it in the English-language *Buenos Aires Herald*. It was reported that the entire Altman family had disappeared. The government claimed they had been involved in a massive fraud on the foreign exchange market and had since fled the country.

And still no one came to the apartment to ask about the Altmans or their children. It was as if Reuben and Rosa had existed in a vacuum.

From the morning following her parents' disappearance, the child cried incessantly. Nothing seemed to pacify her. Mercedes took her to a local doctor, pretending the child was her own. The doctor could find nothing physically wrong with her. He prescribed sedatives.

The Barringtons' housekeeper and maid, Maria, was told what had happened that night and sworn to secrecy. But even though she was on hand to help, Mercedes insisted on nursing the infant herself.

Stephen looked on, knowing there was more than simple Christian charity at work here. One day, about a week after the Altmans' disappearance, he found his wife bent over the child's makeshift cot, changing her clothes. For once she had stopped crying. Mercedes was singing to her, softly, her face lit with rapture.

They had always wanted another child. But Luke was almost six years old now and there had been three miscarriages in the intervening years. Their doctor had told him he did not think Mercedes would carry to full term again.

There was a danger, Stephen knew, that his wife might grow too attached to this baby. Every day the bond between them grew stronger. Luke had been tended mainly by Maria; perhaps because he had appeared so quickly in their marriage and she had taken him for granted. Now time was running out for her and her mothering came not only from love but from desperation. Mercedes hardly left the infant alone for a moment, night or day.

But her devotion had brought results. The child had settled and although she still cried often the sound of Mercedes' voice always quietened her. And because they did not know the child's name Mercedes had started calling her 'Gabriella', the name they had agreed on for their first daughter.

After two weeks Stephen announced that they could not continue this way. 'We must find out if the Altmans have a family somewhere.'

'We know nothing about them. If we start asking questions we put *ourselves* in danger.'

'We have to inform the authorities of our situation. What we are doing is illegal.'

'And what was done to her parents, was that *legal*? Think about it. Think about the child. What will happen to her if we call the police?'

Stephen rubbed a hand across his face. He knew she was right. 'But she's not ours.'

'She has to belong to *someone*.'

She is right, he thought. What can we do?

He looked up, saw Luke listening at the doorway. 'This is your new sister,' he said to him.

27

In spring the pink buds appear again on the *palo borracho* trees. The warm sunshine brings the neighbourhood mothers back to the plaza at Recoleta, small children in tow.

Mercedes sat on one of the benches, in the shade of the great *ombú* tree, watching the joggers and the professional dog walkers, the *paseadores*, who came here to exercise the pedigree Afghans and Airedales on the grass. Luke was staring wide-eyed at two old men in dark suits and trilbies, singing *milongas* outside La Bielá, busking for coins.

She stared at the child beside her in the stroller. A miracle. A gift from God when she had all but given up all hope.

She loved Luke of course. But she had desperately wanted a daughter. Boys grew up and went away. Little girls were yours for ever.

Gabriella looked up at her and grinned and suddenly it was as if there was a nest of warm puppies squirming inside her. She wanted to pick her up and squeeze her. At times it was easy to forget that Gabriella was not her own. In fact, she had been surprised at how easy it had been for herself and her husband to obtain a forged birth certificate. They had told family and friends they had adopted her.

The thought of giving her up now was inconceivable.

The fuzz on top of her head had turned into a mop of thick, dark hair. She had huge brown eyes, olive skin and a delightful heart-shaped mouth. She was a beautiful child, an angel, the daughter she had always dreamed of. The first word she had spoken, one morning when Mercedes came to fetch her from her cot, was: 'Mama.'

Mercedes reached out her hand and the child gripped her finger tightly, putting it in her mouth. Gabriella grinned up at her. She had one tooth.

Mercedes felt the sting of a tear in her eyes. '*Chiquita*,' she whispered. 'You're mine now. I won't ever let *anyone* take you away from me. Not *ever*.'

Domingo Gonsalvez hesitated. Beside the front doors of the Edificio San Martín there was a bank of dark green buttons with the apartment numbers engraved above each one on the brass backplate. He pushed the button under number 402.

A metallic voice with an English accent demanded his name and business in Spanish.

'My name is Domingo Gonsalvez. I have come about my sister, Rosa Altman. She used to live in apartment 401.'

There was a long silence. Finally the disembodied voice said: 'You had better come up.' He heard a buzz as the lock was released. He pushed open the door and went inside.

Stephen felt a chill hand squeeze his chest. So. He had been waiting for this moment for almost six months. Recently there had been times when he thought that it might not come, after all.

He waited by the door, took a breath, checked his reflection in the hall mirror, fighting down a wave of panic. Six months, and still he was not prepared. He wished there had been some warning so that he could decide what to say, how to behave. He wished Mercedes were here.

He stared at the man in the mirror, the tall, rather thin Englishman in the blazer and tie, with the wings of grey at his temples. He had a pinched, sallow face and a rather prominent Adam's apple that bobbed in his throat when he was nervous. As he was now.

A knock on the door. Their maid, Maria, led the visitor into the living room. Stephen stepped forward to greet him.

He was perhaps thirty years old, Stephen guessed, with the dark complexion of a *mestizo* and the large coarse hands of a working man. He wore running shoes and an open-necked white shirt that was stained with sweat. His brown suit was a size too small. There was a fresh pink scar over his left eye.

'Stephen Barrington.'

'Domingo Gonsalvez, señor.' He looked around, ill at ease.

'You wish me to help you?' Stephen said, taking the advantage immediately.

'Yes, señor. It is a personal matter. I hope I am not imposing on your time.' He hesitated. 'My sister and her husband lived next door, in apartment 401. You knew them?'

'Not well.'

The other man hesitated again, staring at the chintz curtains and chesterfield sofas and the framed photographs of horses and prints of English hunting scenes. Stephen could not fathom his expression. Envy or resentment? Perhaps both.

Stephen had no idea how to proceed with the interview. He waved his visitor towards one of the two chesterfields and invited him to sit down. Domingo perched on the very edge of the sofa, as if he might be ordered back to his feet at any moment.

Stephen asked Maria to fetch a pot of tea. He sat down. 'My wife is not here. She likes to take the children to the park on Saturday mornings.'

Domingo nodded and stared at his hands.

'You live in Buenos Aires?'

'Yes, señor. In Avellaneda. But I was born in Córdoba.'

'I see.' There was a shuffling silence. The man was staring at a sepia photograph on the wall. 'My wife's grandfather,' Stephen explained. 'With the Prince of Wales. He visited their *estancián* when he came here in the thirties.'

The other man nodded, without comprehension. With every second that passed Stephen felt increasingly ashamed. He had often wondered how he would react when finally faced with this situation. Now he realised he did not intend to volunteer the truth, that he would only produce as much information as he was asked for, like a man hoping to keep a misplaced wallet.

'My sister . . . has disappeared.'

Another pause. A dangerous conversation to be having these days, Stephen thought, even in private. He cleared his throat. 'I know.'

'You were here?'

Stephen nodded.

'You saw it?'

'We heard . . . noises. There were two cars . . . a number of armed men.' Stephen hesitated. 'This was over six months ago. No one else has been to the apartment as far as we know. It's been relet.'

Domingo nodded. 'A friend of Rosa's rang me the next day to tell me what had happened. So I made my way straight here. I was arrested downstairs in the lobby. They beat me and put me in prison. Why? I still don't know. I don't even know what my sister is supposed to have done. She had nothing to do with the *comunistas*, I swear it.'

The tea arrived, in a cottage china service of English floral pattern. There were scones nestled in a lace cloth and a small pot of raspberry jam. Domingo stared in bewilderment at this alien offering, unsure how to proceed.

Maria poured two cups of tea, added milk and sugar and handed one cup to Stephen and the other to Domingo, who remained poised on the edge of the chesterfield, the tiny cup balanced on his knees.

'This has been very hard for me and my family. No one can tell me what has happened to my sister or her husband. She had two baby daughters. Did you know that, señor?'

'Yes. Sometimes we heard a baby crying.'

'Our parents are both dead, señor. Now there are just the two of us. But since we moved here to the city I did not see her very much. I think she was ashamed, you know? She married this big-shot guy, and perhaps she wanted to forget about Avellaneda.'

Stephen did not know what to say. The silence seemed to go on for ever. 'So why were you arrested?'

'They wanted to know where to find Señor Altman. You know Reuben? My sister's husband?'

'We spoke once or twice. In the lobby.'

'Why wasn't he here that night?' Domingo wondered aloud. 'Did you see him, Señor Barrington?'

'My memories are very vague, I'm afraid.'

He heard the front door of the apartment open. He looked up. It was Mercedes. He got to his feet and Domingo hurried to do the same, almost spilling his tea.

His wife's smile fell away when she saw Domingo. She looked at Stephen, their eyes met. In the silent code of couples married for many years, he gave her fair warning.

Mercedes took Gabriella from her stroller and handed her to Maria. Luke rushed into the room, where Stephen adroitly headed him off. 'Can you take him to his room, please?' he said to Maria.

He was bundled away with promises of *dulce con leche*.

Stephen introduced his wife to Domingo, who solemnly took her hand and gave a slight bow. 'Señor Gonsalvez is Rosa Altman's brother,' he said to her, in Spanish. 'He is hoping to discover what happened to her and her family.' So now they must give Gabriella back. They had known this would happen one day.

'I see.'

'We have to tell him the truth,' he added in whispered English.

Mercedes did not respond but assumed the expression of an expansive hostess. She was a formidable woman, his wife. She had the demeanour of a Conservative politician, her English accent laced with heavy inflexions, even when speaking Spanish, as she was now. Her Latin looks and small stature disguised a will of massive proportions.

She draped herself elegantly beside Stephen on the sofa and he poured her a cup of tea from the pot. She gave Domingo the same friendly, but impossibly distant, smile she kept for social guests, such as Luke's music teacher and Stephen's business associates.

'Señor Gonsalvez informed me that he came here the day after the Altmans were taken away. But he, too, was arrested. Downstairs, in the lobby.'

Mercedes sipped her tea. 'You realise we are taking a very great risk even in *talking* to you,' she said to Domingo. 'We could just deny we even saw or heard anything. That is what *most* people would have done.'

'Yes, I understand. You are very kind.'

Stephen heard Gabriella crying in the nursery. 'But we were here,' he said. 'And we did see, we did hear.'

'Yes, as you say, we were here. What can we tell you, Señor Gonsalvez?'

'Anything you know may be a help. All I know for now is that my sister and her whole family are gone.'

Mercedes looked at her husband, then turned back to Domingo. 'We were woken by the sound of cars braking to a stop outside. They used plastic explosives to blow the lock off the security gate. Then we heard men running up the stairs. You understand that my husband and I were very frightened. There was *nothing* we could do.'

Domingo nodded his understanding. 'What time was this?'

'A little after three.'

'And then?'

Gabriella was crying even louder now.

'A short while later we saw the cars drive *off* again. We went into your sister's apartment to investigate.'

'And what . . . what did you find?'

A long silence. This is it, Stephen thought. Now we must tell him. No matter how much pain it causes us. He was about to answer but to his astonishment Mercedes talked over the top of him. 'The front door had been kicked off its hinges,' she was saying. 'We went inside but the apartment was empty. The desk and the filing cabinet in the study had been completely emptied out and in the bedroom everything had been thrown on the floor. It was . . . *terrifying.*'

'They had taken everyone?'

'Yes, *everyone.*'

Stephen stared at her, aghast at her perfidy. He had never known his wife to be anything less than honest, had never caught her out in a lie before. This is not right, he thought. We must tell him. We must tell him the truth.

'No, not everyone,' Domingo said. 'They did not take everyone.'

You see? Stephen thought. He knows! We cannot do this! We, who have so much, will we now rob this poor peasant of one of his family?

'They did not take Reuben.'

'Reuben?' Stephen echoed.

'My sister's husband. Reuben Altman. When I was arrested, all the police kept asking me, "Where is Reuben?" At three o'clock in the morning, he should have been here with his wife and his children. Yes?'

'Perhaps he went away on business.'

'And never came back.' Domingo's attitude of humility dropped away and Stephen saw the raw hatred it concealed. 'He abandoned his wife and children.'

'No man would do such a thing deliberately.'

'You think they would have taken my sister if he had been here? All they wanted was Reuben.' Domingo stopped and looked up. Maria was standing there, holding Gabriella in her arms.

'Excuse me, señora. I did everything I could. She will not stop crying.'

Mercedes stood up. 'It's all right, Maria, I'll take her.' She took

Gabriella from her arms. She cooed to her and immediately the
child began to settle.

'What is her name?' Domingo asked.

'Gabriella,' Mercedes said. 'Her name is Gabriella.'

28

'Gabriella,' Domingo said. 'It is a pretty name. How old is she?'

'She is eight months old now.'

'My little nieces will be the same age. If they are still alive.'

This is your niece. But Stephen could not make himself say the words. He looked up at his wife. Her eyes were like flint. He knew that look. Christ, I can't believe we're doing this.

'You have other daughters?'

'We have a son, six years old, little Luca. He was the tornado who swept into the room when I came home. And we have little Gabriella here. That's all.'

'Just one daughter, then,' he murmured. He looked up at Stephen and their eyes locked. What in God's name is he thinking? Has he guessed? 'For myself I have six children. It is too many. I cannot feed them all. Life can be very hard.'

Stephen had not meant to maintain this lie. He had always prided himself on his integrity. Now he felt his cheeks burning hot with guilt.

'You are British, Señor Barrington?'

'Yes. Yes, I am. I represent a British publishing house. Textbooks, manuals, that sort of thing.'

'You speak very good Spanish.'

'Thank you. I have lived here a long time. My wife's family has been here for four generations.' He looked up at Mercedes, aware of the shifting nuances of this conversation. In his own mind their dissembling had afforded Domingo the moral high ground. Now he felt almost as if he were being interviewed for a job. As what? A foster parent? Mercedes gentled Gabriella in her arms. She held her husband's gaze, willing him to maintain the deception.

'You have a fine apartment. This is more than I can ever dream of.'

What does he want? Money? Is he trying to blackmail me?

Domingo smiled at the baby girl now falling back to sleep on Mercedes' shoulder. 'There is something about a woman with a child. It is almost holy, is it not, Señor Barrington? A bond that should never be broken.' He got to his feet. 'I should go now. You must excuse me for taking so much of your time. You have been very kind.'

Stephen stood up too, bewildered. The blow had not fallen, Domingo had not claimed her. 'You haven't drunk your tea,' he stammered.

'We must not keep Señor Gonsalvez,' Mercedes said. 'Not if he has other places to *go*.'

Domingo reached out and gently touched Gabriella's head with one brown and callused finger. 'Your daughter is very lucky. She will have a good life. We all wish more for our children, but I am afraid my own daughters can never hope for as much.'

Stephen could only shrug his shoulders helplessly. What was there to say in the face of such philosophy?

'I must go. Señor. Señora Barrington.' He turned towards the door.

'Wait. You have suffered a great deal. Isn't there something we can do?'

'You did not take my sister. You cannot bring her back.'

'I am not a poor man, as you say. Perhaps . . . some financial compensation?'

'Compensation, señor? For what will you compensate me?'

Domingo's eyes glittered. Anger and pride. Stephen cursed himself. The man wanted only to retain his dignity and he, in his clumsiness and his guilt, had taken it from him.

'Thank you again for seeing me. I am sorry to have troubled you.'

Stephen watched from the window as Domingo made his way back up the tree-lined street. He did not look back. Stephen felt both overjoyed and deeply ashamed. He looked at his wife.

She bit her lip. 'I thought we were going to lose our *baby*,' she said, and a bright, shining tear made its way down her cheek.

The cool blue skies of spring gave way to the broiling white clouds of summer. The streets of the capital boiled, the *pampero* winds bringing with them the fetid, hot breath of the Equator. By January

the *porteños* were getting ready to escape to the coast, leaving behind
for a short while the baking concrete, the fear and the graffiti:

Where are the disappeared?

Stephen had been in Argentina for almost a decade but he had
still not grown accustomed to the heat, or the inversion of the
seasons. His body still told him that the Christmas season should
be cold. But every January he, along with most of Buenos Aires,
fled to the coast, where his wife's family owned a small villa at
Nicochea.

Mercedes' family was part of the British enclave, old money. The
family name was Devereux. Her grandfather had come to Argentina
just before the First World War as an engineer and had stayed when
he married a *criolla*. Mercedes' own father had been a founding
member of the British Community Council in 1939 and retained
a lifelong passion for gins and tonic and British royalty, although
he had not been to England more than half a dozen times. Spanish
was not spoken in Mercedes' home and she had had to learn the
national language at school.

The Devereux family were proud of their adopted country but
yet somehow remained slightly aloof from its politics, retaining
an inbred superiority that two generations had not diluted. When
the junta imposed a law making Catholic education obligatory
in secondary schools, it caused no more than a raised eyebrow
among them. Mercedes could not see how her profession could
be considered a threat, that the military perceived Freudian ideas
as alien to Catholicism and their own holy crusade.

So it came as a shock to all the family, especially Stephen, when,
just after New Year, with the white dust covers thrown over the
furniture in their apartment and their luggage packed and ready
in the hallway, Mercedes was abducted by two armed men outside
her consulting rooms on Paraguay.

29

They had been waiting for her. As she came through the doors and out on to the pavement two men came towards her from opposite sides. They each took an arm and marched her towards a green Ford Falcon that was parked by the kerb, its motor running.

She could not have run even if she had tried. The shock turned the muscles in her legs to water and she would have collapsed if they had not held her upright. It was too unexpected, too bizarre. She saw people staring from both sides of the crowded street, but no one made any move to help her. She remembered her own terror the night the Altmans' apartment had been raided. All she could do was shout out her name and address, in the vain hope that someone in that crowd would know her and report her disappearance.

They bundled her into the back of the car and one of them threw a blanket over her and pushed her down on to the floor. She lay there, too terrified to move or make a sound.

This had to be a mistake. Her husband was a British national and her own family were not without consequence. They would not dare harm her.

She felt the stop and start of the car through the city streets, heard the horns and noise of heavy traffic. Then they turned on to a long stretch of open road and she guessed it was the new motorway the government was building out towards the airport.

Even then, she did not think she was going to die. By some trick of the mind she was unable to think of anything except the pain in her back where one of the men had his boot pressed into her; that, and her own dire need to go to the lavatory.

Finally the car began to slow and she heard heavy gates creaking open. A few moments later the car stopped and the driver turned off the engine. While they were on the motorway she had begun to feel calm, lulled by the motion of the car; now that irrational sense of security disappeared instantly.

The blanket was pulled away as they jerked her to her feet and she saw that she was outside some sort of barracks. But then someone forced a hood over her face. She stumbled blindly forwards. Somewhere she had lost her shoes. She felt gravel under her feet then concrete. A door slammed behind her.

A man demanded her name and she stammered out an answer. Then she was ordered to take off her clothes.

30

'She was taken in the street, in the middle of the city and in broad daylight by armed men. You don't expect me to believe that someone in this government doesn't know where she is?'

The young man sitting across the desk from him gave him a chill and supercilious smile. His hair, it seemed to Stephen, had been parted with a slide rule. He exuded an air of vague embarrassment. 'We don't actually know that the men who abducted your wife have any association with the government of Argentina. They might be leftists. They could be anyone.'

Stephen leaned forward. 'She was driven away in a green Ford Falcon. Everyone in this city knows what that means.'

'Because she was seen being placed in a certain kind of vehicle means nothing, I'm afraid. It would hardly stand as evidence in a court of law.'

'Perhaps you haven't noticed, but the rule of law no longer applies in Argentina.'

The young man's face creased into a rather strange expression – it might have been a smile or a grimace – and he picked up the white china cup and took a sip of tea. 'Her Majesty's Government will of course do all it can to help you, but . . .'

'It's been three days and you haven't done anything!'

'With respect, Mr Barrington, there is very little we *can* do. We have contacted the Foreign Ministry and they have made exhaustive enquiries on our behalf. They say that the Interior Minister has informed them that he has absolutely no information about your wife's whereabouts. According to Ministry records there is no record of any arrest being made by either the police or the military.'

'Of course there isn't. That doesn't mean to say it didn't happen.'

'I'm afraid we have a situation of *no locus standi* – there is no conceivable grounds for our embassy to take any action.'

Stephen wanted to reach across the table and put his hands around the man's neck. Junior officials, he had discovered, were the same the world over. Put a little power into the hands of a young man who has only recently been a school prefect and he takes on the demeanour and attitude of a dictator.

'I understand how you must be feeling, of course . . .'

'No, you don't understand! You couldn't possibly understand! You're barely out of school, you unctuous little squirt! You don't have a wife, I doubt if you've ever had a girlfriend! How could you possibly know what I'm going through? So, don't say you understand, because you don't, you don't even want to!'

There was a long silence in the room. The young man took another sip of his tea. The colour rose in his cheeks. After a few moments he opened the manila file that lay on the table in front of him.

'I see you failed to notify our embassy of your recent change of address. Neither have you registered the details of your marriage. Let's see, that was . . . eight years ago? Perhaps we should catch up on our paperwork. If you would like to . . .'

'Go to hell,' Barrington said. He got to his feet and walked out.

The lights fell on the red velvet plush of the Teatro Colón amid the soaring, grandiose anthems of Puccini. Angeli settled in his seat and the curtain rose on the brooding darkness of the Attavanti chapel in the church of San'Andrea della Valle in Rome. It was the setting for the first act of *Tosca*, an opera that romanticised republican rebels in the grip of a repressive government in eighteenth-century Rome. He was surprised that Videla had allowed the performance to go on. He watched, irritable and restless, Puccini's score failing to move him as it usually did.

Francesca leaned closer to his shoulder. He shifted his weight slightly, away from her. He closed his eyes, safe here in the darkness, was instantly back in the barracks at Ezeiza, felt the thrill in his gut, a visceral sensation, both chill and resonant. He found now he could conjure his dark secrets just by the power of his own imagination. Sweat beaded on his forehead.

His eyes blinked open quickly. No, not here. Francesca, unaware of his sudden discomfort, gripped his hand and smiled up at him in

the darkness. He smiled back at her and returned his attention to
the opera.

For the second act the action moved away from the chapel to the
Farnese Palace. The chief of the secret police, Scarpia, suspected
that an artist named Cavaradossi knew the whereabouts of a
republican rebel who had escaped his custody.

Cavaradossi's screams as he underwent torture were heard from
off stage. Angeli shifted uncomfortably in his seat, his eyes riveted
on Tosca, Cavaradossi's lover, as she listened in anguish to his cries.
Angeli felt sweat beading on his forehead and an oily warmth in his
groin. He realised he was getting an erection.

Finally Tosca broke, whispering the escaped prisoner's whereabouts in order to release her lover from the torturers. Angeli
smiled to himself. *Yes. They all broke in the end.* He wiped the
palms of his hands on the velvet arms of his seat.

Finally Scarpia and Tosca were left together on the stage. He
knew what would happen next, of course. He had seen the opera
countless times. Always he found himself wishing for a different
ending.

Scarpia raised the wine glass to his lips. Could he not see the
paring knife concealed in Tosca's hand? How could so ruthless a
man also be so ingenuous?

He lifted his eyes to the great domed ceiling, bored and frustrated
by Scarpia's sentimentality. When he looked back at the stage
Scarpia was dead, Tosca standing over him with the knife.

She washed the blood from her hands in a basin, arranged her
hair in a mirror, extinguished the lights at the supper table. Two
candles still burned on Scarpia's desk. She placed one on each
side of Scarpia's body, then took a crucifix down from the wall
and placed it on his breast.

The lights came up for the end of the second act.

Francesca looked up at him, her face serene. 'It's beautiful,
isn't it?'

Angeli bought a coffee in the gallery during the interval and
was late returning to his seat. As the curtain rose on the final
act he decided he would have to speak to Videla and ask him
to have the performances stopped. The opera was nothing short
of sedition.

*   *   *

By the time they arrived home from the opera Simone was asleep. Angeli crept into the bedroom and watched her in the glow of the bedside lamp. Her hair was damp, her lips parted slightly, forming the shape of a heart. Angeli leaned over the cot and tucked the quilt under her chin.

'My princess.' He kissed her softly on the forehead, turned off the night-light and went out.

Francesca was waiting for him at the top of the stairs, still in her opera gown. 'Are you coming to bed, *caro*?'

He shook his head. 'I'm not tired.'

What was that look on her face? Hurt? Disappointment? Concern? It was gone almost as soon as it had appeared. She went into the bedroom and the door closed gently behind her.

He went downstairs and stared out of the French windows at the floodlit lawn. He picked up his packet of cigarettes and lit one.

Antonia appeared in the doorway. 'Would you like supper, señor?'

Angeli waved a hand, dismissively. 'No, thank you, Antonia. Good night.'

'Good night, Señor Angeli.' She went out, closing the door behind her.

He rubbed a hand across his face, exhaled a thin stream of smoke through his nostrils. He looked around at the polished parquet floors, the marble-topped tables. None of it gave him any pleasure. It was like a mausoleum.

He went to the cocktail cabinet and took out a bottle of Chivas Regal. He splashed some of the amber fluid into a crystal glass. He should be tired. In the last few weeks he had been getting just two or three hours' sleep a night. He had left for the barracks at five o'clock this morning and now – he looked at his watch – it was almost midnight and still he felt this terrible compulsion to return.

Tonight was the first evening he had spent with his wife for months. Most nights he came home long after Francesca had gone to bed, ate his supper at the long dining table alone. Not that it mattered. Francesca was always tired these days. She spent so much of her time with the baby. She would not let Antonia do anything for her, she was like a child with a new doll.

He swallowed the Chivas Regal, felt it burn the back of his throat. He closed his eyes. He didn't want to think any more, didn't want to analyse these compulsions. He would instead cling to duty.

He called for Jorge. 'Get my coat. You can tell the señora that I have had to go back to work.'

'She is asleep, señor.'

'Then it doesn't matter. Just my coat, then.'

He telephoned for his car. The black Mercedes arrived promptly, ten minutes later.

31

There were few cars at this time of night. His driver turned off the motorway just before the airport and drove along a narrow unlit road. The barracks appeared ahead, a lonely jumble of lights in the darkness. A guard opened the front gates and Angeli felt his excitement start to build. Here was his private pleasure dome, its haunting and terrible secrets beckoning him to another long and heady descent into his own darkness.

Tonight he would claim his own Tosca and have his satisfaction in pain and possession.

She had been given a thin cotton dress and thrown into a cell so narrow she was unable to stretch out her arms either side of her. There was a mattress on the floor with a single rough woollen blanket and a hole in the cement floor for her to urinate and defecate into. On the third day it had overflowed and now the floor and the mattress were permanently wet. She had rolled the mattress up and sat on the one part of it that was not soiled, but this meant she had to sleep sitting up. She could not manage sleep in this position for more than one or two hours at a time. She kept the blanket around her shoulders day and night to keep it dry.

She could not see her fellow prisoners but she could hear them. Loudspeakers had been mounted in the corridor and when a torture session was taking place they played Rachmaninov records to cover the sounds of the screams. But it could not drown them out completely and when it was going on she huddled shivering in her blanket and put her fingers in her ears.

Once, in the middle of the night, she was woken by a cracked and strident voice screaming at her in a foreign language. She gasped and sat upright, terrified. Then she realised what the voice was. Instead of Rachmaninov, someone had placed a recording of Hitler's Nuremberg Rally on the turntable and they were playing it at full volume. A good joke.

There were no windows in her cell; the only light came from a small crack in the door which acted as an air vent. The faint glow of a single low-wattage bulb, which was left on day and night, eliminated the idea of time for her. The light was extinguished only once when they used too much electricity on a prisoner and overloaded the system. On that occasion they blacked out the entire barracks for several minutes.

She guessed she was somewhere near the airport. Several times she thought she heard the scream of airliners landing and taking off. Once she even imagined she could hear the rumble of an undercarriage as a jet came in to land at Ezeiza. She started playing mind games with herself, imagining she was on board one of the passenger jets, flying away to another country where once again she could be free.

When she had first been brought to the barracks she had been interrogated. A hood, a *capucha*, was thrown over her head so that she had no idea who her interrogators were or how many of them there were. They asked her bizarre questions: Did she have any contacts in Israel? Was she aware of a Zionist conspiracy in Argentina?

Finally she was taken back to her cell. She had crouched there in the darkness, shivering with fear, waiting for them to return. But hours and days went by and now it seemed she had been forgotten. She comforted herself with the thought that somehow Stephen, or one of her own family, would soon engineer her release.

She saw only one of her fellow prisoners.

He was being held in the cell across the corridor from hers. It seemed that he was a priest. She had heard one of the guards calling to him when they had come to fetch him for a torture session: *Time to say your prayers, Father*.

Once, with her eye pressed against the air vent in the door, she saw them dragging him back to his cell. A small man, and wiry, much of his body covered with a fine pelt of black hair. He was naked and she saw the black marks on his skin where they had burned him with the electricity. A long rope of saliva hung from his chin and the muscles in his body were still jerking in spasm. The guards thought that was funny.

Their eyes met for a moment. She saw the man's lips move

but she could not hear the words. But she knew what he had said.

Have faith.

Angeli stood at the back of the room smoking a cigarette. Turturro was using the *picana*. He preferred it, he said it was not as impersonal as the machine.

Angeli nodded for him to stop. Turturro looked disappointed but he and the doctor silently left the room. Angeli locked the door from the inside.

He stubbed out his cigarette on the floor. He saw the tiny movements in the black hood, in time with the woman's breathing. The muscles in her legs and shoulders were in spasm. He checked her name on Turturro's file. When he touched her he felt her stiffen, heard her gasp. Then she sighed and relaxed when the expected pain did not come. He smiled.

He slowly began to undress. Then he took off the woman's hood. He liked them to see him. It was not the same if he could not see their eyes.

32

Stephen received the telephone call five days after Mercedes had disappeared. A voice on the other end of the line said that he wanted to speak with him about his wife. He would meet him for coffee the next day at La Bielá. And then he hung up.

La Bielá faced on to an elegant plaza opposite the entrance to La Recoleta cemetery. It was home to the smart set of Buenos Aires and had been a regular target for bombings. A part of the bar was still cordoned off to allow builders to repair the damage caused by the most recent outrage.

Stephen arrived promptly at ten o'clock the next day. A waiter led him to a corner table. His host for the rendezvous was not the thug he had expected. He had fair hair and ice-blue eyes set in a handsome and smiling face. He wore tan slacks and a green Pierre Cardin polo shirt. He could have been a film star.

When he saw Stephen he stood up and held out his hand.

Stephen had hardly eaten or slept for five days. He was conscious of his own haggard appearance and felt overdressed in his charcoal woollen suit. Now he hesitated, unsure whether to ignore the proffered handshake.

He took the stranger's hand. A grip that could break bone.

'Señor Barrington. I am delighted you could come. Please, sit down. Would you like a drink?'

Stephen shook his head. 'I didn't catch your name.'

'I didn't give it,' Angeli said, still smiling.

'Where's my wife?'

Angeli picked up the menu and pretended to study it. 'Have you had breakfast?'

'What do you know about Mercedes?'

'You have to eat.'

'I'm not hungry.'

Angeli summoned a waiter with a movement of his eyebrow. He ordered three *media lunas* and a *café con leche*. Then he took out his cigarettes and lit one. He did not ask Stephen's permission and he did not offer him one.

Stephen waited. This man was in charge of the situation. If he offended him he might never see his wife again. Who was he? Police? Military? It was possible that Mercedes was already dead and this was some brutal game. But he had to go along with it, there was no choice. He fought to control his anger. Losing his temper would gain him nothing. It might even be what this stranger wanted.

The man with the blue eyes began a long monologue, a comparative study on the cafés and *confiterías* of Buenos Aires. Perhaps he is trying to impress me with his cosmopolitan tastes, Stephen thought. 'Please,' he said, interrupting him, 'if you know anything about my wife, you have to tell me.'

At that moment the waiter brought Angeli's breakfast. 'You do not want some coffee?'

Stephen shook his head.

'Not hungry, not thirsty. What would please you, Señor Barrington?'

Angeli tore one of the croissants in half and dipped it in his coffee. 'You are English, am I correct?'

'Yes.'

'Your wife. Mercedes Devereux. A very distinguished name.'

'Her grandfather came here from London in 1913.'

'Yes, I know.' He smiled again.

'How much do you know?'

'I know many things about many people. It is my job.'

'It must be very rewarding work.'

Angeli sipped his coffee. 'I am a professional, señor. As you are. You sell information. I collect it. But, unlike you, my talents are used in the service of my country. Yours are employed in the service of yourself. Is that not so?'

'What exactly is your position?'

'I cannot tell you that. But I am committed to defending your way of life, señor. Many people would rather not think about that. They accuse the present government of certain crimes but when the *comunistas* are planting bombs on the trains, who do they look to for help?'

'Where's my wife?'

Angeli ignored the question. 'You have an apartment here in La Recoleta. A very pleasant district. You also have a home in Great Britain. In Berkshire.' He said the last word slowly and carefully, struggling with the foreign word.

'It was my father's. I'm keeping it as an investment.'

'That is good. A man should have investments. He should provide for himself and his family. You are a wealthy man.'

'My father inherited some money from his uncle. We are not millionaires.'

'But you do very well for a bookseller.'

'What is all this about? Do you know where my wife is being held?'

'Your wife. She is the psychiatrist?'

'She had a practice on Paraguay. The last few months she has been working part time. We have young children.'

Angeli nodded. 'She teaches Freud.'

Stephen felt his nerves becoming frayed. 'What has this got to do with her disappearance?'

'Freud,' Angeli said, 'the Zionist.'

Stephen blinked. 'I don't understand.'

'There is a Zionist conspiracy to overthrow Christianity in Argentina, Señor Barrington. Freud was a Jew, a Zionist. One of the ways this subversion is spread is through psychiatry.'

If the situation had not been so dire, Stephen would have laughed in his face. It was a bizarre suggestion. He felt the other man's ice-blue eyes studying him. 'My wife . . . has no interest in politics.'

Angeli sat back, looked around the restaurant, lit another cigarette. He delicately wiped his mouth with a napkin. 'I know where your wife is, señor.'

Stephen stared at him, waiting.

'I might be able to help you get her back.'

'What is it you want?' Stephen asked him, his voice tight.

'Fifty thousand dollars.'

33

'What?'

'You may have to sell your apartment in Recoleta but you can afford it. As you say, you have a large inheritance. I knew about this already, however.' He paused, to allow this information to be digested. 'I imagine whether or not you choose to pay my fee depends on how you feel about your wife. Some men, of course, would like to see their wives disappear.' He smiled at his joke.

Stephen could not breathe. 'Where is she?'

Angeli gave him a sympathetic smile. 'That I cannot tell you. But once I have the money I can have her returned to you within twenty-four hours. In good condition.'

'Has she been . . . hurt?'

Angeli drew on his cigarette and said nothing.

'I swear to God . . .' Stephen breathed, but the empty threat died stillborn. He would just make himself look a fool.

'Fifty thousand dollars.'

'How do I know that if I pay you this ridiculous sum of money I will see my wife again?'

'You must trust me.'

'Trust you?'

'You have no choice.'

No, he's right. Don't argue. You have no choice.

'I will call you in three days. We can make the arrangements.'

Stephen lurched to his feet. He felt so utterly powerless. It was difficult to breathe.

Angeli held out his hand. 'Be careful, señor. These are dangerous times.'

Stephen hurried out of the restaurant. Fifty thousand dollars. How could he raise such a huge sum of money?

* * *

Three men came into her cell, without warning, and hauled her to her feet. They cuffed her wrists behind her back. She was dragged out into the corridor, but this time not in the direction of the latrines or the torture cells.

'Where are you taking me?' she shouted.

'Don't worry. No one's going to hurt you.'

And that was when she knew she was going to die.

She felt hot gravel under her bare feet. There was the taint of warm diesel in the air and she could see a faint aura of light through the cloth hood. She was pushed forward on to her face, something slammed shut close to her ear and she was consigned to the cramped darkness. She smelled leather and petrol. She guessed she had been thrown into the boot of a car.

She said a final prayer to God, enumerating her sins, then whispered a silent goodbye to her husband, and to Luke. She thought of little Gabriella. May God forgive me . . .

She began to cry.

Impossible to tell how far they drove. Finally the car came to a halt, she heard the men get out and walk around to the boot. Light flooded through the thin black material of the *capucha* as the boot was thrown open.

They hauled her out by her arms. One of the men unlocked the cuffs on her wrists. She didn't struggle. There was no point. She stood there, waiting, knowing it was useless to run, wondering if she would hear the sound of the pistol shot that ended her life.

34

Doors slammed, she heard the car drive away. She waited.

She heard dogs barking, the voices of children. She put her hands up to her face. They were shaking so hard it took her some moments to finally tear the hood away and breathe in the cool, clean air.

She was standing in front of the park in Recoleta, the same park where she brought Luke and Gabriella on Saturday mornings. Across the road she saw two of her neighbours drinking espressos by the window of La Bielá. A *paseador* with a dozen yapping charges on the end of long leads stared at her in surprise as he went past.

She slumped down on the granite kerbstone and started to cry. She rocked slowly backward and forward on her haunches, her hands clasped around her knees. Two mothers with strollers stared at her but did not stop.

'*Pobrecita*,' one of them whispered. 'Poor thing.'

Poor thing.

Stephen stood by the window, holding a glass of single malt whisky. So, what was he to do now? For months he had tried not to think, to carry on despite the daily numbing terror that had insinuated itself into their lives. Even after what had happened to the Altmans he had tried to convince himself that it was an aberration, that things would get better. Perhaps what the blue-eyed man in the restaurant had told him was right; he paid lip service to liberal sentiments but he still somehow believed the junta was defending his way of life. He had friends who were Peronists, others with connections to the army and the far right. He had avoided the issue by never discussing politics, not such an easy thing to do in Argentina as it was in his own country.

Now he had felt the hot breath of the colonels on his own neck.

He had thought himself immune, supposed that if he lived his own strictly circumscribed life and hoped for better days that he could remain untouched. Now, as he looked down over the city with the new perspective of his own fear and outrage, he experienced a deep sense of shame.

He was not after all a good man, as he had always told himself. He was instead a frightened one, as he had always been.

Mercedes arrived home, loaded down with shopping bags bearing the names of the elegant shops on Florida – Calvin Klein, Yves St Laurent, Christian Dior. Just two weeks ago she had been lying half naked and manacled to a bed frame. Now she behaved as if nothing had happened. After her dramatic return to the apartment, dressed in rags and hysterical with fear, he had immediately called the family doctor. He had prescribed her some sedatives. The next day, when she woke from a fourteen-hour sleep, she refused even to talk about her experience. And that was the way it had been for two weeks.

Stephen was deeply disturbed and wanted to seek professional advice. But almost every psychiatrist in the city had disappeared or fled, the latest victims of the *Proceso*. This in a city that had more trained psychiatrists per head than New York. These days the man who sold you your morning newspaper at one of the *kioscos* in the street was most likely better educated than you were. To be a doctor or a lawyer or a teacher or a journalist in Argentina these days was to live more dangerously than a soldier.

'Come and see what I *bought*!' Mercedes said, eager as a child. She paraded her purchases in front of him. Stephen let her chatter on but his gaze never left the window and she was so delighted with the success of her expedition that she did not seem to notice that his attention was elsewhere.

'Stop it,' he said.

Mercedes looked up, surprised. 'Stephen?'

'Just stop it. Stop.'

She let the new dress she was holding slip to the floor. 'What's *wrong*?'

He stared at her. She was like a child in a fantasy game. 'I have made arrangements for us to fly to London. We leave in two weeks.'

'Leave?'

'We cannot stay here. It is too dangerous for you. It is too dangerous for anyone to live here. I want the children to grow up somewhere they can feel safe.'

Mercedes stared at him. 'But this *apartment*.'

'How many times do I have to tell you this? This apartment was mortgaged to buy back your freedom. I have listed it for sale. When we find a purchaser there will hopefully be enough to pay off the bank. The company has arranged for me to transfer back to our head office in Oxford.'

'My *family* are here.'

'I have spoken to your family. They are as eager as I am that I take you somewhere where you will be safe.'

'What are you *saying*?'

'What I am saying is that we cannot stay in Argentina. Not until this madness is over.'

Mercedes sat down heavily on the sofa. She seemed quite unable to comprehend what he was telling her.

'You must trust me,' he said.

'Well, all *right*. But I still can't see why we have to go. Don't you *like* it here?'

II

Mexico and Argentina, 1983

35

Mexico City, December 1983

The police were crashing up the stairs.

Rifle butts slammed against the door. It splintered on its hinges, burst open with a sound like a gunshot. But it was Rosa standing there, holding something in her arms, a blanket. It was sodden with blood.

He backed away. The bundle she was holding fell on to the floor and the blanket unravelled. Inside were two babies, smeared with blood, as they had been the day they were born . . .

Rosa stepped towards him, her bloody hands outstretched. He kept backing away, felt himself falling.

He sat up in bed, breathing hard. He groped for the light beside the bed, heard the lamp crash to the floor. He scrambled out of bed and stumbled across the dark room, his hands fumbling for the light switch.

Isabel stared at him, bewildered. 'Reuben? What's wrong?'

He stood panting and naked by the bedroom door. The red digital numbers on the clock beside the bed showed 2.13. He slid down the wall on to his haunches.

'*Por Dios*. The sheets are soaking. Are you ill?'

He shivered in the mortuary chill of the air-conditioning, felt the oily sweat cooling quickly on his skin. His heart wanted to burst out of his chest. *Just a dream*. Yet the images were so vivid, so real.

Isabel jumped out of bed. 'Reuben, it's okay.' She knelt down beside him, her arms folded across her chest. She seemed afraid to touch him, as if she too might become infected by this dread disease that stalked his nights.

'You were screaming.'

Reuben blinked, clawing his way out of the dream.

Isabel stroked his hair. 'Same dream?'

He nodded slowly. 'Same dream.'

'Come back to bed.'

He shook his head.

'This happened last night.' She ran her fingers through his hair.

He reached for her, needed her to hold him.

'Do you often have these dreams?'

Often? His last good sleep was eight years ago, in Carmen's bed. But he hadn't had this particular dream for months, had even stopped taking the sleeping tablets. They had saved him many times in the past, delivered him to a numbing blackness from which he woke in the mornings hung over and irritable. Many times he had thought about committing himself to the blackness for good.

He stood up, found a pair of track pants and an old sweatshirt on a chair next to the bed. He padded downstairs in his bare feet. There was a bottle of Bushmills in a kitchen cabinet and he splashed some into a tumbler, drank it neat. He turned on the radio: a mariachi band on an all-night AM station, the music battling against the static of a distant electric storm.

He heard a sound behind him. Isabel had followed him downstairs and was watching him from the kitchen doorway. She was wearing one of his old shirts.

'Are you sure you're okay?'

He nodded.

'Does this happen every night?'

'Not every night.'

'So you only have nightmares when I sleep with you?'

He swallowed the whisky and poured another.

'I've slept here three times and every time you've woken up screaming.' When he didn't answer, she said: 'It's not me, is it?' She forced a smile.

'It's not you.' He wished she'd just go back to bed and leave him alone.

'Is this because of what happened to you in Argentina?'

'What do you mean – *happened* to me?'

'I'm not dumb, Reuben.'

He took another slug of whisky.

'Do you think you need to talk to someone?'

'A shrink, you mean?'

'This is not normal.'

'I don't want to talk about it right now.' He went into the other room and turned on the television. His jacket was hanging over the back of one of the chairs. He took out his wallet, opened it. Inside there was a picture of Rosa and the girls, crumpled with age, worn like some ancient religious icon. He stared at it for a long time. It was all he had left of that other life and it was so long ago now he might have been looking at the photographs of complete strangers in a magazine. All that endured was the guilt.

36

But Isabel was right, it wasn't normal. He had forgotten what normal was. Was anyone normal? Normal was a fantasy, an illusion, a place you were before the real world intruded and left its mark on you.

Normal was a place you could come from, but once you had left, you could never return. He knew, because he had tried, for the last seven years he had tried. For a political exile, he supposed he lived a very comfortable life. He had a job in the foreign exchange division of a large national bank and owned a comfortable apartment in San Angel. From the outside his life was almost as it was before. But life was not lived from the outside.

Inside him there was the constant fear; staring at people sitting in cars parked at the kerbside to reassure yourself they were not armed and waiting for you; seeing a policeman in the street and instinctively catching your breath. These were the patterns of terror that continued long after you remembered you were safe from them.

They had broken him, without interrogation, without pain. They had violated his family, and when that happens life is no longer plausible. Consolation and tenderness had become impossible for him.

Since Mexico there had been other relationships with other women, but none of them had lasted. Give it time, he had told himself. Just hold on, life is simply a matter of remembering to breathe. What happened was not your fault. There is nothing you can do to change the past. You have to get on with the rest of your life.

But his life was stalled. Every day he was lapped once more by the world going on without him. He knew that night in 1976 would go on for ever.

Perhaps, he told himself, it would be easier if there was

someone to blame, someone to hate. If he knew who had betrayed them.

He had been over it in his mind countless times. He was sure there was no one in Argentina who knew what they were doing, outside of the family. Just his father, his brother, himself. The weak link was Havana, with Mario Firmenich and the leadership of the Montoneros. Firmenich had told them he was the only one who knew about their arrangement but they only had his word. It had been folly from the beginning.

There was no one to blame, no one to hate. Except himself.

He was walking through Alameda Park one Friday after finishing work. He sat down on a bench to listen to a man strumming his guitar. The man had his back resting against the trunk of a poplar tree, his wife beside him, his suit jacket a pillow under her. The song was a *milonga* from the *pampa* and he was singing in *lunfardo*, the unmistakable patois of Buenos Aires. They were exiles, he realised, exiles like himself.

'Altman. Reuben Altman.'

Reuben turned, fighting down the sudden thrill of fear he always experienced on being recognised. It was a constant danger in Mexico City. They said almost a quarter of a million of his countrymen had fled here during the seventies. You never knew when you might stumble across an acquaintance from that former life. He dreaded their unwanted reminiscences and condolescences, the unsolicited invitations to reunions he habitually avoided.

'It is you, isn't it?' the voice demanded.

Reuben had a well-rehearsed performance for such occasions; at first, pretend not to know the person, then remain vague and finally break away as soon as possible. On this occasion his mystification was not a difficult thing to fabricate. The stranger was a priest, but that in itself was not enough of a clue.

'I'm sorry. I don't think I know you.'

'Father Paolo Salvatore. We met once at your home. You married Rosa Gonsalvez.'

The invoking of her name made him feel physically ill. 'Yes. Of course.' He did not remember him at all.

'What are you doing in Mexico? Is your wife with you?'

Reuben shook his head.

Immediately the priest looked troubled. 'Surely not. Not you?'

Reuben gave him a chill smile.

'Oh, my God,' the man said, but not in the normal way that oaths were made by laymen. He seemed to be genuinely invoking the compassion of the deity. 'I'm sorry. Poor Rosa. Why?'

'Does there have to be a reason?'

'Rosa, Rosa. I knew her since she was a child. I gave her her first communion in Córdoba.' He was silent a long time. 'And the little girls?'

Reuben looked away.

'Dear God have mercy.'

'I don't think He does.'

Salvatore ignored the blasphemy. 'This is terrible, terrible.'

Why did people always do this to him? Just let me get through the days. I don't need to glimpse my pain through a new pair of eyes every few months.

'I am an exile here too,' Salvatore told him, though Reuben did not remember asking. He just wanted to escape. 'You must bear a terrible amount of guilt.'

Reuben stared at him. 'Why should I feel guilty?'

'The survivor always feels guilt. It is the same with me. I sometimes wish I could have died. It would have been easier. I feel they are laughing at me, that this is just another aspect of the torture.'

Reuben shrugged his shoulders. He did not trust his voice.

'I always think people are wondering why I was spared. That perhaps I made a deal with them, that I did not have the strength to resist. I think that is why my new bishop sent me here, to a poor little barrio. But I like it here. I am comfortable with the poor.' Salvatore was no longer looking at him. His eyes were fixed on the middle distance, some private reverie. Then the light returned suddenly to his eyes. 'Poor, poor Rosa. I shall say a prayer. I shall say a prayer for all of you.'

He held out his hand. Reuben was expecting an offer of help, some lantern of friendship he had neither demanded nor needed. But instead Salvatore said: 'I should go now, I can see you want to be with your thoughts. God be with you, Reuben. Your God and mine.'

He started to walk away.

Reuben did not know why he did it. Perhaps he was attracted by the other man's pain, because he had not offered him his help, only a kindred suffering. But he heard himself say: 'Perhaps we can talk again, Father.'

The priest turned, as surprised at receiving this request as Reuben was at having made it. His face creased into a slow smile. 'Of course. If you think it would help. I will give you the name of my church.'

The party was in Cuernavaca, on the patio of a friend's villa, the coloured lights gaudy and cheap against the backdrop of a bloody Aztec moon, newly risen over the distant volcanoes. Many of the guests were émigrés, like himself.

During his eight years in Mexico Reuben had, as much as he was able, avoided anyone from his old life. Exiles sought out the same accents, exchanging anecdotes of shared friends and places. There was always someone who recognised him, or thought they did. Some of them even thought him a hero; if only they knew.

Isabel had persuaded him to come. The party was to celebrate the first free elections in their native country for almost a decade. The military junta had eventually foundered on spiralling inflation and the national humiliation in the Malvinas. Their final act had been to pass a law excusing themselves for the crimes they had committed during their eight-year tenure before scuttling into waiting black limousines behind the Casa Rosada. The Peronists were proclaiming victory, even before the counting had started.

There was a forced air of gaiety. He saw a woman he knew, an artist who had lost her husband and son to the death squads in 1976. She arrived hand in hand with a Miami property developer, wearing large red sunglasses and a black hooped skirt. She was laughing too hard, like everyone else here. Over there was a lawyer who had had electrodes taped to his balls in a military prison; he had a blue-and-white Argentine flag draped over his shoulders, and was already drunk. That woman there had lost both her brothers in the Dirty War, as they were now calling it, disappeared because of their membership of a trade union. She was dancing with a New York commodities broker.

'Reuben Altman!'

For the second time that day he turned around to be confronted by someone he thought to be a total stranger. It took him a few moments to put the vague memory of the man's face into context. And then it came to him: the University of Buenos Aires. The man had been a friend of Julio Castro's, had studied journalism with him.

'Daniel Facchetti,' Reuben said. He had changed. He had lost some hair, and a few extra pounds around the middle had put pressure on the buttons of his shirt.

The man grinned. He was holding a bottle of Corona beer and appeared to be a little drunk. 'You have a good memory.'

'So do you.' Reuben hoped he would not have to listen to any more harrowing tales of others' misfortunes, or more dreams of a roseate future for Argentina.

'Not likely to forget going to university with one of the Altmans. Last time I saw you must have been . . . '73. Ten years. My God. The things we've seen, right?'

Reuben gave him a tight smile. 'How are things?'

Facchetti gave a shrug. How could you sum up such a decade in a few words? 'I'm doing my best. Like everyone here. I heard you were in Mexico.'

Reuben nodded. 'Got here in 1976. What about you?'

'Two years ago. I spent six years before that in Lima. I have a job working on *El Día*. You?'

'Banamex. Foreign exchange department.'

Facchetti hesitated, as exiles always did after the small talk, like a swimmer taking a breath before plunging into icy water. 'They really screwed you, didn't they?'

'They screwed a lot of people.'

'You were the only one to get out, huh?'

It was said innocently enough, but Reuben bristled at the imagined criticism. 'I was lucky.'

Facchetti sipped his drink. 'Bastards. Why did they go after you?'

'We were Jews.'

Facchetti shrugged again. 'That's the story I heard. Crazy.' He gulped the rest of his Corona. 'You going back? After the elections?'

'I don't think so.'

'I'm going back. In fact, I was there last month.'

'Buenos Aires?'

'Sure. I still have some of my family there.'

'What's it like?'

Facchetti smiled. 'The military spent a hundred million dollars

building a fun park. And they say Galtieri doesn't have a sense
of humour.'

Reuben searched the room for Isabel. He wanted this conversation to end. He was about to excuse himself when Facchetti said:
'Guess who I saw when I was there?'

'Who?'

'An old friend of yours. Julio. Julio Castro. Do you remember him?'

37

Facchetti finished his beer, belched, looked around for another.

'Julio's back in Buenos Aires?' Reuben asked him.

'Don't think he ever left. He's still working for *La Prensa*. That guy breaks me up. Remember what a radical he used to be? I thought he was the first one the military would have picked up. But there he was tapping away on an old Remington in his little cubby-hole. The guy's a survivor, no doubt about it.'

Reuben shook his head. He remembered their last conversation, after Jorge Albrecht had been arrested. He had always assumed that Julio was dead or an exile like himself, living in Caracas or Lima. Instead he had spent the last eight years hunched over his typewriter, spinning the party line. Incredible.

Reuben saw Isabel waving to him from the other side of the room. He turned to Facchetti. 'My girlfriend wants me to dance. Catch up with you later, okay?'

He moved away into the crowd. But he didn't feel like dancing and he didn't want to wait around for the results of the election. He didn't give a shit about Argentina any more. He left the party early with Isabel and drove back to Mexico City.

Reuben was walking through the Alameda Park on the way to the Metro when he lost his last link with Rosa.

He saw them from a hundred yards away. There were perhaps half a dozen of them, beggar boys with broad grins and bad teeth, dressed in filthy T-shirts and shorts. They were kicking a can along the gravel, laughing and shouting. As they got closer he assumed they would run around him, but the first two boys had their backs to him and finally he saw that a collision was inevitable. He felt the bump and suddenly they were all around him, charging into him as if he wasn't there, one of them even kicking the can at his legs.

And then, just as suddenly, they were gone, still laughing,

the tin can there at his feet. They all ran off in different directions.

And then he realised what had happened. He felt in his jacket pocket for his wallet. Gone. He didn't care about the credit cards, the money, only the photograph of Rosa and the girls, beyond value, irreplaceable. He ran blindly, searching for one of the pick-pockets, bumping through the crowds of strollers, deaf to their shouts and curses. Finally, out of breath and lathered in sweat, he slumped down on to a bench.

They were gone.

He had lost his last link with Rosa and the girls. Not even their ghosts remained.

38

Reuben watched the hawkers working the jam of traffic on Reforma, pressing flowers against the windows of the stalled cars, washing windscreens for a few coins. In front of him a matron with Ralph Lauren and Ruben Torres shopping bags examined her reflection in the coffee shop window as she ate strawberries and vanilla ice cream from a glass bowl.

Reuben nursed his espresso and tried to concentrate on the newspaper. Lech Walensa's wife, Danuka, had accepted the Nobel peace prize on his behalf in Oslo and Raul Alfonsín was set to become Argentina's first civilian president in eight years. His Radical Party – who were actually moderates, Reuben thought with a smile, but try explaining that to someone who had not been born in Argentina – had confounded all the pundits and defeated the Peronists. The article went on to enumerate the problems Alfonsín would face when the euphoria of his election had disappeared; the military junta had left the country with spiralling international debt and an annual inflation rate of just under one thousand per cent.

'Reuben.'

He looked up. Isabel. She was wearing a navy blue suit over a cream blouse; a gold chain nestled in the tan hollow of her throat. Her long dark hair was braided down her back in a ponytail. A beautiful woman. He had always been lucky in love, or so they told him.

She sat down. She smiled and he tried to smile back. These situations were always difficult, knowing how to behave. He wished now that he had not arranged to meet her here, that he had done this over the telephone. Once he had never thought of himself as a coward. Now it seemed to be second nature to him.

He ordered two espressos. 'How was your day?' He could not meet her eyes, tried to keep some distance between them.

'Little Hector died.'

Hector, he remembered, was a little boy who had come under her care in the paediatric ward of the hospital where she was employed as a doctor. He had been brought in a few weeks before with respiratory disease and she had taken over his case and grown fond of him. Bad timing for Isabel. Bad timing for little Hector too, he supposed. Wasn't God supposed to care for little children? That had not been his experience. Perhaps he should put this off.

'You okay?'

'Sure. What about you?'

She shrugged her shoulders. 'I knew he was going to die some time. It's better sooner than later. The resident says I can't afford to get so attached to my patients. People die every day. It's a fact. Even children.'

'Yes. Even children.'

The espressos arrived. He stirred sugar into his coffee, his mind elsewhere.

'So. Alfonsín won.'

He nodded.

'Are you going back?'

'No. No, I don't think so.'

She looked relieved. 'So why such a long face? Are you a closet Peronist?'

'I don't give a damn about politics any more.'

'Sure. So what's wrong?'

'I've been thinking.' He took a deep breath. 'I don't think it's a good idea if we see each other any more.'

A long, angry silence. 'What?'

'I know what you're thinking. But it's better we do this now. I don't know any other way to tell you.'

'What are you talking about, you bastard?'

The woman at the next table had finished her ice cream and was staring at them. He stared back at her and she turned her head. If she wanted entertainment she could pay the pavement buskers.

'I'm sorry, Isabel.'

Her eyes had filled with tears, her anger evaporating as quickly as it had come. 'But I thought we . . . What is it? What have I done?'

'You haven't done anything. But there's no future in this for either of us. It's not you, it's me.'

'What's that supposed to mean?'

'I owe you an explanation but I don't have one. I was wrong. I thought this would work and it won't. Don't ask me to give you reasons because none of them will make any sense, not even to me. I didn't mean to hurt you.'

'You just wanted to sleep with me?'

He had considered telling her the truth. But that would only make things worse. She would want to heal him and help him and then he would never get rid of her. He knew because it had happened to him before. Better to tell a lie. After all, what did it matter what she thought of him? She could not despise him more than he despised himself.

'I just wanted to sleep with you.'

To give her credit, she didn't slap him or throw her coffee in his lap, did nothing that might have embarrassed them both. Instead she reached into her purse and put some coins on the table. Then she stood up and hitched her bag over her shoulder. 'Thanks for the coffee. Keep the change.'

Reuben watched her walk away. A part of him wanted to run after her, wanted to explain. He felt a terrible cold pain deep in his belly. This would be worse, he knew. Losing Isabel would hurt him more than losing any of the other women he had known and left. Except Rosa, of course.

Well, good. He only wished it hurt more. He should suffer more.

He deserved it.

It was a poor barrio scarred by factories and concrete apartments. The air stank of sulphur from a nearby chemical plant. The church was made of red brick, ugly, modern, utilitarian. At the rear was a high wall topped with broken glass. A small boy in a white surplice with a bronze, pockmarked face opened a wire mesh gate and led him through a small garden of roses.

The roar of traffic on the nearby highway was muted by the wall.

Salvatore was seated on a stone bench. He looked up and smiled. 'Ah, my confessor.' He turned to the small boy. 'Thank you, Raimundo. That will be all for today. Tell the others they can go home. We are not yet ready to challenge the choir in the Sistine Chapel but if we practise, and with God's help, who knows?'

The boy nodded and walked away.

Reuben sat down on the bench beside the priest.

'So, what brings you out here to the playgrounds of the Devil?'

'I'm going back.'

Salvatore nodded. 'I thought you would. I have toyed with this idea, also. But I am not sure if my old bishop wants me. You, however, have the power of choice.' He reached inside his cassock, brought out a packet of cheap cigarettes and lit one, holding it in two fingers and a thumb, sighting it like a pistol. 'Why have you come to see me?'

'Do you think it's a good idea?'

'You want my advice?'

He nodded his head.

'Hear that, blessed Mother?' he said to the statue of the Virgin, in her niche in the wall above the roses. 'If I convert this Jew here will you send me back to La Boca?'

'I want to look for my daughters.'

Salvatore took a deep breath, let it out slowly. 'What do you want me to say to you?'

'As a priest. What do you think?'

'As a priest? As a priest I have to ask you what it is you're afraid of.'

'I'm afraid that I'll find them.'

Salvatore thought about this and when he finally spoke again his voice was very soft. 'Why does that remote prospect frighten you, Reuben?'

'There are things I have not told you.'

'I can hear your confession, Reuben, if that is what you want. Unofficially, of course. I cannot give you absolution, naturally. But God will hear you and I am sure He does not distinguish between faiths, as we do down here.'

'I don't want to be forgiven for anything. I just want to be sure I am doing . . . the right thing.'

'We can never be sure of that. It is what makes life interesting.'

Reuben rested his elbows on his knees. 'To live your life successfully you have to be the hero of your own story. When

you are the villain, or the coward, it is impossible.' He put his
face in his hands. 'Did they torture you, Father?'

'Yes.'

'What was it like?'

'Why do you want to know?'

'I cannot stop thinking about Rosa. What they did to her.'

'I see. You want me to add to your torment.'

'They must have wanted to know where I was.' He clenched his
hands together. The knuckles cracked. 'I keep telling myself that
she told them. That it was over quickly.'

'Did she know where you were?'

'I was with another woman. And yes, she knew.'

'Dear God.'

'Just tell me what it's like.'

'Reuben . . .'

He looked into the priest's eyes. At some stage they had broken
him, he realised. Peel away all the layers of a tortured man and
you find only fear.

The priest drew on his cigarette. 'One day I will find my courage
again. One day my hands will stop shaking like this. I will stand
up to them again. Like you will.'

'If you run once, do you run for ever? There must be some way
to win.'

'Yes. Yes, there must be a way to win, as you say. I shall let
you know.'

Reuben got to his feet.

'I know it's impossible. I wouldn't even know what they look
like now, if they're still alive.'

'I shall light a candle for you.'

'Thank you for listening.'

'Thank you for coming. God be with you.'

'Yours or mine?'

Salvatore smiled. 'Oh, I think He'll probably turn out to be the
same guy, don't you?'

Reuben made his way home. That evening he sat down
in front of the television with the bottle of Bushmills balanced between his knees. The news bulletin carried pictures of
Argentina's new president, Raul Alfonsín, accepting the plau-
dits of the crowd from the balcony of the Casa Rosada. He
listened to him promise to bring the former military rulers to

justice for spreading death, terror and pain through Argentine society.

Yes. Yes, there has to be an accounting. For the perpetrators and for the victims as well. There must be justice.

What he had told Salvatore was right. He had to go back. It was time.

It was time to go home.

Buenos Aires

He arrived home, as he always did, in a black limousine. The driver
wore an army uniform and the car was escorted by a motorcycle
rider travelling behind. It always seemed to Simone that her father
must be very important to merit such attention.

She watched him get out of the car and run up the front steps
of the house. She supposed that God must look something like
her father, blue-eyed and massive and important and beautiful.
She waited for him under the portico, beside Antonia. When he
shouted her name she ran to meet him and he scooped her up in
his arms.

He carried her into his study so that she could tell him about
her day; about the picture she had drawn at school, the games she
had played with her friends, how Antonia had taught her to make
dulce con leche.

'What did you do today, *Papito*?' she asked him.

'Nothing that was nearly as much fun.'

'Mama says you're in the army. Do you fight wars, like on
television?'

He laughed. 'I spend all day in an office looking at files and
reading reports.'

'You won't get hurt, will you, Papa? You won't get shot?'

'No, *cara*. There are no wars here in Argentina. Not any
more.'

'I want to be in the army when I grow up.'

He smiled again. 'We'll see, *chiquita*. We'll see.'

Francesca appeared at the doorway. 'Simone, Antonia is calling
for you. It's time for your bath.'

'Yes, Mama.' She leaned towards him and whispered: 'Mama
says we are going away.'

'Yes, *chiquita*. We have to leave Argentina.'

'Are you coming too?'

He laughed. 'Of course. I would not go anywhere without you and Mama.'

'And Antonia?'

'No. Antonia has to stay here. We will find someone else to look after you.'

Simone looked sulky. 'I don't want to go.'

'You'll like it in the new place. I promise.'

Francesca clapped her hands. 'Simone. Come on. Your bath is getting cold.'

Simone ran from the room. Angeli watched her go, the smile freezing on his face. Those bastards. They had chased him out of his own country. Like a criminal. If he had committed any crime at all it was that he had made this country safe for the little ones.

The Aerolineas Argentinas flight from Mexico City touched down at Ezeiza on a hot January night. As he stepped on to the runway the heat and humidity turned his shirt into a sodden rag in minutes. Summer in Buenos Aires, a bad time to arrive; most *porteños* would already have taken off for the beaches.

As he stepped inside the terminal the knot that had been in his stomach since they started their descent became suddenly unbearable. Hard to believe they were not waiting to arrest him, that it really was safe now. He looked around at the armed policemen in the terminal and fought down a wave of panic.

There was a queue at the immigration desk. A policeman stamped the disembarkation cards and passed them to an elegant young woman who checked the documents. His new passport was perused with only fleeting interest.

He walked out of the arrivals lounge, still anticipating a death squad waiting for him in the car park, smirking and lounging on a dark Ford Falcon. He had to keep reminding himself: *The junta is finished, we have democracy again now*.

He jumped in a black-and-yellow taxi. The driver did not take the new motorway downtown. 'Who can afford the toll?' he said. He became garrulous when he discovered that Reuben was a fellow *porteño*. He told him he had once been a teacher, but the school where he had worked had been closed down by the military in 1976. Since then he had been unable to get another job. Still, he

was lucky. Most of the teachers he had worked with had been
disappeared.

But things would change now. Those dirty bastards were gone,
Alfonsín would get the country back on its feet. For himself he
hoped he would find another teaching job somewhere.

Reuben stared out of the window. Steel-and-concrete skeletons
left to rot, remnants of the unfinished motorway like great ramps
leading nowhere, throwing ink shadows against the night sky. In
the distance he made out the silhouettes of the Interama Park, the
giant Ferris wheel a monument to the junta's folly. Two hundred
million dollars in credits, raised by the city, had been invested in
the project, and most of it had finished up in numbered deposit
accounts in Switzerland and Luxembourg.

It reminded Reuben of the old joke: when God created the earth
he discovered he had given Argentina too much. He had blessed
the country with oil, the fertile *pampa*, the Andes, the River Plate.
So to balance the ledger, he also gave it the Argentinians.

The broad avenues gave way to the cobbled streets and curlicued
Parisian apartments of the old quarter. Reuben had booked into
the grand old Alvear Palace Hotel, just a few blocks from where
he had once lived. Returning to these familiar streets brought on
an intense pain deep in his chest. It was not like being home; more
like revisiting the scene of a crime.

He checked into his room and sat down on the bed. Now he
was here he felt curiously reluctant to begin. In his pocket was
a list of names and telephone numbers that might well be useless
now. What was it that he hoped to achieve. Vindication? There
was none. Redemption? No.

The only thing that could save him now was to turn back
the clock.

Those idiots, Angeli thought.

He stood in the garden, looking back at the house. It was
one of the finest houses in Palermo, with green shuttered windows, air-conditioning, ten rooms. He had done well for a
man whose grandfather had been a Calabrian peasant, whose
grandmother had started life in the slums of Genoa. His own
father had risen no higher than corporal under Perón. Angeli
had received his education not at St Andrew's or St George's,
but at a secondary school run by the army. He had devoted

his life to the service of Argentina and he had been well rewarded.

But now the wheel had turned and it was time to return to Italy. One of Alfonsín's judges had ordered him to appear in court to answer charges of kidnapping, torture and homicide. It was outrageous.

He would not give the bastards the satisfaction. He would shake the dust from his shoes and leave.

Because of those idiots. Those ungrateful bastards.

He was proud of what he had done, of everything he had achieved. World War III had been fought and won in Buenos Aires; he and his brother officers had demonstrated that the communists could be defeated if one had the will, if one was strong enough. History would vindicate them.

What they had not been able to overcome was incompetence; the stupid economic policies of Videla's Economics Minister, del Hoy, and the grand folly of the military misadventure in the Islas Malvinas – what the British called the Falklands. They had been humiliated there in the eyes of the nation and of the world. That was what had broken them in the end, not the *locas*, the crazy women in the Plaza de Mayo. It was one thousand per cent inflation and seeing their flag trampled in the mud at Port Stanley.

Because of that fool Galtieri.

He threw his cigarette in the pool.

Well, he could still serve Argentina and the grand designs of anti-communism, only he would have to do it from elsewhere. He was no longer just a functionary of the military; he had made powerful friends during his career and now he had his own power base. This was not the end for César Angeli. It was just the beginning.

40

Ghosts everywhere.

Reuben stood outside his old apartment in Recoleta and stared at the brass backplate. It was as if there were a steel band around his chest. He couldn't breathe.

A jogger, wearing Nike runners and loose silky blue shorts, came out of the front door and gave him a suspicious glance. But she did not stop. She ran down the steps and set off down the tree-lined avenue.

He looked beyond the black iron grille to the foyer. The ancient lift was still there, the wrought-iron stairs, a vase of flowers reflected in the mirrored hallway. Everything as he remembered it. He thought of Rosa the first night he had brought her here, heard her laughing as he shut the iron gates. She kissed him while the old lift wheezed its way up to the fourth floor.

He blinked and the image was gone. He heard the sound of a baby crying from somewhere above him. Eva and Simone in their cot, dust suspended in a bolt of sunlight through the open shutters, the tinny jangle of a nursery rhyme playing on the mobile he had hung from the nursery ceiling.

He looked up. The crying stopped. Perhaps he had imagined it.

He turned and walked away.

The worst of it was, you never knew. His parents, his brother, his wife, his children, they were all gone. *Desaparecidos*. That was the real cruelty. There was no body to grieve over, not even a cold certainty that they were dead. Even now, those bastards still tortured you with hope.

Eva and Simone would be eight years old now. If they had lived. He could not imagine what fate had overtaken them. Perhaps one or even both of them had survived. Stories had begun to surface of how the children of death squad victims were sometimes given or sold to officers in the regime without children of their own. If that had happened to his daughters, how would he ever find them? He doubted that Alfonsín's new commission would help. So what would he do?

He thought about Rosa. Had she been tortured before she died? Raped? He shut his eyes, tried to dismiss the images that came unbidden to his mind.

He found himself standing outside the Recoleta cemetery and without thinking he walked through the gates. Even in death, Argentina's élite strove for supremacy. They were all here, the long-dead aristocracy entombed in their fantastic temples, competing with each other for novelty and lavish expense. Here were the mausoleums of Aramburu and Alvear, and, tucked away along one of the less celebrated avenues of the famous dead, Santa Evita herself. Even her husband, the great Perón, had not been allowed a tomb here; he had been buried across town in less fashionable Chacarita. There was a saying that it was cheaper to live extravagantly all one's life than to spend one's death in Recoleta.

Here they all mouldered in their palaces to mortality, guarded by great marble angels who looked down with unfounded compassion on the peace of the great and the mighty.

The entrances to these mausoleums were barred with iron gates, but a few were in disrepair, the glass doors smashed and, beyond, the casual visitor could view the great coffins with their ornate silver trimmings piled on top of each other like cordwood. Reuben put his face against the bars and sniffed at the musty taint of corruption.

For my Rosa, he thought, not even a headstone.

The stories of the disappeared were being told now and there were more revelations every day. It seemed the navy had coated their victims' bodies in cement and dumped them into the River Plate; the air force pushed them out of helicopters high over the Atlantic or over the jungles of Tucumán, sometimes when they were still alive; the army, without access to such convenient dumping grounds, had simply bulldozed their *desaparecidos* into mass graves, marked 'NN' – *No Nombres*, No Names.

So. Not even a grave to weep over. Nothing at all.

* * *

He had relived that moment a thousand times, knew every action, every word, like a litany. He had woken to the clamour of the telephone, heard Carmen swear softly as she picked up the receiver.

'*It's Rosa.*'

He remembered the terror and panic in his wife's voice, one of the twins crying in the background. He could still summon that same cold clutch of dread in his guts.

'*The police are here!*'

It was all she had said. It was something he could not get past, even if he could forgive himself for everything that had gone before and after; Rosa had known he was in another woman's bed but still she had thought to warn him.

'*What's going on?*' *Carmen had shouted as he threw on his clothes.*

'*I don't know,*' *he told her, but he did know. He knew about the twenty-one million dollars of Montoneros money that had been funnelled to Havana through the Altman Group. He knew they weren't after Rosa, they were after him.*

'*You can't go back there.*'

'*I have to.*'

'*What good is it going to do? Perhaps they forced her to make the phone call! It's you they want, isn't it?*'

'*Yes.*'

'*What have you done?*'

'*The less you know, the better for you.*'

'*It's a trap. Think about it! You're no good to your family dead!*'

'*I have to go to Rosa!*'

He had left Carmen's apartment intending to go straight to Recoleta, but somewhere on the way he had changed his mind, convinced himself that what Carmen had told him was true. It was a set-up. A trap.

So instead of going home he went to the Mexican embassy. He saved himself. They died.

He sat on the dusty steps of some long-dead general's tomb and hung his head and wept.

41

The Plaza de Mayo was at the heart of the city. The great edifice of the Banco de Nación, the metropolitan cathedral, the ancient *cabildo*, all faced the square with its palms and flower gardens, the white obelisk at its centre. The park reflected the mood of the city: the grass was withered, there were brown splotches of dust, a litter of paper and discarded *gaseosa* cans.

It was almost five o'clock and the pink stone of the Casa Rosada, the Presidential Palace, was lent a softer coral hue by the late afternoon sun. Reuben picked out the balcony where Perón and Evita had waved to adoring crowds of more than a million, where Galtieri had accepted the cheers of the crowds after the invasion of the Malvinas, where more recently Alfonsín had waved to his jubilant supporters after the elections that had given him victory.

The bells in the cathedral chimed the hour. Soon the monument was encircled by a throng of shuffling, solemn women. The Mothers of the Plaza, *Las Locas*, 'the crazy women', as the military had labelled them. They carried placards around their necks, with blurred photographs – here a teenage girl with a violin, there a serious young man with neatly combed hair in his first suit – and underneath a date and the word *DESAPARECIDO*. A few of the women were dressed in expensive suits and sweaters, most had heavy-heeled, sensible shoes and drab clothes, but they all wore on their heads the symbol of peaceful outrage that united them – a white scarf.

Reuben wondered if this new government would bring them justice, would end their torment of not knowing. He wondered, too, if they would ever discover the fate of their children and if it would be some consolation to them.

He wondered if he would ever discover the fate of his own.

*   *   *

This was another Buenos Aires: there were no brightly lit boutiques and restaurants and cafés here. Reuben sniffed the dank and oily breath of the docks. The cranes and gantries and container ships of the Richuelo waterfront were silhouetted against a dirty orange sky. The streets were littered with garbage, the domain of pi-dogs and filthy barefoot children.

Even after eight years he knew there was a good chance he would still be here in Avellaneda. Many *porteños* lived in the same house all their lives. He climbed the cement stairwell, recoiled at the stink from the dark corners. This was the kind of apartment block where Rosa had grown up. He remembered what his father had said: *She's only marrying you for your money. You're her passport to an easy life.* If that was true there was a savage irony to it.

He hesitated outside the door, took a deep breath, preparing himself for the confrontation. He heard a television blaring the dialogue of a Brazilian soap opera. He balled his right hand into a fist and banged twice on the door.

A few moments later it swung open and Reuben found himself staring into the face of a teenage boy in a white vest and badly fitting jeans.

'I'm looking for Domingo Gonsalvez,' Reuben said.

42

The boy looked him over, took in the polo shirt and Italian loafers and neatly pressed grey slacks. His expression was an unnerving mixture of suspicion and contempt.

'Tell him it's his brother-in-law.'

The boy turned away, leaving the door open. Reuben was afforded a glimpse of peeling plaster walls, a black-and-white television, a calendar with a photograph of the Boca Juniors football team. Over the blare of the television he heard an urgent conference taking place in the kitchen.

Then Domingo appeared in the hallway.

He was just as Reuben remembered him, except that now his peasant pride had set into his manner like iron. He was a little greyer, his weather-beaten face had a few more lines, but he was still lean, his body wiry and hard underneath the white vest. There was the same truculence in his grey eyes; poverty had made him no more amenable to his in-laws.

'You.'

'Domingo. It's been a long time.'

He leaned on the door jamb. 'I don't believe it.'

'You thought I was dead.'

'No, I knew you weren't dead.'

'Can I come in?'

Domingo looked down at Reuben's shoes, the Rolex on his wrist. 'You put one foot inside here and I'll slit your throat.'

They stared at each other. 'What happened wasn't my fault,' Reuben said.

'What did you come back here for?'

'I want to find out what happened to Rosa and the girls.'

Domingo gave a short bark of laughter. 'You are really something.'

'*Por Dios*. Please, Domingo. I need your help.'

'You think if one of your daughters was alive, she would want to see you? After you ran out on her and her mother?'

'I didn't run out on—'

'Fuck off!' He hawked deep in his throat and spat at him, slamming the door. Reuben looked down at the thick glob of saliva on his polo shirt. So, there was his answer. His misgivings had been correct. He should not have come back.

Reuben stripped off his clothes and climbed into the shower, washing away the grime of Avellaneda. He closed his eyes, his head resting against the tiles. What else could I have done that night? he asked himself, as he had done countless times before. If I had gone back to the apartment in Recoleta they would have killed me. I never thought they would take Rosa and the girls. I intended to send for them as soon as I reached Mexico. How was I to know?

He got out of the shower, wrapped a towel around his waist and sat on the edge of the bed. He stared at the list of names he had brought with him. Old friends of his family's, former business associates, team-mates from the rugby fifteen, friends from university. Suddenly he had lost enthusiasm for it. He wondered if anyone would be able to tell him anything, anything at all.

Or perhaps there was one man who might still be able to help him. If anyone would be able to find out what had happened to Rosa and the girls, it would be a journalist.

His old friend, Julio Castro.

43

The *La Prensa* offices were on Azopardo, down towards the old San Telmo district. There were linoleum floors, Formica-topped tables supporting yellowing piles of discarded copy and back issues, dreary striplights. The air stank of stale cigarette smoke, shirt-sleeved journalists toiled over ancient typewriters.

Reuben found him on the first floor in a partitioned cubicle behind a bank of metal filing cabinets. He walked right past him, almost close enough to touch, and did not recognise him. Julio had put on weight and lost a lot of hair. He was dressed conservatively, in a dark suit and white shirt, his hair cut much shorter now. But then everyone had grown more conservative under military rule, it seemed. It was a tactic of survival. Long hair and untidy clothes branded you as a leftist.

Still, it was somehow sad to see his friend so quickly in the throes of middle age.

'Julio!'

Julio looked up from his typewriter, startled. Surprise alone, Reuben thought, did not account for his expression. What was it? It was gone before he could identify it. Then he jumped to his feet, his arms outstretched. He wrapped them around his neck, hugged him with what seemed to Reuben like desperation. 'Reuben? Reuben!'

Reuben grinned and returned the embrace.

'I thought you were dead!' Julio shouted.

'No, they didn't get me.'

People were staring at them, all around the office.

'I don't believe it. I thought you'd been disappeared.'

Reuben grinned but something was nagging at him, some intuition he could not define.

'To hell with work,' Julio was saying. 'Let's go and get a drink.'

*   *   *

They went into the *whiskería* on the corner of Azopardo and Belgrano. It was five o'clock and the bar was hot and crowded. Around them the hubbub of conversation and laughter, the clatter of cups and glasses, the steamy hiss of the espresso machine.

'*Por Dios*,' Julio was saying. 'They were bad days. It's still hard to believe it's over.'

'For some of us it will never be over.' Reuben finished his *ginebra*, Dutch gin, and ordered two more. Julio insisted on paying for them.

'So many of our friends were disappeared.' Julio stared moodily into the liquid in his glass. 'Marcello Bolsi. You remember Marcello? Alfredo Gil, Pola Albrecht, Sixto Reboratti. Those dirty bastards in the military . . . but we mustn't think about that any more, right? Now it's over, our new president has promised to get those fascist *cretinos*, every one of them. He's set up a National Commission on the Disappeared.'

Reuben shrugged. He would rejoice when he saw the results.

'You remember Victor Marta, at university? He played hooker that year we won the Inter-University Cup. They sent him to the Malvinas. Some British paratrooper shot him in the back. He's in a wheelchair now. You should see him. Just sits there in his own shit. His mother has to clean him up.' It was nervous chatter. He noticed Julio's hands were shaking. 'But we should think about the future now. So, what about you? You've come back to Argentina to live?'

'I don't know. I haven't made up my mind.'

'How do you like Mexico, huh?'

Reuben shrugged. 'It's the biggest smog bowl in the world. My eyes burn all the time and I have a chronic sore throat.'

Julio ordered two more drinks, still would not let Reuben pay. 'This is a celebration, Reuben! I thought we'd lost you! You keep your hands in your pockets!' He laughed again, a little too loud. 'So, tell me what you've been doing.'

'I'm working in a big Mexican bank. I have a quiet life. That's all. There's nothing to tell.'

Julio looked away. 'You married again?'

Reuben shook his head.

'Shit, I'm sorry, Reuben. What happened to Rosa—'

'It's okay. You don't have to say anything.' He didn't want his sympathy.

'When I heard what happened . . . how did you get away?'

'I got a telephone call.' He hesitated. In the retelling the justifications for what he had done never seemed quite as reasonable, or as sound. 'I didn't go home that night. I didn't think – I thought they were after me, not Rosa. I thought they would be safe.'

A burst of laughter from a group of journalists in the corner. Reuben stared at his reflection in the mirror behind the bar.

'You were right to do what you did.'

Of course I was right, Reuben thought. And I don't remember asking for your opinion.

'Who would have thought they would do something like that?'

Reuben stared into his glass. 'So you're a big-shot journalist at *La Prensa* now?'

'Sure. You see my new office? I have a great view of the air-conditioner, right?'

Reuben drained his glass. Julio ordered two more *ginebras*. Reuben felt himself getting a little drunk. Well, the hell with it. Why not? Let Julio pay if he wants to. He'd bought him enough drinks at the bars in La Boca in their student days.

'Married?'

Julio gave him a curious smile and nodded. 'Four kids. Imagine it. Me! I was the one who was never going to get tied down with a wife and kids!' He realised what he'd said and the laughter died in his throat. 'I'm sorry.'

'It's okay.' Strange, talking about it now, this way. Like it was a big rugby game they had lost. 'So. They never found those articles you wrote, huh?'

Julio lowered his eyes. 'No. I was lucky, I guess.'

'You remember how you came round that afternoon? You were shitting yourself.'

'Sure. I remember.'

'I told you to go to the Mexican embassy.' He gave a hollow laugh. 'Funny how things turn out.'

Julio concentrated on his drink.

'How come they never arrested you?' Reuben said. He was surprised to hear the bitterness in his own voice.

'I don't know.' He raised his glass in toast. 'To the disappeared.'

They drank. It was suddenly too hot and airless in the little bar. He saw Julio loosen his tie. 'It's good to see you again, Julio.'

'It's good to see you too. Look at you. You haven't changed a bit. Not like me, huh?' He patted his stomach. 'Too much of my wife's good cooking. You're lucky, too, you've still got all your hair. I woke up one morning and someone had stuck this shiny soup plate on the back of my head.' He laughed at this little joke against himself. 'This drink is making me light-headed. I can't even get drunk like I used to. Remember those times we had at university? We'd drink all night and still be on our feet next morning.'

'If we keep this up I'll be lucky to be on my feet in another half-hour.'

'What we need is some food inside us. You got any plans for tonight? You have to come back and have dinner.'

Reuben nodded. 'All right.'

Julio slapped him on the shoulder. 'Good. Come on, let's go and find a cab. You can meet my wife. Maybe you remember her.' He gave Reuben another smile.

'What's her name?'

'Carmen. She used to be a friend of Rosa's.'

'Sure,' Reuben said. 'I remember Carmen.'

44

Like Julio, Carmen too had changed. There were four children around her legs and from his first glimpse of her it was evident that the strain of child-rearing had taken its toll. Her figure had gone and even her smile looked tired.

In the taxi from the bar he had worried over meeting her again. He had even thought about making some last-minute excuse to Julio, avoiding this unfortunate reunion. Carmen was etched in his memory in pain and in guilt.

But this wasn't Carmen, not the Carmen he remembered. When she saw him she kissed him on the cheek as casually as she would an old friend and gave no sign that there had ever been more between them. Reuben wondered if Julio knew, or had guessed. He asked himself if it even mattered now, after so many years and all that had happened.

The children were all boys, one of six, another four, and twins, almost a year old.

'You've been busy,' Reuben said to Julio, who smiled, as if it were a compliment.

They lived in Acasuso, a middle-class dormitory suburb half an hour north of the city. The house was comfortable, but not extravagant. There were three bedrooms, a garden with a pit for the *asado*, a Fiat in the garage. Julio was not a rich man, but he had survived. More than many had done during the seventies.

The nervous habits Julio had acquired in the intervening years were even more pronounced in his home. He chain-smoked cigarettes and chewed his fingernails. Not like the Julio he remembered at all. He wondered what pressures Julio had been living with for the last seven years. Perhaps it was only when Alfonsín took over in December that he finally believed that those articles he had written in his student days could no longer hurt him.

They sat on the patio, the air strong with the scent of jasmine flower. An old pepper tree had dropped red berries on the flagstones. They drank beer and talked while Carmen put the children to bed and then prepared their dinner in the kitchen. Reuben looked up occasionally, wondering if she might try to make eye contact with him through the window, but she largely ignored him.

He supposed that was a good thing.

Julio lit the *asado*, the barbecue pit, and Carmen brought out some beef ribs which they grilled over the coals and ate with pimento, onions, bread and a bottle of white wine.

For Reuben it was like being in a house with ghosts. There was a sense of unreality to it all. These two people belonged to a nightmare past he had enshrined in his memory. It shocked him to find them still alive, living ordinary lives, growing older, forgetting.

He felt sorry, too, for Carmen. Look at her now. He wondered if she ever felt as if life had somehow cheated her.

After dinner she packed up the plates and left them alone on the patio. Julio talked, a beery monologue on rugby, the economy, politics. And the subject that Reuben wanted most to talk of was carefully avoided.

They drank some more Quilmes and Julio got very drunk. He began to slur his words. 'So. You're going to come back and live in Buenos Aires?' he asked him for the third time that evening.

Why did it sound as if he hoped he wouldn't? 'I told you, I don't know. All I want to do for now is try and find out what happened to Rosa and my daughters.'

'Perhaps once they get this commission under way.'

'Perhaps.'

A long difficult silence. 'They say Mexico City is full of exiles.'

'I suppose. But it's a big city and I don't mix much any more. I have my own apartment, I go to work each day, I come home at night, I go to cafés, I read. It's a quiet life but then I guess you don't appreciate peace until you have lived without it.'

'You didn't get married again?'

'No. I don't think I'll ever marry again. Besides—' He stopped, tried to find the words. 'I don't think I can ever forgive myself.'

'What are you talking about?'

He took a deep breath. 'I should have come back for her.'

'Reuben. That wouldn't have done any good.'

'If they had me, they might have let them go.'

'Those bastards never . . .' Julio stopped. 'What happened to the rest of your family? Your parents, your brother?'

'All gone.'

'*Por Dios*,' Julio murmured. 'I never understood why you did it. You were the last people I thought would have helped the *comunistas*.'

Reuben drained his beer. Something was nagging at him. 'When did you find out?'

There was a strange look in Julio's eyes, like that of a cornered animal. 'There were rumours. They started the next day.'

'Yeah. Where did you hear them?'

Julio hesitated. 'At *La Prensa*.'

'I thought the government kept a lid on it, said it was a foreign exchange fraud.'

'We still heard stories. We couldn't print them.'

Something was still not right. 'Is there something you're not telling me, Julio? If there's anything, anything at all, please . . .'

'Shit, Reuben. You think I'd hold out on you about something like this?'

Reuben felt blurry from drink. 'No. No, of course not.'

Carmen brought out the coffees then, and the talk turned to other things, to children, inflation, the problems of owning a car. Carmen avoided his eyes. The secrets gathered around this table, he thought, the hideous ways all our lives have intertwined. To talk about Rosa was fraught with danger for all of them. We would have to talk about passions best left buried and so we talk of inconsequential things while we keep our eyes from each other.

Finally, Reuben said: 'I have to go now.' He stood up. Julio stood too, unsteady on his feet. He put a hand on Reuben's shoulder. 'You don't know how good it is to see you again.' He embraced him. 'How long are you going to be in Buenos Aires?'

'I can't stay too long. I still have a job in Mexico. I have to go back next week.'

'Call me up tomorrow. We're heading to the beaches the day after tomorrow for the summer holidays but we'll have another drink before I go, okay?'

'Sure.'

'Hey, I'm too loaded to drive. I'll phone for a taxi.'

'No, Julio,' Carmen said. 'I'll take him back to his hotel.'

A look passed between them, but Julio was unwilling to confront his wife in front of Reuben.

'It's okay,' Reuben said. 'A cab is fine.'

'No,' Carmen said. 'We haven't seen you in seven years and then we let you take a taxi home? I won't hear of it.'

She went inside to fetch the car keys. Julio looked at Reuben. 'Women.'

'Yes,' Reuben answered, avoiding his eyes. 'Women.'

45

They drove for a long time in silence. Finally, Carmen said, 'It's all right. He knows about us.'

'You told him?'

'I wanted to hurt him. Like he hurt me.' A racing change through the gears as she sped through a red light.

Reuben studied her in the glow of the dashboard light. The jeans and dark jumper she wore did not flatter her. Hard to remember they were once lovers. 'You didn't do anything wrong. He was playing around with other women all the time.'

'It wasn't just Julio. I did it because I was jealous of Rosa.'

A hollow laugh. 'And I always thought it was me.'

'You were beautiful. You still are.' She took a packet of cigarettes from the console, put one in her mouth, fumbled in the glove box for a lighter. 'I always promised myself I would marry him one day. And I did it, too. Now I wonder why I thought it was such a big deal.'

'George Bernard Shaw said there were two tragedies in life. One was losing your heart's desire, the other was getting it.'

Carmen kept her eyes on the road, but her lips parted in a sly smile. 'Perhaps I should have gone to university like you. I would have known the trouble I was asking for.'

'University doesn't stop you making trouble for yourself, Carmen. It just helps you explain it afterwards.'

She turned to look at him a moment. 'You look great, Reuben.'

'So do you.'

'You're a liar.' She looked at her reflection in the rear-vision mirror. 'Look at me. I was never as beautiful as Rosa, but I didn't look too bad. Now I'm fat, I've got four screaming kids and a shit of a husband. I suppose it's no better than I deserve.' She touched his knee lightly with her hand.

Reuben wondered where this was leading. Hot in the car. A warm
night, the smell of heat and gasoline. There was a lot of traffic on
the road, *porteños* heading into the city for the restaurants and
the clubs.

'I still lie awake at night thinking about it. She was my best
friend. And there I was, fucking her husband.'

He hesitated. 'There's something I've been wanting to ask you.
After . . . after that night. Did the police come?'

She shook her head. Well, of course not, he thought. If the police
had found out about Carmen, she would have disappeared too.

So. Rosa had not given up Carmen's address. Extraordinary.
Even when she knew what he had done she had not betrayed
Carmen, as she had not betrayed him. He closed his eyes and
filed this burden away with his other sins.

'Why did you come back, Reuben?'

'Like I told Julio, to try and find out what happened to Rosa
and my daughters.'

'You think you'll ever find out?'

'I have to try.'

They reached the centre of the city. The broad boulevards gave
way to *fin de siècle* apartments and cobbled streets. Reuben stared
out of the window; yellow haloes around the streetlamps, a couple
pressed close together in the doorway of an apartment building.

'Rosa told me what you were doing. About the money going
to Cuba.'

He felt as if he had been punched in the chest. No, wait a minute.
That wasn't possible. 'But she didn't know.'

'The same way she didn't know about you and me?'

It took a few moments to find his voice. 'But how?' he said,
finally.

'Perhaps she heard you talking on the telephone some time.
Perhaps you left some papers lying around. I don't know.'

They were back in Recoleta. Carmen turned into the forecourt
of the Alvear Palace. Reuben made no move to get out.

'You never knew?' she said.

He shook his head. 'She shouldn't have told you. She shouldn't
have told anyone.'

'She was frightened. She needed to talk to someone.'

'Well, it makes no difference now.' He closed his eyes. 'I should
have gone back to the apartment.' He clenched his fists in his

lap as if trying to will himself back in time. 'I should have gone *back*.'

'And if you had they would have taken Rosa and the girls anyway.'

'Or maybe they wouldn't have.' He couldn't get past this. There were some things that happened to you, he thought, you couldn't get over. You might as well be dead. 'I keep thinking that perhaps they're still alive somewhere.'

'Reuben, disappeared is the same as dead. Stop torturing yourself.'

'I shouldn't have been with you that night.'

'You think I don't think that same thing every day?'

'I don't know. Do you?'

'I see. You're the only one in the whole world with a conscience?'

He didn't know what to say to that.

'If it's any consolation, I'm not happy.'

'You think I want you to be miserable?'

'I don't know. But perhaps it's justice. *Por Dios*. He's changed so much, Reuben. I don't even know if I love him any more.'

His head was spinning. Whiskies, beers, wine. He was in no state to make any sense of this. Suddenly Carmen leaned over, took his face in her hands and kissed him on the lips. He did not try to stop her. Her kiss had a terrible, desperate urgency and he could feel her disappointment when he did not respond.

Finally, she pulled away. 'I'm sorry.'

'I can't, Carmen.'

'You don't want me any more. I don't blame you.'

'You're married now. Julio's my friend.'

She looked at him, the green glow of the dashboard light throwing her face into shadow. There was an odd smile on her face. 'It never stopped me, did it?' She turned away, put both her hands on the wheel. 'It never stopped Julio either.'

'What?'

'It doesn't matter.'

He grabbed her wrist. 'What did you mean by that?'

'You're hurting me, Reuben.'

'Tell me!'

'She never told you, did she?'

'Told me what?'

'About Julio. What he did to her.'

The world stopped. He didn't think he wanted to hear this.

'He raped her, Reuben. Oh, it was before you. He was sleeping with me at the time. I was the one he betrayed. But I still wanted him, even after I found out. Isn't it sad, Reuben? Isn't it pathetic?'

This was too much to take in. For so long he had supposed he had cornered the market on disgust; hard to spare some now for someone else. 'I don't believe you.'

She shrugged her shoulders. 'Okay.'

'Carmen?'

'What, you think I'm making it up?'

'Rosa would have told me.'

'And you would have married her, after you knew your best friend had had her first?'

He didn't answer her.

'You see?' She angrily brushed away a tear. 'Goodbye, Reuben.' She leaned across the car, threw open the door. 'Goodbye,' she repeated.

He got out of the car. He watched the Fiat pull away from the kerb and merge with the traffic on Ayacuso. Holy Mother of God. He could not believe what he had just heard. Even his friends were enemies. All those years he had lived with his own secrets, he never considered that others might be keeping things from him. What else did he still have to learn?

When she got back Julio was still sitting on the patio, drinking. She stood at the French doors, watching him. She wondered how she could once have found this man so wildly attractive.

'He's all tucked up in bed?' Julio said.

'I don't know. I only took him as far as the front door.'

Julio poured some more wine into his glass. 'What a surprise seeing him again.'

'You knew he would come back. You said so yourself.'

'Still. Seeing him, in the flesh. It brings back memories. What did you tell him?'

'I didn't tell him anything.' He knew by the tilt of her head and the way she lowered her eyes that she was lying to him. 'Are you going to sit there drinking all night?'

'I'll do what I damn well please. Just like you do.' He expected she had thrown herself at him in the car. He could imagine the scene. He thought Reuben would have done it too, out of spite.

She shrugged her shoulders. 'I'm going to bed.' She went back inside. Julio looked at his watch, tried to remember what time she had left, if there had been time. If I went up to the bedroom now, I bet I would smell him on her, he thought.

He threw back his head, stared up at the night sky. Sometimes he wished he could just let this thing go. He could not go on living like this. He had unburdened himself only once, with Carmen. He had been drunk and he had immediately regretted it the next morning. But he had had to tell someone.

It hadn't done any good. He had only told her half of it anyway. Even when he was drunk he knew he couldn't trust his wife with everything. And besides, he was not sure she would understand. How could you explain something as complicated as the truth?

46

They met in the *whiskería* on Azopardo where they had gone the previous evening. There was no air-conditioning in the bar and the ceiling fans barely moved the air, which was thick and warm as treacle. The bar was crowded with businessmen on their way home from work, a few journalists from the *Herald* with their clipped Home Counties accents.

Julio shambled in almost half an hour late.

'Reuben. Sorry. What a day.'

Reuben ordered two gins and tonic.

'I can only stay for a while. I have to get home. We're leaving early in the morning.'

The forced bonhomie of the previous evening had vanished. They made stilted conversation, two complete strangers pretending they were friends. Julio forced the pace with more news of tenuous mutual acquaintances, another unenthusiastic interrogation about life in Mexico, a discourse on politics. This was a different Julio to the one from the previous evening. They were both aware of undercurrents at play here and the talk only papered over the increasingly uneasy silences between them.

At one point, Julio said: 'I had a big fight with Carmen last night.'

'What about?'

'Our marriage is not so good. I suppose you knew that.'

'Why would I know that?'

Julio shrugged. 'I thought she would have told you all about it in the car.'

Reuben did not respond.

'I think she's still burning a candle for you.'

'*Por Dios.*'

'I'm not accusing you of anything,' Julio said. 'I knew about the two of you. I'm not upset about it.' He drained his glass and ordered two more gins. Reuben was still nursing his first.

He's not accusing me, Reuben thought. Well, that's good of him, considering. He did not understand his own reaction, why he felt so angry. The rape had happened nine, ten years ago, before he had met Rosa. All he knew was that yesterday when Carmen had told him what Julio had done, he had wanted to break his neck.

Julio looked pointedly at his watch. 'Look, I have to get home and pack. How much longer are you going to be in Buenos Aires?'

Reuben shrugged. 'I don't know.'

'We'll be gone about a week. If you're still here when we get back, give us a call, okay? You have to give me your address, so we can keep in touch. Come on, I'll give you a lift back to your hotel.'

They finished their drinks and Reuben followed Julio out of the bar, into the sweating January night.

47

Julio's Fiat was parked about a hundred yards away. They sat there in silence. Taxis and buses passed them in the street, most driving with just their parking lights, some without lights at all. It was a peculiarly Argentine habit; *porteños* believed using headlights made it harder to see at night.

Julio held a match to yet another cigarette before he started the engine.

'Carmen told me what you did.'

Julio reacted as if he had been slapped. He dropped the lit cigarette on to the floor well. 'What?'

'She told me what you did.'

'*Por Dios*. You don't believe her?' He started to get out of the car. Reuben grabbed him by the shirt front and dragged him back in. 'Reuben! Please! I had no choice! They tortured me! I'm lucky to be alive!'

Reuben stared at him. He had no idea what he was talking about. 'Who tortured you?'

It was dark in the car. The nearest streetlamp was twenty metres away. But Reuben could still make out the play of emotion on his friend's face, the terrible realisation that he had said too much, too soon. He made a little whimpering sound from fear.

The answer came slowly, with a crawling of the flesh and a cold settling of rage. 'You. It was you,' he said, slowly, wonderingly. He felt like a child; the world had been explained to him and he had lost at once both his innocence and his confusion.

'There was nothing I could do. You don't know what they do to you, Reuben . . .'

'How did you know?'

'Carmen.'

'Carmen?'

'Rosa used to tell her everything. Reuben, they dragged me off the street . . .'

He didn't listen to the rest of it. In his mind he was putting together the pieces of the puzzle. Rosa. She had shared her dread secret with her friend and her friend had whispered it to her lover.

Julio had finished his story of the tortures and outrages that had been done to him and had started to cry. It was all a lie. He was still alive, so it had to be a lie.

'Stop it,' Reuben said.

'You think I don't suffer every day? They made me tell them, Reuben. You don't know the things they do to you. I resisted them as long as I could. You have to believe me. Reuben?'

Julio had tried ringing Rosa's apartment the next morning but the line was disconnected. He drove straight there. The security lock on the wrought-iron gate was gone and the glass door had been smashed in. He ran up to the fourth floor. The apartment was empty. It had been ransacked.

A neighbour told him the death squad had taken everyone. He stumbled back into the street, numb with disbelief. This was not the way it was supposed to be.

He had not gone further than a hundred yards when two men grabbed him and pulled him into a car. A blanket was thrown over him and when he tried to protest, they kicked him until he was quiet.

He thought that after everything they were still going to murder him because of those articles he had written. It was only later he found out they were Angeli's men. They had been watching the apartment, waiting for Reuben or any of his friends or family to show up.

He had no idea where they took him. They stripped him and handcuffed him to a bed.

But he was lucky. It was Angeli who interrogated him. He could not see his face, for they had thrown a hood over his head. But he recognised his voice.

When he had first offered his services as an informer, it was Angeli himself who had questioned him. Julio had thought it would guarantee his entrée into the golden circle, vouchsafe immunity from the death squads. To seal the pact he had given Angeli the Altmans.

At the time he had congratulated himself on the genius of his solution. His name off the death list. And Rosa, alone, afraid, unprotected. He would be there for her.

But now he knew himself for a Judas and a fool.

Angeli seemed angry that Julio had been brought there and berated his two guards. Julio had listened, naked and helpless, shivering with cold and with terror.

Finally Angeli said to him: 'What were you doing at the apartment?'

'I wanted to talk to Rosa.'

'Rosa Altman is no concern of yours.'

'But she's innocent. It's her husband you want! I told you that!'

'So that was your reason for informing on Reuben Altman? And we thought you were a good patriot.'

'But Rosa is innocent!'

Julio had waited, ears attuned to every small sound, wondering what they were going to do to him. It was not beyond possibility that they would torture and kill him anyway.

'Where is Reuben Altman?' he heard Angeli say.

'I don't understand. You've got Altman.'

'He was not at his apartment last night. We are looking for him now.'

Not at his apartment? Julio did not understand. He heard a whispered conversation between Angeli and the guards, knew his own fate was being decided at that moment. He wanted to say something but his throat seemed to close up and he was unable to speak.

Rough hands lifted him to his feet and led him down a corridor. The hood was removed and a uniformed guard threw his clothes at him. 'Get dressed,' he said. When the men came back they tugged the hood back over his face and he was led out to a waiting car. He was thrown into the gutter in the middle of the city, just a block from the Plaza de Mayo.

And he had spent the rest of his life living in fear.

48

'May you rot in hell,' Reuben breathed.

'Don't presume to judge me, you pompous bastard! If I rot in hell, you'll rot with me! Maybe your family would still be alive if you hadn't run away! They wanted you, not Rosa, not the babies. He took them to try and get you! You were the one to blame, not me!'

Reuben did not remember what happened next. The rage bubbled up in him, driven by the same accusations he had flung at himself for the last seven years. Julio was right. *He was to blame.*

The next thing he knew he was staring down at the ruins of Julio's face. Dark blood dribbled from his nose and mouth. His hands were still locked around his throat. He wasn't moving.

Reuben took his hands away and Julio slumped over the wheel.

He sat there, paralysed, unsure what to do next. He felt completely disorientated. The tattered remnants of his rage competed for his attention with a terrible, numbing fear. In the space of a few minutes the world had turned on its head.

Julio had betrayed him and his family to the military.

He kept turning this thought in his head, like a child examining some new object, trying to make sense of it.

And now Julio is dead.

He did not know how long he sat there. A bus rumbled past. A young man and woman passed on the footpath, arm in arm, kissing as they walked. They did not spare a glance at the car.

It took an effort of will to move. He reached over, felt for a pulse at Julio's throat. Nothing. I've murdered him. No, impossible. I'm not a murderer. Any moment Julio would stir, try to sit up.

I've murdered him.

He started to hyperventilate, lose control. He wanted just to get

out of the car and run away but he forced himself to be calm. He
heard the soft drip of blood on to the floor.

I have to get him away from here.

He got out, went around the car to the driver's side and
manhandled Julio's body out of the seat. He got in behind the
wheel. *Por Dios*, sticky blood on the seat, the dashboard. What
was he going to do? He couldn't leave Julio here. Someone would
find him, if not tonight, then first thing in the morning. He made
a decision, turned on the ignition and drove away towards the
Paseo Colón.

He drove badly, unable to concentrate on what he was doing. Not
that it mattered, not in Buenos Aires. Everyone drove that way.
Reuben had no idea where he was going. Then he remembered
how, in the days of Isabelita, bodies were often left on one of
the garbage dumps on the outskirts of the city. He turned the
car around and headed out towards the airport. He turned on to
Avenida Riccieri, towards the speedway out to Ezeiza.

He passed the gates of an army barracks, saw the lights of the
international airport in the distance. Justice, he thought to himself.
Julio is travelling the same road as Rosa.

He drove down a dirt road, littered with the mouldering wrecks
of cars. He stopped, turned off the ignition and the headlights. He
wound down the window, was immediately assailed by the ripe
smell of garbage. He held his breath and listened.

The only sounds were the chirrup of crickets in the trees and
a scuttering among the shadows, rats perhaps. Now that he had
stopped he found again that he could not move. He put his head
on the steering wheel and sat there for a long time. It took an
effort of will to force himself out of the car.

He opened the passenger door, reached in and dragged Julio's
body out of the car. He threw open the boot. Then he took Julio
under the arms and lifted the top half of his torso into the boot,
then lifted his legs so that his body rolled in.

He leaned against the car, panting hard.

He thought about Carmen, about the four young children he
had seen just last night. He rubbed a hand across his face. But
Julio deserved this for what he did. And yet . . .

But right now he could not think about this. Perhaps later he would find a way to justify this, to take succour from this vengeance and to nurse his soul for the terrible thing he had just done. Another desperate voice whispered to him about survival now, that same devil who had assumed his life in crisis once before, the demon that had sent his feet scurrying towards Arcos Street and the Mexican embassy instead of his own home in Recoleta.

He found a jack and a crowbar in the toolkit. He used the crowbar to lever off the registration plates. He threw them on top of Julio's body and slammed the boot shut. He spent the next half-hour fumbling in the darkness with the jack, removing all the tyres, leaving the Fiat resting on its hubs. Then he calmly walked around the car, smashing in all the windows and hammering the metal coachwork with the crowbar. When he had finished he felt satisfied that when the sun rose in the morning the Fiat would look just like every other wreck rusting away there, as if it had been there for months.

It was a long walk back to the road. He flagged down a taxi to take him back to his hotel. He told the driver his car had broken down.

If the desk clerk thought his appearance unusual he did not remark on it. He got in to his room and examined his reflection in the bathroom mirror. There were dark stains on his suit jacket, crusted blood under his fingernails. Reuben stared at the face in the mirror; eight years ago the mirror had shown him a coward, now it showed him the face of a murderer.

He turned off the light and lay down on the bed, still fully clothed. But he knew there was no chance of sleep. He wanted simply to be alone in the darkness with his demons, to try to come to terms with his own guilt as well as that of his wife and his best friend.

49

The next morning at just after eleven o'clock Reuben stared out
of the cabin window of an Aerolineas Argentinas 747 *en route*
to Mexico City. He had claimed a stand-by seat in the economy
section. His eyes were red-rimmed from lack of sleep, his cheeks
unshaven. As the airliner banked over the city he thought he saw
a garbage tip among the trees just below, the glint of metal from
a rusting car.

What had he done? It had been a revenge of sorts, but even if
he could claim it as a sort of rough justice, Rosa was still as dead
as she was before, and he was no closer to finding his daughters,
if they were still alive. Did Julio's death absolve him of his own
guilt? Did two evils lead to redemption?

While others dozed in their seats or stared at the in-flight
movie, Reuben Altman flicked endlessly through the channels
on his headset, the volume turned high, trying to drown the
endless cacophony of his own thoughts.

III

Europe and South America
Summer 1994

50

Rome, Italy

He called her his princess, *mia principessa*.

They lived in an apartment on the top floor of a palazzo that had been built for Pope Innocent X and his family. Even as a child she drank from glasses fashioned by master craftsmen at Murano, ate from chinaware designed by Giò Ponti. Her communion dress was commissioned to Valentino Garavani.

As the years went past her memories of Buenos Aires became vague. She remembered the great house in Palermo with its echoing marble foyer and the aquamarine swimming pool in the back garden, remembered the dinner parties and peeping through the balustrades at the top of the stairs as the guests arrived, the men dressed in braided uniforms, their wives in sumptuous gowns, glittering with diamonds. They were like scenes from a fairy tale and for many years, even after they came to Italy, she thought she really *was* a princess.

Her parents sent her for riding lessons to a private club just outside Rome. On her tenth birthday Angeli bought her her own pony. She threw her arms around his neck and swore that he was the most wonderful father in the whole world. 'Anything for you, *mia principessa*,' he whispered. 'Anything for you.'

She was driven every day to a private school in Trastevere in a white Mercedes by her father's chauffeur.

It was not until she was thirteen years old that one of the other girls whispered to her that her father made his living by selling guns. The claim was so outrageous that Simone demanded to know where she had obtained such stupid information. She replied that it had come from her own father; he made his living by buying them from Angeli and trading them on.

After a week of sleepless nights Simone dismissed this information from her mind. But as hard as she tried, the roseate world of her childhood was gone for ever. From that time on it became a habit with her never to examine her life too closely. But like a mosquito in a darkened room, this unwanted knowledge nagged at her constantly.

After all, he was her father; and every daughter loves her father.

César Angeli and his guest sat at one of the tables clustered on the cobblestones of the Piazza Campo dei Fiori, watching the fruit and flower sellers pack away their stalls after the morning market. It was a warm summer day, the sky a clear washed blue. The tourist season was at its height and in the hubbub around him Angeli heard the drawl of American tourists mixed with the *romanaccio* of the locals.

He summoned a white-jacketed waiter and ordered two *digestivi*.

Angeli's guest wore just a simple black clerical suit with a silver pectoral cross. He was a tall, powerfully built man in his sixties, with the blunt fingers of a peasant. His teeth and the first and second fingers of his left hand were stained with tobacco. He spoke Italian with a heavy accent that revealed him as an East European. There were no other clues to his identity, nothing to betray him as an archbishop in the Roman Catholic Church and one of the most powerful men in the Vatican.

'My associates will not be happy with this latest rise in the charges,' Angeli was saying.

The archbishop took a black Egyptian cigarette from an engraved silver case. 'Two per cent.' He waved a hand airily. 'Nothing.'

'Two per cent of a hundred lire is nothing. Two per cent of a hundred billion lire is quite a lot of money.'

'Tell them to think of it as a donation to the Church. Peter's Pence will not pay for everything.'

'I will pass on your sentiments.'

As they sipped their *digestivi* the archbishop looked across the square at the cowled figure of Giordano Bruno, his likeness now dominating the piazza where he had died in agony. The Inquisition had burned him alive on that very spot for heresy.

Angeli nodded in the direction of the statue. 'They knew how to deal with subversives in those days.'

'Before the Church got soft. No wonder young people lose their way.'

'We could have killed those bastards in the Plaza de Mayo, right in front of everyone. The Archbishop of Buenos Aires should have stood there to give us his blessings as we did it. We were defending Christianity.'

The archbishop nodded. 'Now we have priests in league with the *comunistas*.'

'Well, at least we showed them how it should be done. And we'll do it again, if we have to. *Saluta!*'

They finished their *digestivi* and called for the bill. Angeli did not notice one of the waiters standing by the cash register, staring at him.

He does not recognise me, the man thought. But I know him. I'd know him anywhere. It had been seventeen years since they had last served together but you didn't forget someone like that. He was heavier and maybe a little fuller in the face, but it *had* to be him.

He remembered those bastards, all of them. Okay, he had done some things he wasn't proud of, but not as bad as most. He was just taking orders, doing what he was told. *They* were the ones responsible.

He still remembered how this one had thrown him against a wall, for no reason, nearly choked him. He could still remember what his breath smelled like.

One of the other waiters returned with the man's American Express card. Turturro called him over. 'I know him.'

'Yeah?'

'I knew him in Argentina.'

The waiter shrugged, processed the card. As he put it back on the tray Turturro glanced at it. *Gregorini*. So that was the name he was using now. But it was still him, it was still Colonel César Angeli.

He checked the list of bookings, found the name 'Gregorini'. There was a telephone number beside it, and Turturro scribbled it down. He looked up. Angeli and his guest had got up to leave. Turturro took off his white jacket and walked out of the restaurant after them. His colleague stared after him open-mouthed as he scurried away across the Campo dei Fiori leaving him alone with a restaurant full of customers.

*   *   *

Turturro followed, at a discreet distance, prayed they were not going to jump in a taxi on the Corso Vittorio Emanuele. His luck held. He saw them cross the busy street and walk side by side, still deep in conversation, up the Corso dei Rinascimento. They went into an expensive security apartment on the other side of the Piazza Navona, in the Via della Pace.

He took careful note of the address, checked the name on the brass plate beside the front door. *Gregorini*. On his way back to the Corso Vittorio Emanuele he decided to celebrate with a grappa in the Bevitoria Navona. He had served his last day as a waiter.

51

Just before Turturro left the Command Action Group at the end of 1977 he was ordered to shred certain documents. Most of them were records of interrogation, giving the identity of the prisoner, the times of interrogation, the name of the interrogator – which was always a code word – and the result of the interview. This was invariably logged as either NORMAL or DEAD.

Among the documents were the personnel files of every member of the Command Action Group, including the three files of his superior officers. At great risk Turturro did not shred these papers as he had been ordered to do but instead smuggled them out of the barracks concealed in his clothing.

For many years, until the end of military rule in 1983, they had lain concealed in a metal box buried in his garden. When Alfonsín had announced the National Commission on the Disappeared, Turturro had congratulated himself on his foresight. He had imagined that the documents would now be worth a great deal of money, if properly utilised.

But the commission had turned out to be toothless, a sap for the masses. After three years no convictions had been recorded, and the commission had been ordered to wind up its investigations in 1986. Only two of the junta's leaders, General Jorge Videla and Admiral Emilio Massera, had been imprisoned, and Alfonsín then proclaimed the Law of Due Obedience, which had in fact turned out to be a blanket pardon for everyone else.

Then, two years ago, he had been involved in a bar-room brawl in La Boca. Another soldier, a sergeant, had died. Over the years he had made many friends in the army and they ensured that his arrest warrant was delayed until he had had the chance to escape to Montevideo. From there Turturro had decided to go to Italy where he still had distant relatives. One of them owned a restaurant in Rome. Out of the kindness of his heart the owner of the Casa Latina had given his long-lost cousin a job as a waiter, on the minimum wage.

But Turturro did not give up hope. He still had his files. And now, thanks to fate, he would finally be able to cash in.

When he got back to his tiny apartment in the suburbs later that evening, he was stumbling from the effects of too much grappa and immediately fell asleep on the sofa. But the next morning when he woke up and had lit his first cigarette of the day, he fumbled in his shirt pocket for the piece of paper with Angeli's telephone number. He unfolded it and laid it out on the coffee table.

The cat was mewing around his legs for food but he kicked it away. Nothing had gone right since he had come to this stinking country but perhaps now his luck had changed. His head was aching from the grappa but he had never felt so good.

Simone answered the phone on the second ring. '*Pronto.*'

'May I speak with Signor Gregorini?'

'Who is calling, please?'

'Just tell him it's an old friend.'

Angeli threw down that morning's edition of *La Repubblica* and stalked into the hallway from the dining room. He did not like being disturbed during breakfast. '*Qui parla César Gregorini.*'

'Colonel Angeli?'

Angeli felt his heart bound in his chest. Even his oldest friends and associates did not call him by that name any more. 'Who is this?'

'Maybe you don't remember me. I worked for you in the old days. We made a lot of those *subversivos* disappear together. Do you remember, Colonel?'

It never crossed Angeli's mind to deny his identity for one moment. It would have been pointless. The fact that this person knew him by his real name proved that. 'What do you want?'

'I was hoping we could sit down and talk about old times.'

He saw his wife and daughter watching him from the breakfast table. He turned his back towards them and lowered his voice. 'To what purpose?'

'It's good for old friends to keep in touch, don't you think, Colonel?'

'I have no interest in the past.'

'Others may not share your view. There's a café opposite the

church of Sant'Agnese di Agone. I'll see you there at ten
o'clock.'

'How will I know who you are?' Angeli hissed into the phone.

'Don't worry. I'll recognise you.' The caller hung up.

52

Francesca looked up. 'What's wrong?'

Angeli stood in the hall, his hands in his pockets, staring at the telephone. 'I think I'm being blackmailed.'

She didn't seem as surprised as he thought she would be. She stared at him for a few moments, her hands clasped in front of her. 'Who is it?'

'I don't know. I'm about to find out, I think.'

'Someone from the old days?'

He nodded. He had often wondered how much his wife knew, or had guessed. He had never told her about his role in the Command Action Group in the seventies. He imagined she did not want to know, and that was how it should be. She came from a military family and she knew certain questions were never asked.

She had been a beauty when he had married her, a prize. Back then he had been a junior officer without money or influence and her family had been scandalised when she had chosen him over a dozen more eligible suitors. He still did not know why. Perhaps even then she had recognised an ambition in him that matched her own. If so, he had not disappointed her.

'Are you worried?' she asked him.

'No. I'm not worried.'

She smiled. She expected him to take care of these things. And as long as he did, he would get her loyalty and support, whatever means he chose. That was the tacit agreement between them.

Angeli went back into the dining room to finish his breakfast. He stared moodily at his newspaper but he read the same sentence three times and still could make no sense of it. His mind was preoccupied with the telephone call. The last time he had confronted one of these spectres from the past had been almost six years ago, in a restaurant in Piazza di Spagna. A man had stood in front of his table and started shouting at him. Deranged, the proprietor had

said after they had shunted him out of the door. But the man was
still outside when he left, screaming insults.

Angeli had his driver teach him some manners.

Still, it made him nervous, knowing there were people who knew
him in that other life. Not that he gave a damn about any of
them. They should have got rid of all of those dirty bastards.
Unfortunately a few had been kept alive through expediency,
either as bait to trap other *comunistas*, or because they were
foreign nationals. He would have thought they would have been
grateful.

He looked around. His apartment had cost him several million
dollars. It had murals on the ceiling that dated from the eighteenth
century and the Renaissance brickwork in the hallway had been
worked around an ancient Roman Ionic column. Francesca had
decorated much of the apartment, in baroque style. There were
antique vases and alabaster *putti* on pedestals in the entrance
and hall, polished marble-tiled floors, gilt chandeliers, brocade
chairs and marble-topped tables. On the walls eighteenth- and
nineteenth-century European paintings hung in gilt frames next
to wrought-iron sconces.

This was his palace, something his grandfather in the slums of
Genoa could only have dreamed of. Such domains were not founded
on weakness; they were the preserve of brutality and power, as they
had always been, since the days of the caesars. His only fault was
that he had been unable to distance himself from the tortures and
the murders. He still had blood under his fingernails. As with all
dynasties it would be his offspring who would inherit the veneer
of respectability.

What disturbed him was Simone. She had been just a child when
they had been forced to leave Argentina and he did not think she
would really understand these things about his past. The foreign
press had championed those crazy *madres de Mayo*, had painted
the generals in the junta as monsters. It was easy to distort things
when you lived in Europe, when you did not have bombs going
off every day right on your doorstep, when your friends and your
family were not being kidnapped and murdered by leftists.

When she was a child he had not foreseen such dilemmas. What
Francesca had wanted, had needed then, was a baby. When he
had arranged Simone's adoption he had not imagined her as a
fully grown woman, had not foreseen the day when she might

judge for herself what he had done. Nor had he anticipated that her opinions might one day become paramount to him.

He was still sometimes troubled by his memories. A car might backfire in the street, with a sound very like a gunshot, and an image would come to him, unbidden, of a woman's naked and tortured body jerking on the end of a rope. He would again see the splatter of blood and brain matter on the wall.

He looked up at his daughter, so beautiful, so gentle. And his. *His* daughter. He felt an overwhelming urge to protect her, from men, from politics, from life. He realised he loved her, as much as, perhaps more than, his own wife. Every man has a weakness, he used to tell his junior officers in the Command Action Group. You will always find some way to break them if you look hard enough. Every man has a weakness.

He had a sudden premonition that Simone was his.

She looked up from her breakfast. 'Are you okay, *Papito*?'

'Yes, I'm okay. Just tired.'

'Your coffee's cold. Shall I ask Sylvia to make some more?'

'No, it's all right. I have to go out now.'

He kissed her and went down the hall to the bedroom to change. Of course, Simone could never discover that she was not their child, would never learn what had happened to her real mother. But still. He wanted her to be proud of him, as every father wants respect and affection from his children. But if his past ever came to light, he wondered what she might think of him then. It would be so easy to misunderstand.

Turturro. He knew him straight away.

The beef had run to fat and his hair was reduced to a few oily strands brushed back over his balding pate, but Angeli remembered him. He was wearing a cheap suit and a white shirt, unbuttoned at the collar. He sat down at Angeli's table, grinning, as if he thought he was a real big shot dragging the colonel out of his warm apartment into the rain.

The storm had moved in overnight. Rain drummed on the canvas umbrellas that had been set up on the cobbles to keep the customers dry. Angeli put aside his newspaper and raised a hand languidly in the air. Angeli was a regular patron of the cafés in the piazza and the waiter immediately scurried away to fetch two more espressos.

'Colonel Angeli.'

'I am no longer a colonel,' Angeli reminded him.

'I am no longer a sergeant.'

'That doesn't make us equals,' Angeli said, leaning towards him. 'What the fuck do you want?'

Turturro's smile slipped a little. 'First, let me remind you who I am, Colonel . . .'

'I am not a colonel. If you call me that again I will break your jaw. And I am not here to play games with you or to be pleasant. Do you understand me?' Well, that seemed to do it. The smile fell away completely and the man's cheeks flushed with anger. 'Didn't I see you in the restaurant in Campo dei Fiori yesterday?'

'You do remember.'

'I thought there was something familiar about you. I couldn't place you at the time. But I remember you now. You worked for me in the Command Action Group. You were the fat one who typed up the interrogation reports and sometimes helped us out with the beatings. You were very good with the *picana*.'

'I only did what I was told.'

'Of course you did.'

'When I got the information, I stopped. I didn't keep going like some of those other bastards.'

'Okay, so you were a great guy. What do you want?'

The espressos arrived. Angeli smiled and handed the waiter a ten-thousand-lire note.

'You've done well for yourself,' Turturro said.

'And you look like a bag of shit. What are you doing in Rome?'

'That's my business.'

Turturro did not seem to like the way the conversation was going. He had expected to be in control. Oh, Angeli knew how to deal with scum like this. He opened a packet of sugar and emptied it into his cup. 'You're in trouble.'

'No, you are.' Turturro had recovered his bravado.

'Oh? How?'

'I have something you want.'

'I doubt it.'

'Why are you talking to me like this? We were comrades. We fought the Montos together. We saved Argentina from the communists.' Turturro took his cigarettes from his pocket. He was about to light one when Angeli snatched it from his fingers and threw it on the wet cobblestones.

'I don't like people smoking. Now that you have established we are almost blood brothers, get to the point.'

Turturro looked shaken. 'Okay, I've just doubled the price.'

'On what?'

'I have some files, names of the people we interrogated, names of the ones who died. It has our section name at the top: Command Action Group.'

Angeli raised an eyebrow. 'So?'

'I also have the file of a certain Colonel César Angeli. It has your rank, your date of birth and orders for secondment to the Command Action Group as commander. Best of all it has your photograph. Unlike me, you haven't changed a great deal . . . Colonel. Hardly at all.'

Angeli did not allow his dismay to register on his face. He sipped his coffee, giving himself time to consider. 'And how did you obtain this file?'

'It was supposed to be shredded. I was in charge of the shredding.'

'So what are you going to do with this piece of paper?'

'I am going to sell it.'

'To whom?'

'*Gente* perhaps. They pay big bucks for any hint of scandal.'

'They might be interested if I was royalty, or a movie star or something. You don't think you're frightening me with this?'

It was not the reaction that Turturro had been expecting. For the first time he looked a little unsure of himself. 'Do you want to find out?'

Angeli stared at him. He knew he could not allow this. Even if he could live with being pilloried in public and bear the ostracism of certain of his friends, he would not risk having his daughter exposed to it. 'You forget, I have done nothing illegal. They even passed a law in Argentina so that we could not be prosecuted. I could go home tomorrow, a free man. What about you?'

The rain stopped and a weak, yellow sun brought little wisps of steam from the cobbles. The hawkers were already hurrying from the plaza to exchange their umbrellas for postcards. An artist was setting up his finished canvases on makeshift easels in front of Bernini's Fontana dei Fumi.

'How much do you think you'll get for these bits of paper?'

Angeli asked, wondering which particular idiot had allowed his files to pass into the hands of a man like Turturro.

'I want a hundred million lire.'

Angeli laughed in genuine amusement. 'We all want a hundred million lire. That doesn't mean we're going to get it.' The value Turturro had placed on the files took his breath away. The lower classes never knew the real worth of anything. That was why they were poor.

Turturro's face was flushed with humiliation. 'It's my last offer.'

'It would be simpler to have you tossed in a beef mincer and let my dog eat you for breakfast.'

'Then what about the files?'

'What about them?'

'You think I'm stupid? I took a dozen copies and gave them to a lawyer. Anything happens to me, there's a copy sent to every scandal sheet in Italy.'

Angeli finished his coffee. It was possible this moron was telling the truth. If it wasn't for Simone he might be tempted to take the risk. What the hell was he going to do?

53

Angeli regarded his tormentor. One hundred million lire. Ridiculous. The skill in being a successful blackmailer was to ask only for what your target could comfortably afford. More than that and you put yourself in danger. He should know these things; hadn't he financed his present operation by leaning on rich subversives during the seventies?

He wondered about the files, if they did in fact exist, if it wasn't just a bluff. He had no doubt the scandal sheets Turturro was referring to would publish them if Turturro passed them on. The media in this country were like that, they did not care about news, they printed stories. They treated information as if it were soap opera.

It might be easier to have Turturro find his way to the bottom of the Tiber. But what if he wasn't bluffing? What if he had copies of the files hidden in a lawyer's office somewhere, as he said?

'I'll give you a million, you turd. That's my last offer.'

'Ten million.'

'One million. That's it. Be here tomorrow at the same time and you'll get your money. If you ever show your face in the Piazza Navona after that I'll rip off your balls and shove them down your throat. Do we understand each other?'

Angeli's chair scraped on the cobblestones as he stood up. He stalked away across the piazza in a rage. He had known this would happen one day. No matter what you did the past was always there, right behind you, dogging your heels like a beggar.

On that day, 19 July 1994, a car bomb exploded outside the headquarters of the Argentine Jewish Mutual Association on Pasteur Street in Buenos Aires, destroying the building. Ninety-six people were reported dead and more than two hundred injured. Simone stared at the television and watched the dead and wounded being carried out of the rubble, heard the sirens of the ambulances and the screams of the wounded almost as if she were there.

When her father came into the room he turned on the lamp on the bookcase against the wall and saw that she was crying.

'*Cara*. What is wrong?'

Simone wiped her face. 'All those people.'

Something changed in his expression. 'Oh, that. They're just Jews.'

She had heard his views on the Zionist threat before. But that was politics. This was innocent people being murdered.

A body, limp as rag, was carried from the wreckage, covered with a bloodied blanket. 'How could someone do something like that?'

He shrugged his shoulders. 'They got what they deserved.'

And he walked out of the room.

54

I have not come to bring peace, but a sword, Christ had said; it seemed to Luke that little had changed in two thousands years. Carabinieri with machine pistols now patrolled St Peter's Square in the place where the first Bishop of Rome had been crucified, a few yards from where, just a few years before, a Turkish gunman had gunned down the incumbent Pope. Nothing in the world as divisive as religion.

He sat at one of the plastic tables outside a café on the Via di Porta Angelica, watching the tourist buses crawl through the traffic towards St Peter's. The hot *ferragusto* gusted through the avenue, pulling at the clip-on tablecloths. On the pavements black hawkers kept up a game of brinksmanship with the police, pushing their trashy icons in the faces of the tourists before running off down an alley with an enraged carabiniere in pursuit.

It was almost ten o'clock on a baking September morning and already the square was filling with pilgrims and tourists.

He saw Jeremy Dexter strolling through the crowd. He waved and Jeremy raised a languid hand in response.

He was a tall, slight young man with fair hair and a slightly effeminate voice. Because of this, and the fact that he worked for the Foreign Office, people often made the mistake of thinking he was homosexual. In fact, Jeremy had told him once, he was omnisexual. 'Roger anything, old chum. Anywhere. Have to keep one's options open at all times.'

He was wearing a dark woollen suit and navy blue tie even in the sulphurous heat of the Roman summer. 'Luke. *Buon giorno*, old chum.'

He and Jeremy had been to Cambridge together, but there all similarities in their backgrounds ended. Jeremy had been educated at Westminster and his family claimed Princess Diana as a distant relative. In fact it amused Luke that Jeremy considered him a friend. Perhaps it was his Latin ancestry that attracted him. In their university days he had shown him off to his Sloane Square set as if he were an exotic South American pet.

After Cambridge Jeremy had departed, inevitably, for the foreign service, while Luke entered the world of journalism in grimy East London. Against all Luke's expectations, their friendship had continued and Jeremy, now stationed in Rome, occasionally fed him interesting news pieces.

This time Jeremy had arranged informal interviews for Luke inside the Vatican itself to help him with a feature he was writing for the Sunday supplements on the future of the Catholic Church. His editor had approved a junket for him in Rome, his first overseas.

Luke ordered two espressos and they made small talk, exchanging news of mutual friends, European politics, English prospects in the coming season's Five Nations rugby championships, and, of course, the weather.

Finally Jeremy sat back and crossed his legs. 'Look at all these *fucking* tourists.' He used the obscenity precisely, emphasising the second syllable so that it sounded almost as if it were polite usage.

'All package deals lead to Rome.'

'I mean, what is it they hope to find? The Pietà. Looks like a mannequin in a shop window. One can't sit in silent contemplation in St Peter's for the yellow hordes waving their Sonycams in one's face. Can't get close enough to peruse the Last Judgment. Have to be seven feet tall.' He finished his coffee. 'One can't look at Rome. One has to taste it. Squeeze it. Rome is about moral decay. Corruption. Have to feel the juice running down one's chin. Always been that way, ever since the caesars. Since the wolf with the big titties.'

Luke smiled and ordered two more espressos. Table service in Rome cost a small fortune. He wondered what the accountant would say when he got home and he put in his chitty for four coffees.

'Which leads one inevitably to the subject.' Luke leaned forward. 'The gentleman you're about to meet this morning. Assistant to the Under-Secretary of State for the Vatican. Name's Salvatore. From Argentina. Former countryman of yours. Ran foul of the junta in the seventies, ended up in Mexico. Came under the jurisdiction of the Archbishop of Puebla at some stage, Don Cardinal Comacho.

Must have been impressed with him because when he was promoted to Rome he brought Salvatore with him as his interpreter. Fluent in Italian, Spanish and English evidently. Now he's Comacho's private secretary.'

'And he's happy to talk to me?'

'Wants to use you as much as you want to use him.'

'For what purpose?'

'Flying kites.' An American passed them on the footpath wearing a Leonardo da Vinci T-shirt and voluminous shorts. He was complaining about the heat. Jeremy raised one laconic eyebrow but said nothing. 'Between you and me and the rest of the Catholic world, *Il Papa*'s on the way out. Passed his use-by date. Absolutely. Man of the moment during the Cold War. Bit of an embarrassment now. They're all lining up for a crack at the big hat.'

'He's dying?'

'We're all dying. Nothing imminent. One year, five years. Blink of an eye in the life of the Vatican.'

'Who are the likely candidates?'

'Curia want another Italian. One of their own. Martini perhaps, from Milan. Except he's progressive. Bad form. The Third World's gathering pace. A lot of Church thinkers want someone from outside Rome. Unite the social concerns of the Third World with the traditional values of the Church, all of that.'

'Is there someone?'

'Gantin perhaps, from Benin. Didn't get a sniff last time. Because he's black. Only difference between the curias and the Klan is the colour of the frocks. Who else is there this time? Old Gianpaolo's spent the last two decades loading the deck. Most of the College are all die-hard conservatives now. Neves in Brazil, Lustiger in France. No abortion, no thingies on your todger. Really.'

'Is there a compromise candidate?'

'Comacho.'

'I see.'

'Intellect. Man of the people. Also reasonable chap. Won't ban contraception and abortion. Just won't make a big issue of it like the incumbent.' He looked at his watch. 'That's your briefing. Now to have it from the horse's mouth. Time to go. Can't keep the Church waiting.'

They dodged the cars and tourist buses around the Largo dei

Colonnato. Barriers had been erected to funnel the nuns and tourists and pilgrims towards the colonnades and around the square. Jeremy and Luke followed the right-hand colonnade to the Bronze Door. A Swiss Guard with a halberd and a medieval costume of blue, orange and red stripes snapped to attention. An officer of the guard met them on the steps and led them through the portals of the Vatican to the reception desk.

Paolo Salvatore was nothing like Luke had expected. He was a slight man, unusually pale for a Latin, with dark, intelligent eyes and a quick smile. He ushered them into his office with the businesslike manner of a busy insurance salesman.

The interview took place below a smiling picture of the current Pope. In fact, it had been more like a debriefing session than an interview. Without waiting for Luke's questions Salvatore had expounded on several subjects, such as the moral arguments against the doctrine of liberation theology, the on-going debate over celibacy among the priesthood and the ordination of women priests. He spoke passionately about the need of the Church to serve the Third World, if it was not to become an anachronism in a rapidly changing world.

He also gave Luke some insights into the current infighting inside the Vatican over the Pope's successor. It was at that point that Archbishop Comacho's name was raised.

'An illuminating article in your newspaper on the Archbishop's career to this point cannot do any harm,' Salvatore had said.

But it was near the end of the interview that he made the remark that piqued Luke's interest the most.

'Of course,' he had said, 'should Cardinal Comacho become Vicar of Rome we shall perhaps see an investigation into these persistent rumours of financial irregularities in the Institute for Religious Works.'

Luke raised his eyebrows. 'I thought all that ended with Calvi in the eighties.'

Salvatore smiled. 'Oh, is that what you believed?'

'What sort of irregularities?'

But Salvatore seemed to feel he had already said too much. 'Nothing I am at liberty to speak of, I'm afraid.' He looked at his watch. 'You must excuse me. I have an appointment with the

Under-Secretary in a few minutes. I am afraid I shall have to bring our interview to an end.'

'Thank you for your time, Father.'

'But I have not given you any time,' Salvatore said, with a mischievous smile. 'I must remain your unidentified source inside the Vatican, no?'

Luke returned his smile. 'I understand,' he said.

Afterwards they drove back across the choking, engine-revving madness of the Ponte Vittorio Emanuele. Jeremy dropped him off opposite the church of Sant'Andrea della Valle. To appease the accountants at the newspaper Luke had spurned the luxury hotels of the Via Veneto for the faded glamour of the Campo dei Fiori.

'What did he mean?' he asked Jeremy. 'That remark about financial irregularities?'

'Always rumours, old chum. Who knows what he meant? Now don't forget I'll pick you up at five. I've managed to organise invitations to the investiture of this new orphanage in Esquiline. There'll be a few people there I think you should meet.'

Luke crossed the busy Corso, his mind preoccupied with everything Salvatore had told him. He was excited. This would be his first big feature.

The narrow streets echoed with the hammer of mopeds and the tinny rattle of Fiats as they sped over the cobbles of the Piazza dei Biscione. He was looking forward to the reception this afternoon. Jeremy had promised it would yield some priceless contacts. He would perhaps have viewed the engagement with far greater trepidation if he had known that fate was about to bring Simone Angeli into his life.

The Casa di Santa Maria had been commissioned by a sixteenth-century cardinal as a college for religious education. It had been a hotel for a short while in the nineteenth century – Byron was reputed to have stayed there – and had more recently fallen into disrepair.

Now the ochre stucco had been repainted, the ornate cornices and faded frescoes of Polidoro da Caravaggio carefully restored. The Casa di Santa Maria's latest designation was as an orphanage to be administered by nuns of the Franciscan order. It had been the brainchild of Archbishop Tomaszcewski and the freehold of the building was now invested in the Catholic Church. But it had not cost the IOR a cent; the funds had been raised privately, from many of the wealthy guests at that afternoon's reception.

White-jacketed waiters carrying silver trays with flutes of French champagne moved around the loggias and vaulted marble hall. Luke found himself standing shoulder to shoulder with the rich and powerful of Rome, businessmen and industrialists in ardent conversation with highly placed members of the Curia, an unlikely – or so it seemed to Luke, with his naïve Protestant upbringing – mingling of God and money. The men wore tuxedos and Gianni Versace suits, the women gowns from Renato Balestra, Gianfranco Ferrè and Mila Schön. The glitter of gold and diamonds everywhere.

'The money in this room,' he murmured to Jeremy. 'Jesus, Mary and Joseph.'

'No, they're not here. They probably couldn't afford it.' He sipped his champagne. 'This afternoon's your chance to see some of the main players. That's Martini over there, from Milan. Strong candidate for the big hat.'

'Any chance of talking to him?'

'Better chance of getting an exclusive with God. See that chap

over there, looks like a Chicago dentist? That's Regan. Must meet
him. Used to be a priest, now he's a writer. Populist stuff. The
Vatican and Catholic politics, all that. Plugging a new book at
the moment. He'd *adore* to talk to you. Luke, are you listening?'

But Luke had not heard a word. He was staring through the crowd
at a young woman on the other side of the vaulted marble room.

'Are you all right?'

Luke's face was ashen.

'Luke?'

'Do you know that girl?'

'Not here to pick up women, old sport. Maybe later.'

'Who is she?'

Jeremy caught the urgency in his voice and turned his head. He
frowned. 'Forget it. Out of your league. Christ, what is it? Look
like you've seen a ghost.'

'What's her name?'

'Her father's very rich and very unpleasant. Luke. Please.'

'Her *name*.'

'Gregorini. Simone Gregorini, but . . .'

Suddenly he was gone, pushing his way through the crowds
towards her.

She was deep in conversation with a curial secretary, a young
man with a florid complexion and a small, neat bald spot on the
crown of his head, like a monk's tonsure. Luke took two flutes
of champagne from the tray of a passing steward. He held one
out to her.

'Simone! There you are!' he said in his formal Italian. 'I found
you a drink.' He turned to the young cleric. 'Can you give us a
moment, please? We have something very important to discuss.'

Luke felt his heart hammering against his ribs. He did not feel
nearly as confident as he sounded. He wondered if the bluff would
work. But the cleric smiled graciously and turned away.

Simone Gregorini was staring at him, her expression betraying
both anger and amusement.

'I think he likes you,' Luke said. 'Did you get his phone
number?'

'What are you doing?'

'You looked bored. I thought I'd rescue you.'

'Do I know you?'

'No, you don't know me. But I'm trying to remedy that right now.' He put out his hand. 'My name's Luke. I'm a journalist with an English newspaper.'

Her hand was soft and cool to the touch. 'You seem to know *my* name,' she said.

'I made a point of asking.'

'You speak good Italian for an Englishman.'

'Thank you. I have an affinity for Latin languages. I was born in Argentina. We spoke Spanish as well as English at home until I was seven.'

Her expression softened. 'Where were you born? In Buenos Aires?'

'That's right.'

'So was I.'

'Well,' he said, 'what a coincidence.'

He gave her his best smile and she smiled back. And all the time his mind was racing ahead, trying to make some sense of this. He felt as if he had crossed some twilight border of reality. It was uncanny. It *was* her, his sister Gabriella, from the sculpture of her bones to the smallest gesture. Her voice was the same, in its tone and inflections, even some of her mannerisms were the same, the way she played with a loose lock of her hair at her cheek, the way his sister did when she was nervous.

There was a theory that everyone in the world had a *doppelgänger*, a double, but that had always seemed a fanciful idea to him and he gave it no credence. Surely no one could have this close a resemblance.

This girl and Gabby could be from the same mould.

The same mould.

'How old were you when you left Buenos Aires?' he asked her, but before she could answer, an older woman appeared suddenly at his elbow. She was dressed expensively, but without much good taste, Luke thought, and her make-up might have been applied with a trowel. She wore a large diamond necklace at her throat. Her face registered both surprise and disapproval when she saw Luke.

'We are leaving now,' she said to Simone.

'I'm coming, Mama.' She turned back to Luke. 'It was nice to meet you.'

'May I see you again?' Luke said, aware of the tone of desperation in his voice.

A soft and apologetic smile. 'I don't think so.'

A flood of panic. 'But I must.'

'I'm sure you have a lot of girlfriends already,' she said, and then she turned and moved away through the crowd. The woman with the necklace gave him a poisonous smile.

He watched her from the loggia. She and her mother disappeared into a white Mercedes. Luke glimpsed briefly a handsome and impeccably dressed man climbing into the back of the limousine after them. And then she was gone.

56

'Only met her father once,' Jeremy was saying. 'Very much part of the local colour. If you understand my meaning.'

They were in a restaurant in the piazza di San' Maria in Trastevere. Tables and chairs spilled on to the cobbled piazza under apricot-coloured awnings, while above them vines cascaded down the faded ochre walls. A hot afternoon, the square echoing to the pop music from the radios of the teenagers gathered by the fountain and the tinny rattle of their Vespas. The statues of four of Rome's sixteenth-century popes looking down disapprovingly from beneath the basilica's campanile.

'Mafia?'

'Overused word. Means anything. Not talking men in expensive suits with bad haircuts. More sophisticated. His connections run to Opus Dei and P2. Heard of them?'

Luke nodded. Opus Dei was a supposedly secret organisation inside the Roman Catholic Church, right wing, dedicated to assuming control of the Church. It was said to have an international membership, with some extremely rich and powerful people among its members and patrons. During the seventies its activities had become intertwined with those of P2, a fascist organisation now believed responsible for a number of terrorist bombings and murders around Italy. As with Opus Dei, P2's membership was thought to include many of Italy's most powerful men: high-ranking members of the police and the armed forces, as well as television executives, bankers and politicians.

'Remember Licio Gelli?' Jeremy went on. 'Helped the Argies get their Exocets during the Falklands bother. Calvi helped him out. God bless him. All part of the Vatican Bank business. The left-footers bankrolled Galtieri. Never mind, must forgive and forget. Gelli got very chummy with certain chaps in the Argies' military. After the Vatican Bank thing broke he decided to take his summer hols in Buenos Aires. Permanently. Waved to a few colonels going the other way. Which brings us to Signor Gregorini.'

'Her father.'

'Real name's César Angeli. Former colonel in the Argentine Army. Not one for marching, evidently. Very creative with electricity, if you get my meaning. Liked the cloak and dagger. Early seventies he was issued a diplomatic passport. Showed up in Madrid and Barcelona. Assassinating South American political exiles. Multi-talented.'

Luke blinked at him. His own speculations suddenly seemed less unlikely. Even on this warm afternoon he felt a sudden chill in his bones.

'Old mate. Please. Daydreaming. Must pay attention.'

'Sorry,' Luke said. 'So her father was a colonel. Why did he come to Rome?'

'Panicked. Argies had a brief attack of democracy in 1983. He decided it was time to see Europe. Could go back now, if he wanted to. No point any more. Doing jolly well where he is.'

'Doing what?'

'Arms deals, money laundering. Classic. Certain members of the Argentine military smuggling nose candy out of Buenos Aires. That sort of thing. Ship it to the Camorra and the N'dranghetta, launder the proceeds through the Vatican Bank. Handsome commissions, of course. Use the profits to buy arms, sell them to the Middle East. Use Argentine end-user certificates for the weapons, the aircraft go into Germany, are rerouted to Amman or Damascus. Putting a little nuclear material and some technological back-up the way of the Syrians as well. The money's all going through the Holy City. Praise the Lord.'

'Why Angeli?'

'Gelli gave him the contacts. P2, Opus Dei, the whole club. Became Gelli's front man. When in Rome, as they say.'

'And the money is channelled through him?'

'Swiss bank accounts actually. Angeli does jolly well. Sticky fingers when it comes to money. Learned to diversify. Financier to the whole world. Well, if one is of the right political persuasion. Two years ago police uncovered plans for a military coup, right here in Italy. Large amount of shit and absolutely huge fan. Tremendous. Mafia, neo-fascists, army generals, all fell out of the same bed. Ugly. Someone blew the whistle. Still looking for the banker.'

'Her father.'

'Must be a story in it. Wouldn't if I were you. Bad for the health.' The waiter brought another chilled bottle of Orvieto Classico. Jeremy sipped it, appreciatively. 'Make no mistake. Talking serious establishment here. Knight of Malta. Pope even made him a Gentleman of His Holiness. Whole box of goods. Still want to escort his daughter to dinner dances?'

Luke shook his head. 'Oh, Jesus.'

'He won't help you. Not in this town.'

'I have to see her again, Jeremy.'

'May one ask why?'

'I can't tell you that. Not right now.'

'Lovely-looking girl. Absolutely. But really, Luca.' He was the only one of his friends who called him that.

'Just help me on this one.'

'Want my advice?'

'No.'

'Well, I'll give it to you anyway. Forget it.'

'Get me her address and telephone number. Please.'

'Think about this.'

'I have thought about it. I have to see her again.'

Jeremy shook his head. 'Your funeral.'

Jeremy offered Luke a lift back to his hotel but Luke said he'd prefer to walk. He stood on the Ponte Sisto for a long time, staring into the brown waters of the Tiber. His head was spinning.

Some twist of fate had led him here, to this girl. The question was: what was he going to do about it?

He turned the puzzle over in his mind. It was like the tumblers of a lock slotting into place. His parents had adopted Gabriella in Argentina. This girl, too, claimed to have been born there. Was it really possible that they were sisters? Looking at them, they could even be twins.

Was it possible?

He was tempted to ring his father and tell him about this but he was reluctant to do that, at least for now. First he would find this girl again, talk to her, find out more about her. Next time he would be more prepared.

He could not let this go. But Jeremy was right. He would have to be very careful.

57

Luke sat on the bed, a towel around his waist, the telephone on his lap. It was not yet seven o'clock but already he heard the shouts and clatter from the piazza as the traders set up their stalls for the morning market in the Campo dei Fiori. He picked up the receiver and punched in a number in Trastevere. He knew it off by heart. He had rung the number half a dozen times the previous evening but had got the answerphone and he had hung up each time without leaving a message.

This time a woman's sleepy voice said: '*Pronto.*'

'Simone? It's me, Luke. Luke Barrington. You remember? We met the other evening at the reception at the Casa di Santa Maria.'

A pause. 'How did you get my number?'

'I have influential sources in the government.' How Jeremy had got the number, he could only guess. When she didn't reply, he said: 'I have to see you again.'

'I don't think it's a good idea.'

'How about lunch?'

'I'm sorry.'

'I was hoping you'd show me some of Rome.'

'Get a guidebook.'

He found himself staring at the receiver. She had hung up on him.

A solitary figure in a black tracksuit padded through the twisting cobblestoned streets of the Trastevere. Her dark ponytail was tied with a pink band, her Nike joggers as big as diving boots on the slight frame. A cat mewed and darted away, leaving the scrap of meal it had found, waste from one of the streetside trattorias. Washing fluttered from the balconies above the alleys, red peppers drying alongside, vivid against the honey-brown stucco walls.

Simone avoided the traffic, keeping to the back streets. She pushed herself harder than usual, trying to run out the feelings of anger and disruption left by Luke's telephone call. She felt both flattered and outraged. How had he got her number?

Anyway, she had no use for a casual lover. She had had only one real relationship in her life, with a boy she had known since she was seventeen. When that affair had ended six months before, she had been distraught. She had thought it would last for ever.

Most of her friends went through boyfriends as if they were tissues, but she was not like that. She wanted a man who would love her for good. So why waste time on this Englishman? He only wanted to bed her, then he would fly back to London and forget all about her.

And yet she could not forget about *him*. The tenacity with which he had pursued her both frightened and fascinated her.

Oh, don't be a fool, Simone.

Don't be a fool.

When she got back to her apartment he was sitting on the steps in the courtyard.

'There's something wrong with your telephone. When I was talking to you this morning the line suddenly went dead.'

He smiled at her. To die for, he thought. Her track top was tied around her waist, her white T-shirt was wet with perspiration, almost transparent. She was breathing hard and there was a sheen of moisture on her forehead and her lip. Something about a woman panting and soaked in sweat. He swept the thought aside. Somehow almost incestuous, thinking that way. That wasn't why he was here.

She put her hands on her hips. 'How did you get here?'

'I walked across the Ponte Sisto.'

'I mean how did you know where I lived?'

'I'm an investigative journalist. It's what I do.'

'That friend of yours. From the embassy.'

He shrugged his shoulders, confirming her suspicions.

'What do you want?'

'I lied about being a reporter. I sell antiperspirant. Can I order you a truckload?'

Her expression reminded him of Gabriella when he teased her; her eyes blazed for a moment, her lips compressed in a thin white line. She shouldered past him, pressed some digits on a panel by the heavy door and pushed it open.

I blew it again, he thought.

She stopped and looked at him from the doorway. 'Do you want a cup of coffee?'

'Are you offering?'

'It sounded like I did.'

He grinned and followed her inside.

58

Her apartment was at the top of two flights of stone stairs. The crumbling honey-coloured stucco and Renaissance façade belied a modern two-bedroom apartment with terracotta tiles on the floor, soft white leather sofas, a huge glass coffee table, tubular steel-and-leather chairs. The main living area was decorated in fashionable tonings of black, taupes and creams.

She led him through to the kitchen, set two cups on a worktop of black-veined marble. She poured coffee into the grinder. 'I thought you were only going to be in Rome for a few days.'

'That was before I met you.'

'Am I supposed to be flattered?'

'I don't know. Are you?'

She tossed an errant lock of hair from her face with an angry flick of her hand.

'I told you I didn't want to see you. Now you show up on my doorstep. Perhaps I should call the police.'

'Let's have coffee first. I can't deal with the police until I've had at least one cup of coffee.'

If she hated the thought of me following her here, he thought, she wouldn't have asked me up to her apartment.

She put the coffee pot on the stove. 'Take it off the range when it's boiling. As you so delicately pointed out, I need a shower.'

He heard water running in the bathroom. While he waited he wandered around the apartment, looking for clues. Some silver-framed photographs on the coffee table, Simone with a tanned fair-haired man in a polo shirt, a handsome, older woman wearing too much jewellery, the same woman he had seen at the Casa di Santa Maria. The man and woman figured in two other portraits: Simone as a teenager, another even younger in a white communion dress.

He examined the photographs more closely, paying careful

attention to the fair-haired man in the polo shirt. So, this was
César Angeli. He was not at all what he had been expecting. Not
the face of a torturer. Hair neatly brushed, clear eyes, a face unlined
by age. Looking for Charles Bronson, he had stumbled on Robert
Redford.

Well, repression had been good to him.

A large lacquered bookshelf stood against one wall. Textbooks
on human biology and genetics were juxtaposed with Alessandro
Manzoni and translations of Shelley, Byron and Keats.

The bathroom door opened behind him.

'Found anything interesting?'

He turned around. She had changed into jeans and a dark silk
shirt. Her hair was still wet and she dabbed at it with a towel.

'Let us have wine and women, life and laughter, sermons and
soda water the day after.'

'*Don Juan*. You read Byron?'

'My sister. She's a great reader of the classics.'

Simone went into the kitchen and took the coffee off the range.
'Well, you were no help. A typical Englishman. Didn't you know
that you should never over-boil coffee?'

He picked up one of the framed photographs on the coffee table.
'Is this your father?'

'Yes. Why?'

'Just curious.'

'He's almost sixty years old. Doesn't look it, does he?'

'Clean living. That's what I'll look like when I'm sixty.'

She raised an eyebrow and he smiled.

'What?'

'That thing you did. With your eyebrow.'

She poured the coffee into two cups. 'I practised a lot when I
was a child.' She crossed the room and handed him his coffee.
'You're very persistent.'

He shrugged his shoulders in acknowledgment.

She turned away from him and went to the window. The
apartment looked over a small piazza with stuccoed butterscotch
walls and green-shuttered windows. Two storeys below the awnings
and planter boxes of restaurants spilled on to the cobbles. A handful
of teenagers crossed the square in stonewashed denims and designer
basketball shoes, shouting and laughing, on their way to school.

'I have lectures all morning,' she said.

'Perhaps I could see you this afternoon.'

She turned around. 'What do you want from me?'

A good question. Do I want to know the truth about you for Gabriella's sake? Or do I also want the story on your father? It was as if he were keeping a certain distance from himself, like a player in an arcade video game, interested but not completely involved. Running it out to see what would happen. As if even he didn't want to understand his own motives. He couldn't keep up this charade for much longer. Every moment he maintained this duplicity would make it harder to explain should he decide finally to tell her the truth.

'Dinner. No strings attached, no complications.'

She picked up her towel. 'I have to dry my hair. I can drop you off at your hotel if you want.' She took her coffee back to the bathroom.

'And dinner tonight?' he called to her.

'I'm still thinking about it.'

The door closed.

She dropped him off on the Via di Giubbonari. Like all Romans she knew only one way to drive: with the accelerator pedal jammed to the floor. When he got out his hands were shaking.

He leaned in through the passenger window. 'So now what?'

He kept his fingers hooked around the window, watching her make up her mind.

'I'll pick you up at your hotel at seven o'clock,' she said, and drove away, the throaty roar of the Lancia's exhaust echoing on the cobbles and the ancient walls of the Palazzo Pia Righetti.

59

The restaurant was off the Via Nazionale near the Termini station in a badly lit side street. No light escaped the heavy curtains and the two imposing wooden doors suggested an illegal gambling hall rather than a restaurant.

But inside it was a bedlam of noise and cigarette smoke, scurrying waiters and shouted conversations. There were black-and-white framed photographs on the walls, apparently taken fifty or sixty years before, showing the same vaulted ceiling, bentwood chairs, timber-panelled walls.

The patrons were mostly Roman. At one table there were three wealthy, middle-class Italian couples, all wearing expensive watches and with *telefonini* in their pockets, shouting at each other over their antipasto. At another was an old man in a threadbare brown suit, his cane hooked over the back of his chair, crumbling a piece of bread into his soup.

They were shown to a table in the corner. The proprietor came over to welcome the Signorita Gregorini personally, brought a complimentary bottle of *rosso* and asked her to pass his felicity to her father. Luke remembered what Jeremy had told him. He was swimming in the water with sharks.

Simone looked stunning. She wore a short black cocktail dress, cut low at the back, as simple as it was effective. She wore no jewellery except for a gold broken-heart motif at her throat. Her long blue-black hair was tied back in a French braid, her skin light olive. The impression of casual elegance was emphasised by her fingernails which were long and well manicured but unvarnished.

He thought about Gabriella, rarely out of jeans and baggy, ill-fitting jumpers, her hair loose around her shoulders. She rarely wore make-up. Like Cinderella, in two separate incarnations.

He raised his glass in a toast. 'To the orphans,' he said.

She sipped the *rosso*. Her lips glistened with wine. 'Are you really English? You don't look English.'

'My real name's Luca. My mother's part Spanish. I have her looks, my father's shy English reserve.'

She smiled at that, at least.

He was very good-looking, Simone thought, but in an obvious way. Not the kind of man she was usually attracted to. The designer ponytail hinted at excessive vanity. But he also had charm, she had to admit. She was intrigued.

'So. You are a journalist. You are writing about Rome?'

'I'm doing a story about the Pope.'

'Is it a scandal? He has been sleeping with the Duchess of York?'

He grinned. 'I'm not that kind of journalist.'

'You want your readers to respect you in the morning?'

'Exactly.'

'So what are you writing about *Il Papa*?'

'Really, it's an article on the next Pope.'

She regarded him seriously. 'But Gianpaolo is not dead.'

'But he's getting old.'

'Surely God will decide our next *Papa*, not your newspaper?'

'God reads the *Guardian*,' he said.

As they ate he told her about himself, about the newspaper he worked for – he called it a 'broadsheet' – in London. This was his first major assignment, he said, and he was hoping eventually to work as a foreign correspondent, perhaps with one of the international news bureaus. He was trying to impress her, of course. Still, he talked like a journalist. He certainly knew a lot about Italian politics and about Rome.

'How long will you stay in Rome?' she asked him.

'Just a few days.'

Just a few days. He was after a casual romance, someone to help him pass away a few idle evenings. The intense way he stared at her was unnerving. Perhaps this had not been such a good idea.

He asked her about her early life in Argentina, wanted to know everything about her. She told him about her memories of the big house in Buenos Aires, the *estanción* her father had owned just outside Córdoba. He was one of the best listeners she had ever met. He was even interested in the novels she liked to read and the name she gave to her pony when she was a child.

'What do you do?'

'I'm a student, at the university. I'm in my last year.'

'What are you studying?'

'I'm doing a science degree. I'm hoping to go into medical research. Perhaps genetics.' She looked up from her tiramisu, saw the expression on his face. 'Why are you looking at me like that? You think that is too hard for a woman?'

'No, of course not. I have a . . . friend in England. She's studying genetics, too. Coincidence.'

'Your girlfriend?'

'No, just a friend.'

'You're not married, are you?' she asked him.

'Of course not.' He laughed. She should have suspected then, should have listened to her intuition. But then he was asking her about her parents and what they did and she let the moment pass.

'My father is . . . a business consultant. I don't know exactly. He is always having lunch or dinner with some businessman or some politician. I think he is some kind of, you know, lobbyist.' She forced a laugh. 'I think he's honest. I'm not sure.'

'No brothers and sisters?'

She shook her head. 'My mother had some problem when I was born. She couldn't have any more children.' She could not decipher the expression on his face. 'What?'

He looked at her over the rim of his glass. 'Nothing.'

'You are thinking something.'

'Indigestion.' He laughed.

'You cannot get indigestion here. This is the best pizzeria in Rome.'

She realised he had allowed her to do all the talking. He knew everything about her, she knew almost nothing about him. She asked him about Buenos Aires, learned that like her he had left there when he was just a child.

'Where did you grow up?' she asked him.

'It's a place called Market Dene. Just outside Oxford. My father inherited this big house. It's big and cold and draughty but it was the best place to play hide and seek when I was a kid.'

'You had a big family?'

'No. It was just me and my sister.'

'What is she like?'

'Oh . . . I don't know. She's a lot like you.'

They finished their meal. The coffees came and there was a sudden and awkward silence between them. There was an undercurrent here, something she did not understand. This was more than a faltering attempt at seduction. He both intrigued and scared her, and she was not sure why. She looked at her watch. 'I should go now. I have a lecture tomorrow.' She stood up. She did not know what to make of this man. She did not know what to make of him at all.

60

Luke sat on the balcony of his room, staring over the red-tiled rooftops, the dome of Sant'Andrea della Valle, the great white monument of Il Vitoriano, 'the typewriter' as the Romans derisively referred to it, in the distance. He leaned on the balcony rail, wondered desperately what to do.

He went inside, picked up the telephone beside the bed, placed a call to his editor in London. 'Martin. It's Luke.' He could imagine Martin in his office, sitting in front of his VDU, his ashtray overflowing, surrounded by a litter of discarded copy and polystyrene coffee cups.

'Luke. How's *la dolce vita*?' he said in his broad Cockney.

'They don't have that here any more. They haven't for years.'

'Good. You're supposed to be working.'

'Martin, I need a few more days.'

'Fuck off.'

'Martin, I'm serious. I've stumbled across a big story. Arms smuggling, right-wing extremists, Italian businessmen with links to South American dictatorships.'

Silence on the end of the line.

'Martin.'

'Who the fuck do you think you are, Peter Arnett?'

'Another few days. It's a great story. I mean it.'

'Jesus.' Luke held his breath. 'On *your* money, son. If we like the story, we'll reimburse you. And be back Friday or your job's in the classifieds Saturday morning.'

He hung up. The second time someone had done that to him in two days.

Well, he still had his credit card.

His hand again reached for the dial pad. Many times he had been about to call his parents in Berkshire, each time he had slammed the receiver back on its cradle. Should he tell Stephen and Mercedes about this girl?

It would bear thinking about. He would have to tread cautiously here, for his parents' sake, and for Gabriella's.

He was convinced that he had stumbled on his sister's twin. Was it possible, he wondered, that his parents already knew about this? Had they deliberately held back that knowledge? And if they had – why?

But if they did not know, how had Gabriella and Simone been separated?

Would his mother and father, would Gabriella, want to know the answer?

So many possibilities, so many overgrown paths led away from this point, back to the Argentina of the seventies, the thick of the so-called dirty war. He knew the sort of things that had happened in those days. He had read about the atrocities, had never thought they would touch his own life.

He should know where this might lead before he burdened his family with it. He replaced the receiver, put the telephone back on the bedside table and went back to the window. He stared over the rooftops of Rome. He was sweating. He supposed he would just let things play out and see what happened.

In even the most mundane corners of the city, Rome's history was piled on top of itself, the time lines of the past layered one on top of the other like strata in a rock. The city was careless with its antiquities; like a millionaire leaving canvases by Reubens stacked in the garden shed next to the potting mix. The courtyard of Simone's apartment in Trastevere was a litter of jarring images: a Roman pilaster long ago built into a doorway by a Renaissance architect, a medieval baronial crest above an archway, beneath it a motorcycle leaning against a faded butterscotch-coloured wall.

Simone came through the glass door carrying a bowl of warm milk. As soon as she appeared a small cat darted across the cobbles towards her. She bent down and put the milk on the step and the cat, one of Trastevere's countless population of strays, began to lap hungrily.

Simone stroked its back, felt it arch and purr. 'What am I going to do?' she whispered. 'This strange man. Should I be frightened of him? You know I don't go out with just any man, don't you, little Gabby? So why do I waste so much time thinking about this crazy Englishman?'

She had adopted the stray as a kitten, had tamed it with affection and warm milk. In return it had become an unwitting sounding board, a mute ear to all her troubles and doubts. 'I don't know why I am so interested in this man,' she whispered, as it lapped at the milk. 'Perhaps I am as crazy as he is. What do you think? What am I going to do about him? What am I going to do?'

61

They had lunch on the cobblestones in a small trattoria off the Piazza di San Cosimato. They ate risotto stuffed with clams, shrimp and squid, and drank a chilled bottle of white Frecciarossa, and watched the traders from the local market and the matrons in their floral frocks argue and shout and laugh, their hands describing a thousand gestures in the air.

'You know what Orson Welles said?' she said to him. 'All Italians are natural actors. Except the ones working in the film industry.'

He laughed.

The next day she took him to the Vatican Museum, hurried him along the Gallery of Tapestries and the Gallery of Maps to the Sistine Chapel. The sombre and windowless room was stifling hot, crowded with tourists, most of them staring up at the west wall and Michelangelo's terrifying vision of the Last Judgment.

They stood there a long time, in silence.

Finally she pointed to one of the figures low in the right-hand corner. 'There is Minos, the infernal judge. Some people wonder why he has been painted with a pair of asses' ears. It is actually a portrait of a man called Biagio da Cesena, one of the Pope's courtiers. He objected to the nudes in the fresco and tried to have them covered up. This was Michelangelo's revenge. As it was, da Cesena had his way ten years later. Another painter was commissioned to paint in the strategically positioned cloaks so that innocent virgins like myself would not be corrupted by the sight of so much holy and martyred male flesh.'

Luke smiled.

'That one is Christ, and all around him his saints, each bearing the instrument of their own martyrdom. That one there is St Bartholomew. He was flayed alive. The face is actually a self-portrait, the artist himself, tormented in death and mocked

by his God. Poor Michelangelo. He lived in mortal terror of his
own faith.'

'What man doesn't?'

'Look at our Lord. He has no sympathy for anyone. He waves
away the protests of his saints, spares no tears for the damned as
they fall towards the demons waiting for them in hell. And still they
rise, the souls of the dead, torn from their graves to face Christ the
judge. How many of us could sleep again if Michelangelo's vision
were true, if we must account for all our sins in front of such a
judge at the end of our lives?'

After a while Luke said: 'Fortunately, I don't believe in it.'

She smiled, breaking the tension of the moment. 'No, I don't
believe in it either.'

That night they drove up the hairpin curves of the Via Garibaldi to
the hill above Trastevere. The lookout was a favourite assignation
for lovers, and there were half a dozen cars dotted around the
square, their lights off, windows misted.

They got out of the car. A fat moon hung over the city. The
night was cool. Rome glittered in front of them, the appalling
Vittorio Emanuele monument bathed in phosphorescent halogen,
demeaning the lesser glow of the Duomo and the ruins of the
Palatine.

She turned her face to look up at him. He thought she wanted him
to kiss her and for a moment he panicked. Instead, she whispered:
'I've told Papa all about you. He's *dying* to meet you.'

62

Angeli examined his reflection in the gold-framed Venetian mirror. Simone had had only a handful of boyfriends, to his knowledge, and the advent of a new ... supplicant, he thought with a wry smile ... was not an event to be dismissed lightly. There had been one boy, Paolo, the son of one of his friends, who had escorted her for almost three years, since she was sixteen. Since then he had been gratified to note that she had chosen her acquaintances with great propriety. He had been concerned that as soon as she had her own apartment she might behave with less discretion, but she had not disappointed him. He was as confident as a father ever could be that she was still a virgin. And now there was at last a new man in her life, one important enough for her to bring home for their inspection.

Well, we'll see.

He looked around the salon, satisfied. There were fresh flowers in the vases, Rachmaninov on the stereo.

The buzzer to the apartment sounded and their maid hurried to open the door.

He heard their guests in the hallway. Francesca was already there to welcome them. Angeli held back. He was afforded a view of a tall man with hair straggling over the collar of his linen jacket, long-legged, wearing denim jeans. He was good-looking – *too* good-looking – and there was a leather bracelet on his wrist. He wore boots instead of shoes. Soft, Angeli thought. Vain. Probably an opportunist.

He put his smile in place and stepped forward, hand outstretched, the perfect host.

They ate in the formal dining room, gathered around the great oak table with its gilded Renaissance chairs. The cook had prepared *penne all'arrabbiata* to start, an antipasto of artichoke hearts, roasted peppers, basil and black olives and for the main course a whole grilled bass, which she filleted at the table. To complement the meal Angeli had produced three bottles of a Vigneta Torricella Orvieto.

But he did not let the food distract him from the business at hand. He kept his eyes on his daughter during the meal, noted the way she looked at this young man. There was a glow about her, something he had never seen in her before. It occurred to him that perhaps this interloper had already slept with her. It made him angry just thinking about it, as if he himself had been violated. Well, he would have to discover if this Luca was suitable. He doubted it.

For a young man being presented to a girl's family for the first time, he asked a lot of questions. He wanted to know too much about Argentina particularly, where they lived, what they did there. He felt as if he were being interrogated. In his own home.

His knuckles clamped around the arms of his chair as they sometimes did during a turbulent air flight. Fortunately Francesca managed to change the subject, was now explaining to this Luca about the problems of renovating Renaissance apartments. Five-year waiting list, she was saying. For a good tradesman. Fortunately my husband has connections and when we bought this apartment it was done in a few weeks.

The arrogant little shit again seized on this opening. 'Yes, Simone told me you are a business consultant.'

Angeli bowed his head in acknowledgment.

'It sounds interesting.'

'I don't know if it's interesting. It is what I do.'

There was a delicate pause. 'What sort of businesses?'

'A wide variety. Businessmen consult me on their financial arrangements.'

'So. Kind of an accountant?'

Angeli did not answer. He sipped his wine.

He glanced at Francesca, who took her cue. 'And what about you, Luca? Where do your family live?'

Luca, he thought. What kind of name is that for an Englishman? A Spanish mother, he had said. Something was not right here.

'We live just outside London. Near Oxford.'

'Simone tells me you are a journalist,' Angeli said. He spoke the word with distaste, as if it were 'garbage collector' or 'pest exterminator'.

'That's right.'

'And what are you doing here in Rome?'

'I was sent here to write a feature. I have been interviewing various members of the Curia, certain Vatican commentators, getting opinions on who is likely to succeed the current Pope.'

'Oh? And who *is* likely to succeed him?'

'It depends who gets their way. The conservatives or the liberals.'

'You make it sound like politics.'

He smirked. 'Isn't it?'

'Ah, but I am a traditionalist. I still believe the choice of a pope is divinely inspired.'

'You don't think He gets a little help?'

Angeli laughed easily. 'That is why we are here, surely. To help God's cause?' He could feel his daughter's eyes on him, willing him to drop this. He refused to meet her eye. 'So who, in your opinion, are the front-runners among the *papabile*?'

'The conservatives want another Wojtyla. For once the prime conservative candidates are from the Third World. Trujillo of Colombia and Neves from Brazil are their front-runners. The Italian candidate, for once, is a progressive. Martini. Or perhaps there'll be a compromise as usual.'

'Who?'

'Comacho.'

'Comacho? The Mexican?'

'Wojtyla was a man for his time. It was considered a masterstroke to have a Polish pope during a time of so much upheaval in the communist bloc. But the Church needs someone who will address the problems of the modern Church in the Third World. Poverty. Repression. Overpopulation.'

It was painful to keep his smile in place. He felt his jaw muscles freeze. He poured Luke some more wine. 'Is that what you think? You think because Russia is dead there are no more communists?'

'Not as a world force. It's a label right-wing governments use to justify repression.'

'So now the Church must condone terrorism? In your opinion?'

'Papa,' Simone said, sensing the turn the conversation had taken.

'I am interested in the young man's opinions.'

'It depends on your definition of a terrorist.'

'A terrorist is anyone who spreads ideas contrary to Western and Christian civilisation.'

'In Latin America a lot of priests support these so-called terrorists. Liberation theology weakened the Church in Latin America. That is why many people think we need a pope from that continent to bring the Church together again.'

'To tell the Church to forget about civilised values? To break down all order in society? To take away everything a man has worked for all his life, give it to rabble? To break down all respect for the Church and for authority? To allow women to have abortions? Is this bringing the Church together again?'

There was a long silence. Luke's face was flushed. He stared into his wine, unable or unwilling to answer. Simone and Francesca had found something of interest on the ceiling. Angeli threw his napkin on the table in disgust and went up to the roof terrace to light a cigarette.

Simone found him leaning on the balustrade, staring over the red-tiled Renaissance roofs of Piazza Navona. Luke had made his apologies and left. Simone was not sure how she felt, if she was angry with him, or her father, or both of them. She had wanted so much that they should like each other.

She did not often see her father angry. His temper seldom flared at it had tonight.

They stood side by side for a long time, not speaking.

'Be careful of him,' Angeli said, finally.

'I like him very much.'

'I can see that for myself. How long is he staying in Rome?'

She shrugged her shoulders.

'He will go back to England and you will never see him again. Why are you wasting your time on this boy?'

'I don't know.'

'If he hurts you, let me know.'

Something in his voice alarmed her. 'I'm cold,' she said, and she turned away from him and went back inside.

'Where did you get this information on Gregorini and P2?' Luke asked. They were in Jeremy's apartment in the Via Veneto, all marble and chrome, sixteen floors up. Jeremy opened another bottle of Barolo and refilled his glass. Luke flicked through the several printed pages on his lap.

'Rumour. Innuendo. Cocktail parties at the embassy are like Mothers' Union meetings. Really. Of course, you can't publish any of that stuff. Libellous.'

'There must be someone who can give me more.'

'Could try the cemetery.'

'Thanks.'

'Anyone has connections, it's you. Rogering his daughter, for God's sake.'

'I'm not sleeping with her.'

'Hopeless. Lost your touch.'

Luke felt a flush of guilt. Not that he hadn't thought about it. Jesus. Incest by proxy. That wasn't why he was here.

'Thought you were invited to lunch.'

'I blew it.'

Jeremy made a tutting noise with his tongue and shook his head, obviously amused. 'Old mate. Really.'

'Behind that urbane exterior the guy's a psycho. We were talking about the Vatican and he went ballistic.'

'Never discuss religion and politics. First rule of polite society.'

'Names. There must be someone.'

Jeremy gave a theatrical sigh. 'Well. All right. One's an Italian. Maldini. Prints this fringe newspaper. Back yard. Rumour is he's a disaffected P2. Give you his number. Other chap's a New Zealander. Arthur Fox. Drinks too much. National curse, I suppose. Good journalist, when he's sober. Been in Rome for ever. Met Caligula. Buy him lunch and he'll talk for days.'

Luke grinned. 'Thanks for your help, Jeremy. It's been invaluable.'

'Everything has a value. Your case, lunch. What expense accounts are for.'

'Sure. You make the booking. I'll pay.' Luke had the grace not to mention that his expense account had expired as of the previous evening.

'Just be careful. Murky waters. Watch what you print.' He held up the bottle. 'Another?'

By Thursday Luke had run his credit card almost to its limit. He remembered Martin's warning. Get back to London by the next day or he wouldn't have a job to go back to.

He had tracked Maldini to a grimy flat in the southern suburbs and entertained Arthur Fox over lunch and numerous bottles of wine at a trattoria in Piazza di Spagna. He filled four ninety-minute cassettes with his conversations with the two men, and at the end of it he felt he knew as much as any man alive about César Angeli-Gregorini.

Except how he came to have a daughter who was a mirror image of his own sister.

But he could guess.

'I don't remember much of Buenos Aires now. I remember we lived in this huge house in Palermo. There was a garden and a swimming pool and this great marble staircase.'

They were in a restaurant in Campo dei Fiori, lingering over a bottle of Colle Gaio. Drapes billowed from the ceiling; the restaurant was lit by candles that flickered in the breeze from the open windows. Luke and Simone lingered over their *digestivi*, the last couple in the restaurant, their lives suspended for that moment, trapped in the spell of the wine and the food.

'I remember whenever my parents had a dinner party I'd sneak out of bed and crouch at the top of the stairs in the dark to watch people arrive. Everyone looks so much bigger when you're small. My father was in the army then and I remember the men in their caps and uniforms and the women in their beautiful dresses and jewellery. It just looked so glamorous.'

'What did your father do in the army?' he asked, as casually as he could.

'I don't know. He hardly ever talks about it. I think he is perhaps a little ashamed. He is a very honest man and he does not like what happened in his country during that time.'

And you believed him. Of course. What choice did you have?

'Why did he leave?'

'He said it was the war with Britain that made up his mind. When we were humiliated in the Malvinas.' She used the Argentine term for what he knew as the Falklands.

'Have you ever been back?'

She shook her head. 'We still have family there. Sometimes they visit us in Rome. My father goes to Buenos Aires, on business. But he never takes us.'

She looked at him over the rim of her glass. I wonder what she's thinking. I wonder if she has ever asked herself if her father is telling her the whole truth. Perhaps the doubt always lurks there at the back of her mind. It must be easier to accept the lies and half-truths than to search too deeply into the past.

'What are you thinking?' she asked him.

I was wondering what my parents will say when I show them the photographs of you that I took outside St Peter's and in the Piazza di Spagna. I was wondering what my sister Gabriella will think when she discovers she has a twin. I don't know if I should tell you everything I know right now. I am wishing I had never come to Rome, that I had never seen you, that I never had to make this decision.

'Nothing,' he said.

'I know you are thinking something. You have this look in your eyes.'

Her eyes were too wide. This was leading somewhere he had never intended it to go. He felt a thrill of panic and looked away.

'I was thinking I did not make such a great impression on your family the other day,' he said, trying to break the tension between them. He picked up the bottle of wine. Empty. 'I'm sorry.'

'You should never talk politics to Papa. He is like some men are with football.' She pushed away her wine glass.

'I came on too strong, I suppose.'

'He is a strong character. So are you.'

'I should mind my manners more.'

Her eyes shone in the candlelight. Too much wine. 'You are a strange guy. I can't figure you out.'

'In what way?'

'When I say no to you, you chase me all over Rome. When I say yes and I come to dinner with you, you look all around the restaurant, out of the window, anywhere but look at me. It is like you are frightened of me.'

Truer than you know, he thought. 'I have to go back to London the day after tomorrow. I don't want to hurt you, I guess.'

'It's a little late to worry about that now.'

'No, it's not.'

She gave him a curious smile and stared at him for a long time. Finally, she said: 'I think I want to go home now.'

Her back was to him as she stood at the shuttered window, looking over the piazza. It had been raining and the cobbles were slick and black, splashed with the yellow reflections of the streetlamps. The rattle of a Vespa echoed along the alleyway, the shouts of a group of teenagers carried through the open windows. A breeze stirred the net curtain. There was a radio playing somewhere.

He stood closer, breathed in the scent of her perfume, felt the warmth of her through his shirt. She was wearing a sheer black dress, cut low at the back. He watched the ripple of her shoulder blades beneath her skin. He traced the curve of her spine with his finger. He heard her catch her breath.

What the hell am I doing?

She turned around, put her arms around his neck. He felt like an animal, hypnotised by the lights of an oncoming car. Nothing he could do now to stop. He stroked her hair, kissed her neck, very gently. There was a sheen of sweat between her breasts.

He couldn't help himself.

64

He woke in the middle of the night to a feeling of panic. The bedroom door threw a shaft of light across the bed. She lay on her stomach, asleep, her hair splayed across the white pillowslip.

What had he done?

He slipped out of bed, gathered his clothes and walked naked into the bathroom. He stood under the shower for a long time, the hot needles of water playing over his scalp and shoulders. He had not meant this to happen. He tried to project the consequences in his mind. He wondered what his parents would think when they found out, what Gabriella would think. He closed his eyes and groaned aloud.

When he got out of the shower Simone was in the kitchen, making coffee. She was wearing a silk housecoat, her hair mussed from sleep. She gave him a nervous smile which quickly faded. 'It's stopped raining.'

He nodded.

'I can run you back to your hotel in the car, if you like.'

'I'll walk.'

She pushed a cup across the marble counter. 'I made you a cup of coffee.'

'Thanks.'

She watched him, hugged herself, shivering in the cool of the morning. 'So. Are you disappointed?'

'It's not that.' I've done nothing wrong, he reminded himself. You're not my sister. Neither, for that matter, is Gabriella. Not by blood.

'I've only had one other boyfriend. I went out with him for nearly three years. I'm a good Catholic girl and he was afraid of my father, I think. We only slept together twice.'

'I'm not disappointed.' He sipped his coffee. There were tears in her eyes. 'What's the matter?'

'Nothing.' She swallowed hard.

'It's just that I have to go back to London.'

'So I won't ever see you again?'

He almost told her then, almost spilled it out.

But she was the first to break the silence. 'Will I see you before you go?'

'Of course.' He put the coffee cup back on the counter. 'How about lunch tomorrow?'

'What time?'

'One o'clock. Will you pick me up from the hotel?'

'Okay.' She reached across the counter, touched his fingertips. 'You won't go without saying goodbye?'

'What kind of a question is that?'

He kissed her, pulled away when he felt the answering pressure of her lips. 'See you tomorrow,' he whispered. He turned for the door, shut it gently behind him. He did not look back as he crossed the square, knew she was watching him from the window.

He walked with his head down against the cool night wind, across the Ponte Sisto and through the dark streets to his hotel. When he got there he went up to his room, packed his case and called for a taxi. He got to Fiumicino just as dawn was breaking over the city and booked himself on the eight o'clock British Airways flight to Heathrow.

65

Market Dene, Berkshire, England

They lived in a farmhouse that had seen a succession of owners. There had been a dwelling on the site since the Domesday-book and parts of the laundry dated from the original cottage built in those days by medieval farmers. The house itself had been left to Stephen by his own father, inherited three generations before.

It had been extended piecemeal over the years, a circumstance attested to by the different types and colours of brick. This oddity was partly disguised by the ivy that had taken hold on three of the four walls. There were grey stone tiles on the roof and gabled windows that looked out over a cobblestone yard, a byre and a pond on one side, stables and outbuildings on the other. The house had six bedrooms, a library and even a billiard room. It was too large for their needs, and far too expensive to heat in winter, but it was the house where Stephen had grown up and he could not bear to sell it. Besides, it was an indulgence he could afford.

He was now the general manager of the publishing house that he had worked for in Buenos Aires. He drove into the Oxford headquarters three days a week, on the others he worked at home in his study. But Stephen's wealth did not come from publishing, it came from the money and estate left to him by his father, who had amassed a modest fortune on the stock market.

When Luke arrived there was a yellow Volvo parked in the yard, outside the kitchen door. There was a pink Volkswagen beside it; Gabriella was down from university.

'Luca!'

Mercedes came out of the house. Ten o'clock, but she was still in her dressing gown. Wisps of hair hung about her face.

'Ma,' he said.

She hugged him. 'When did you get back from Rome?'

'Yesterday morning.'

'You had a good trip?'

'Sure.'

He heard the sound of voices behind the house. 'Gabby's down for the weekend,' she said. 'Are you *staying*?'

'I have to go back to London tonight. Deadlines.'

She took his arm. 'Pity. Never mind. Come on, your father's *dying* to see you. And Gabby. They're playing tennis. It might be a good time to break it up. Your father is *losing*, by the sounds of it.'

There was a clay tennis court at the rear of the house, surrounded by a green mesh fence. As they came around the corner he saw his father first. He was greyer these days, and wiry in his tennis whites, but still very fit even though he was well into his fifties. He had always been a good tennis player but this morning he was getting a run for his money.

Gabriella had her back to him, lean and brown in white shorts over a Lycra bodysuit. The outsized running shoes she wore instantly took him back to another young woman jogging in the Trastevere. She stretched across the net to win the point they were playing with a crisp backhand drop volley.

Stephen shook his head. 'Your set.' Luke could tell it was all he could do to stop himself slamming the spare ball in his hand into the net. He was the consummate Englishman until he played tennis and then he wanted to be John McEnroe.

Gabriella turned around, saw him and waved. 'Luke!'

He felt an unpleasant, oily sensation in the pit of his stomach. The world jarring out of plane, like seeing a ghost. The hairs prickled on the back of his neck as they had when he first saw Simone in Casa di Santa Maria. But now there was the added burden of guilt, deep in his gut.

He heard a voice saying: '*You won't go without saying goodbye?*'

'Hello, Gabby.'

How the hell am I going to do this? he asked himself. How am I going to tell them about Simone?

66

They had breakfast on the patio at the rear of the house. There was toast and muffins and home-made jam that Mercedes had bought from an old lady in the village. She brought out a pot of Earl Grey tea and some freshly brewed coffee.

A wasp committed suicide in the strawberry jam while small brown sparrows darted around the stone flags looking for crumbs, bigger starlings hovering at a more discreet distance on the lawn.

Gabriella was buttering some toast. The gold broken-heart pendant at her throat flashed in the morning sunlight.

She felt Luke's eyes on her. 'What?'

'Nothing,' he said. 'How are things at Cambridge?'

Gabriella shrugged. 'Okay.'

'I saw an old friend of mine in Rome. I told him my sister was studying genetics. He thought it was probably too difficult for a girl.'

She made a face.

'I told him you were smarter than you looked.'

'Well, so are you. But for you it's easy, for me it's a real achievement.'

Stephen put down the newspaper. He was a *Times* reader but had switched to the *Guardian* out of loyalty to his son. 'How was Rome?'

'Okay.'

'A junket,' Gabriella said.

'He's doing a feature on the *Vatican*,' Mercedes told her.

'Did you talk to the Pope?' Gabriella asked him. 'Did he tell you all his dark secrets?'

'Secrets?'

They all looked up at him and waited for him to continue. Instead he jumped to his feet and gathered up the breakfast plates. 'I'll wash up,' he said.

Stephen stared after him as he went back inside the house. 'Well, that's something new,' he said.

The house was quiet, Stephen was working in his study and Mercedes was upstairs, taking her afternoon nap. He wandered out on to the patio, found Gabriella lying face down on one of the sun chairs. She was wearing a white bikini and the sight of her stopped him in his tracks. He stood there for a few moments, watching her, remembering.

You damned idiot, Luke.

He came to stand beside her, letting his shadow fall over the page of her book.

'What are you reading?'

She showed him the cover.

'Byron? I thought at last Jilly Cooper or Shirley Conran.'

'Byron's a romantic, Luke. You wouldn't understand.'

'I can be romantic. Just not with my sister.'

She raised an eyebrow.

'How do you do that?'

'Do what?'

'Raise one eyebrow like that?'

'I don't know. It's a gift.' She returned her attention to her book. 'Could you rub some more oil into my back?'

He hesitated. 'Yes, your ladyship.' He sat on the edge of the sun chair, picked up the bottle. He poured some of the coconut-scented oil on to his palm and rubbed it gingerly into her shoulders.

'Are you okay, Luke?'

'Sure. Why?'

'I don't know. I just get the feeling something's up.' When he didn't answer her, she went on. 'There's nothing wrong, is there? You've not got some poor girl pregnant?'

'I'm fine.'

He was standing behind her at the shuttered window, looking over the piazza. There was a radio playing somewhere. She was wearing a sheer black dress, cut low at the back. He watched the ripple of her shoulder blades beneath her skin. He traced the curve of her spine with his finger.

'There, that should see you cooked for another hour.'

She twisted her head to look up at him. 'You sure you're not in any kind of trouble?'

'What the hell are you talking about?'

'You've just got this look on your face.'

'You sure you want to do genetics? Maybe you should be a shrink, like Ma.'

'Something happened in Rome.'

'Nothing happened in Rome,' he said, and went inside. He had never been a good liar, not with his family. Gabriella was right. His face always gave him away.

Luke watched his mother's face twitch in her sleep, her limbs starting occasionally at the spectres that sometimes haunted her dreams. She was in the bentwood rocker, by the window, taking her afternoon nap. She seemed to spend most of her life asleep, or lying quietly in dark rooms. He could not remember when it had ever been different.

He had seen photographs of her taken in Buenos Aires, when he was still a small child. He did not recognise the confident, smiling woman on his father's arm. Stephen said she had something called depression, which had overtaken her soon after they arrived in England from Argentina. Over the years Ma's depression had become a fact of life, like the weather. All his life he remembered having to creep around the house in the middle of the afternoon because his mother had another of her 'migraines'.

She had been a psychiatrist once, in Argentina. It was hard to equate the picture his father painted with this sickly and pale woman he knew. He had been told that she had been abducted during the Dirty War, that his father had paid a big ransòm to get her back, that everyone considered her fortunate to have survived. He had been told all this as a child, in the most simplistic terms; but his mother had never spoken of it with him, ever, and his father always changed the subject whenever he brought it up. It had become a family taboo.

He listened to the murmur of insects in the garden. The breeze was laced with the aroma of the honeysuckle that grew wild along the fence.

He heard the tinny rattle of the Volkswagen coming to life. Gabriella was on her way into town, to pick up some groceries for the evening meal. He had perhaps half an hour. He gently nudged his mother awake.

'Ma,' he whispered. 'Ma.'

Mercedes' eyes flickered open, dull from sleep. It took a few
moments for her to focus, remember where she was.

'Luca. I must have dropped *off*.'

'Come downstairs, Ma. There's something I have to tell you
and Dad.'

67

Stephen stared at the glossy photograph between his fingers. His hands were shaking, his face ashen.

'It was taken in the Piazza Navona, three days ago. Her name's Simone.'

Mercedes sat on the other side of the kitchen table, thumbing through the rest of the prints. She put them down and pushed them across the table to her husband. She wrapped her cardigan more tightly around her shoulders as if she were cold.

'Did you know?' Luke asked them.

He saw the look that passed between them. It told him everything. 'We suspected,' Stephen said. 'That's all.'

'Did you . . . *tell* this girl anything?' Mercedes asked him.

He shook his head.

His father gave him an enquiring look.

'I thought I should talk to you first.'

A look of relief passed across his face. 'Thank you.'

A long silence. Mercedes pushed at the edges of the photographs, as if she were trying to put as much distance as she could between herself and these unwelcome images. He waited for them to ask him the obvious question, but they seemed reluctant to know.

Finally he reached into the brown manila envelope at his elbow. 'There's more,' he said.

Stephen slowly nodded his head.

'I met her parents.'

'Her parents?' Mercedes repeated, her voice a raw whisper.

'She thinks they're her real parents.'

Stephen cleared his throat. 'Her real parents went by the name of Reuben and Rosa Altman. They were murdered by the Argentine authorities in 1975.'

'You knew their names?'

'Does that change anything?'

'You never told Gabriella?'

'I don't see how that would *help* her,' Mercedes answered. 'They don't even have a *grave*.'

Luke brought out the grainy colour photograph of César Gregorini, in green polo shirt and tan slacks, his arms around his wife and daughter, the photograph he had removed from its frame that last night in Simone's apartment.

He slid it across the table to his father. Stephen picked it up and gave a hiss of recognition. He slammed it down on the table with the flat of his hand and pushed it away from him as if it were poison.

'You recognise him?' Luke asked.

Stephen was looking at his wife. 'It's him,' he whispered to her. 'The man in the café.'

'You're sure?'

Stephen nodded.

'What man?' Luke asked.

Stephen did not answer him. Instead he asked: 'What do you know about him?'

Luke pushed the envelope towards him. 'It's a feature article. I researched it while I was in Rome. I can't publish it, never will. It has everything about him, his activities, his *alleged* so-called businesses, past and present. It's mainly about his activities in Italy. His life in Argentina is still pretty much a mystery. The only thing I know for sure is that he was a colonel in the army, and that he left for Italy soon after Alfonsín's victory in 1983.'

'I met him once,' Stephen said, almost dreamily. 'In Buenos Aires. He tried to blackmail me.'

'Blackmail you?' Luke was astonished. 'How?'

Stephen shook his head. 'It was a business matter. It was a long time ago. It doesn't matter now.'

Luke looked up at his mother. She was staring at the photograph of César and the two women as if hypnotised. 'I feel sick,' she said. She was shaking. Stephen and Luke both had to help her to her feet. She staggered to the downstairs toilet and they heard her being violently ill.

Then they heard the rattle of the Volkswagen outside. Gabriella was back.

'Not a word,' Stephen said.

68

Stephen's study was the most untidy room in the whole house, a jumble of manuscripts loosely tied with string and rubber bands, filing cabinets, a copier, two fax machines, a computer, telephones, a corkboard. Stephen regarded it as his private bolthole. He came here when he needed to think, needed to be alone. As he did today.

Luke had gone, had driven back to London. So much they had to explain to him. But that would have to wait for another day. Gabriella was in the kitchen, preparing supper. Of course, she knew something was wrong. Mercedes' sudden indisposition would have to make do as an excuse for now.

Stephen sat behind the antique bureau, staring out of the lattice window, the sun low in the afternoon sky, birdsong in the garden. But the sounds his mind replayed were less pleasant: the crash of boots on the stairs, a woman's screams, a car roaring away in the night.

Now fate had brought that night screaming back into their lives. The fact of Gabriella's twinship could not be denied. The question now was what they should do about it.

'We have to talk.'

He looked up, startled. He had not heard his wife coming up the stairs. She stood in the doorway, playing with the jewellery on her wedding finger. She had never been still since her ordeal in Buenos Aires. She was like a sparrow, always on the move, twisting a handkerchief between her fingers or touching her face as if searching for some imaginary wound. Her nails had long ago been bitten down to the quick.

'What did you *tell* her?'

'I haven't told her anything. Not yet.'

'And we will *not* tell her anything.'

He looked up at her. 'She has a right to know.'

'What good will it do?' Her voice had risen, strident, desperate. If frightened him.

'I don't know.'

'She must not know. Not ever. This never happened. Do you understand?'

'But it did happen.'

'No! It did not!' She slammed her fist on his desk.

He had not seen her as animated since . . . since Buenos Aires. A face like a madwoman. He stood up, put out a hand to try to calm her. 'Darling, hush, Gabriella will hear us . . .'

She twisted away from his outstretched hand. 'You will not tell her anything. You will not tell Luca anything. We are going to go on as if this had never happened. Do you understand me, Stephen?'

'I don't know if that's the right thing to do.'

'If you love me . . . if you want to continue loving me, you will do this for me.'

She turned and walked out of the study. He watched her retreat down the landing to the bedroom. He stood there, his hands hanging uselessly at his sides. He supposed his wife was right. If they told Gabriella the truth, little good could come of it. Besides, in the circumstances, it didn't seem he had much choice.

Mercedes lay on the bed, the curtains drawn, her eyes closed, the phantoms once again invading her darkness. She saw a man in a green polo shirt and tan slacks, a broad smile, golden, immaculately parted hair, strong jaw, perfect smile. The face of a doctor perhaps, or a stage actor. Not the face of a torturer. Not the face of the man who had raped her on five different occasions in the barracks at Ezeiza, while she lay helpless and strapped to a table.

She would not invite that monster back into her life. They had a good life now. The nightmare had been buried in the past. And there it would stay.

69

Rome

Angeli had always considered himself a good Catholic if not an ardent one. But recently he had begun attending Mass twice or even three times a week. He became agitated these days when he watched the television, shouting at newsreaders when they read stories about communist activities in Latin America, switched channels if the current US President, Bill Clinton, appeared.

He was having trouble sleeping. He often woke in the middle of the night, would get up and spend hours sitting alone in the darkened living room. He told himself it was because of Simone. He had doted on her when she was a child and as she grew he had spent many evenings with her, playing arcade games on the computer or bent over long and intricate games of chess which they both took very seriously. Now she was gone and he suddenly felt old and lost.

She had moved out against his wishes. He had bought her the apartment in Trastevere, not to show his approval for her decision, but to retain some control over her life. She was never one for crowds and staying out late at parties but she still insisted on far more independence than Francesca had when she was her age. Than she did now, in fact.

But he had to accept that times had changed. Simone wore jeans with tears at the knees which she said were fashionable, bathing costumes that concealed absolutely nothing. At least, unlike many girls her age, she displayed some modesty about her choice of boyfriends. He clung to the hope that she was still a virgin. But who could tell these days?

They had argued about her behaviour many times. She had never forgiven him for the way he had treated that last boyfriend, the English reporter. What was his name? Luke.

Simone, Simone. His daughter had made him weak. He had been ensnared by his own portrayal of her father. In truth, there were two César Angelis. He knew a very different one and he wondered what she would think if she met this other man.

Some secrets could not be kept for ever. One day, he guessed, there would have to be a reckoning.

Simone stopped at Gino's on the way home. It was empty except for a teenager listlessly playing the pinball machine in the corner. The waiter's name was Riccardo. He was alone behind the bar, wiping glasses and lining them up on the zinc counter top.

She sat down on one of the stools. '*Ciao*.'

'*Ciao*, Simone.'

'Just an espresso.'

He brought it over to her. 'What's the matter?'

'Nothing.'

'Haven't see you around much lately. You heard from that Englishman?'

She shook her head. She opened a sachet of sugar, spilt the contents on the counter top.

'That *stronzo*. He's got to be crazy, dumping a girl like you.'

Two Americans came into the bar and Riccardo slipped away to pour two cappuccinos. He brought them over to the tourists, who had seated themselves at one of the tables outside. Then he came and sat on the stool beside her at the bar.

'Is that why you're so down?' he asked her.

She shrugged her shoulders.

'Perhaps you should go out with me.'

She gave him a rueful smile. 'Why didn't you ever ask me before?'

'I'm asking you now.'

She shook her head. 'I heard you're going out with Claudia Tombetti.'

'I'm not a monk.'

'Far from it, the way I hear it.'

'Claudia is just a friend,' he said, his expression sulky. 'Still. That's not it, is it? I guess you don't want to go out with someone who's just a waiter, right?'

'That's not it, Riccardo.'

'Your father wouldn't let you anyway.'

'My father doesn't run my life.'

He smiled. They both knew that wasn't completely true. 'I won't always be a waiter.'

She touched his cheek. 'You're sweet. I'd like to go out with you. But . . . I've had enough of boys for a while. Okay?'

'What are you doing,' a voice growled, 'you trying to send me bankrupt?' Gino rolled in, his florid face lathered in sweat.

'It's the first time I've sat down all day.'

'Sure it is. Look at these glasses. Is this where they live, huh, on the counter top?'

Riccardo went back behind the bar and started slamming glasses around. Gino winked at Simone. But she was not in the mood for the by-play today. She finished her espresso. '*Ciao*, Riccardo,' she said, and walked out.

He stared after her. '*Ciao*, Simone,' he said, softly. He watched her until she had disappeared inside her apartment. 'I'm going to kill myself,' Riccardo said.

'Not on my time. You want to kill yourself, do it out of work hours.'

'She is so beautiful.'

'I don't know why you torment yourself that way. You don't have a hope. Now are you going to stand there with that moon face all morning or can we have some cloths on the tables out there?'

It was all that Angeli could do, as he walked into his study, to keep from slamming the door. He sat down, his fists in his lap, the knuckles white.

The *stronzo* reporter was writing an article about him, naming him as a fascist and an illegal arms dealer. He had just found out that the little prick had been talking to Maldini, asking all kinds of questions about him. He had had himself invited into his home for lunch, maybe slept with his daughter. No doubt he picked up some useful snippets of information there. He knew he had stolen a photograph from Simone's apartment. Oh, she didn't tell him about that, she didn't have the nerve, but Francesca did.

Just a parting insult, no doubt. He does all this and thinks he can get away with it. Thinks he's so fucking smart, so fucking clever. He had taken advantage of Simone's gentle nature for his own purposes. But what offended him most was that this young buck thought he could insult him without consequence.

He took several deep breaths to calm the shaking in his hands and then he picked up the telephone. He made five calls, three long distance and two local, and when he finally hung up the telephone everything was arranged.

70

Farringdon Road, EC1, London

The rumble of a train leaving the nearby Underground station shook the bare wooden boards in the Betsy Trotwood. Martin Harris chewed his Cumberland sausage standing up at the bar, washed it down with a long draught of Bishop's Finger. He was a big man, with a fleshy face and a loud, braying voice. The cloying smell of beer and nicotine clung to his well-worn three-piece suit. 'So where's this big story you were promising me?'

Luke shook his head. 'It's just not going to hang together.'

'Jesus Christ.' A piece of well-chewed sausage landed on the dark, polished bar. 'What are you trying to do to me?'

Luke shrugged his shoulders helplessly.

'What was it, then, this big story you were chasing in Rome? A bit of rumpy-pumpy, was it? A bit of foreign?'

'I couldn't get the research together. The story's too thin. There're too many libels.'

'Let me be the judge of that.'

'I haven't written it.'

'What about your notes, then?' When Luke still didn't answer him Martin finished his pint and ordered two more. 'You said your spotter over there had given you leads on arms dealing and money laundering inside the Vatican. That's what you told me.'

'That's what I thought I had.'

'Look, my son, if you could produce a story like that, it's the sort of thing gets careers moving. You with me? No one gives a fuck about the next pope until this one's dead. The Sunday readers. The fuckers who watch BBC2. But scandal and war stories get you your own office. Your bylines in caps. If you want to kick-start your career you're going to have to finish off someone else's.'

'Martin, I told you, I couldn't get the material together.'

Martin drew on his pint. 'Well, fuck me,' he said. 'That's not what you said on the phone. You remember? When you were in Rome? All that desperate fucking urgency.'

Luke thought about Simone; he thought about his father's hands shaking as he stared at the photographs, listened to his mother choking up her grief through the bathroom door. Yes, he could write the story but what would it do to his family? What would it do to Simone? 'It was all dead ends,' he said.

Martin said nothing for a moment. Luke could feel the other man's eyes boring into him. 'You holding out on me, old son?'

Luke shook his head.

'I put my fucking neck out for you. The boss is going to be dead chuffed when he finds out I've come up a blank on this.'

'The article on the Vatican was all right, wasn't it?'

'Very professional. Very interesting. Very Channel Four. But that was the first week you were there. You stayed on four more days.'

'At my own expense.'

'There was work to be done here. And you promised me a big fucking story, my old mate.'

'I did my best. I told you. It just didn't pan out.'

Martin finished his sausages and took out a packet of cigarettes. 'Well, fucking hell.'

Luke finished his beer. 'I'd better be getting home.'

'I don't know how I'm going to square this away with the boss,' Martin said.

'I'm sorry, Martin,' Luke said. 'I'll make it up to you.'

'I don't see how.'

'I'll see you tomorrow.'

Martin raised his eyebrows and said nothing.

It was raining on Farringdon Road. Luke turned up his collar. Summer in England. What a joke. He started across the road.

A splash of light on the wet pavement, a moment's swelling of noise as the pub door swung open and a man ran across the road, his jacket held over his head to keep off the worst of the rain.

He never saw the car that hit him; he was a little careless because of the rain and besides, it had no lights. It accelerated quickly, struck him from the left side, the force of the impact breaking both his legs just above the knee. He flipped over the bonnet and

landed head first on the tarmac, twisting his neck and fracturing
his skull just above the right temple, avulsing a large flap of skin
from his scalp.

The driver of the car did not stop. He sped north up Farringdon
Road, the lights still extinguished.

The drinkers in the bar of the Betsy Trotwood heard the squeal
of tyres and the sound Luke's body made as it hit the bonnet.
Martin, knowing in his bones what had happened, was the first
to reach him. He was still breathing, but his face was covered in
blood and his left leg was at a bizarre angle to his body.

'Oh, Christ, oh Christ,' he moaned. 'Luke!' He turned around,
looked up at the bystanders who had followed him out of the saloon
bar, gaping in horror. 'Somebody call a fucking ambulance!'

71

Stephen stood at the window, watching the rain weep down the pane, leaving a trail of grime. He had always thought himself a sentimental man, and the fact that he felt nothing while his only son lay fighting for his life surprised him.

'We are being punished.'

His wife looked up. She sat on a hard plastic seat on the other side of the corridor, twisting a handkerchief between her fingers. She had not cried either.

'Punished?'

'That time in Buenos Aires. We should have told that man the truth. We dissembled. She is not ours, by law or by right, and now we are being punished. Through Luke.'

Mercedes stared at the tiled floor, twisting the handkerchief into even tighter knots in her lap. 'You mean *God* is doing this? Is *that* what you believe?'

'I don't know. Perhaps it's a sort of wild justice.'

'We did nothing *wrong*. We gave shelter to an abandoned child.'

'We hid her from her family.'

'That man did not want her. He practically *said* as much. If he had *wanted* her he would not have gone away.'

'Perhaps we intimidated him.'

Mercedes was silent for a long time. 'I still think we did nothing *wrong*.'

Stephen turned back to the solace of the rain and grey skies.

He intoned a silent prayer: *Please, God, don't let him die.* But as he prayed another part of him thought: *This is what you deserved. You always knew this would happen one day.*

They heard footsteps echo in the corridor.

They both looked up and saw one of Luke's doctors, the neurological surgeon, Caldow. Stephen tried to decipher his

expression, steeled himself for bad news. Mercedes got slowly
to her feet, reached for Stephen's hand.

'Is he going to be all right?' Stephen heard himself say.

Waiting-room coffee, brown and foul. Gabriella cradled the
polystyrene cup in both hands, stared at the dull heavy-duty
carpet. There were four mismatched chairs, a coffee machine, a
crucifix high on the wall. She felt as if there were a great weight
pressing on her chest.

The door opened.

'Pa,' she said. She stood up and he took her in his arms and
held her. They stayed that way for a long time.

'I've just seen the doctor, pudding,' he said, using the nickname
he had given her as a child. His voice sounded as if it were about
to break.

'Is he going to be all right?'

'We must be brave.'

They sat for a long time in silence, listening to the hospital
sounds, the clatter of a drugs trolley in the corridor outside, the
beep of a doctor's belt pager.

Gabriella was the first to break the silence. 'How did it
happen?'

'The car was stolen. The police found it abandoned about two
miles away. Just kids, they think.'

It was all so senseless, Gabriella thought. 'Where's Ma?'

'The doctors gave her something to help her sleep.'

Gabriella felt the strength go out of her. She leaned against her
father's shoulder, buried her face in the rough wool of his jacket.
'He won't die, will he?'

'No,' Stephen said, without conviction. 'He won't die.'

72

The rented BMW turned into the driveway of the old house, the tyres crunching on the gravel. Jeremy turned off the ignition and sat for a time staring at the imposing gables of the house and stables, the mossy grey tiles. There were no other cars in the courtyard. He wondered perhaps if both the Barringtons were out.

He looked in the rear-vision mirror. In the far distance he could make out the spire of the village church in Market Dene through the green stands of oak and beech. Peaceful here.

The curtains moved at the front of the house. Well, someone was here. He got out of the car, walked across the yard and rapped twice on the kitchen door.

Mercedes Barrington looked sunken and frail. She was still in her dressing gown, though it was after three in the afternoon. Her hair was unkempt, and long strands with long grey roots straggled around her cheeks.

'Mrs Barrington. Name's Dexter, Jeremy Dexter. Friend of Luke's. From Rome.'

She nodded, a sign of vague recollection. 'Yes. I remember. He spoke about you.' She stepped aside. 'Please. Come in.'

'Thanks.'

The house was dark, shut up, as if the owners were away. Which in a sense they were, he thought. She led him through to the drawing room. She slumped into one of the wing chairs.

'Please, sit down.'

He sat, his hands between his knees, feeling awkward, wishing he had not come. He wasn't looking forward to this, but he had told himself that there were certain things that Luke's parents should know. He wondered now if that were true.

'It was good of you to come,' Mercedes said.

'Needed to talk to you. Your husband not here?'

'He's at work. In Oxford.'

'Ah.'

'I'm afraid he won't be back until *late*. Perhaps seven.'

'I see.' He looked around the room, at a photograph on the mantelpiece, Luke with his parents, arm in arm. An icon of happier times.

Jeremy leaned forward. He didn't know where to start, knew he just had to get this done, finished with. 'It's about Luke. Should have spoken to you at the funeral. Didn't seem the right time.'

'You were at the funeral, Jeremy?'

He nodded.

'I'm sorry. I don't remember.' Her air of vague politeness was unsettling. Perhaps she's taking antidepressants, he thought. 'I hope I wasn't *rude*.'

'No. Not rude. Not at all. A sad time . . .' He trailed off.

He listened to the loud ticking of the grandfather clock in the hallway.

'Knew what he was doing in Rome, did you?'

'He was writing an *article*, he said. On the *Pope*.'

'There was some other business. He did tell you?'

She stared right through him.

'Gregorini,' he prompted.

A long silence. 'Yes?'

'You did know?'

An almost imperceptible nod of the head.

'You see, thing is, I wonder if you've considered. This accident, I mean.'

'That it wasn't an *accident*?'

He nodded, relieved she had said the words for him.

Another long silence. Finally, she said: 'There is nothing you or I could *do* about that, is there?'

Jeremy flinched. 'Well, suppose not.'

'Is this a *mea culpa*, Jeremy?'

He looked away. 'My fault, really. Encouraged him. Told him things it was better he didn't know.'

'You're not to blame,' she said softly.

'Think I am. Actually.'

Mercedes rose slowly from her chair and went to the sideboard in the corner of the room. She picked up a framed photograph and brought it over.

She switched on the lamp on the corner table and handed it to him. Jeremy stared in blank incomprehension at the smiling faces of the Barringtons, Luke . . . and Simone Gregorini.

'Don't understand.'

'That is my *daughter*, Gabriella,' she said. 'She didn't go to the funeral. She couldn't face it. They were very close.'

He looked at the portrait photograph for a long time. 'Oh, my God,' he breathed.

'If you loved Luke, and if you have *any* concern for the feelings of myself and my husband, then you will not tell a *soul* about this. Do you understand?'

'Yes. I understand,' he said. But he did not understand. He did not understand at all.

IV

Europe and South America
Winter 1995

73

Mexico City

Reuben sat on a tubular chrome chair, listlessly turning the pages of a magazine. He changed seats, looked at his watch, picked up another magazine. *Newsweek* carried a report from Rome on the crisis inside the Vatican. The Catholic faith, it was reported, was facing mass defections in Latin America because of its habit of supporting repressive regimes. Now Seventh Day Adventist and other Protestant churches were gaining ground there. It was reported that the Catholic Church might lose as many as eighty million adherents to Protestant congregations in Latin America alone by the year 2000.

There were also concerns about the health of the Pope. The Vatican was trying to dispel rumours about Parkinson's disease or even bowel cancer. A spokesman had denied there was pressure on the Pontiff to step aside.

Death is not far away, Reuben thought grimly, not even for the Vicar of Christ. It never is. And on Judgment Day, God will ask you why you never thought it holy or just to stand by the tortured in Latin America. Why you never spoke out for your murdered priests and nuns as you did in Poland.

I'll see you in hell.

He tossed the magazine aside.

It was the end of the rainy season. The sky was the colour of lead and a late afternoon downpour had temporarily leached the smog from the air. The jutting concrete nightmare of Mexico City was bathed in greenish light.

The receptionist called his name. 'Dr Calderón will see you now.'

He knew what Calderón was about to say, but it is human nature to hope for the best. But the tests only confirmed for him what he already knew, in his soul. He had wondered, these last few days, if there was a psychological cause for his affliction, that perhaps what had been eating at him in spirit had now begun devouring his body too.

Last night he had dreamed he was back in Argentina. It was late at night and the cobbled streets were dark and empty, closing in on him from all sides. A green Ford Falcon, its lights off, was cruising silently towards him. He had woken from the dream in a lather of sweat. He knew what was waiting for him behind the darkened windows of the car.

Calderón wore an expensive grey double-breasted suit, purchased, no doubt, in the Zona Rosa. The suit was complemented by a powder-blue shirt and navy tie. His hair and fingernails were immaculately groomed. Reuben guessed his age at around fifty-five.

Older than I am, though he has much longer to live.

Calderón produced the X-rays from a large grey envelope and hung them on an opaque backlit screen. Like a teacher explaining a complex mathematical problem, he pointed out to him the shadow on his liver. He heard the word 'tumour'.

'How much time do I have?' Reuben asked him.

Calderón seemed bewildered by the interruption. 'One cannot be sure in such cases.'

'Just tell me how much time.'

The doctor took his time with his verdict. It was difficult to say. They could try radiotherapy. He would do his best to make him comfortable.

'How much time?' he repeated.

Pressed, he gave his verdict. Six months. Reuben might be able to function normally using self-administered analgesia for half of that time. After that he might require hospitalisation. Reuben was not without means. He could be assured of the very best medical care.

Reuben was surprised by his own reaction. He felt quite calm. In fact, it was a relief in many ways. For the past twenty years he had lived every day tormented by ghosts. Now he could join them.

That was not to say he was not afraid. Of course he was afraid. He did not believe there was anyone alive who was not afraid to die. We live, and we become accustomed to life. No one is sure what is on the other side and it is terrible for the ego to contemplate oblivion.

He realised Calderón had spoken to him. 'I beg your pardon?'

'I asked if there is any family.'

Reuben shook his head. 'No. No family.'

Calderón seemed anxious. Perhaps because Reuben appeared so calm, or perhaps he was thinking about his next patient. 'What will you do, Señor Altman?'

'Did you hear about the patient who went to his doctor, and the doctor says: "I have some good news and some bad news." And the patient says: "Let me have the bad news."

'And the doctor says: "I'm afraid you only have a week to live." And the patient stares at him and shouts: "Oh my God, what's the good news?"

'The doctor says: "Well, did you see that beautiful new receptionist I've hired, the young girl with the absolutely fantastic breasts? I fucked her last night."'

The doctor blinked, shocked perhaps, and then realised the insult. He slowly closed Reuben's file. 'If there's anything I can do.'

Reuben shook his head. 'I shall be going overseas for a while. I will need a good supply of painkillers. I must know how I can obtain more while I am away. Can you help me with that?'

74

In the street a small boy was playing the accordion, a green plastic bowl on the pavement between his bare legs. Reuben opened his wallet and dropped a wad of notes into the bowl. He wouldn't be needing the money any more. The boy snatched up the bank-notes and hid them in his pocket before some other, older urchin saw what had happened and tried to steal them. He shouted benedictions at Reuben's retreating back.

A curious kind of liberty that death bestows, Reuben thought. Our own desperate need for life keeps our spirit chained. Once the urgency of survival is removed, one could be a good man again.

If only he had gone home that night instead of to the Mexican embassy.

He stood in the living room of his apartment, gazing around helplessly, as if searching for something he had lost. Finally he took a bottle of Bushmills from the cabinet and fetched a crystal tumbler from the kitchen. He slumped on the sofa, switched on the television with the remote. He turned down the volume and surfed through the channels: an Italian football match, a gringo soap opera, a music channel, Luis Miguel.

Shadows crept towards him from the window, the skyline etched in violet. He could hear police sirens in the distance.

How quickly we join the ranks of the damned and the dead. Only yesterday he was at university, young, full of sex and hope and promise. Suddenly his life had been lived and it seemed no more than a moment.

He tried not to think about Julio.

It was the way his life had been lived for nearly twenty years, trying not to think, to reflect. He worked fourteen, sixteen hours a day, sometimes even on weekends. To drown himself in the desperate act of forgetting. He had thought that with time he would find some way to proceed, some redemption, some hope.

He had found none.

He stared at the telephone. One phrase echoed over and over in his mind as it had done for the last thirteen years: *You think if one of your daughters was alive, she would want to see you? After you ran out on her and her mother?*

Why did Domingo say that? *One of your daughters.* Not *either* of your daughters. *One* of them. As if he knew that one of them *had* survived. Was it possible that he knew more than he was willing to say? Perhaps it was time to find out. There were some things he could face in death that he could never face in life.

He picked up the receiver.

Money would not be a problem. The bank had paid him well over the years and he had never spent extravagantly, had not even taken holidays. He knew how to invest his savings; it was one lesson his father had taught him well. Now he would spend what he needed on this last pilgrimage.

He used his credit card to book an air ticket. One way, to Buenos Aires.

75

Buenos Aires

He expected to be arrested at the airport, just as he had the last time he had landed at Ezeiza. This time, he thought, it is just to be afraid; this time I have a real crime on my head. But the official behind the desk stamped his passport and waved him through with no more than a cursory glance.

As he sat in the taxi riding the motorway into central Buenos Aires he allowed himself a glance out of the window and tried to pinpoint the exact location where he had left Julio's body. He wondered how long it had taken to find him, decomposing in the boot of his car.

Or perhaps he's still there.

For months afterwards he had lived in dread. Every day he expected the police to appear at his apartment or at the bank with an extradition warrant. When they did not come it finally occurred to him that Carmen had, for her own reasons, kept silent about Reuben's presence in Buenos Aires, in their home. She was the only one who could link him directly to Julio's disappearance, could have given the police a name.

It made him wonder again about her motives. Why had she told him about the rape, that night in the car? She surely could not have anticipated where that revelation would lead. And yet.

It was warm for the time of the year. The weather in Argentina had been slowly changing ever since 1980, something to do with the destruction of the Amazon rainforests. The political climate had changed, too. The Peronists had won power again in 1987, under Carlos Menem. Inflation continued to spiral, and reached five thousand per cent a year in 1989. It was said that some people renegotiated their annual salary on a daily basis; prices were not marked in supermarkets and increased not only by the day but by the hour. Finally, the Economic Minister, Domingo Cavallo, passed a 'convertibility' law pegging the peso to the US dollar. The previous year inflation had been brought down to just four per cent.

Menem had further reduced budget deficits by selling off state-run dinosaurs such as Aerolineas Argentinas, the oil monopoly and ENTel, the telephone company. The parks were once again green and freshly mowed, having been taken over by *La Nación* and the Banco de Galicia. There were new hotels and shopping malls and the smell of money had returned to the Microcentro.

But on other fronts the news was not as good.

Just after Christmas 1990 Menem had distinguished himself by handing pardons to Videla and Massera for their part in the Dirty War. They had served just four years of their life sentences, most under house arrest in their own palatial homes in Buenos Aires. Alfonsín's administration had already passed a 'law of due obedience' allowing lower-ranking officers to escape prosecution by claiming they were 'only following orders', as well as establishing, in 1986, the 'Punto Final' beyond which no prosecutions could take place. It seemed that the only ones who would suffer for the Dirty War were the families of those who went missing. The Madres de la Plaza still marched every Thursday afternoon around the obelisk in front of the Casa Rosada, still wearing their white scarves and bearing the ancient photographs of their disappeared. Menem continued to ignore their pleas for justice.

Reuben stared at the graffiti on the walls. 'IMF OUT OF ARGENTINA.' Well, that was something. In 1975 you could be shot for painting slogans in public. Now people were free to write on the walls again, but they had wisely decided to blame their problems on someone *outside* the country.

This time he stayed in the Claridge in Tucumán. He went straight up to his room on the fourth floor, stood at the window and reviewed his plans, such as they were. He had considered making an attempt to contact Carmen. But there were some questions better left unanswered. She had known too much, spoken too freely. Perhaps her only crime was thoughtlessness.

Or perhaps not.

Besides, she would not want to see him again, a spectre at the feast. She might even have remarried. Let her have her life back.

She had had enough Reuben Altmans for one lifetime. And, for him, there had certainly been enough Carmens.

He winced at a sharp and sudden pain and lay down on the bed. The pains had become more frequent in the last week. He reached for the morphine tablets he had placed within easy reach on the bedside table. In a way he was thankful for the pain. It was a constant reminder to him that time was short and he must hurry on with what he had to do.

He had climbed this same stairwell thirteen years before. The dank smells of the docks permeated everything, as he remembered. He stopped in front of Domingo's apartment, stared at the cracked and peeling paint on the door.

What if he had moved on? How would he find him after so long? Gonsalvez was not an unusual name. Must he track down every Gonsalvez in Buenos Aires? But what if he had left the city, gone back to Córdoba, moved to any of the other dozen provincial cities? He wasn't a private investigator. This could take months, months he did not have.

He took a deep breath and knocked on the door. After a few moments it opened. He found himself looking up at a tall young man in a white T-shirt and jeans. There was a few days' growth of stubble on his chin.

'Does Domingo Gonsalvez live here?'

He saw an expression of both envy and mistrust in the young man's eyes as he took in Reuben's Italian leather shoes, his Swiss wristwatch. A stranger at the door dressed like this could only be bad news.

'Who are you?' The question confirmed for him that Domingo was still here. This hulking brute – my nephew, he reminded himself – was probably just a child peering from behind his mother's skirts the last time I came.

'My name is Reuben Altman. Your father will remember me.'

The door closed in his face. He waited.

When it was thrown open again, Domingo stood there, legs akimbo, glaring up at him. The brown face was deeply lined now, years of despair and hard work carved into his skin. He had also lost a lot of his hair. He wore a white vest, the badge of his class, and a pair of baggy black trousers. The muscles of his arms and shoulders were stringy and hard, like knots in the old manila ropes by the docks. His teeth were bad. Reuben imagined there was little money in this household for dentists.

If he had thought that over time Domingo would have forgiven him, one look told him he was wrong.

'*Por Dios*. Is it you?'

'Domingo.'

'You look sick.'

'I am sick.'

'Good. I hope you die. Now get away from me and my family.'

He tried to shut the door. Reuben put out his hand, held it open. 'But I must talk to you. I came all the way from Mexico.'

'You should have saved your money. We have nothing to say. Now get away from here or I'll have my boys throw you down the stairs.'

The door slammed in his face, as it had done thirteen years before. All that was missing this time was the spit.

76

Reuben hired a Fiat from a Hertz agency and drove to Avellaneda very early the next morning. He parked opposite the apartment block and waited. Just after seven o'clock Domingo came out of the building and jumped on one of the gaudy *colectivos* that plied the city. He followed the rattling Mercedes bus to the Avellaneda bridge, saw him walk up the concrete stairwell to the iron-and-cement footbridge. Reuben followed, at a distance. He was still halfway across when he saw Domingo cross the dock-front on the Boca side and walk into a tyre fitter's not a hundred yards from the Avenida Almirante Brown.

He came back later that afternoon, took up a position on the bridge where he had a clear view of the workshop. It was almost dark when a man in a blue vest and overalls closed and padlocked the wooden doors. Reuben had guessed that Domingo would not go straight home and he was right. He saw him walk with the owner of the workshop to a bar not ten yards away on the street corner.

Reuben came down off the bridge, took up position in a doorway on the opposite side of the street. More waiting.

He wondered if he had the nerve to do this.

Hours passed. The shadows lengthened, yellow light spilled into the darkened street and the rough laughter of men's voices inside the bar grew louder. He smelled the savoury aromas of the *asado*, saw the flicker of the television screen, the men inside cheering the game. Boca Juniors were playing San Lorenzo. Reuben took a handful of morphine, swallowed the pills down with brandy from his hip flask. Give me strength for this, he prayed, to no god in particular.

Finally he saw him come out, alone, heading back towards the bridge. Reuben followed.

It was dark on the bridge. It shook whenever a heavy truck

rumbled past, a few yards above their heads. The terrible smell
of the river, sewage and diesel, permeated everything.

They were halfway across when Domingo sensed Reuben behind
him. He stopped and turned around, bleary with drink. His face
registered a moment's fear, which quickly transformed itself into
disbelief when he saw the knife in Reuben's hand.

Reuben grabbed his arm and pushed him against the metal
guardrail. He pressed the knife against Domingo's kidneys through
the threadbare brown workman's jacket.

'You haven't got the guts to use that,' Domingo said.

Reuben smelled the whisky on his breath. Hard to think of him
now as Rosa's brother. 'You want to find out?'

Domingo did not even try to get free of Reuben's grip. The
fear had vanished quickly, there was almost a swagger about
him. Perhaps it was the drink, perhaps his contempt for Reuben.
Perhaps both. 'What is it you want from me?'

'I want to find my daughters.'

'It's twenty years too late to worry about them.'

'You know something. You lied to me.'

'I don't know a fucking thing. They disappeared. That's it.' He
grinned. 'So, what are you going to do?'

Reuben stared at him. This was not going the way he had planned.
What am I going to do? Put the knife in his back? He had come all
this way, invested so much of his hope on a turn of phrase.

He just stood there feeling like a fool.

And it would have been all over except Domingo tried to take
the knife away.

He twisted around and grabbed Reuben's wrist. Reuben twisted
free and heard Domingo gasp in pain. He froze, thinking he had
stabbed him. Immediately Domingo lashed out with his good arm,
punching Reuben hard in the right shoulder. Reuben's hand went
numb and he heard the knife clatter on to the bridge. Domingo
crowded him back against the rail and hit him double-handed on
his ears. Reuben screamed and found himself lying on his back.

Domingo kicked the knife away before clutching at his own
hand. Blood dripped steadily from the tips of his fingers. The
knife had sliced open his palm. 'You stupid little shit,' he
growled.

Reuben was too stunned to move. He was hurting, there was
terrible pain in his ears and his shoulder. He watched Domingo

take a handkerchief from his pocket and wrap it around his
bleeding hand.

'Where did you get such a stupid little knife?'

Reuben groaned and leaned forward, holding his shoulder with
his left hand. His ears were ringing with the force of the blow.
'From my hotel . . . room. The fruit bowl.'

'I'm bleeding like a pig.'

He reached down, grabbed Reuben by the hair. 'I ought to kill
you right now. I wanted to do it last time. I've always promised
myself I would, if I saw you again. I should get that knife right
now and cut you throat with it.'

'Do it, then.'

Reuben felt his hot, whisky breath on his face. 'That's too good
for you.'

'You don't have the guts either.'

'Don't talk to me about guts. I wasn't the one who ran out on
his wife and kids!'

Domingo turned his back to him, tightened the makeshift
bandage around his hand. Reuben saw the glint of the knife
blade. He reached for it.

When Domingo looked around Reuben was back on his feet,
the knife held in his left hand. His expression changed from anger
to disbelief. 'What the hell are you doing?'

'You do know something.'

'Even if I did. What good will it do now?'

'I'm dying. I have a tumour on the liver. The doctors can't do
anything for me. So I don't care what happens to me any more, I
just want to know what happened to my daughters. If you know
something, for God's sake, tell me.'

'Why?'

'Because I've suffered for twenty years. That's long enough.'

'You haven't suffered like Rosa suffered.' Domingo returned
his attentions to his injured hand. 'Stick it in my back if you like.
That's the kind of thing I'd expect from you. Fuck you. I don't
know anything.'

Reuben slipped down the cement wall on to his haunches. He
put his head on his knees and wept.

Domingo stepped over him and started to walk away.

77

Domingo was almost at the stairwell when he stopped and turned around. 'What if I *did* know something?'

'For God's sake. Please.'

Domingo stood there for a long time, silhouetted by the light from the stairwell. When he spoke again his voice was so soft Reuben could hardly hear him. 'His name was Barrington. Stephen Barrington. You remember him? He lived in the apartment next door. Somehow he saved one of your girls. I don't know which one. I let him take her, God forgive me. I had no choice. I couldn't even feed the kids I had. He gave her a far better life than I ever could.'

So. At least one of them was alive. Was this what he wanted to hear? Or, rather, what he had dreaded? 'You knew. All this time.'

Domingo shrugged his shoulders. 'What difference does it make? I don't know what happened to him, or your daughter. The other twin, I don't know, maybe she's dead, maybe one of the army took her. You know the things they did in those days. For God's sake, that's it. Let it be. You won't do her any favours if you show up now, even if you did find her.'

'But I have to find her. I have to.'

Domingo swore at the pain in his hand. 'Fuck you. Look what you've done. I can't work like this.'

Reuben fumbled in his wallet. 'Here. Take something. For medical expenses. For your family.'

'Fuck you and your money. I'd rather choke on dog vomit than take anything from you now.'

'Please, Domingo. Forgive me. For everything.'

'Never. Not if I live to be a hundred years old.'

And he was gone.

*   *   *

Reuben stood in his hotel bathroom and slipped off his clothes. God alone knew what the concierge and the other guests in the lobby had thought when he staggered in from the street, blood and dirt all over his suit. He showered, slipped on a dressing gown and rang room service. He ordered a bottle of Malbec with his dinner. He had decided to get drunk. A celebration, of sorts.

Barrington. The name stirred vague memories, but he could not put a face to it. He had met the man and his wife a few times in the elevator and the lobby. He remembered he was British, the representative of some English company in Buenos Aires. That was all he remembered.

He rang down to the concierge and asked for a copy of the telephone directory to be sent up to his room. When it arrived he put it down by the window and went through the private listings for Barrington. There were none.

He drank the bottle of Malbec and tried desperately to recall the name of the company Barrington worked for. But it was no good. After his solitary dinner he went into the bathroom and vomited. He stared at his reflection in the bathroom mirror in the harsh light of the fluorescent strip above the vanity unit. He was losing weight and there was a faint yellowish tinge to his skin.

He looked into the eyes that stared back at him from the mirror. Why are you doing this? he asked himself. Is it for you, or for them? 'Every child has a right to know their father,' he said aloud, as if trying to convince himself.

But in truth he knew why he had embarked on this search. He was looking for forgiveness. *Still thinking of me first, after all this time. Nothing has changed.*

He sat bolt upright in bed. 'It was a publishing company,' he said aloud, and fumbled for the switch on the bedside lamp. He looked at his watch. Almost three o'clock.

He got out of bed, found the telephone directory on the table next to the window. He checked the names of all the publishing companies with offices in Buenos Aires. Ah, there it was. University Publishing. That was it, he was sure of it. He copied down the address and the telephone number.

He could not sleep. He sat there by the window all night, anxious for the dawn.

*   *   *

The office was on Paraguay and Junin. There was a display window with medical and scientific textbooks and manuals and a glass door that led to a carpeted reception area. Beyond the reception was a strip-lit office with cheap partitions. A young Argentine in a suit and tie saw him and came out.

He told him he was looking for an old friend; that his name was Stephen Barrington, and that he had once worked for the company. The man asked him to wait. A few minutes later another man came out of the back office. He was older and dressed in a grey suit and dark blue rugby club tie. He spoke Spanish with a pronounced English accent.

When Reuben told him his business he appeared a little wary. 'Barrington, you say? A friend of yours?'

'That's right. I believe he used to work for you.'

He looked amused. 'Yes, he is still with the company. He's our managing director.'

Reuben tried to conceal his excitement.

'Look, I can't give you his personal address. Company policy. But I can give you the address and telephone number of our head office in Oxford. You can write him a letter, ring him there, whatever you like. If you're old friends I'm sure he'll be delighted to hear from you.' He gave Reuben a white printed card with the address and telephone number of the company's English headquarters printed on it.

Reuben assured him he would call. He tucked the card carefully in his wallet and went back to his hotel. He immediately checked out his luggage, drove to the airport and caught the next flight to London Heathrow.

He slept on the plane, dreamed of his daughter, a girl with dark eyes, like Rosa. She was standing on the bridge at Avellaneda in the misty darkness, the yellow glow of a lamp throwing an aura of light behind her. She had her arms open and she was beckoning him. He fell into her embrace, she stroked his hair and they wept.

78

Rome

The air had turned cold. Manger scenes, what the Romans called *presepi*, had begun to appear in the churches and piazzas. The *Befana*, the Christmas market, had opened in the Piazza Navona, the square alive with balloons, the stalls glittering with festive decorations.

Turturro sat in front of the television in his vest and shorts, watching the Premio Roma from the Ippodromo delle Capannelle. It was cloyingly hot in the small apartment. A two-bar electric heater and a white saucer, full of cigarette ash, lay on the carpet by his feet. He swore as the horses flashed across the screen. Not even a place. One afternoon off a week and all I do is lose more money. He tore up the gambling slip and dropped the pieces on to the floor. He wrinkled his nostrils at the stale stink of his own sweat.

People had been afraid of him once. Now what was there left for him? He deserved better than this. He put his hand down his shorts and massaged his erection. It had been a long time since he had been able to afford a woman. He remembered those days at the barracks at Ezeiza and smiled.

He had done whatever he had wanted then.

He thought about Angeli, all the money he had, and here he was paying him shit. Well, things were going to change. He knew all about his dirty little secrets and now Angeli was going to start rewarding him properly for his loyalty.

A diffuse light filtered through the white net curtains on the high windows. Salvatore had often considered that Heaven itself would be backlit with this same intense, milky light that illuminated the Under-Secretary of State's office. He sometimes wondered, too, if St Peter would have three telephones on his desk and a large wooden crucifix on the white wall above it.

He fidgeted in the straight-backed Renaissance chair as His Eminence read the single-spaced typewritten report in his hands.

It had been prepared for the Secretariat by a concerned official in a bank called the Credito Cattolica Privata. It was a small and largely inconsequential institution except for the fact that its majority shareholder was the Institute for Religious Works, the Vatican Bank.

The IOR, far from being an institute for religious works, was one of the largest players in the world money markets. It had funded, among other projects, Washington's Watergate complex, and held real estate and stock portfolios valued in billions of dollars.

It was also, thanks to a deal done in 1929 between Mussolini and Pope Pius X, immune to Italian banking laws.

The report Comacho held in his hands detailed how the IOR had channelled tens of millions of dollars to a Swiss holding company called Belgrano AG. The money, the report noted, was then wired to a branch of the Banco Cattolica di Argentina Overseas (Ltd) in Nassau, whose main shareholders were César Gregorini and Archbishop Stanislaw Tomaszcewski.

The report further speculated on the source of the money. The author claimed that the funds were profits derived from cocaine and weapons deals put together by this César Gregorini and financed with loans from the IOR.

Don Cardinal Comacho took off his spectacles and placed them carefully on his desk beside the typed report. The two men looked at each other.

'What does this mean?' Salvatore said.

'It means those entrusted with the finances of the Church have learned nothing from the scandals of the eighties.'

Salvatore knew he was referring to the Banco Ambrosiano scandal, when the Vatican had lost over a hundred million dollars investing money in a crooked bank. 'Does the Holy Father not know about this?' he asked.

Comacho pursed his lips and did not answer.

'And he does nothing?'

'I do not know if he knows or not. But the stewardship of the IOR is a papal appointment.'

'But what does Tomaszcewski want with all this money?'

'One of his predecessors had a saying: "You cannot run the Church on Hail Marys." He thinks what he does is for the best.'

'With money from drugs, from weapons? It is tainted with blood.'

'You are naïve, Paolo. It is what makes you a good person. It is also what makes you unsuited for Rome.'

'Then what are we to do?'

Don Enrique Cardinal Comacho considered. He had been appointed to the College of Cardinals by Gianpaolo in 1986, and had been made Prefect of the Congregation for Religious and Secular Institutes. He had risen to his present rank of Under-Secretary of State despite the fact that the Curia suspected him of being a liberal; a terrible stain on his character which was confirmed for them when he made Salvatore his private secretary.

But Comacho was above all else a conciliator and a consummate politician. He only fought those battles he knew he could win. That was how he had attained his present exalted rank.

'We shall do nothing,' he said. 'Because, Paolo, there is nothing we can do.'

Angeli took the steps two at a time, left the bedlam of the Corso Vittorio Emanuele behind as he entered the echoing vault of San'Andrea della Valle. The day's last sunlight filtered in through high windows in dusty yellow shafts. He sat down in one of the pews, folded his hands neatly in his lap. Cold in here, cold as the grave. Christ stared back at him, face drawn in agony on his cross. He knew about agony. How many times had he pinned men to an iron table in similar fashion?

He had never liked this particular church, it was too gloomy and dark, but he was always drawn to it when the black dog was on his back. He closed his eyes. Puccini had set the first act of *Tosca* here. This was where the escaped prisoner, Angelotti, had come to hide, where the police chief had come in pursuit. He closed his eyes, heard Puccini's soaring arias, heard Cavaradossi's screams from the torture chamber.

His eyes snapped open. Sweat erupted like cold grease on his forehead. Opera was opera. Life was life.

He wished only to put away his memories. He was nearly sixty years old and the vista of his own life was no longer a broad flat plain with limitless horizons. Some things you did when you were a young man were more troubling as you got older.

But he had no regrets. He had done his duty in the best interests of his country, had protected the Church and served his God faithfully. Sometimes a man was called on to do those things that a priest could not do. The answers were simple. Countries needed strong leaders who would act in the best interests of all. Men like himself. He had protected his Church and his country at its time of darkest danger, knew in his heart he was a hero.

It should have been enough. But still the spectre of his own death clung to him like a damp and clinging mist.

As he was about to leave he passed a statue of the Virgin and Child and for some reason he found himself thinking of the Altman woman again. He pushed away thoughts of his own judgment and hurried out through the heavy door, back into the world of light, and traffic, and noise.

79

A chill fine morning. The white Mercedes was parked on the cobbles outside Laura Biagiotti on the Via Borgognona. Angeli sat in the back seat, wrapped against the cold in a David Cenci overcoat, reading *L'Osservatore Romano*. The rest of that morning's newspapers were folded on the seat beside him. The car's engine was running, the heater on. His driver, Marco, was buffing the coachwork with a soft cloth.

Angeli saw Turturro appear through the crowd, wearing a brown leather jacket, his pants too tight for his fat gut. He had the look of a cheap gangster, which, Angeli supposed, was what he was. He opened the door and slid into the back seat.

Angeli recoiled at the smell of sweat and tobacco that accompanied him. There was a web of broken veins on his nose, a slight but definite tremor in his hands.

This was the fourth time he had agreed to meet with Turturro. On each occasion he told him this was the last time. But Turturro always came back, demanding an even more outrageous sum of money to keep silent.

He was drunk, he could smell it on his breath. 'So. How is life treating you, Colonel?'

Angeli did not look up from his newspaper. 'I'm not going to discuss anything about my life with shit like you. What do you want?'

'I need another loan.'

Angeli put down the newspaper. 'How much this time?' He wondered again if Turturro really did have an envelope tucked away somewhere or if it was all an elaborate charade. Was all this really worth it, anyway? There was a time when he didn't give a damn what polite society thought of him. Since he had been in Rome he had grown accustomed to the cocktail parties and the opening nights at the opera and invitations to embassy dinners. Everyone knew he was an arms dealer. That had never been any obstacle to his entrée in polite society. But to be revealed as a torturer and assassin, while no longer indictable, would make him a social pariah, even among those who privately sympathised with him.

And there was still his daughter to consider.

'I need one hundred million lire.'

Angeli laughed and went back to his papers.

Turturro looked offended. Pride took over and his eyes became sulky. 'I have gambling debts.'

'That is no problem of mine.'

'I could make it your problem.' Turturro ran a finger under his shirt collar as if it were too tight for him. A muscle in his cheek jerked. 'You've been getting away cheap. You've given me small change so far. Now I want proper payment. Give me what I want and I'll give you the files and we'll have an end to it.'

Angeli experienced a swell of anger. This piece of shit. Who does he think he's talking to?

'If you don't, I'll see how much some magazine editor will pay me for those files.'

The files. How could it happen that someone like Turturro was given the final responsibility for shredding them? Or was he bluffing? Had the files been destroyed after all, as he had ordered?

'If I give you a hundred million lire, what will you do? In another six months you'll need more money. You throw everything away on brandy and bookmakers. You're one of life's losers, Turturro. I'm not giving you another penny.'

'What will your pretty daughter say when she reads about the things you did?' His voice was shrill.

'I'm not giving you another penny.'

'I'll tell them everything. I mean it. You remember that woman you shot in the head? The way her brains sprayed up the wall? That should get you a few paragraphs in *La Repubblica* even. What will your daughter think of you then? And your wife?'

'My wife already knows,' Angeli growled. 'As for everyone else they'll never believe you. Look at you. You're a drunk, a gambler, a loser; who will pay any attention to you?'

'You're a fucking murderer and I can prove it.'

Angeli saw his wife come out of the showroom with two shopping bags. 'Get out,' he said to Turturro.

'I'll fucking show you!' Turturro shouted back at him. At Angeli's signal Marco opened the back door and hauled him out of the car. He threw him on to the footpath, at the feet of some startled shoppers. Francesca, to her credit, hardly broke her stride. She stepped adroitly over him and climbed into the back of the Mercedes, the seat already warmed by Turturro's ample behind. She was still chatting to a friend on her mobile telephone.

'George's,' Angeli said to Marco as he got behind the wheel.

Turturro got to his feet and made an obscene gesture through the passenger-side window as they drove away.

I will have to do something about you very soon.

Very soon indeed.

80

Simone hurried through the glass doors of the apartment. There was ice on the cobblestones. She zipped up the mauve ski jacket and hefted the day pack on to her shoulder, at the same time fumbling in her pocket for the keys to the Lancia parked in the courtyard.

She stopped. Someone had slipped a brown manila envelope under the windscreen wiper of her car. She opened it, puzzled. Inside were some photostat pages. She flipped through them quickly. Some appeared to be taken from a handwritten ledger, others had photographs, printed forms with typewritten inserts.

'I thought you might like to give those to your father,' a voice said.

She turned around. A heavy-set, balding man in a leather jacket and thick black polo-neck sweater stood in the arched gateway, his hands in the pockets of the jacket. It was early in the morning, not yet seven, but she detected the taint of grappa on his breath. She felt a thrill of fear.

'What is this?'

'Like I told you. It is something for your father. Your father, the fucking murderer.'

The little bitch was terrified. Good. He could see her measuring the distance to the apartment door, wondering whether to run or brazen it out. He grinned, enjoying her discomfort.

The grappa in the hip flask in his pocket had made him feel brave and truculent. He didn't want any shit from this girl. He had taken enough from her father.

'What did you say?'

'Have another look at what's in the envelope. Do you know what your *papito* did in the Dirty War? You must have guessed. Don't tell me Colonel Angeli's little girl is that fucking stupid.'

'I don't know what you're talking about.'

'I'm talking about your father's career in the army. Ask him how many of the junta's enemies he disappeared. How many leftists he tortured and murdered.'

'He had nothing to do with that.'

'Is that what he told you?'

She was just standing there, staring at him, her face the colour of chalk. Poor stupid little rich girl. 'Don't look so shocked. Go on. Look at that stuff. It's his file from the Command Action Group. Did he ever tell you about that? The other stuff is good night-time reading. They're our records of interrogation. You'll notice all of our clients ended up one way.'

'I don't believe you.'

'Of course you do. You just don't want to hear it.'

She backed away towards the glass doors. 'Why are you telling me this?'

'Don't you want to know what a big hero he was?'

'Who are you?'

'My name's Turturro. Sergeant Raoul Turturro. Ask him, he'll remember me. I was there. I worked for him. I wasn't a sadist like some of them. I just did the paperwork. I helped a lot of them, massaged their legs and arms after they had been tortured with the electricity. I tried to stop the worst of it. Sometimes your father tortured them so badly they couldn't speak, their voices had gone they had been screaming so hard . . .'

'Shut up!'

'There were a lot of bad ones, but he was the worst. Sometimes he stayed in the torture room for twenty-four hours, sometimes more. He'd go home but a couple of hours later he'd be back again. He couldn't stay away. He loved it. Sometimes, if we were interrogating young girls, maybe the same age as you are now, he'd make the doctor and everyone else leave the room and lock the door. I don't know what he did in there, but when we came back in the girls were dripping wet.' He leered at her. 'You know, down there.' He lowered his voice. 'He'd fuck them then he'd shoot them in the head!'

She turned and fumbled with the security lock on the apartment door. If he had wanted to, he could have stopped her, made her listen to more. Instead he just stood there, his hands in his pockets, watching her. He almost felt sorry for her.

The door clanged shut. A kitten darted away into the shadows.

He turned and walked back towards the piazza. He felt a curious sense of anticlimax. Baiting her hadn't been as much fun as he had thought. In fact he felt suddenly nauseous. He had imagined this moment for so long, clung to this fantasy of revenge so desperately, that now it was done he felt curiously empty and afraid.

Angeli was in the dining room, eating lunch alone; Francesca had gone to her health club. His housekeeper, Fulvia, had prepared *coda alla vaccinara* served with a half-bottle of Barolo. He heard the front door slam, looked up in surprise.

As soon as he saw her he knew something was wrong. She was breathing hard, as if she had been running. Her face was flushed, her eyes unfocused. His first thought was that she had been in a car accident or had been attacked in the street.

He jumped up and put his arms around her. She was cold, her body as unyielding as marble. '*Cara*. What's wrong?'

She did not respond.

'Simone?'

'Why did we leave Argentina?' she asked him in a voice he barely recognised.

At once he realised what had happened: Turturro. He felt a numbing chill in his heart and cursed himself for a fool. He had underestimated the man's vindictiveness. And vastly overestimated his intelligence.

'Papa?'

'I have told you many times. After the Malvinas . . .'

'You're lying to me.' She shook herself free, stood with her back against the wall. There was a strange light in her eyes.

'*Cara*. What are you saying?'

'This man was at my apartment. He said he knew you. He gave me this.' She threw a brown manila envelope on the table. Angeli picked it up, flicked through the photostat pages inside. Son of a whore. Turturro had not been bluffing.

'Did you enjoy it?'

'Enjoy? Enjoy what?'

'Enjoy torturing all those people. Those girls.'

He stared at her for a long time. 'You are not well. I am going to call the doctor.' He went to pick up the telephone.

Simone threw the papers at him. They scattered on the floor. 'What is this all about?'

'Simone?'

'He said you were in charge of one of the death squads. He said he used to work for you.'

'What?'

'Is it true?'

He ran a hand across his face. When he spoke again his voice was very soft. 'How can you ask me this question? What sort of a man do you think I am?'

'He said he took orders from you at one of the detention centres. That you were his commander.'

'You believe him?'

'I don't know! Who was he?'

'*Cara.*' He stepped towards her, his arms open.

'Don't touch me.' She backed away. 'He said you tortured people. He said you raped the girls and murdered them when you were finished with them.'

'You believe these lies?'

'Are they lies?'

'Of course! Of course they are lies! You think your father is a monster?'

'I don't know. I don't know!'

'Did this man give you his name?'

'Yes. I think so. I can't remember.'

'Because, you know, a man, especially a wealthy man, gains many enemies in a lifetime. There are many people who would like to hurt me. They can hurt me most of all through you.'

Simone pointed to the papers scattered on the floor. 'But what about those!'

He sighed, let his arms hang limp at his sides, a gesture of resignation. 'I was in charge of some of the arrests. All right. Yes. But what happened after that . . . that was not my concern. We were fighting a war. That is what you have to understand. The important thing was gathering information. The people I arrested, they were not civilians. The Montoneros bombed our barracks, I had seen my friends and their wives and their children blown to pieces. These people were evil. But I did not torture or murder anyone. I just did my job.'

She shook her head. She wanted so much to believe him.

'It is the truth. Please.'

The tears came then. He held her in his arms, felt the great juddering sobs course through her body. He kissed her, held her, stroked her hair.

'I am innocent of these things,' he whispered. 'You must believe me. I give you my word. I am innocent.'

81

Turturro hurried across the echoing departure hall towards the Alitalia desk, his luggage on a stainless steel trolley, the carpet bag with its precious contents draped over his left shoulder. A flight was leaving for Milan in half an hour and he intended to be on it. Now he had sobered up, he was cursing himself for his impetuosity.

He was so preoccupied with his self-recrimination that he did not notice the two policemen until they were just a few yards away. The white cross-belt on their uniforms and the red stripes on their trousers indentified them as carabinieri.

'Turturro?' one of them said. 'Raoul Turturro?'

He felt an oily spread of panic in his guts. These men are not police, he thought. Nothing in their manner or their dress betrayed them. But one of them looked vaguely familiar. He knew.

He tried to run but one of them grabbed him and wrestled him to the ground. Everyone in the terminus was staring and he shouted for help. But even as he did it he realised no one was going to interfere with two policemen going about their business. It was the same psychology that had enabled their Command Action Group to abduct so many people in broad daylight in Buenos Aires; no one challenges authority, no one wants to become a victim too.

They frogmarched him towards the doors. He heard himself calling out to people to call the police, even though he knew how ridiculous that must sound. Faces were staring at him with those particular expressions of revulsion reserved for madmen. It was hopeless. He was lost.

There was a dark blue Fiat parked in the forecourt, a beacon on its roof, CARABINIERI written on the doors in large white letters. They handcuffed him and bundled him into the back seat.

One of the carabinieri went back inside the terminus to retrieve the cap he had lost in the struggle and the carpet bag Turturro had dropped. Turturro recognised him now. It was Angeli's driver.

He saw one of the airport security men hand Marco the carpet bag.

His colleague jumped behind the wheel of the Fiat. 'I wouldn't be in your shoes for anything,' he said to Turturro. 'Signor Gregorini is a very unhappy man.'

A fool was a fool for life, Angeli thought. You could never save a man from himself. Greed, anger, lust, these were the true sins. And they led you to disaster.

The room was over a garage and machine repair works. It reminded him of one of the detention centres they had used in Buenos Aires, at Orletti. In those days they had owned the garage themselves, had a corporal race the engines to cover the sound of the screams when there was a torture session in progress. But this would do just as well.

He ran up the flight of metal steps to a padlocked wooden door. He took a key from his pocket, unlocked it and went inside.

Turturro woke to the smell of oil and grease, the howl of a revving engine. He could not move his arms or legs. When he moved his head he felt as if he was going to vomit.

He remembered now. Those bastards had injected him with some sort of drug in the back of their fake police car.

There was someone standing over him, but he could not see him clearly, his vision still blurred.

'You still think it was a good idea to say those things to my daughter?'

Por Dios. Angeli.

He wanted to sit up, but his wrists and ankles were tied to some sort of frame. He tried to scream. There was something in his mouth and no sound came. His own panic threatened to overwhelm him. He thought he was going to faint.

Angeli yawned, a release of tension rather than fatigue. He looked around.

There were four bare brick walls, no windows. The room was lit by a single bulb hanging on a worn piece of flex. Old car parts, rusted exhausts, empty oil cans, ancient carburettors, a dented mudguard, all piled in one corner. A bed frame and a single chair, both metal, had been placed in the middle. A brand-new battery-operated cassette player sat on the dusty floorboards, its newness in jarring contrast to everything else in that room.

Turturro was spreadeagled on the bed frame, his wrists and ankles secured with thick wire. He was naked. He looked, Angeli thought, like some hairy whale. His genitals, blue and frozen by cold and fear, looked ridiculous, dwarfed by the flaccid mound of his belly. There was a gag over his mouth and his nostrils flared as he tried to breathe. His eyes were as big as soup plates and even in the dank chill of the room Angeli could smell the sweat coming off him. The scent reminded him of the barracks at Ezeiza, poignant as the perfume of an old lover.

Angeli was carrying a briefcase. He set it on the floor and sat down on the chair beside the bed, crossing his legs. He leaned back, making himself comfortable. 'Well, my friend. How many times have you done this to someone? Now it's your turn.'

'Do you remember the old days?' Angeli was saying. 'You used to have a lot of fun with the *picana*.'

Turturro was shaking his head.

'You don't remember? Or you don't want to remember? Or are you trying to tell me something else?' He shook his head, like a teacher with a recalcitrant pupil. 'I did not kill you straight away, I gave you a little money, I was indulgent. But you were greedy. You tried to ruin my life. You have no gratitude.' He smiled. 'Gratitude is not something we are born with. It must be learned.' He leaned forward and lowered his voice. 'I am going to remove the gag for a moment. But if you scream, I shall have to hurt you. Do you understand?'

Turturro nodded his head, desperately.

Angeli pressed the 'play' button on the cassette recorder. A precaution in case Turturro made too much noise. He turned up the volume. Abba: 'Dancing Queen'. Turturro's eyes darted frantically in his head, trying to understand the significance of the music. It was a joke, of course. But the joke was on him.

Angeli ripped off the sticking plaster, pulled the rag out of Turturro's mouth.

The words came in a rush, like popping the cork from a bottle of champagne. 'Please don't hurt me, don't hurt me, don't kill me.

I have a lawyer. He has copies of everything. Anything happens to me, he sends them to all the newspapers. Just let me go, I'll give you everything. I swear . . .'

Angeli did not have time for this. He stuffed the rag back in Turturro's mouth and snapped off the cassette player. 'What you are telling me could be true or it could be bullshit.' He snapped open the briefcase, took out a handful of yellowing pieces of paper. 'These were in your bag at the airport.' He flicked through them, as if seeing them for the first time. There were career files on dozens of officers and enlisted men in the Command Action Group that he had once directed. There were also records of interrogation of some of their victims, enough to do him considerable damage in the public arena should they find their way into the wrong hands. Already some of these documents had damaged his relationship with his own daughter. How much damage, time alone would tell.

He held up one of the pages. There it was, his own face staring back at him, unsmiling, from a black-and-white photograph, together with his service record, official and unofficial. How had Turturro smuggled these out? He would not have given him credit for such ingenuity.

'Originals,' he said. 'Now if I were you, these are the ones I would have lodged with a lawyer.' He nodded slowly, his lips pursed, as if considering some deep mathematical problem. 'But perhaps you did make copies and had *those* lodged somewhere. Perhaps. But how can I be sure?'

He leaned over and from his briefcase produced a neatly folded butcher's apron. He put it on. Then he snapped on a pair of white rubber gloves. The last item he produced was a filleting knife.

Turturro's chest was heaving. Angeli heard a high keening sound escaping the gag. He leaned over the bed and turned the blade under Turturro's eyes, so that it caught the light. 'Do you see this? You used to have one like this. Do you remember?'

Turturro was bucking up and down on the bed, his belly quivering like jelly.

'Listen to me, Turturro. Are you listening?' The bucking stopped. He leaned across him. 'Now, it's very simple. I am going to remove the gag. If you scream I shall castrate you. Do you understand?'

Turturro nodded. There was sweat running down his face, into his eyes.

'I am going to ask you if there are any copies, and if there are, I want you to tell me the name of the person you gave them to. If you don't tell me, I shall replace the gag and cut off two of your toes. Just like that. Do you understand?'

Angeli pressed 'play' on the cassette player. He hummed along with the tune. Turturro fouled himself. The stench filled the room.

Angeli removed the gag.

Turturro answered in a babble of Spanish and Italian, his voice no more than a squeak. 'Please, Colonel, it was a bluff, there was no lawyer, please, please, believe me, there is no one, please don't hurt me, you have everything, I didn't give anything to—'

Angeli replaced the gag. He sat very still for a moment, considering. Then he carefully removed two of the toes on Turturro's left foot. It was a disgusting business and he was glad when it was done. Meanwhile Turturro had fainted.

Angeli sat down, waited patiently in the chair, listening to the steady drip of blood on the floor. Finally he grew impatient and woke him, digging his fingernails into Turturro's earlobe.

Turturro's eyes were rolling around in his head, the muscles in his bloated white body quivering under the disgusting mat of hair. Angeli screwed his face up in distaste and removed the gag.

'No lawyer,' Turturro mumbled, 'believe . . . no lawyer . . . please.'

Angeli replaced the gag once more. 'I don't believe you. I am going to castrate you now.' Turturro bucked and rocked on the bed. Angeli waited until he had exhausted himself. Then he leaned forward, squeezed Turturro's testicles in his fist, ensuring that he had a good grip. He removed the gag. 'Is there anything you want to tell me?'

Turturro let loose a babble of words: 'No, please, believe me, there are no copies, please don't, please, please, please, please . . .'

Angeli made one small incision with his knife and Turturro fainted again.

He was satisfied. If there was a lawyer somewhere, with photocopies, Turturro would have broken. He was convinced there was nothing now to connect him to the past.

He replaced the gag and turned off the cassette player. He roused Turturro, who immediately started moaning and crying. 'It's all right, they're still there,' Angeli told him, knowing he could not see over the great bulge of his belly.

He snapped off the gloves and removed the apron. Then he picked up the files. 'Now I want you to eat these,' he said. He leaned forward and stuffed the first sheet of paper into Turturro's mouth.

It took the best part of three hours. He had to go downstairs several times and fill an old wine bottle with water from a rusted tap to help Turturro swallow them all down. He kept his own file, with its pasted photograph, for the final act.

When it was done he let Turturro's head sag back on to the frame and replaced the gag for the final time. Then he stood up, snapped shut the briefcase and picked up the cassette player. 'Turturro, you are a fool. I gave you a few lire because I felt sorry for you. I threw money at you like I would throw coins at a beggar. You do not think I feared you for one moment? You wanted to play with me, now we have played and I have won. I hope you understand.'

It stank in here. Faeces and blood. He wondered how he had endured the smell all those years at Ezeiza. Back then he had been paid to do a job, to shield decent people from such things. He supposed, in a way, it was a higher calling. Almost like the priesthood.

'I will say goodbye to you now,' Angeli said. 'We will not be talking to each other again. I shall now give you some time to reflect on your treachery.'

And he went out, padlocking the door behind him.

82

Near Gatwick Airport, England

It was the phone call he had always dreaded. His secretary patched it through to his mobile from his office. He was on his way to Kent on the M25 but when he heard the man's name and recognised the accent he pulled his Range Rover on to the hard shoulder and stopped the engine.

The car shook as a heavy lorry roared past. 'Who did you say you were?'

'My name is Altman, Reuben Altman. We were neighbours in Buenos Aires in 1976.'

His heart hammered painfully against his ribs. 'Where are you calling from?'

'I am in London, señor. I came here from Argentina to see you.'

His mind raced. Stall him somehow. 'To see me?'

'Don't you remember me?'

'Should I? It was a very long time ago.'

'I would like very much to see you. I believe it is important.'

'Yes. Well, I'm not sure that's possible. What did you want to see me about?' There was a long silence on the other end of the line. 'Mr Altman?'

'It is about my daughter. I think you know what I mean. Please, Señor Barrington. I don't want to do anyone any harm. I just need to talk to you. Please.'

After so long, having this happen, out of the blue. First this business in Rome, then Luke. Now this. The fabric of his life was unravelling.

The car shook as another lorry roared past. He sat there, staring at the brown fields, rutted with frost. The downland on this side of the road had been fenced with post and wire, a NO

TRESPASSING sign nailed to a nearby oak. *No trespassing*. You could fence off a field, you couldn't fence off a life, no matter how hard you tried.

'Señor Barrington?'

'Have you got a pen there? I'd better give you the address.'

Stephen cancelled the rest of that day's appointments and drove back to Market Dene. It was just after midday. He found Mercedes in the kitchen, holding a book in one hand, stirring the soup on the stove with the other. A Joanna Trollope novel.

She was still in her dressing gown.

She looked at him over the rim of her spectacles. 'Good *Lord*. Whatever's *wrong*. You're white as a *ghost*.'

He set his briefcase on the table. 'Is there any tea?'

'The pot's still warm. Stephen, what are you doing home at *this* time of the day?'

There were times when this fragile bird of a woman seemed so imperturbable. He had once imagined telling her that World War III had started. 'Oh *dear*,' he had pictured her saying, 'whatever do you think they were *thinking* of,' and she would return her attention to the book on her lap. He supposed it was all part of the distance she had created between herself and the world; like her afternoon naps, her voracious reading, her migraines. She still had not grieved for Luke, had not even wept at the funeral.

'I have some news.' He went to the worktop, poured some tea into a cup with milk and three sugars. Then he changed his mind, went to the cupboard and took down a bottle of single malt. He splashed some into a glass.

Mercedes watched him down the length of her nose. 'Nothing bad, I hope.'

'I had a phone call today.' He downed half of the whisky. Her eyebrows went up.

'Well, are you going to *tell* me, or do I just stand here and *die* of curiosity?'

'It was a man. Spoke good English. Heavy accent. Claimed to be Gabriella's father.'

The spoon disappeared into the soup. Mercedes closed her book and laid it on the counter-top beside the range. Her face went ashen and for a moment he thought she was about to faint. For a long time neither of them spoke.

'What did you *tell* him?'

A shrug of the shoulders. 'What could I tell him?'

She put one hand on her hip, a combative stance familiar to him through many of their fights, the signal for him to retreat. But this time he could not withdraw, his boats were already burned. 'Stephen. You *didn't*.'

'What would you have me do?'

She took off her glasses. 'You *stupid* bastard.'

There had been many fights over the years. No more, no less, than any other marriage, he supposed; fights over money, over the children, over sex. Especially over sex. But she had never sworn at him, had never resorted to name-calling. He found it juvenile and shocking. 'I couldn't lie to him. She's almost twenty years old now, for God's sake. What are you afraid of?'

The fight went out of her, suddenly. One arm fell to her side, the other clung to the worktop, as if for support. 'We could lose those twenty *years*. Oh, damn you, Stephen. *Damn* you. You don't understand, *do* you?'

'He's coming down tomorrow morning. I gave him our address.'

She shook her head, bestowed on him the same look she had given Luke or Gabriella when they were children and they had spilled the milk over the tablecloth or dropped the sugar jar on the floor. 'Couldn't you *lie*?'

He swirled the whisky in the glass. 'Why should I do that?'

'Oh, Stephen.' She picked up her glasses and her book and turned to leave the room. She stopped in the doorway. 'If we lose our little girl, I'll *never* forgive you. You do *know* that?'

And she walked out.

83

Reuben consulted his map and took the A34 on to Oxford. The morning sky was overcast, the air bitingly cold, there was mud-stained slush and ice beside the road. He wiped at the condensation on the windscreen of the rented Range Rover. How did people live in such a climate? He saw a sign: Market Dene, two miles. Exhaust fumes formed a little cloud on the still air as he changed down the gears to negotiate a steep incline. As he reached the crest of the hill he saw a brass plate attached to one of a pair of ancient and imposing red brick gateposts: *The Gables*.

Up ahead the yellow glow of a lamp through a latticed window, a thin skein of smoke rising from a red brick chimney. The Range Rover's tyres crunched on frozen, rutted mud. He parked by the stables and got out, his breath crystallising on the air, rising in thin, white trails of vapour. The surrounding fields were dusted with frost and he was afforded a glimpse of the snow-dusted downs beyond the house before the mist rolled in again.

His heart was bounding in his chest. Barrington had not made it clear if Gabriella would be here to meet him. He had rehearsed what he was going to say over and over but suddenly his mind was blank. He fought the urge to get back in the car and drive away.

Domingo was right. What did he hope to achieve?

He did not recognise them. He supposed there was no reason why he should.

Stephen Barrington was a tall, distinguished-looking man with trimmed, grey hair. He was dressed in a dark suit with a polo-necked jumper underneath. His wife stood beside him, close but not touching, neat and compact in a dark blue tailored suit with a white silk blouse. They looked as if they were mourners at a funeral.

They welcomed him at the door with excruciating formality and led the way inside.

They showed him into what they called the drawing room. It was dominated by a huge mantelpiece lined with framed photographs and sporting an expensive ormolu clock. There was a log fire crackling in the grate but it barely took the chill from the room. Winged armchairs were ranged around the hearth and Persian rugs were scattered around the floor. There were framed watercolours on the cream-and-gold-striped walls.

'How was your journey?'

The English, Reuben thought. Always so polite. These people assuredly hate me and would like to toss me bodily into a ditch. But they make small talk so easily.

'I was very careful. Because of the ice.'

'We thought you might get lost,' the woman said, with heavy irony.

'I asked for your house in the post office. They knew you straight away. Their directions were very clear.'

'The house has been in my family for a long time,' Stephen said. 'The name's well known in the village. Would you like some tea?'

A table had been set by the window, laid out with a formal English tea. There were pastries on doilies, a silver teapot, a lace cloth edged with pink flowers. Reuben sat by the window. As Mercedes poured the tea he stared at the photographs on the mantelpiece: one of the Barringtons, taken outside the house, apparently quite recently; beside it another much older photograph, monochrome in a heavy silver frame. He recognised the Plaza de Mayo in the background.

There were others, portraits and holiday snaps of varying age. A young woman featured in several of them. I wonder if it's her? he thought. It had to be. The resemblance to Rosa was uncanny: the same mane of dark hair, the brown eyes, heart-shaped mouth. It was an effort of will to tear his gaze away and when he turned back to his hosts they were both staring at him. Reuben felt abashed, as if they had caught him pocketing their silverware.

After Mercedes had poured the tea, and Reuben had politely accepted one of the proffered pastries, Stephen leaned forward, his fingers steepled in front of him. 'You've come about Gabriella.'

Reuben was relieved that all pretence had finally been shunted aside. 'My daughters were named Eva and Simone.' He looked from one to the other. 'You know she *is* my daughter?'

Mercedes put her face in her hands. Stephen sighed as if a great burden had been lifted from his shoulders.

Suddenly there was nothing to say. He had feared that they would lie to him, try to deny him in some way. But now the tension drained out of him and he felt quite empty. 'Is she well?' he said. That sounded ridiculous. He could not believe he had said it. But he could not think of anything else to say.

'She's at university.' Stephen hesitated. 'Cambridge. She's an extremely intelligent young girl. We're very proud of her.' He stopped himself, almost as if that were the wrong thing to say. 'We haven't told her yet. About you, I mean.'

He nodded. 'I see.' He took a deep breath. 'There's one thing I have to know. They were twins. My other daughter . . .'

Their faces told him what he wanted to know. So, one of them was gone for ever.

There was a long silence.

'How did you find us?' Stephen asked.

'It's a long story. My brother-in-law Domingo told me about you.'

Stephen nodded. 'Yes, we remember him.'

'Why *now*?' Mercedes asked.

How do I explain it? 'I have been in exile. I did not see him for many years.' It was part of the truth. He did not know how to explain all of it.

Mercedes' cup rattled in its saucer as she set it down. 'We've always treated her well. We never *meant* to keep her. Not at first. We always thought that someone would *come* and when they didn't . . .'

He raised his hand. 'Please. It is not like that. I did not come here to accuse. On the contrary, I owe you a great debt.'

'She's a wonderful girl. Wonderful. Stephen is right. We're *so* proud of her.'

Stephen told him about the events of that night, how they had found Gabriella in her cot and taken her in. When he had finished there was a long silence.

'I just want to see her again,' Reuben said, finally.

Stephen cleared his throat. 'It's just that we don't know if that's such a good idea.'

'I am her father. I have a right to see her.'

'What will you say to her?' Stephen asked him.

'I don't know.'

'You see, we haven't *told* her,' Mercedes said. 'She *knows* she is adopted but we have never told her the exact *circumstances*. We thought . . . well, we didn't see what *good* it would do.'

Reuben nodded.

'We felt it was for the best.'

Stephen leaned towards him. 'She thinks her parents are dead.'

'I have to see her.'

'What is it you *want*?' Mercedes asked. 'Absolution?'

There was a shocked silence. Stephen looked away.

Reuben met her eyes. 'Perhaps. Perhaps just to see for myself that she is okay. That my failure was not so great. And also I think every child has a right to know their own history. Don't you?'

'Why did you have to come?' Mercedes whispered. 'You'll only *hurt* her.'

'Believe me, that is not my intention.'

Stephen shook his head. 'We've come to think of her as our own now. We were not able to have more children of our own after Luke. We wanted her to think of us as her real parents. We still do.'

'But she isn't.'

'No. No, she isn't.' Stephen bowed his head in resignation. 'I suppose I always knew it would come to this one day. When I came home yesterday and told my wife about your call she told me I should have tried to put you off, lie to you. But I suppose in the end I agree with you. Every child has a right to their own history.' He reached for the teapot. 'Well. I suppose it's decided. Would you like some more tea?'

84

Stephen persuaded Mercedes to fetch the photograph albums,
allowed Reuben a Kodachrome glimpse of his daughter's life. As
she paraded Gabriella's achievements for their guest, Mercedes
thawed a little. Stephen was relieved. It seemed to him there was
nothing to be gained from further denial and hostility. The die
was cast now.

Reuben, Mercedes could tell, was not a well man. His face had a
greenish pallor and his cheeks shone in the light of the table lamp,
the skin stretched tight across the bones. His wrists were painfully
thin. But he wore good clothes, Italian leather shoes and a tailored
suit. There was a Rolex Oyster on his wrist. He was obviously not
without means.

She watched his face as he leafed through the photograph
album: here a picture of Gabriella as a small girl, her face
sticky with ice cream; another of her on her pony when she
was five years old; in her school uniform, lying on the lawn
with her arm around her pet Border collie; a school portrait of
her with her classmates in her last year of primary school. The
fragments of a life he had witnessed at its beginning but had never
shared.

She supposed she could not even begin to imagine his pain.

'May I have this one?' he asked, pointing to a recent photograph
of Gabriella outside the house with Stephen and Mercedes.

'Yes. Yes, why not? I can always have a *copy* made.'

He wanted to know everything. What she was good at at school,
how old she was when she learned to walk, who her heroes were, if
she made friends easily, what sports she played. She told him about
her scholarship to Cambridge, her love of chemistry and biology, the
resolve it had taken to succeed in subjects traditionally dominated
by boys.

'And this is your son?' he asked her, pointing to one of the photographs.

Mercedes could not find her voice. She nodded.

'A fine young man.'

'Was. I'm afraid . . . we lost him.'

Reuben looked away. 'I'm sorry.'

There was an embarrassed silence as he absorbed the implications of this. Gabriella, then, was their only surviving child.

He put the album aside and sat for a long time staring out of the window at the lonely downs. She wondered what he was thinking. So far from Argentina here, so far from those terrible days.

Stephen came back into the room.

'They were twins,' Reuben said, his face still turned to the window, 'identical twins. Simone was born first, a fine, healthy baby. Her sister was smaller, she almost died that first day. We put Simone in the crib with her. From that moment she started to get better. It was a miracle. A miracle.' His eyes were unfocused, fixed on scenes of that long-ago drama. 'Your Gabriella. I don't even know which one she is.'

Mercedes thought about what Luke had told them. She shot a warning glance at her husband, shook her head.

'Has she ever hinted to you that she . . . knew?'

'Knew?'

'Sometimes twins have some sense that they have been separated. Do you think she felt that?'

Mercedes looked at her husband. 'No. No, I don't *think* so.'

A log fell in the grate and a flurry of icy rain spattered against the window. Stephen felt a cold draught against his legs. A strange twist to life. Sitting here on this winter's morning listening to the moan of the wind and talking with a stranger about things that happened twenty years ago in a hot country on the other side of the world.

Reuben's hands clenched into fists. 'If I could find just one of the men . . . but what is the point of thinking about that?' He turned away from the window.

'When can I see . . . Gabriella?'

Stephen looked at his wife. 'We will call her and ask her to come down. You have to let us talk to her first. This is going to be a great shock for her.'

Reuben nodded. After all this time he supposed he could wait a day or so longer.

Stephen walked with Reuben to his car. He was staying at a hotel in London, he said. In Bloomsbury. Stephen promised to call him the next day, after they had had the chance to talk to Gabriella.

When he came back into the house he found Mercedes in the kitchen, hunched by the warmth of the Aga cooker.

'I don't *like* him,' she said.

'He is her father. We must put our own selfish thoughts aside.'

'What do you think Gabby is going to say when she finds *out* about him?'

'She will probably react the same way as you did when I told you about it. She will be shocked. She might be very angry. I don't know. I hope she will see that everything we did, we did for her own good. But we have to be prepared for the fact that she may not see it that way at first.'

Mercedes rocked gently backwards and forwards. 'Why is this happening to us *now*?'

'I don't know. But it is and we just have to face it.'

'I don't *want* to face it.'

Stephen put his hands into his pockets. 'We have to tell him about this other girl in Rome.'

'We don't *have* to do *anything*.'

'For God's sake!'

'No!' Her voice rose hysterically. 'You won't tell him *anything*!'

'Why not?'

Their eyes locked, a silent battle of wills. Stephen looked away.

'If you tell him,' she said, in control again now, her voice no more than a whisper, 'I will leave you. I mean it, Stephen. You are *not* to tell him about her.'

'That is unbelievably cruel.'

'I mean what I say.'

Stephen knew he could not deal with this right now. He went out, shutting the kitchen door behind him.

85

Stephen was in his study when he heard the distinctive lawnmower rattle of the Volkswagen Beetle as it pulled into the courtyard. He slipped on his jacket and boots and hurried across the hall and out into the courtyard. Gabriella got out of the car dressed in a ski jacket and boots, one of Luke's university scarves round her neck, her cheeks pink with cold.

She slammed the door on the Volkswagen. 'Hi, Dad.'

'Hello, pudding,' he said.

Her face was etched with worry and, yes, with fear. All he had told her when he had called was that he and Mercedes had to talk to her urgently.

No, neither of us is ill. It's nothing like that.

It's not something I can talk about over the telephone.

She looked small and lost. His heart ached for her. He had never loved her as much as he did at that moment.

Altman had said he was her father. But that was not true. *He* was her father. He was the one who had seen her through the tumult of her schooldays, had sat up late when she had been out on dates, had paid for her fees, had ferried her to all the hockey games. He wondered whether all that would count for anything now.

She stood there, her hands in the pockets of her jacket. 'So. What's up?'

'Why don't we have a wander?'

Gabriella looked past him at the house and her face fell. 'Is Ma okay?'

He fixed a smile on his face. 'Yes, yes. I told you, it's nothing like that. We're both fine. Come on.' He put an arm around her shoulders and led her down the path behind the stables.

There was ice on the pond and nothing moved in the skeletal branches of the oaks and hazels. The only sound was the distant, plaintive call of a crow from the fields.

'Okay. What's the big mystery?'

He had rehearsed the words so many times since Reuben had left. Now he couldn't remember a single word he had meant to say. 'Can I just say this . . .?'

He took a deep breath. He watched her, committing this moment to memory. From now, he told himself, everything changes.

'I just want you to know that we've always loved you, like our own. You know that, don't you? Nothing can ever alter that.'

'Dad. What is it? Just tell me.'

'It's about . . . about your parents.'

The blood drained out of her face. 'My parents?'

'Gabriella, we told you certain things. They weren't completely true.'

Nervous laughter bubbled up in her throat. 'You mean you lied to me?'

'We thought it was for the best at the time.'

She watched his face.

'We said your parents were dead and we said we didn't know who they were. That was the lie. So now I'm going to tell you the truth.'

86

Gabriella did not remember Argentina. She had grown up far from the pampas and the tango clubs as the daughter of a comfortable conservative British family, in the shadow of the Berkshire Downs. Her mother still had family over there. They received Christmas cards from Buenos Aires every year.

She remembered going there once, when she was about nine years old. They had stayed with her mother's brother in San Isidro and a lot of people had made a fuss of her. She remembered being surprised that everyone in her uncle's family spoke English and had big afternoon cream teas. But her abiding memories were of the heat, the toothpicks on restaurant tables, the smells of garlic and strong breath.

The fact that she was adopted had never bothered her before. Sometimes, especially in her early teens, she had tried to imagine her parents, what they had been like, why they had died. It was a mind game, a game she had resigned herself to play for the rest of her life. Each night, if she wished it, she could conjure up a new set of parents with different names and different faces.

In her fantasies her father had been dark and big-shouldered with a broad, expansive grin and a loud voice. In fact he was completely different to Stephen, the man she had called her father for twenty years.

No, her dream father was not like Stephen at all; neither was he like the pale and sallow stranger her father led into the room that next morning.

They stood facing each other, awkward, a few paces apart. Finally he held out his hand. It was soft and there was no strength in it.

A long silence.

Her mother rescued her. 'Why don't we all sit down?' she said, and led the way into the drawing room. She started to pour them all tea.

Reuben stood by the fire, an uncertain smile on his face. He had his overcoat draped over his arm as if he were in an overheated railway waiting room. Gabriella stared at him, looked for some resemblance in his face and her own and found none. The moment seemed unreal. She had expected some spark of recognition, an unspoken connection of some sort. Instead it was like being trapped in an elevator with a total stranger.

None of them knew what to say. Stephen and Mercedes exchanged an uneasy glance.

'So this is Gabriella,' Reuben said, finally.

She had no idea how to respond. She felt like an actor on stage who had forgotten her lines.

'You look so much like your mother,' he managed.

She looked at Stephen and Mercedes. She felt as if she were betraying them just by talking to this man. They were all looking at her but still she could not find her voice.

Reuben turned to Stephen, as if looking for support. But he was lost, too.

'Why did you wait so long?' Gabriella heard herself say.

'I have not been able to find you until now. It is a long story.'

He told her everything, filled in the gaps in the terrible tale her father had told her the previous evening by the byre; a mother abducted, tortured and murdered, a twin sister she never knew she had, lost now, apparently for ever.

Stephen had been right, she decided. It was a past she did not want. She stared at the stranger who had brought her this burden and experienced a sudden upwelling of rage. Her hands shook and her teacup rattled off the saucer on to the floor.

Stephen jumped to his feet and put his arms around her. 'It's all right, Gabby.'

'I don't want to talk to him.'

'Gabriella?'

She pushed him away and jumped to her feet. 'I don't want to do this!' she shouted, and ran out of the room. Her reaction was as sudden as it was unexpected. Stephen looked at his wife, then at Reuben, who had also jumped to his feet and now stood by the fireplace, his face stricken.

The front door slammed. Gabriella ran across the yard towards the stables.

'I'd better go after her,' Stephen said.

Reuben was about to follow. Mercedes put a restraining hand on his arm. 'No. I think it's best if you stay here.'

'You were right. This was a mistake. I should go.'

'No. Sit down. *Please.*'

The expression on her face, the compassion he had not expected to see there, stopped him. 'I'm sorry,' he repeated. 'I'm so sorry.'

There was nothing from here, nowhere to go. What had he imagined? That there would be redemption at the end of this? He slumped back into his chair.

'What did you *expect*?' she asked him, echoing his own thoughts.

'Please,' he said. 'Don't taunt me.'

'That was not my intention, believe me. But you have been so *desperate* to see her you have not been able to imagine what it is like for *her*. You have missed her for twenty years. She did not even know you *existed*. It's going to take her some time to deal with this.'

'You hated me from the first. Now you feel sorry for me.'

'I don't feel sorry for you.'

'No?'

He felt the pain coming again. He reached into his pocket, found the morphine tablets, swallowed two of them dry.

'What are they?'

'Morphine sulphate. Painkillers.'

'What for?'

'I'm dying. There. Does that make it easier for you now?'

She stared at him.

'I have a tumour on the liver. In four more months I will be dead. So you see why I am in such a hurry.'

'I'm . . . I'm sorry.'

'It's not the end of the world.' A bitter smile. 'Well, perhaps for me.'

'That's why you came looking for her now?'

'Yes.'

'Why didn't you *tell* us?'

'So you would all feel sorry for me?'

Mercedes looked out of the window, towards the stables. 'What are you going to *do*?'

'I don't know.'

'She *will* want to talk to you again. An hour. A day. Next week.'

'I don't think so.'

'She will.'

He put his head in his hands. 'I should not have come.' He jumped to his feet. 'I have to get back to London.'

'She is upset now. But she *will* want to talk to you again.'

'Perhaps she will call me at the hotel. Thank you for your kindness. I know it was hard for you.'

'I'm not kind. I hated you, I have always *hated* you, even before I found out you were still alive. I was afraid you were going to take her *away* from me.'

'She is a grown woman now. No one is going to take her away from you.'

Reuben could not read her expression, could only watch as she struggled with some private dilemma.

'Do you believe in heaven and hell?' she asked him, finally.

Reuben waited, not knowing where this might be leading.

'I'm glad you've come now. Perhaps this is my chance to get this *over* with.'

Reuben held his breath.

'Señor Altman, what would you do if you found the man who murdered your wife?'

'I'd kill him.'

She studied his face intently. 'Without hesitation? I mean, *would* you? It is easy to say, standing here by a warm fire. But would you *really* kill him?'

'What is this?'

'Just answer me.'

'Of course I would kill him. I would die happy if I could find him.' He hoped it was true. Or perhaps Domingo was right. *You don't have the stomach for it.*

'Only you don't *look* like a killer to me.'

'What does a killer look like?' He leaned closer. 'You know something.'

She stared back at him, her eyes unfathomable.

'Please,' he said.

'I wonder if I can *trust* you with this.'

Reuben wanted to reach out and shake her.

'The thing is,' Mercedes said, 'I think I can help you find your other daughter.'

'For God's sake,' Reuben said. 'You know where she is?'

Mercedes sipped her tea. The cup rattled in its saucer.

'How?'

'It doesn't matter *how*.' Their eyes locked. 'She is living in Rome. The man she thinks is her father was once in the military in Argentina. I expect you to kill him, as you *said* you would. You have ample reasons. And it appears you have *nothing* to lose.'

'I don't understand.'

She leaned forward. 'He also murdered my son.'

'What? What are you telling me?'

'I'm telling you what you wanted to know. What you said you came all this way to find *out*. You don't look like the fist of God to me but you're all I've *got*.'

'I shall do it for myself. Not for you.'

'I don't care *why* you do it. But I only ask that you do not tell Gabriella about this . . . sister . . . until it is all over. *Please*.'

Reuben nodded his agreement. He was not sure how he felt. He had never thought he would find the one man who could answer all his questions, the scapegoat for all his sins. Certainly not in such bizarre circumstances. Excitement, revulsion, bewilderment, all battled for his attention. 'You were not going to tell me?'

'I've told you *now*, that's all that matters. We have made our bargain. I expect you to *keep* it.'

Even after all these years of standing empty the old taproom still retained a unique perfume of its own, a piquant mix of leather and dung. It was the place where she had always come to hide as a child, whenever she got into trouble. Now she ran into one of the loose boxes, put her head against the wall, her hands balled into fists on the cold stone. She was wearing only a thin jumper over her blouse and she shivered with cold.

She did not know why she had reacted that way. Just the shock of transformation perhaps, for there was no doubt that the sun would go down on a world vastly different to the one she had woken to. Her whole life had been turned on its head. They had rewritten her history. She felt like a blind woman in a room where all the furniture had been moved around. Now she blundered in alien darkness, no longer sure of anything. It would be like learning to walk again, having to test every new step, regain her balance.

After a while she heard her father's footsteps on the cobblestones.
'Pudding?'
She hid her face in the crook of her arm and said nothing.
'I'm sorry. I'm so sorry.'
'I just want to be on my own for a while.'
He slipped off his jacket and put it over her shoulders. He stood for a long time in his shirtsleeves, not speaking, then finally turned and walked slowly back to the house.

And so.
She had journeyed to the dark side of the moon, had discovered that the heroic heritage she had imagined for herself was possessed by a far grimmer reality. The father of her birth had not died a hero after all. She had also to accept the fact that she was a twin. A dubious gift. A part of her immediately resented the fact that she was not, like most other people on the planet, unique. Yet this

startling and unexpected knowledge was also somehow comforting. She was not alone; there was someone else out there who looked just like her, perhaps felt and saw things just the way she did. Someone else who shared this terrible history and this appalling secret.

It was still too soon after Luke's death to absorb any of this. She had a father she did not want, a twin she had never suspected. What was she supposed to think, to feel?

After a while she heard Reuben drive away. She stayed in the taproom for a long time, thinking. She would have to talk to him eventually. But at that moment she felt lonely and adrift, a small boat on a large sea, with no lights ahead or astern.

Rome

Near the Porta Sant'Anna, in a seventeenth-century tower leading off the courtyard of Sixtus V, a brass plate set into an arched entranceway announces the offices of the Instituto per le Opere di Religione, the IOR, better known as the Vatican Bank. It had been created by Pope Pius XII during the Second World War to facilitate the transfer of funds from fascist Italy to Catholic organisations around the world. After Mussolini's overthrow it had financed the founding of the Christian Democratic Party to ensure that the communists did not gain power in Italy. More recently it had channelled one hundred million dollars to Solidarity in Poland.

Unfortunately, during the eighties, it had also become embroiled in the activities of Mafia and P2 figures such as Michel Sindona and Roberto Calvi. It was Vatican money that had paid for the Exocet missiles that Catholic Argentina had used against the British Navy during the Falklands War.

The bank may fairly be described as a unique institution in the world of finance and is answerable in this world only to the Pope himself. It has also been described as an offshore tax haven in the middle of the Tiber and has attracted, over the years, many individuals such as César Angeli as its clients.

A Swiss Guard, in steel helmet and starched neck ruffs, guarded the entrance to the Porta Sant'Anna. Angeli nodded to him as he strolled through the entrance, one hand in his pocket, the other holding a large black leather briefcase. In the briefcase was three billion lire in cash.

He pushed through the frosted glass swing doors of the IOR and crossed the echoing marble floors where blue-uniformed ushers escorted wealthy clients to the polished wooden counters.

Archbishop Stanislaw Tomaszcewski – more commonly known as The Bear among his secular associates – greeted Angeli in his spacious modern office above the banking hall. The two men settled themselves on a black leather sofa and an usher brought them coffees laced with a little black sambuca.

'I have been hearing rumours about the Pope's health,' Angeli said after the small matter of the three billion lire had been attended to.

'The old goat will outlive us all.'

'You believe that?'

Tomaszcewski carefully placed his cigar on the edge of a heavy onyx ashtray. 'I believe that talk of a new pope always makes me nervous.'

'Should we be nervous? *Il Papa* has made a number of appointments to the College of Cardinals over the last few years. Surely he has ensured a smooth transition?'

Tomaszcewski sipped his coffee. 'Perhaps it will work that way. We all hope so. But for now we have a more immediate problem. That is why I needed to see you.'

'Yes. You said it was urgent.'

'The problem is a certain priest, right here in the Apostolic Palace. A countryman of yours. His name is Paolo Salvatore.'

'I have never heard of him.'

'He is private secretary to Cardinal Comacho. Somehow he has obtained a copy of an unofficial report that was passed to the Secretary of State by a senior official in the Credito Cattolica Privata. It was properly suppressed by Comacho but now this priest has taken it upon himself to pass a copy to the Holy Father – in person.'

'I assume he has been found a small parish in Patagonia that urgently requires pastoral care only he can provide.'

'Comacho still wishes to protect him. I cannot even be sure Comacho himself did not encourage him. As it stands it would be no great cause for concern, nothing I cannot deal with. But the priest has taken the matter further and given a copy of the report to a journalist.'

Angeli's face set like stone. 'How did you find out about this?'

'I have many friends in Rome. This particular journalist is one of them. Do not concern yourself, the story will not be published. But who knows who else this meddlesome priest may choose to talk to? Should a copy of the report find its way into the wrong hands it will be very damaging.'

'Leave it to me,' Angeli said. 'I will take care of it.'

London

The city was blanketed by grey overcast. The taxicabs had their headlights on, table lamps glowed in the windows of the Regency buildings around the square. A cold drizzle drifted down through the haloes of the streetlamps.

The hotel was in London's Bloomsbury, two streets from the British Museum. It appeared nondescript from the street, only the brass nameplate on the white portico distinguishing it from the exclusive offices and apartments around it. Gabriella stood outside, collecting her thoughts, summoning her courage. She went up the steps.

The foyer had been refurbished in period with gold leaf moulding, gilt mirrors and limed oak panels. There was an antique reception desk to the left of the foyer. On the other side was a small salon with a Chippendale fireplace and Queen Anne chairs, soft-lit by the Lalique sconces on the walls.

She asked for him at the reception and sat down to wait in the parlour, perched nervously on the edge of one of the chairs. She felt like a schoolgirl again, waiting outside the headmistress's office.

She heard someone come into the room and she looked up.

'Gabriella,' Reuben said.

He was wearing a grey double-breasted woollen suit and a white open-necked silk shirt. But his physical appearance did not match his impressive clothes. His face was gaunt and he had not shaved. There was a fine grey stubble on his chin.

He held out his hand. It was shaking. She took it in both of hers. It felt deathly cold.

'Please,' he said, 'sit down.' He settled himself in one of the wing chairs beside her.

They both started to speak at once.

Reuben smiled. 'No, you first.'

'I came to apologise.'

'I am the one who should apologise. It was a great shock for you. I'm . . . I'm just so . . . relieved that you've come. I was afraid you might not.'

There was a silence. They stared at each other.

'I don't know where to start.'

'First, I shall see if they will make us a cup of tea. It's the English thing to do. I would ask for coffee but I don't trust the way they make it. You have to be a Latin to know how to make coffee.' He grinned. 'Like us.'

She made him tell her everything. She wanted to know what her mother was like, where she was from, where he had met her, where they had lived in Buenos Aires. He told her about her twin and the mysterious bond that had developed between them in the desperate days after their birth.

He held back nothing. 'I told your parents that the night the police came I was away on business in Montevideo. That was not true. I was with another woman. Your mother . . . knew . . . and she rang me to warn me. Instead of going home I went to the Mexican embassy and asked for asylum. There. Now you know it all. Your father is an adulterer and a coward.' He held his head up and looked her in the eye and he said it, as if daring her to hate him, vilify him. As if he wanted her disgust as punishment.

He looked into her face expecting to find contempt and saw only sorrow. 'If it's any consolation,' he added, 'my life since then has been a misery.'

'Oh, Reuben.'

'I abandoned you. I abandoned you and your sister and your mother.'

She reached across the table and touched his hand. 'But it wouldn't have made any difference.'

It broke then, the dam he had built over the years finally collapsed. He wept. He wept in shame and regret and grief, for the wife he had lost and the children he had never seen grow. He wept for all those wasted, wasted years. He wept because he had been given so much and he had never appreciated any of it until it had been taken away. He wept most of all for the absolution she had given him, without question, as if it were his by right.

When it was done he looked up and saw the registrations clerk and two German businessmen on the other side of the parlour staring at him. He didn't care. He had found his daughter and she was safe and she was happy.

'Where do we go from here?' she whispered.

'You already have a father,' he said. 'I am just a footnote to your life.'

He felt a sudden stab of pain, and a sheen of sweat erupted on his skin. She still did not know about his medical condition, the one secret best held back for now.

'Are you all right?'

'I am just tired.'

'You're sick.'

'This climate. I picked up some sort of virus.' His hand went instinctively to his pocket, where he kept his pills, then he stopped himself.

'You're sure you're okay?'

'Yes.' He forced a smile. 'Yes, it's nothing.'

They sat and talked for almost an hour. He wanted to know about her studies, her friends at university, her plans for the future. He suggested they go out for dinner but as he got out of the chair he felt the room start to spin and his whole body felt suddenly as if it had been immersed in cold grease.

'Oh, God. Look at you.'

'I think I need to lie down.'

'I'll have the concierge ring a doctor.'

'No. No, really. It's not that bad. Just a chill. I have some antibiotics in my room. I'll be fine after a night's rest.'

He got up and escorted her into the foyer.

'How long will you be here?'

'Oh, a few more days.'

'I'll call again in the morning.'

'Thank you.' He took a last look at her. So beautiful. Just like Rosa. He had anticipated bitterness, had hoped for love. Instead what he saw in her eyes was awkwardness, curiosity, concern. But no more than that. How could it be? What he had said to her was the truth. She already had a father.

Unexpectedly she put her arms around him and held him.

It was a clumsy gesture, but he understood she meant well by it. Then she pushed herself away. 'Goodbye, Reuben.' He watched her from the foyer. She paused in the portico to turn up her collar against the biting wind.

And then she was gone.

As she walked through the cold streets she tried to understand what she was feeling. When she held him he had felt curiously light, a husk. It somehow reinforced the curious sensation that none of this was real.

She tried to imagine her mother, as he had painted her; both heroine and martyr. She searched inside herself for some scraps of rage for what was done to her. But it was impossible to conjure hate from nothing. To hate, you have first to love, and it was impossible to love a ghost.

She wondered instead about this twin she had never seen.

Somewhere in the world there was a mirror image of herself. She wondered what she was like. Would they be as Reuben insisted, identical twins? If they should meet, would they discover that they had always liked the same things, done the same things, even had the same thoughts?

But there was no point thinking about that. Finding her now was against all odds.

She rang the hotel the next morning. But when she asked for Reuben the clerk at the desk told her that Mr Altman had checked out of the hotel at seven o'clock that morning. He himself had arranged a taxi to take him to Heathrow. He was sorry but he had no idea where he had gone and he had left no messages.

90

Mar del Plata, Buenos Aires Province

The yacht clubs were clustered around the naval base to the south of the town. Bastions of the privileged élite, they had their own private beaches, dotted with shade huts made from canvas and timber, for the exclusive use of their members.

The name above one of the huts read: 'ANGELI, César L.'

He sat on a wicker chair in a pair of running shorts, his clothes neatly folded on the table beside him. He was muscular and lean for his fifty-nine years, his handsome face well tanned, his hair thick and immaculately groomed. A small gold crucifix glistened in the gold-and-grey hairs on his chest. Several bikini-clad women, wives of officers at the nearby naval base, looked in his direction. One or two of them smiled. He ignored them.

He saw Massini loping along the beach. He was scrawny, with too much hair for his body, the perpetual frown on his face giving him the look of a harried husband. His skin had been burned mahogany by the sun, so that he could have been mistaken for a *mestizo*. But the chunks of gold on his fingers, the Oyster Perpetual on his wrist and the bright three-tone shorts jarred with this impression.

'Colonel.'

Angeli did not get up. He pointed to one of the wicker chairs beside him.

Giorgio Massini was nothing like a harried husband. He had been trained by the Argentine Secret Service in the early seventies and had worked for Angeli in the Dirty War. In the eighties he had been employed by General García Meza's military junta in Bolivia where he had worked closely with Klaus Barbie and Arce Gómez, Bolivia's chief of military intelligence, running cocaine to the United States and Europe in drugs-for-weapons deals. These days he was semi-retired but still took contracts from selected clients, usually for those with ties to P2.

'You have a job for me.'

Angeli took a brown envelope from his shirt on the table and handed it to Massini.

'Everything is in there, photographs of the target, his habits. There will be minimum security, you should have no problem.'

Massini flicked through the contents. 'A priest.'

'A communist.'

Massini frowned. 'How much?'

'The usual fee. If you accept, half will be transferred to whatever account you specify immediately. The rest when the job is completed.'

Massini nodded. He looked down the beach, scratched his chest. 'Look at the ass on that one over there. Wouldn't you like a piece of that?' A girl with long brown hair halfway down her back was wading into the water. She was wearing what the Argentines called a cola-less bikini, a few scraps of material that hardly covered anything.

He picked up the envelope and stood up. 'I'll be in touch.' He sauntered away, staring at the girls.

91

Rome

She had arranged to meet her mother in Babington's Tea Rooms, by the Spanish Steps. When she arrived Francesca was already there, waiting. Shopping bags from Fratelli Rossetti and Salvatore Ferragamo lay on the floor by her feet. That was her life these days: shopping, coffee, dinner parties, the opera, health clubs.

She was staring at *la passaggiata*, her face set in that determinedly cheerful expression Simone hated so desperately.

'*Cara*,' she said, when she saw Simone, and she got to her feet, her face immediately registering disapproval of the jeans, the day pack, the long shapeless jumper.

'*Mama*.' She kissed her on the cheek. Simone sat down and Francesca ordered English tea – Earl Grey – and muffins.

Francesca gave her a fierce smile. 'I love it here. I like to pretend I have an assignation with Shelley.'

'Shelley died a hundred years before this place was built. And he was a poet. He could never have afforded the prices here.'

The smile disappeared from Francesca's face. She had hurt her. She couldn't help it, her mother was an irresistible goad. Simone hated this delusional world she had built, as if she weren't aware of what was going on under her nose. *As I have been doing myself for the last twenty years.* Perhaps that's why I hate her so much.

Francesca pursed her lips, a sulky expression, like a little girl who has been scolded by a parent. 'You should dress better.' Francesca herself wore a mink coat. There were Mikimoto pearls at her throat and the air around her was rich with expensive perfume.

'I dress to please myself.'

'You are easily pleased.' Simone let that one go.

The tea and cakes arrived and Francesca braced herself for

the object of their meeting. 'Simone, what's the matter with you?'

Simone stirred milk into her tea. She did not respond. She could not talk to her mother about this. There was no point. Her eyes travelled listlessly around the room – the mirror, the potted plant, the flower curtains, an old woman examining a copy of the London *Times* through half-moon glasses.

'*Cara*,' Francesca persisted. 'What have we done to deserve this? What has your father ever done except been a fine father and a wonderful husband?'

There was no answer to that. All she had were her instincts, an intuition that it was her father, not the man in the leather jacket, who had been lying to her. Her mother treated her like a little girl who understood nothing. 'Just tell me it isn't true,' Simone said.

'Of course it isn't true. How could you even think it?'

She was lying. They were both lying. There was something they had not told her. 'You will make up with your *papito*. Promise me.'

Simone closed her eyes.

'*Cara?*'

'I promise you I'll talk to him.'

'Your father is a good man. You do know that? You don't believe these lies you have heard about him?'

Simone decided to capitulate for now. What else could she do? 'I'll talk to him,' she repeated.

A hesitant smile. 'He's a good man,' Francesca repeated, like a litany, 'you have to believe that.'

A good man. Simone wanted so desperately for her father to be a good man.

Clouds the colour of lead swept over the Roman hills. Reuben looked through the window of a bar, watched a fat lady wrapped in a fur coat spooning cream from a glass of hot chocolate. The fountain in the piazza was festooned with icicles. He shivered, his breath freezing on the air. The pain was bad today.

She came out of the apartment in a tracksuit, a towel wrapped around her neck, a woollen hat pulled low over her ears. Her cheeks and nose were ruddy with the cold. He waited, huddled in the doorway.

It was her.

He resisted the urge to rush over to her, remembered how things had gone with Gabriella, did not expect even as much here in Rome. But he was overwhelmed with relief, even gratitude. The tenuous thread that had connected their lives had survived two decades; the child he last remembered in her cot had grown into this beautiful woman. He watched her jog across the cobblestones, run past him in the direction of the Vicolo dei Piede. She passed within a few feet of him, close enough to touch.

After all this time, he had found the last of his family.

92

A jumble of domes and Renaissance tiled roofs, garden terraces and TV aerials, the silhouettes of pines and cypresses on the distant Roman hills. A watery sun broke through the clouds, reflecting on the ice sheen on the dome of Sant'Agnese di Agone. Simone thrust her fists into the pockets of her jacket. Her parents' roof garden looked sad in winter; the nubs of roses in their pots, the brown stalk of a passion fruit vine.

There had been no answer when she had buzzed the apartment and she remembered it was the maid's day off. She had let herself in with a key. She had decided to talk to her father, as she had promised. It was for her own sake as much as his. She had been taking tablets to help her sleep, was not eating, had lost almost a stone in weight. She had to do something.

She could not forget the stranger in the leather jacket, the things he had said to her.

She knew her father was lying to her, it was only a question of degree. And yet she had always suspected there was more to his past than he had told her. She had never asked too many questions, never wanted to know too much. He had always told her he was never involved in the disappearances, but the way he talked about the communists, the anger he displayed whenever anyone mentioned South American politics, it was clear he was not the kind of man to watch from the sidelines.

Her father's image dissolved through a welling of bitter tears.

In a way it would be better if he told her it was all true: *Yes, I did some terrible things and I'm sorry for it. You must learn never to make my mistakes.* But he had always seemed incapable of shame or introspection. She wondered, too, if evil could be passed on to her, like the colour of her hair or the pigment of her skin. Perhaps she was infected too.

She leaned over the balcony, felt the razor chill of the iron

rail through her coat. She wanted so desperately to believe his
denials. She just wished there was some way she could be sure
of the truth.

She saw her father's white Mercedes pull up in the street below.
Marco got out and hurried to open the rear door. Damn, her
father had someone with him, Tomaszcewski from the Vatican.
She heard their laughter echo around the cobbled courtyard and
then they disappeared inside.

She waited a while, deciding what to do. When she got downstairs
they were already closeted in her father's study. The door was open
and she could hear their voices clearly.

'How is *il Papa*?'

'My guess? He has Parkinson's. Of course, the Press Office
denies it, but you only have to look at him. For an institution
that is supposed to have made the truth sacred, they embarrass
me.' She heard the old archbishop laugh heartily.

'As long as he doesn't get Alzheimer's. Now that would be
embarrassing. Imagine if he came out on to the balcony thinking he
was Mussolini and gave the Sunday faithful the fascist salute!'

The two men laughed again. She couldn't believe it was her
father talking this way. She stopped outside in the hallway and
listened.

The archbishop lowered his voice and she had to strain to hear
him. 'We shouldn't laugh about it. It's not funny. Changes are
not good for business.'

'It will come out all right. The Church doesn't change.'

'I'm still worried about this other business.'

'Salvatore?'

'He could do a lot of harm.'

'I've taken care of it. I believe he will find God very soon. Right
there on the steps of the Palazzo di San Calisto.'

'Divine inspiration?'

Angeli laughed. 'Call it a shot out of the blue. Another
sambuca?'

Simone felt the blood drain out of her face. She crept back along
the hallway and up the steps to the roof garden. She thought she was
going to be sick. The sting of the cold air revived her. She leaned on
the parapet, everything she had heard running round and round in
her head. Well, she had wanted the truth. Now she had it.

*   *   *

Angeli came out on to the roof to smoke a cigarette. A violet dusk
had settled on the skyline, the air frigid and still. As he replaced
the gold Ronson lighter in his pocket he looked up and saw Simone
standing at the end of the terrace, leaning on the parapet. He stared
at her in astonishment.

'Simone?'

'*Ciao, Papa.*'

'I didn't hear you come in.'

'I was here when you got back from lunch with the archbishop.'

He nodded, the implications of what she had said registering in
his mind. 'And you have been up here the whole time.'

She turned her face to look at him. 'Yes,' she said.

'You should have come down.'

'It sounded as if you were busy.'

'Still. You should have come and paid your respects to the
archbishop. But you must be freezing.'

'I wanted to be alone for a while. I needed time to think some
things over.'

'What kind of things?'

She shrugged her shoulders, but didn't answer him.

'You came to see me?' he asked, after a while.

'It's late. Maybe another time. I have to go.'

She kissed him perfunctorily on the cheek. He didn't move. He
knew the game she was playing. What was it she wanted from him?
Confession? He loved her like his own flesh and blood but he wasn't
going to beg. He was her father. She owed him her respect and her
loyalty, at least.

He watched her from the roof as she walked away down the street
towards the Piazza Navona. She said she had been up on the roof
the whole time. He wondered if that was the truth. The cold set
into his bones. The grey of winter embraced the city, embraced
them all.

93

It was the heart of one of the oldest cities in the world and yet it was still little more than a village. When Reuben first appeared in the piazza every eye was on him. When he bought some *suppli* and a slice of pizza in the *panetteria*, the baker watched him leave the shop and take up his position in the doorway across the street; the vendor at the kiosk who sold him the copy of *La Repubblica* saw him walk across the piazza to Gino's and take a seat in a table by the window. Riccardo did not take his eyes off him. He saw that he was there when Señora Bonetti, Simone's neighbour, left to go to the five o'clock Mass and he was there when she got back, and that he had spent the whole time watching the courtyard that led to Simone's apartment.

Señora Bonetti had seen him too. When she spotted Simone walking across the piazza, she hurried to meet her, the pigeons scattering in her wake.

'Signorina Gregorini!'

'*Ciao*, Signora Bonetti!'

'Be careful. A man has been watching the apartment all afternoon. He's sitting in Gino's, over there by the window. Do you see him?'

Simone stared at her, muddled, her mind still preoccupied with the things she had heard in her father's apartment on the Piazza Navona. *I believe he will find God very soon. Right there on the steps of the Palazzo di San Calisto.*

'Do you know him, signorina?'

Simone shook her head.

'The whole piazza has seen him. If he tries to follow you we'll call the carabinieri.'

'You're imagining things. He's just a tourist.'

But she felt the man's eyes on her as she walked into Gino's. She nodded a greeting to Riccardo and asked for an espresso.

The man was openly staring at her now. He was tall, well dressed but with a sickly, sallow complexion. Simone guessed him to be in his mid-fifties.

He got up and started to walk over. Simone glanced nervously at Riccardo. What did he want? Surely he was too old to try a casual pick-up?

He pulled out a chair and sat down. 'Please don't be alarmed,' he told her. He reached into his pocket and put a photograph on the table in front of her. Her own face smiled back at her, wearing a dress she had never owned, sitting on the steps of a house she had never seen before in her life. She stared at the photograph, and then at the stranger, open-mouthed.

'I know this is going to be a shock,' Reuben said, 'but I'm your father.'

94

Simone stood at the window of her apartment, a cup of coffee growing cold in her hands. Her voice was no more than a rasp in her throat. 'When I was a child he was my hero. I remember I used to sit on his lap in his study in Palermo. He had this massive desk, solid mahogany, there were little blue and white Argentine flags at each end and sometimes he let me play with them. He used to tell me I was his princess. Back then I could not imagine any father better than him.'

Reuben listened but said nothing.

She went to the coffee table, picked up the photograph of Gabriella, looked at it again as if reassuring herself that it was real, that it had not disappeared like a mirage. She kept running what he had told her over and over in her mind, trying to refocus her life through this dark new filter. Impossible to grasp it all. She would need time, lots of time.

'What did your father tell you he did in Argentina?'

'He said he was in the military. He admits to arresting a few people on orders. But that's all.'

'Do you believe him?'

'I used to.' She thought about the man in the leather jacket, her father's words that afternoon while he was sitting drinking in his study with the archbishop. *I believe he will find God very soon. Right there on the steps of the Palazzo di San Calisto.* 'A couple of weeks ago this man came up to me in the courtyard as I was getting into my car. He gave me this envelope. There were photocopies of some files. One of them had a photograph of my father. It must have been taken over twenty years ago but I recognised him straight away. My father has aged very gracefully.' She gave him a bitter smile. 'It had his name: Angeli. This man said the papers proved my father was not just a soldier. That he was actually in charge of one of the detention centres. That he was a torturer.'

'Where is this man now?'

'I don't know. I haven't seen him since.'

'What about these papers?'

She shook her head, wondering at her own impetuosity. 'My father has them.' She had thrown them at him that morning because she hadn't wanted to look at them again. 'I went to see my . . .' She was about to say 'my father', but she stopped herself. '. . . to see him. He denied everything. Even then, I wanted to believe him.'

'You knew your real name was Angeli?'

'When we came here from Argentina he explained to us that there were people from the new government who might want to hurt us and that it would be better if we changed our name. I was only eight years old at the time. I suppose it's easy to frighten a child into believing anything. Even when I grew up it seemed to make sense. A soldier makes enemies.'

He gave her a rueful smile. 'Indeed.'

'You see? It's like peeling an onion. One lie layered upon another. After a while you wonder if you're ever going to find the truth, there are so many lies.' She looked at Reuben. He was younger than he looked, she had learned. In his forties. Impossible to think of this stranger as her father. Absurd. 'How did you find me?'

'It wasn't easy.'

'But how?'

'It was chance. I saw you in the street.'

'Another lie. Another layer of the onion. You see?'

He stared at his hands. 'It's better you don't know. Not yet. I promise I will tell you. But not now.'

'I want you to tell me now!'

'You have not had enough shocks for one day?'

She returned her attention to the photograph. She was too shaken to argue. 'Who is she?'

'Her name is Gabriella. It used to be Eva. She is your sister.'

'Gabriella.' She said her name aloud to get accustomed to the sound of it. Her sister. Her twin. 'I want to meet her.'

'You will.'

'When?'

'Soon.'

'*When?*'

Reuben took a deep breath. 'She lives in England, near London. But there is a problem, with her parents.'

'But you're her parent . . . our parent.'

He gave her a tight smile. 'Only on a technicality.'

Simone put her face in her hands. 'Stop it! Just tell me the truth! I just want someone to tell me the truth!'

'Her parents are not eager for her to meet you. Not yet.'

'*Why?*'

He would not look at her. 'I can't tell you that.'

'Why are you lying to me? Why won't you tell me what's going on?'

He shook his head. 'I'm sorry.'

She had a sudden image of her life as a jigsaw. Until today she had forced the pieces into places where they did not belong and wondered to herself why the picture was distorted. Now she was finally discovering where each piece fitted and the result was not pretty. She thought again about the man she had called her father for the last twenty years and wondered if he was a monster.

She felt as if her head were going to burst.

The coffee cup spilled on to the carpet. In a moment she was curled on the floor, her body racked with great, choking sobs. She heard Reuben say her name, but from very far away, as if he were calling to her down a long and very dark tunnel. She was lost on a dark and pitching sea, without friends, without hope, without any one thing that was secure which she could cling to. She knew she was going to drown and they would never find her and her disappearance would not even be accorded the dignity of a name.

95

The Apostolic Palace was as far removed from the rundown parish church in Mexico City where he had last met Salvatore as it was possible to imagine. There were rich stuccoes, mirrored marble floors and great vaults above the corridors bearing the ornate insignias of the popes. Biblical figures in classical poses adorned the ceilings of the entrance hall to the Secretariat of State. Reuben's footsteps echoed in the sacred hush.

Salvatore had not changed. There was a little grey in the hair, a few lines around the eyes, that was all. He still wore the simple black soutane of a cleric.

He stretched out his hand.

'Reuben. I've often thought about you. It's good to see you again.'

Reuben was surprised at the warmth of the greeting and of his own response. 'And you, Father.'

'As you can see they live a little better at headquarters. Come into the nerve centre.'

In contrast to the splendour of the Apostolic Palace, Salvatore's office was simple, even extreme: bare white walls, a wooden crucifix, an idealised painting of the Virgin with a crown of stars and a red heart on her breast, pricked by thorns.

A nun brought in a tray with a silver coffee pot and two china cups. As she poured the coffee, Reuben felt Salvatore watching him. He was smiling but his eyes were clouded with concern. Somehow he knew.

'Only coffee, I'm afraid. I can't get you a kosher sandwich in here.'

Reuben grinned.

'So. How are you?'

'As you can see, my health is not what it was.'

'With your permission, I will pray for you.'

'I don't really believe in it, but as you wish. I suppose it can't do any harm.'

'Cover your bets,' Salvatore said, and smiled.

'So. Business is good?'

'Apparently. Despite all our best efforts.'

'And you've got a promotion?'

'I go where God wills. I even came to Rome for Him.'

'You have not been back to Argentina?'

'It seems He does not need me there. Sometimes I wonder if He goes there Himself.' It was a joke but neither of them smiled. 'So, Reuben, what brings you to Rome?'

Reuben set his coffee cup in its saucer. 'I have found them, Father. I have found my daughters.'

'Thank God.'

'Yes. Thank God.'

'You have spoken to them? They are still together?'

'No. One is in London. But yes, I have spoken to both of them.'

'And?'

'They are total strangers to me. They might as well be dead. I suppose it is a . . . relief to know they are happy. That they came to no harm. But for me – they might as well be dead. Like Rosa. It changes nothing for me.'

Salvatore stared at him for a long time. It was as if he could read his mind. 'How did you find them after all this time?'

'The man who did it. He's here, in Rome.'

Salvatore stared at him. 'You want vengeance.'

'Do not ask me to forgive him.'

'Vengeance crumbles to dust, Reuben. It will change nothing.'

'It's not vengeance. It's justice.'

'So you are to be his judge as well as his executioner? For God's sake, I beg you, don't do it.'

'I have made up my mind.'

'I see.' He sighed, sipped his coffee. 'So, then, why did you come here? You want me to give you my blessing, tell you that it's the right thing to do?'

'He murdered my wife. He took away my children.'

'And taking his life will restore yours to you?'

No, Reuben thought. No one and nothing can restore to me my family, my faith in other men, my faith in myself. They took from me not only my wife and my daughters, they took away my belief in life itself. They tore away my trust, my hopes, my beliefs, my innocence. Like an abused child I am useless for anything now except hate. It is not what they do to your body, it is how they desecrate your soul.

'I want to set the Devil a challenge. He has to make a hell worse than this.'

Salvatore's dark eyes studied him. 'You wanted your revenge on me, too.'

'On you?'

'For not hating them. So you want me to suffer over you.'

'Is that what you think?'

'Why else would you come?'

Reuben stood up. 'It was good of you to see me, Father.'

'For the last time, don't do it. It will solve nothing.'

'If I can rid the world of a plague, how is it a sin?'

'Evil is an intrinsic part of the world. All you will do is create more. I shall pray for you, Reuben. I shall pray for God to take away your strength.'

'I am going to kill that bastard' were Reuben's last words as he left. But later, as he walked across St Peter's Square, he wondered if they were all right about him, that he didn't have the strength to do it after all.

As the door opened she saw her father first. He was about to leave, dressed in a tuxedo and cummerbund, his white scarf and overcoat draped over his arm. He seemed surprised to see her. Marco waited to one side. She noticed the bulge in his jacket, just under the arm.

Angeli came towards her, his arms outstretched. 'Cara,' he said, and embraced her. 'We are just on our way to the opera.' His piercing blue eyes were fixed on hers. When she was small, she remembered, she thought he could tell everything she had done during the day just by looking at her. Even now she felt utterly transparent in his presence. 'But you've been crying. Whatever's wrong?'

She hated her own blindness. No, it wasn't blindness, because she had chosen not to see. Her parents' fictions were more comfortable than the truth. She had been given her own car, her own apartment, her studies had been paid for. She had never asked where the money had come from. Once she had been too young to ask questions. That had ceased to be an excuse many years ago.

'Are you all right?' he repeated.

Her mother appeared in the hallway in a long silk gown and mink wrap. There were jewels at her throat.

'You've been lying to me,' Simone said. He had to strain to hear her. Ever since this afternoon and her meeting with Reuben she had been unable to speak above a whisper.

Angeli took a deep breath. His expression quickly changed to anger. 'What is it now?'

'You're not even my father.'

Francesca gasped aloud.

Angeli looked at his wife. 'I'm getting a little tired of this.'

'This has gone far enough,' Francesca shouted. 'Of course he is your father! What is wrong with you? You're making yourself sick with all this. Listen to you! What has happened to your voice?'

Simone kept her shoulder blades pressed against the door, ensuring her line of retreat. 'What happened to my mother?'

Angeli looked at his watch. 'We have to go. The opera is starting in half an hour. I don't have time for this.'

'You know what happened to my real mother, don't you? My real mother in Argentina.'

'What are you talking about, your real mother?' Francesca screamed at her. 'I'm your real mother!'

'No, you're not.'

'Are you on drugs? Is that what it is? Should we take you to a doctor?'

'What happened to my mother, Papa? Was it you? Did you kill her? Did you order her killed?'

'This is insane! Who have you been talking to?'

'Just tell me the truth! For once in your life.'

Francesca reached for her hand. Her voice became gentle again. '*Cara*. We've loved you all these years. What have we done to deserve this?'

'I'm going to ring the doctor,' Angeli muttered. 'There's something wrong with her.'

Simone threw open the door. As she rushed down the stairs she thought: *Perhaps I am going crazy. Perhaps I am.*

*   *   *

She ran into the street, heard music playing somewhere. They were playing Christmas carols in the Piazza Navona.

She ran blindly through the cobbled streets into the piazza, stopped to catch her breath in a doorway. What had she hoped for? Some final *mea culpa*, a redemption for him, for her? What she had done had been as stupid as it was rash. She choked back another racking sob, deep in her chest. She had loved him. She had known him as her father and she had loved him. She wept for him as much as for herself.

She saw an ambulance pull up next to a carabiniere on the other side of the street. A tramp had frozen to death in the doorway of a toy shop. She watched the ambulance officers load him into a green plastic bag. Like a giant garbage bag with a zip. Here, where the best apartments sold for twenty million dollars, a man had had nowhere to go in the middle of winter and had been allowed to die.

The truth had always been there in front of her. She had just never wanted to see it.

96

Gino rolled up the steel shutters, closed the bar for the night. Riccardo shouted good night, zipped up his black leather jacket and climbed on to the Vespa parked in an alley on the other side of the street. He searched in his jeans pocket for his keys.

The silhouette of a woman detached itself from the shadows and came towards him. '*Ciao*, Riccardo.'

He looked up, startled. 'Simone. What you doing?'

'Just walking.'

'You'll freeze. You okay?'

'Sure. How's that girlfriend of yours?'

'We split up. What happened to your voice?'

'I've got a cold.' She seemed distracted, on the verge of tears. 'Want to walk for a while?'

'Okay.'

He climbed off the moped and followed her into the piazza. The yellow lights of the streetlamps reflected on the black and ice-slick cobbles.

'What is it?' he asked her. 'What's happened?'

She stopped walking, put her hands deep in the pockets of her jacket. 'Imagine the most terrible thing in the world.'

'Okay.'

'Have you got it?'

'Yes.'

'What is it?'

'Well, I can't think of anything. What is this?'

Simone shook her head. She was crying. He stared at her, confused, bewildered. 'Why don't you just tell me what's going on?'

'If you had to choose between your family and your conscience what would you choose?'

It was bitterly cold standing here in the middle of the piazza. 'Can't we go up to your place? I'm freezing.'

'There's someone there. You haven't answered my question.'

He felt a stab of jealousy, looked over his shoulder. The light was on in her apartment. Perhaps there was a man there waiting for her. The man he had seen the other day in the bar. But he was too old for her. And anyway, if he was a lover why was she standing here talking to him this way? 'I already chose between my family and my conscience,' he said to her. 'My father always wanted me to go into the family business. I wanted to be an actor. So I gave up the chance of an easy life and plenty of money to work in a bar for almost nothing. After two years I have been the star of one television commercial for jeans and an extra in a low-budget comedy that never even got released. And I have to watch the girl I'm crazy about going out with other young guys who can afford to buy her dinner. That was my choice. But what kind of choice was that?' She was staring at the fountain, the icy splash of the water. He took her hand. 'What is it, Simone, what's going on?'

'I can't tell you.'

He tried to contain his frustration. 'If you can't tell me anything, then why the hell did you want to talk to me?'

She snatched her hand away. 'I don't know.'

'What is it? Is it your father? Has he got himself involved in some kind of fraud or something? Is he in trouble with the police?'

She put her hands up to her face. 'Look, I can't talk about it. It's too complicated. It doesn't matter. It doesn't matter!'

She ran away across the piazza, leaving him staring after her, utterly bewildered.

A scream from somewhere just off stage.

Don Giovanni stood up from the supper table, the passageway behind him lit by the flame of the candle he held in his hand. For a few moments he disappeared from view and the audience was left to imagine his fate. Suddenly he reappeared, backing away from the graveyard statue of a man he had once killed, now come to life to haunt him.

Angeli felt a droplet of sweat squeeze from his forehead and make its long progress down his cheek.

'Will you come with me to supper?' the apparition asked him.

Angeli felt himself breathing faster. There was a dull pain in his chest.

'Think on your sins, Don Giovanni,' the statue demanded. 'Do you repent them?'

'No,' Angeli whispered. 'Never.'

Don Giovanni shook his head. That's it, Angeli thought. *Spit in his eye.*

The demons rushed from the darkness, dragging him down to the sulphuric world of damnation. As the last dismal notes of Mozart's score faded and the lights went up on the applause, Angeli too slowly put his palms together, and joined in the acclamation for the performance. But there had been no joy in it. His mind now was consumed with the terrible visions of his own impending death.

'Who is he?' Reuben asked, peering through the curtains. The young man stood outside the courtyard, staring up at the window, his hands in the pockets of his black leather jacket.

'His name's Riccardo. He works in the bar on the corner.'

'It's freezing out there. He must be in love with you.'

'He thinks he is.'

'And what about you?'

'I think he is, too.' A wisp of a smile, vanished as quickly as it had come.

She was sitting on the sofa, her body hunched over, her arms folded across her breasts, her long hair falling round her face. As if she were hiding.

'Where were you tonight?'

'I went to see my *papito*,' she said, the last word barely audible.

'Did you tell him about me?'

She shook her head. 'Of course not.'

'But you confronted him with it.'

'I shouldn't have gone. I suppose I was looking for one moment of doubt in his eyes. It would have redeemed him.'

'Will he come here?'

She shook her head. 'He's too proud.'

Reuben turned from the window. Impossible to imagine her

as the little brown infant he had held in his arms two decades ago. Now it was a connection made on faith. That he knew it to be true did not help. They were two strangers trapped inside the same dilemma, held prisoner by a slender thread.

'What am I supposed to feel?' she said, echoing his thoughts. 'You say you're my father. My father was the man who raised me and I'm . . . ashamed of him.'

'Aren't you ashamed of me as well?'

'You want me to be, don't you?'

He turned away, unable to meet her eyes.

'I feel sorry for you. Perhaps that's worse. I feel sorry for all the years you have suffered over this. What else can I feel? I don't know you.' She pushed back her hair with a sweep of her hand. Her eyes shone with tears of hurt and rage. 'Tonight, as I was walking home, I stopped on the bridge and stared into the water. I thought about throwing myself into the river. I just wanted all this to end.'

He stared at her, stricken.

'Why not? Knowing what I know. This is a nightmare and I can't wake up!'

'I didn't mean to hurt you.'

'Oh, for God's sake, stop it! You're not responsible for all the suffering in the whole world! It's not you! It's him! It's him and what he did!' She was panting hard, as if she had been running. 'You know what kept me going? This.' She picked up the photograph of Gabriella from the coffee table. 'My whole world has gone. I've lost my mother and father, I've lost my memories. But I keep telling myself there's one person who will understand what I'm feeling, *exactly* how I'm feeling. Just one.' She stopped and her voice became more gentle. 'Let me talk to her, Reuben.'

'Not yet. I just need a little more time.'

'Why? What are you going to do?'

'I haven't made up my mind.' Another lie. He went back to the window. Riccardo had given up and gone home. 'He's gone,' he said.

'Will you stay here tonight?'

'Are you afraid of him?'

'No. He would never hurt me. I just don't want to be on my own.'

He nodded. 'I'll have to go back and get some things from my hotel.'

After he had gone she sat staring at the telephone for a long time. But the decision was already made. She knew what she had to do.

97

The Palazzo di San Calisto had been built by Pius XI to house curial offices. It was in Trastevere, a long way from San Pietro and the papal palazzo, and was inhabited only by unimportant officials. Salvatore had been given rooms there when he first came to Rome, and though now he could afford better he had grown accustomed to it.

It was his habit to walk across the Ponte Cestio each morning and catch the number 23 bus to the Piazza dei Risorgimento in the Vatican. As he came out, a few minutes after seven o'clock, a man got out of a Fiat parked on the other side of the street, holding a 9mm Beretta pistol inside his jacket. He took it out and fired four shots, three of them hitting Salvatore in the chest.

Almost immediately three men from SID, the Italian secret service, jumped from a van parked twenty metres along the street. They were all wearing bullet armour.

They shouted at the gunman to surrender. He turned and aimed his pistol in their direction and was immediately hit by a hail of fire from their machine pistols. His accomplice drove off but then found the narrow street blocked by the dark blue Fiats of the carabinieri. In the brief gun battle that followed he was wounded in the arm and chest and arrested.

Angeli rubbed at his temples, frowning. No matter what you did, people were never satisfied. It seemed he was always to be disappointed in human nature. Turturro's betrayal he understood. Turturro was an ingrate and a peasant.

But this.

Behind him the roofs of the Piazza Navona faded to shadows in the sunset.

A man sat on the other side of the desk, dressed in a silver-grey Brioni double-breasted suit and a silk tie. He had a pleasant face, languid and benign. His spectacles reflected the fading light from the window. He could have been a dentist or a wealthy accountant.

'The police had been warned,' the man said. 'They were waiting for Massini outside the church. Salvatore had been given a bullet-proof vest. He was wearing it under his soutane. He received three broken ribs but that's all. He's in Gemmelli Hospital under twenty-four-hour guard.'

'Massini's dead?'

The man nodded.

'And his driver?'

'He is in a critical condition in the Policlinico Umberto.'

'Will he talk?'

The man in the grey suit shook his head. He lit another cigarette and his head was wreathed in a cloud of blue-grey smoke. 'My sources tell me the informant was a woman.'

Angeli closed his eyes. Not Simone. No. And yet who else knew about it? She must have been standing right outside the door when he had told Tomaszcewski his plans. And the way she had been behaving lately . . . everything pointed to her.

'Does your source have any other information about this informant?'

He shook his head. 'It was anonymous. But my source is well placed inside the SID itself.' He drew on his cigarette. 'All he knows is that the information was passed on by telephone and that it was a woman. Do you have a mistress?'

'*You should have come down.*'

'*It sounded as if you were busy.*'

'There was something else, which may or may not be significant. Her voice was distinctive, my source believes. Hoarse, as if she had a cold. Of course, that could have been a ploy to put us off the trail.'

Angeli stared out of the window.

'This has caused a great deal of consternation for many people,' the other man went on. 'Massini has a lot of friends. It looks to them as if he was set up. These friends are most unhappy. People are saying rash things.'

'Such as what?'

The other man gave a small, humourless laugh. 'The heat of the moment. They blame you. What do you expect?' When Angeli did not respond, he went on: 'If there is a leak right here in

Rome, on something as important as this, how well can you be trusted?'

'I shall take care of it.'

'You know who it is, then?'

'I will take care of it.'

'César?'

Angeli was the first to break the long silence. 'I believe the information came from my daughter. She has been acting a little irrationally lately. It proves nothing. I will—'

The other man laughed again. 'I know how strangely she has been behaving.'

Angeli stared at him, panicked. How could he know that? And then he thought about Marco. Wheels within wheels. Of course. 'As I said, I will take care of it.'

'May I ask how?'

'Her doctor is coming to see me this evening. I shall arrange for her to spend some time elsewhere. In Switzerland perhaps. Somewhere she can get help.'

'You are having her committed?'

'It will take care of the problem. She needs time to get well. She is . . . confused.'

The other man dropped his conversational tone. 'I'm afraid that is not good enough.'

Angeli stared at him. He was not accustomed to having his decisions questioned. But then he was not accustomed to failure. It seemed it was time to pay the ferryman. 'Then what would you have me do?'

'You have a clear choice. It is not an easy one, for any man. But if she does not pay for what happened to Massini, his friends will ensure that *someone* does. I cannot control them, César. You know what these men are like. They are not civilised people like ourselves.'

A long silence. 'You're not serious?'

'Please understand, this is not my ultimatum. I can merely advise you of what I know to be the case. What you decide to do is up to you.'

Lights were flickering on over the city, in the hills. An early twilight. Spatters of rain hit the window. Bells tolled the angelus.

I cannot.

'César, I am sorry. You have done a lot of good work for us in the past. I would have liked to have helped you. But this is most serious.' He looked at his watch. 'I have to get to the airport. I am flying back to Buenos Aires tonight. Perhaps I will see you in the New Year?'

Angeli got up too, but very slowly. Suddenly he felt all of his fifty-nine years. A room full of ghosts jeering at him. He had served his country and Church faithfully and well, but in the end it all counted for nothing.

The other man put a hand on his shoulder. 'This must be hard for you. God knows it is not a decision I would like to make. Let me talk to them. Perhaps I can persuade them.'

'Thank you,' Angeli heard himself say.

He watched from the window as the limousine pulled away from the kerb. He understood what they were saying to him. The choice was clear. He could save himself or he could save his daughter.

But he couldn't save both.

98

César Angeli looked around his study, the bronze cherubs on the desk, the spines of the quarto volumes of Roman history gleaming like gold in the lamplit room. He picked up a silver-framed photograph of Simone, taken five years ago at a gymkhana just outside Rome. She had won that day, he remembered. Her mother had never wanted her to ride, she had said it was too dangerous. But she had wanted her own pony and in the end she had got it. That horse had become a symbol of her independence, the first time she had gone against their will and won. But then she had always been a wilful child. Not rebellious, just stubborn.

Mia principessa, he whispered.

He sat down behind his desk, stared for a long time at the photograph in his hands. He had a vision of her alone in the apartment that day he had come back here with the archbishop and he knew it had to be her. He just didn't want to believe it.

'I will talk to her,' he murmured to the darkness, but in the end he knew it would not make any difference. He sat for a long time, not moving, staring out of the window at the bitter night.

Reuben sat in his room in the Hassler, watching the lights blink on in the Roman hills. He picked up the pistol and weighed it in his hand. It was a police-regulation Colt .45. He cocked it, held back the hammer, pumped the barrel back and slid it into position, catching the unspent bullet in his other hand. He removed the magazine from the butt, popped the bullet back in with the other five and snapped the magazine home. He did it a dozen more times, getting accustomed to the action and feel until he could perform the process without thought.

It had taken almost three days to get the gun. Three days and almost a million lire. Expensive. He slipped the magazine from the butt, put the pistol in his right jacket pocket, the magazine in his left.

Fragments of conversations came back to him.

You don't have the stomach for it.

You don't look much like the fist of God to me, but you're all I've got.

I shall pray for you, Reuben. I shall pray for God to take away your strength.

He wondered if Domingo and Mercedes were right about him. He supposed he would soon find out.

He thought about Simone. *I keep telling myself there's one person who will understand what I'm feeling, exactly how I'm feeling. Just one.*

She had thought she was in the middle of a nightmare, that it couldn't get any worse. But it would get worse and she would need someone to help her through it. He picked up the telephone and asked for an outside line. He dialled the number Gabriella had given him in Cambridge.

He stood framed in the doorway, in a tan overcoat, a Hermès silk scarf draped around his neck. They stared at each other for a long time. 'Can I come in?' he said finally.

He went to stand in the middle of the living room with his hands deep in the pockets of his coat while she busied herself in the kitchen with the coffee. He was wearing his favourite cologne, a subtle aroma redolent with memory. As a child she used to watch him shave, remembered him splashing the cologne onto his cheeks from the small green bottle he kept on the bathroom vanity unit.

Was it possible to lose an illusion, something that had never existed outside your own mind?

He was standing in profile, the light from the window throwing an aura over the aristocratic features. 'What is this all about?'

'That man.'

'That man. A complete stranger someone sent here to tell lies about me.'

She busied herself pouring the coffee into the cups from the pot on the stove.

'Why do you hurt me this way?'

'I know the things that happened back then.'

'But I had nothing to do with any of that.'

He lied so easily. His eyes were so gentle, his face a study of hurt and bewilderment. It was an awesome portrayal of a man wronged.

'Those papers that man gave me,' she said.

'They were lies. Forgeries. You are not so naïve you think it is hard for someone with a grudge against me to make up things like that?'

She brought his coffee, held the cup and saucer towards him. He ignored it.

'Simone. There's something I have to ask you. The other day in the apartment, were you eavesdropping on me and the archbishop?'

'I was on the roof.'

'It was a long time to be on the roof.'

'I told you, I had a lot to think about.'

He watched her, his hands still in his pockets. His eyes were no longer gentle. They were the hard eyes of the inquisitor; ice blue, they looked right into your head, searching for your secrets. She had never been frightened of him before. But he was no longer her father; she had discovered he was some murderous stranger who had simply played out the role.

'It was you who called the police.'

'What are you talking about, Papa?'

'Just tell me. I can forgive you. But I have to know the truth.'

She feigned a look of bewilderment, feeling like a bad actress in a television soap opera.

'*Mia principessa*,' he whispered. He ignored the coffee. He kissed her softly on the forehead and went to leave. He stopped at the doorway and turned around. 'I love you,' he whispered, and went out.

99

Market Dene

Gabriella parked the Volkswagen by the stables and turned off the engine. There were no other cars in the courtyard. Stephen was not yet home.

She got out of the car and walked over to the house. The brown fields were dusted with frost and a gentle overnight breeze from the north had swept the sky clean, herding the leaves in windrows against the stables. She heard a shrill cry, perhaps a bird, but for no reason she imagined a hare caught in the steel jaw of a trap somewhere in that great hushed landscape.

The kitchen door was open. 'Ma?'

She went through to the drawing room. Mercedes was asleep at the fireside, a blanket over her knees. She looked old and withered, her skin sallow like a husk, all the juice drained out. She felt suddenly unutterably sad for her.

She woke suddenly, her eyes fogged from sleep. 'Gabriella?'

'Hello, Ma.'

'Gabriella. What are you doing home?'

'Reuben called me. From Rome.'

Mercedes didn't say anything. Gabriella sat down. A log sparked in the grate.

'You knew he would.'

'What did he *say* to you?'

'He said he'd found my sister.'

No reaction at all.

'Ma? Ma, *please*.'

'Did he say anything *else*?'

'How did he find her? You *knew*. You told him!'

'He rang you. It must be over, then,' she said, almost to herself.

Gabriella wanted to shake her. She desperately wanted to understand this latest, unfathomable hurt. 'What's over? What?'

Mercedes pulled the blanket further around her legs. 'Are you going to Rome?'

'I came back to get my passport. I'm catching a flight tomorrow morning.'

A strange half-smile. 'Perhaps we can talk about it when you get back.'

'Why won't you tell me?'

'Some things are too *painful*. Better to pretend they never happened. You will be *careful* over there, won't you?'

When Stephen got home he found his wife still sitting in her chair in the drawing room staring at the cold ashes in the grate. She told him about Gabriella, that she had been there earlier that afternoon, that she was flying to Rome.

Mercedes did not tell her husband that it was she who had told Reuben about Simone and about César Angeli. As she had not told him about Jeremy Dexter's suspicions about Luke's death. What good would it have done? It changed nothing. There was no proof. As she had no concrete proof that it was Angeli who had raped her on five different occasions while she was a prisoner at Ezeiza.

But she had known, had recognised him from his photograph. And now it was done. She had been avenged. And Luke, too.

She would not burden Stephen with the truth. Had it really helped Gabriella? Would it help Stephen to know that Angeli was the reason she still could not stand being touched by a man, that it was because of him that she had not slept with her husband for years?

As she had told Gabriella, there were some things that were just too painful to tell anyone.

Rome

She had been asleep on the sofa. She looked ill. She was pale and there were dark rings under her eyes. 'He came here today,' she rasped.

Reuben felt the reassuring weight of the revolver in his jacket pocket. 'What did he want?'

'He thinks I have been talking to the police. He frightened me.'

'Are you all right?'

'I took some pills. I haven't been sleeping.' She put her hands across her face. 'I just wanted to shut everything out.'

He reached out a tentative hand. 'You don't think he would hurt you?'

She shook her head. 'I'm still his daughter.' She gave him a twisted smile. 'And he's right. In a way, I still am. I always will be.'

'I know.'

'What am I going to do?'

'It's going to be all right. I promise you.'

'I can't think any more. I just want to crawl into a hole somewhere and hide.'

She let him put his arms around her. He did it tentatively, as one would to a complete stranger who is in distress. 'I have rung Gabriella,' he whispered. 'She will be here tomorrow.'

'She's coming here?'

'She has your address. She will take care of you after . . .' He stepped away from her. '*Por Dios*, look at you. Have you eaten anything today?'

She shook her head. 'I've been throwing up ever since he left. I just want to sleep now.'

He helped her into the bedroom, threw back the covers and laid her on the bed. She was wearing a tracksuit, a zippered jacket over a white T-shirt. He helped her off with the jacket and threw the covers over her, turned off the lamp. 'If I'm not here when you wake up, just stay where you are. Wait for Gabriella.'

'Where are you going?'

He did not answer her question directly. 'I'll try to be back in time.'

She was too tired to interrogate him further. In the last few weeks she had watched her life unravel like an old jumper. Her body and mind were on overload. She just wanted to sleep.

'Good night.'

'Good night, Simone.'

He closed the bedroom door behind him.

'Goodbye, *cara*,' he whispered. 'I'm sorry. For everything.'

*   *   *

The pain was bad today. He took the vial of morphine sulphate from his pocket and swallowed two of the tablets with a glass of water. The doctor had told him three months but perhaps he was wrong. It felt as if the disease was progressing more rapidly than that. After tomorrow it would be irrelevant anyway.

If he was going to do it, it had to be done now.

100

It was almost eleven o'clock when she woke. The sleeping tablets had rushed her through a black, dreamless sleep and now her head was pounding and she felt as if she had a hangover. She stumbled into the living room. Reuben was gone. Not even a note.

She replayed the messages on her answerphone. Three from her mother. She sounded hysterical. Simone fast-forwarded the tape a few times then switched it off. She made herself coffee, dressed, and sat staring moodily out of the window.

What was she going to do?

Without her father she had nothing. It was his apartment, his car. His life, really. Now she was to cut herself off from him entirely. Where could she go from here?

She had decided she would not ask Reuben for help. He had intimated that he was not a poor man, but perhaps it was time she learned to stand on her own two feet. Like Riccardo.

It was time to grow up.

British Airways flight BA552 from Heathrow arrived at Fiumicino just a few minutes late at a little after half past eleven in the morning. Gabriella had no luggage, just a few changes of clothes in an overnight bag, and so she passed quickly through customs and immigration. She found a cab outside the terminal and handed the driver a slip of paper. On it was the address in Trastevere that Reuben had given her over the telephone.

She fidgeted in the back seat all the way into Rome, impatient, eager, fearful. After twenty years she was coming home.

The man had been sitting in Gino's since it had opened early that morning. He wore a knee-length black overcoat over a polo-necked sweater. Underneath his coat was a shoulder holster and in the holster was a Heckler & Koch automatic pistol.

He took out a photograph from his pocket and studied it once more, to satisfy himself that he would recognise his target when she appeared. He ordered another espresso and settled down to wait.

His motorcycle was parked in an alley on the other side of the piazza. It was easier to get away quickly on two wheels. Especially in Rome. It did not concern him that people in the bar or the piazza might remember his face. By this evening he would be in Switzerland and with the money he made from this contract he had no plans to return.

101

Angeli had Marco bring round the car. He had not had time to replace him as yet but he had made a mental note to do so. There were other things occupying his mind at the moment. He had a luncheon appointment with the archbishop at the Villa Strich at twelve o'clock. They needed to discuss the consequences of the shooting outside the Palazzo di San Calisto.

He looked at his watch, as he had done countless times that morning, wondered if it was done. The man he had employed had come well recommended.

He walked out through the foyer and into the waiting Mercedes. Marco carefully negotiated the back streets, turned on to the Corso Vittorio Emanuele just across from the church of Sant'Andrea della Valle.

'Stop here,' Angeli said.

Marco seemed surprised but he did as he was told. He turned into the Via degli Chiavari and shut off the engine.

'Wait for me,' Angeli told him. He jumped out and walked back up the street to the church. He pushed open the heavy door and went inside. He crossed himself and took a seat in one of the pews halfway along the aisle. He closed his eyes and took a deep breath, composing himself. He did not know what impulse had brought him in here. In the name of God. He was sweating like a virgin.

There was a cavernous hush inside the church. The Renaissance architects knew their art, he thought. They removed you from light and noise and made you face this great emptiness in order to remind you of death. When they had brought you to that state of trepidation they offered you salvation, up there on the dome, out of reach, the angels and the glory; in this case Giovanni Lanfranco's *Glory of Paradise*.

Oh, God. What have I done?

I had no choice, he told himself. And yet there was still time to stop it. He took the mobile telephone from his pocket. He knew the assassin's number by heart, could stop him with one call. His finger hovered over the number pad. Was there another way out of this?

He did not spare a glance for the priest who passed him in the aisle and took a seat in the pew behind him.

Suddenly he heard a voice in his ear. 'If you make one move I don't tell you to make I shall blow away your spine.'

Angeli reacted calmly. His heart beat a little faster but a lifetime of training had taught him self-discipline. So: Massini's friends had wasted no time. He thought about Marco outside in the car. No chance of rescue there. He kept quite still, told himself to relax, to think. His best hope was to negotiate.

'We are in a place of God.'

'Does that mean something to you?'

'Of course. I am a civilised man. I hope you are too.'

'I imagine you do hope that.' The man spoke Italian with a distinctive accent. He recognised it. This man was a *porteño* like himself. Almost certainly one of Massini's friends, then.

'I want you to turn around very slowly. Keep your hands in your pockets. Now look down. Good. Like that. You see what I have here, in my coat. It's a Colt forty-five. You see? I'm not playing games. All right. You can turn back to the altar. Contemplate your sacrifice to God.'

He didn't talk like one of Massini's friends. 'I'm convinced. So. What do we do now?'

'What we do now is this: you are going to get up, very slowly, and walk towards the door. I shall be right behind you. One sudden move and I shall empty the clip into your back. Without hesitation. Do you understand?'

'You are being very clear.'

'Good. When we get outside you will turn to the right and go into the Piazza Vidoni. You will see a black Volkswagen Golf parked there. You will get in behind the wheel. The keys are in the ignition. You are going to drive, and I shall sit behind you. We need to go somewhere a little more private so we can talk.'

Angeli stood up and walked to the great doors at the rear of the church. He tensed, waiting for his chance. But the other man had anticipated him. When they reached the door the man stepped in close, one hand on his arm, the barrel of the weapon

pressed hard against his spine. 'I'll shoot you on the steps if I
have to.'

'That will not be necessary.'

Angeli went down the steps, turned to the right as he had been
ordered to do and saw the Golf parked on the cobblestones a few
yards away. He climbed in behind the wheel and his assailant got
into the back seat directly behind him. He had only glimpsed the
man's face for a moment in the church, but now he had a better
look at him, in the rear-vision mirror; fair hair flecked with silver,
a long, sallow face, bony wrists and hands.

He felt quite calm. If this had been a professional hit, it would
have been over by now, without conversation. Perhaps this had
nothing to do with Massini, after all. He sensed that this could
yet be negotiated.

He found the keys in the ignition, as his assailant had promised.
'You shouldn't leave your keys in the car. Rome is full of crime.
It could have been stolen.'

The man ignored him. 'Turn left out of here. Head towards the
Vaticano, turn left down the Vicolo Sugarelli.'

'Where are we going?'

'Just drive.'

After the gun battle outside the Palazzo di San Calisto, the SID
had traced the assailants to a rented apartment in the suburbs near
the airport. Among the dead man's possessions they found a white
business card with the name of an Argentine bank printed on the
front. A telephone number had been scrawled on the back. It was
traced to a mobile telephone registered to one César Gregorini.

Subsequently two agents, a man and a woman, had been assigned
to watch Angeli's movements. No one had expected the surveillance
to yield such dramatic results so quickly.

They had tracked the white Mercedes from the Piazza Navona
in a white Fiat, followed it into Via degli Chiavari. When they saw
Angeli get out of the Mercedes and start to walk towards them,
they put their training into action and pretended to be a married
couple, feigning a fierce argument in the front seat of the car.

But Angeli never gave them a second glance.

A few minutes later they saw him come out of the church and
get into a black VW Golf, followed by another, unidentified, man.
It was immediately apparent to them what was taking place. They

looked back and saw Angeli's driver, Marco, lounging behind the wheel of the Mercedes casually smoking a cigarette, flicking ash through the partly open window. From his position he could not see the entrance to the church, had no idea what was taking place with his employer.

'Your boss has just been abducted, *stronzo*,' one of the agents hissed under his breath. 'Brainless Mafia shithead.'

As the Golf joined the traffic on the Corso Vittorio Emanuele, the Fiat pulled out to follow. As it did so the woman in the passenger seat read out the Golf's registration plates – she noted that it was a Hertz hire car – into her hand-held radio.

The man in the leather jacket checked his watch, lit another cigarette. The ashtray in front of him was overflowing with discarded butts. Almost midday and still no sign of the girl. Was it possible he had missed her? He nodded to the young man behind the bar, ordered another espresso.

He wondered about trying to get past the apartment security, decided against it. Impatience led you into making mistakes. He would wait. She couldn't stay up there all day.

102

Angeli glanced repeatedly in the rear-vision mirror. He thinks he knows me, Reuben thought. 'Remember me?' he asked.

'Should I?'

'You've never seen me before. I don't think you'd even remember my name.'

'Try me.'

Despite himself, Reuben felt a grudging admiration for the man's nerve. He had hoped for fear, panic, pleas for mercy even. The man's unharried demeanour only increased his doubts. He remembered what Domingo had said: *You don't have the stomach for it.*

'Cast your mind back twenty years.'

He saw, for the first time, a moment of fear on the man's face. 'This isn't about Massini?'

'Try again.' Angeli drove badly. It was perhaps deliberate, trying to draw the attention of the police; more likely he was unaccustomed to being behind the wheel of a car in Rome. 'If we have an accident, I'll shoot you anyway.'

'I'm doing my best. It isn't easy driving in this fucking city even when you haven't got a gun pointed at your back. Do you want to tell me your name?'

'Reuben Altman.'

He watched Angeli's face in the rear-vision mirror. Did he see a flicker of recognition? 'I've never heard of you.'

'You knew my wife. And you know my daughter very well. By the way, what did you do to my wife, Colonel?'

'I wish I knew what you were talking about.'

Reuben leaned back in his seat. His hands were lathered in sweat. They were shaking so badly it was hard to hold the gun. If only he could be sure. He heard Mercedes' voice: *You don't look much like the fist of God to me.*

'Just drive the car.'

*   *   *

If Simone's assassin thought he was invisible, he was wrong. Riccardo was watching him and so was Gino. Another stranger, just like the one they had seen a few days ago. That one had turned out to be a friend, or so she had said. But something about this one did not appear benign. He sat there by the window, pretending he was waiting for someone, but it was obvious to both of them that he was watching the apartment.

They did not take their eyes off him.

Reuben told Angeli to park on the Lungotevere dei Sangallo. They got out and he pointed the way down the stone steps to the muddy walkway by the river. There were no fishermen taking their meagre harvest from the polluted brown water today, and the roar of the traffic was muted by the high floodwalls. They were alone with the timeless river.

Reuben had a black frock-coat around his shoulders, the gun loose at his side. Angeli walked a few paces ahead of him, his hands in his pockets as if he didn't have a care in the world, a businessman out for a stroll. The impression was at odds with the weather. A freezing drizzle had begun to fall from a lowering sky.

'Stop there.'

Angeli turned around. 'What is it you want? You want to kill me? All right. Kill me. If not, I want to get out of this fucking rain.'

'First I want you to tell me what happened to my wife.'

'I don't know who you think I am, but I really have no idea what you're talking about.' He smiled. 'By the way, I take it you're not a priest?'

'No, I'm not a priest and I think you do know what I'm talking about. I'm talking about Simone, my daughter.'

Angeli blinked.

It all seemed like such a long time ago now.

They stripped her, doused her with water and tied her, spreadeagled, to a metal table. Beside the table was a heart monitor with defibrillator paddles and a picana, an electric cattle prod. Turturro was waiting to one side with a white-coated doctor.

Angeli wrinkled his nose in distaste. There were splashes of blood on the bare brick, the air was tainted with the odours of burning and sweat and excrement.

He nodded and Turturro picked up the picana, *grinning. He touched it under her arm.*

When you tortured someone with electricity they didn't moan or scream, they howled. Angeli nodded again to Turturro, a signal to step back. He looked disappointed to be called off so soon. Rosa's body still jolted and shook on the metal frame, her muscles in spasm. The doctor stepped in quickly to pull her tongue out of her mouth to prevent her from choking, put a piece of rubber between her teeth to stop her biting her tongue.

And then they started again: Where is Reuben?

'All right,' Angeli said. 'Okay. I was in the military. But I was a soldier, not a murderer. My wife and I . . . we wanted children, we couldn't have them. So, a friend of mine said to me . . . well, you know what happened in those days. We've given her everything she ever wanted, loved her like she was our own. Is that what this is all about?'

Reuben felt his resolve slipping away. What if he were wrong? What if he killed the wrong man? Did he have the right to redress one wrong with another?

He heard Father Salvatore's voice inside his head. *I shall pray for you, Reuben. I shall pray for God to take away your strength.*

Angeli turned up his collar against the rain. 'Please. Can we go somewhere and have a cup of coffee, talk about this? My health is not so good. If I get a chill, I'll be in bed for weeks. I'm not a murderer. For God's sake. Please.'

Turturro was the sadist. I was only doing my duty. I tried to help her.

'*Look, Rosa, the only obligation you have is to survive. He never came back for you. You know that, don't you? You don't owe him anything. Just tell us where he is hiding and I'll make them stop.*'

'You're lying,' Reuben said.

'No. You have the wrong man.'

He hesitated. Domingo was right. He didn't have the stomach for it.

He couldn't do it.

103

Gabriella got out of the taxi, checked the address she had written on the slip of paper. She looked up. A Renaissance façade, crumbling ochre stucco and green shutters. There was a small entrance courtyard, a glass entry door with a brass backplate beside it, a twentieth-century contrivance built into a medieval arch. She paid the driver and stood there, gathering her composure. Her heart was beating so fast she felt light-headed.

Simone was watching the piazza from the window two storeys above. She jumped to her feet when she saw the taxi pull up outside. A young woman climbed out of the back seat and for a moment she froze, the hairs rising on the back of her neck.

'Gabriella,' she murmured.

It was as if she had stepped out of her body and was staring at herself. This woman even wore her hair the same way. She ran to the door, threw it open and rushed down the stairs, three at a time, laughing and crying at once.

The man in the leather coat leaped to his feet, spilling his coffee. He strode out of the café and across the piazza, reaching inside his jacket for the pistol.

As the taxi drove away the woman stood there on the cobblestones, staring up at the apartment building, hitching a carpet bag over her shoulder. Her long black hair was tied in a ponytail. She was wearing blue jeans and a shapeless black jumper.

He brought out the pistol and aimed it at her head.

The girl stared at him. Her mouth formed a perfect 'O' of surprise. He heard a scream. A girl ran out of the apartment, her arms outstretched. She had long black hair tied in a ponytail. She was wearing blue jeans and a shapeless black jumper.

Both women were identical to the photograph.

Such a situation had not been factored into his preparations. As a result, he did something he had never done in his long career as a professional assassin. He hesitated.

One of the women rushed at him, her hands clawing for the pistol. He slapped her hard with his free hand and she fell back. But then the other girl was on him too, her fingernails raking his face. He heard people screaming in the piazza. The pistol jumped twice in his hand.

He pushed the girl away and staggered back, shaken. He had never been interrupted in the middle of business before. It had all gone wrong so quickly.

He brought up the pistol again, deciding now to kill both women.

One of them already lay on her back on the cobblestones. There was a blossoming of bright red blood on her clothes. As he aimed the pistol at her head the first woman rushed him again, spoiling his aim and pushing him off balance. He tried to pistol-whip her, did not see the waiter from the bar where he had spent the morning rush at him with a scalding pot of milk from his cappuccino machine. He screamed as the man dashed the contents in his face.

The woman sank her teeth into his pistol hand. He felt the weapon drop from his grip and he lumbered away, his hands over his face, half blinded by the scalding milk. Emboldened now, other bystanders rushed at him, beating him with their fists and feet. Even an old matron, carrying vegetables from the market, aimed a kick at him.

The young man from the bar had gone berserk. If a carabiniere had not pulled him away he might have beaten him to death with his bare fists.

The rain was falling more heavily now.

Angeli blinked again, licked his lips. He saw the uncertainty on the other man's face. 'I'm getting cold. Can we please get out of the rain?'

'Tell me about Rosa.'

'You have to believe me. I don't know anything about that.'

Angeli saw a man and a woman run down the stone steps and leap on to the embankment, pistols held two-handed in front of them. Professionals. Not his people, but not Reuben's either.

He smiled.

*   *   *

'Police! Drop the gun and stand clear with your hands in the air!'

Reuben turned around. They were moving towards him, a man in a black zippered jacket, a woman in a dark overcoat. They fanned out on to either side of the pathway to open the field of fire.

'Drop the gun! This is your last warning!'

Reuben turned back to Angeli, who was grinning wolfishly. 'You lose,' Angeli said.

Reuben, standing on the banks of the river, looking towards Trastevere. Death inside him and so many sins on his head. What was one more? He saw the look in Angeli's eyes, cold and blue, the only blue on that grey day, the only hint of sky.

'It *was* you.' He raised the pistol and held his finger on the trigger.

As he emptied the clip into Angeli's chest, the gunfire was answered immediately by the pistols of the two SID officers. It was over in seconds, leaving two bodies twitching in the mud, the priest and the devil, side by side, the blood pools spreading and mingling in the rain.

As he lay on his back in the mud Reuben's mind drifted free of the freezing bonds of death, back to Buenos Aires, his city of the colonels. He saw the Casa Rosada, pink in the late afternoon sun, and a handful of women, wearing white scarves, still walking their vigil around the obelisk in the Plaza de Mayo.

He blinked his eyes for one last time, staring at the hastening sky in bewilderment.

'Rosa,' he murmured.

Then he, too, was swallowed up by that vast and unknowable vault of God, and the silent indifference of heaven.

Epilogue

The elevator doors opened. At the end of the corridor was a small waiting room with vinyl chairs and a vase of faded flowers. She recognised the young waiter who had run from the bar to help them. He sat on one of the chairs, endlessly running his fingers through his hair, whispering some private benediction over and over. He was staring blankly out of the window.

The overcast was breaking up, a shaft of sunlight gleaming on the dome of San Pietro.

A nurse led her into the room. It was in darkness, the blinds shut. The only sounds were the blip of the heart monitor and the rhythmic whoosh of the respirator. Coils of plastic tube snaked in and out of Simone's body, connecting her to the bottles and bags above the bed.

A piece of white tape holding a catheter in place on her forearm had come loose. Gabriella smoothed it down. She sat down beside the bed, stared at the medallion in her fist. She had found it on the cobblestones as they were loading Simone into the ambulance. It was a broken-heart motif, almost the same as her own. She removed her own locket, gently uncurled Simone's fingers and pressed them both into her palm.

The bullet had entered her chest just below her left breast. The doctors said it had punctured her lung and narrowly missed her spine as it exited her body. She had lost a lot of blood.

Gabriella ran a hand across her face.

She wondered if there would ever be a time when life would be normal again, if she would find some way to understand what had happened to her in these last few weeks, to explain to herself and others what had taken place that morning in Trastevere and on the banks of the Tiber a mile or so away. At that moment the tunnel was long and dark and the glimmer of light a long way off.

She looked down at the figure on the bed. 'I don't even know you,' she whispered.

Simone looked so frail. Her face was ashen and there were plum-coloured bruises around her eyes. And yet, when she touched her, it did not feel as if she was touching a stranger.

Gabriella longed for her to open her eyes. There was so much to be said. Perhaps they could even help each other to heal.

She remembered what Reuben had told her about the day they had been born almost twenty years before. She looked around. The nurse had gone.

She took off her shoes and lay down on the bed beside Simone. The most curious of sensations, as if she were lying down next to herself. She touched the hair, the skin, so familiar, so much like her own. She would bring her back from the dying, as Simone had done to her twenty years before.

'Simone,' she whispered. 'I'm back. I'm back and I'm never going to go away again.'

DATE DUE